This is a work of fiction. Names, characters, places, and incidents are either a product of the author's imagination or are used fictitiously. Any resemblance to actual persons, living or dead, businesses, companies, events, or locales, is entirely coincidental.

Child of the Dragon

Inked in Gray Press

InkedinGray.com

Copyright © 2025

All rights reserved.

ISBN Paperback: 978-1-952969-32-4

ISBN Ebook: 978-1-952969-33-1

Cover Design by JV Arts

No part of this book may be used or reproduced in any manner whatsoever without written permission except for the use of brief quotations in a book review.

No part of this book may be used or reproduced in any manner for the purpose of training artificial intelligence technologies or systems. In accordance with Article 4(3) of the Digital Single Market Directive 2019/70, Inked in Gray Press expressively reserves this work from the text and data mining exception. in any form or used by, with, or fed into any electronic or mechanical systems, including information storage and AI, without written permission from the author.

Praise for
Child of the Dragon

"With humor and heart, CHILD OF THE DRAGON is an explosion of adventure. Between fantastical, life-or-death stakes or calculus, I — like Kat — would choose the dragons any day."

— Cass Biehn, author of *Vesuvius*

"A fast-paced adventure where family secrets are exposed, a whole world emerges, and friendships are tested. The representation of disabled and queer characters is refreshing and powerful, the dialogue is fresh and believable, and the plot will keep readers hooked from start to finish. This debut promises to entertain fantasy readers and YA fans alike."

— Erica Rose Eberhart, author of *The Elder Tree Trilogy*

"Equal parts perilous and tender, CHILD OF THE DRAGON unfolds with compelling human — and dragon — stakes, pieced together with all the elements you'd want in a fantasy story: rising magic, the power of friendship, and delightful humor. An evil king, shapeshifting dragons, and high school calculus offer readers adventure at a page-turning pace. Grief, growth, and legacy are interwoven among both the fantastical and a diverse cast sure to win your heart. This story is a comfort read for everyone who ever wanted to spread their wings and fly."

— Courtney Collins, co-author of the award-winning *Vows & Valor Trilogy*

Praise for Child of the Dragon

"CHILD OF THE DRAGON is an exhilarating tale, jam-packed with action, the power of friendship, diverse characters you will want to fight an evil king for, and best of all, dragons. Sheesley's magical debut has all the hallmarks of a fantasy classic."

— Rita A. Rubin, author of *A Ballad for Slayers & Monsters*

"Life is hard when you need to handle homework, teenage hormones and ancient dragon overlords trying to kill you, but Kat, a young dragon shapeshifter faces it bravely. Sheesley weaves an adventurous YA fantasy, skillfully combining everyday challenges of teenage life with dangerous mystery and powerful magic."

— Jelena Dunato, author of *Dark Woods, Deep Water*

CHILD OF THE DRAGON

ASHLEY N.Y. SHEESLEY

For those daydreaming of adventure when they should be paying attention in class . . . let's fight dragons together.

BEFORE YOU READ

The following are the content warnings for *Child of the Dragon*. If you don't like to read content warnings, that's fine! Please skip this page and read on.

Otherwise, know that this book contains content that could be difficult for some readers, including depictions of death, fantasy violence, a short and minor torture scene and references to others, and death of a grandparent. Coleman recounts experienced abuse in his past. There is some minor ableism, but it does not go unchecked.

Please feel free to reach out at contact@inkedingray.com for any clarifying questions or concerns and remember to take care of your mental health.

You matter.

The Council to keep the peace
Will force the war of kings
With two left and all to remain,
All agency shall cease
Until salvation soars on willing wings.
A free dragon, one to break the chains,
Will release them from the snare
And take their place as rightful heir.

The Assassin's Leech

Coleman

Nowhere in my plans for Friday night did I anticipate hiding behind a steel crate in a shipping yard with a dead body at my feet.

Well, I supposed it *might* have included hiding behind a steel crate. Jason and I were supposed to go paintballing. The location and the *dead body at my feet* were just further proof that the universe hated me.

I absentmindedly wiped my bloody sword against my pants, scanning the surroundings for any other threats and making sure the spell I'd put up around the shipping yard to ward us against mortal eyes was still in place. It shimmered blue along the border of the yard and the street where cars zipped carelessly past, completely oblivious to the fight raging inside the ward.

Completely oblivious to the two dragons battling above me.

Meanwhile, *I* was completely oblivious to the fact I'd just wiped my bloody sword all over my *white pants*. I groaned, silently chastising myself. *This is why we can't have nice things, Coleman.*

I supposed it was my own fault for wearing white to a rescue mission, but again, we were supposed to have gone paintballing.

We knew coming here tonight was probably a trap, but our intel said some of King Balaskad's followers had taken a child hostage, and we couldn't ignore that. And besides, we figured the three of us — Jamie, Jason, and I — could handle a few of Balaskad's lackies.

We just weren't expecting King Balaskad herself to be here. And just our luck — there was no child.

Dragon fire lit the night, flashing above me. Jamie clashed with Balaskad in the air. Jamie's white dragon form stood out in stark contrast against the night sky and Balaskad's dark copper and red. Both their scales glistened with blood. I watched, mesmerized for a moment, as the last free dragon and leader of our small resistance fought against one of the two tyrannical kings who kept the rest of the Rhaegynne — shapeshifting dragons — bound to them in our dragon forms.

Somewhere in the distance, Jason screamed my name. Flashes of magic lit the tops of the shipping crates near where his shout had sounded.

My heart pounded as I zigzagged between the shipping crates toward him. Jason had gone searching for the fictitious child. I hadn't seen him since the fight broke out.

I reached for my magic, and a painful, cold but familiar squeeze across my chest and shoulders sucked the breath from my lungs. I flung a ball of crackling, blue-tinged energy upward at the copper-and-blood-colored dragon, barely missing a step while I ran, hoping to give Jamie a little more time.

My spell dispersed against Balaskad's scales. She didn't even glance my way.

The dragon fire above gave the only real light to see by. The few lamps still standing among our battleground cast deep shadows from the shipping crates. The flashing magic near Jason cut off abruptly.

I prayed the fight had ended with Jason still alive.

The sharp, grating squeal of crushing metal and a dragon's roar ripped my attention back to the now-grounded dragon fight. King Balaskad stalked triumphantly forward, flattening steel boxes beneath her taloned feet. Jamie stood against the cruel king, her bloodied white wings stretched out. She reared back on her hind legs. Her mouth sparked with electricity before she shot a lightning bolt at Balaskad.

The lightning illuminated the limp, black-haired form behind her. My stomach fluttered.

Jason!

I rushed forward, reaching out and chanting incantations I knew by heart. My chest burned from the pressure under my skin, but before the spell could leave my hand, the last of Balaskad's soldiers knocked me to the ground.

My head cracked against the pavement. Lights flashed in my vision, and my eyes shifted to my dragon eyes. I clenched my jaw, fighting against the change threatening to overcome me.

You won't do anyone any good if you turn into a murderous puppet for your king right now.

I hissed out a breath, breathing through the pain, and pushed out a small thread of magic to burn off the impending change while I struggled against the form pinning me to the ground.

Balaskad shimmered like a mirage and shifted into her red-haired human form. Her face twisted into a wicked smile before a crack of maroon burst from her hand and slammed into Jamie.

Jamie let out a horrific roar that shook the ground. Lightning sparked at the corners of her maw before it erupted with white-hot dragon flame. She writhed, swinging her head in pain. Her fire ran wild, racing out toward me, but the soldier above me took the brunt of it. He fell screaming and finally freed me from his grasp.

Balaskad stood calmly amidst the flames and reached out a hand to quench the inferno.

Jamie dropped to her knees, her dragon form melting away to reveal an older woman, bloodstained and battered, clutching her side. The king sneered and turned to blow me a kiss when she noticed me in the wreckage before transforming once again and launching into the sky, leaving her dead followers behind.

I struggled to my feet, pushing the charred corpse to the side. My head spun. My hands shook from the cold and pain of so much magic. I almost fell again, but I pushed on. I had to reach Jamie and Jason.

Blood stained Jamie's gray hair and wrinkled face. Her eyes shifted back and forth between pale blue human eyes and diamond-like dragon eyes with slitted pupils. Even cradling the injury at her side and barely clinging to consciousness, she still shielded Jason's body with her own.

"Are you okay?"

Bad question. Jamie looked *old*. She *was* old, I knew that. Considering Rhaegynne dragons age slower than humans, she was probably well over one hundred years old by now. But she wasn't *old*-old. Not like this. I didn't even dare to look at Jason yet.

Jamie tried to smile, but it turned into a grimace. "No. That —" She sucked in a pained breath. "Balaskad hit me with something. I didn't recognize the . . ." She squeezed her eyes shut, and a single tear escaped out the side.

My stomach dropped. In all the years I'd known her, I'd never seen Jamie cry over her injuries. I reached out to her, but she recoiled at my touch.

"I don't know the counter curse, Cole." She took a few deep breaths and whispered the words to a sustaining spell. A white mist plumed out of her mouth, floating into the air around her. A little color returned to her pale face, and her eyes finally settled into her pale blue.

"Let me see," I offered, my mouth dry with fear.

She lifted the side of her shirt. I gasped at the spiraling, spiderweb-like mass writhing along her side. Tendrils of the brown and red curse creeped like a living *thing* across her rib cage and stomach.

"If you have any magic left, heal Jason and get us out of here," she said.

"What? No! What about you?"

She pulled her shirt back down, straightened up, and set her jaw as if pretending she wasn't in pain would somehow convince me she was fine. "We can figure out my curse when we get home."

"But the prophecy—"

"Can be about anyone willing to step up and decide it's about them. Your magic can't help me, but it can save Jason." Her face was already losing the color her spell had given her.

Reluctantly, I turned to Jason.

His lips were purple and quivering — a clear sign of using too much magic — and a massive gash ran through his black hair, the blood dripping across his tan face and running down his neck. His arm was twisted at an impossible angle. I reached for him, my hand already glowing with green healing magic.

I made quick work of his arm, mending the broken bones in

his forearm, then moved to the gash across his face. His blue eyes fluttered open beneath his dark lashes, and I breathed a sigh of relief.

"How bad is it?" Jason asked, feeling along the side of the wound I hadn't closed yet.

I swatted his hand away. "It'll be fine if you don't mess it up!"

He grinned. "Isn't that what I do best though? Mess your spells up?"

I rolled my eyes, fighting back a smile, and directed the magic into the wound, coaxing his light brown skin back together. "What got you? Too much magic or too much blood loss?" I asked, helping him sit up before wrapping my jacket around his shoulders.

"Bit of both," he said as he gazed at the destroyed shipping containers. "So . . . did we win?"

Jamie sighed. "Balaskad got away."

Jason swore and pulled himself to his feet before helping me to mine. "What happened to *your* face, Cole?"

I shrugged and touched a healing spell to my temple. A soothing warmth flooded through my head, clearing my mind and lending me the slightest bit of energy. Yet that cold vise of magic use still tightened around my chest. "Nothing magic can't fix."

Jason reached down and helped Jamie to her feet. She let out a hiss of pain, and he turned to me with an accusing glare. "Why'd you heal me before Jamie?"

"We don't know the counter for my curse, dear," Jamie explained. "I insisted he heal you, so we can get home and do some research."

"Curse?" Jason asked, voice tight with alarm.

"Yeah," I said, pulling my last set of transport beads from my pocket. "I'll explain at the library. Let's get out of here."

I threw the transport beads to the ground where they twisted and formed into an intricate ring of lace-like runes. "Let's go home," I whispered to the beads.

Jason pulled Jamie's arm over his shoulder, and we stepped into the portal together.

Teleporting always felt like that sudden drop in a rollercoaster after a loop the loop: You're already dizzy when you get to it, then your stomach drops so fast you can't scream. Then, it's over.

Some people liked it, but I'd grown too used to it to have an opinion.

We stepped out into Jamie's library. Books floated between dozens of shelves. Pens, typewriters, and computers cranked out notes and novels on their own on the desks around the room. A few other Rhaegynne sat in secluded nooks illuminated with either candles or LED light bulbs searching through piles of books, ancient and modern.

Jamie limped out into the middle of the room. "I need as many books on curses and counter curses as possible," she spoke into the air.

At least twenty books jumped off the shelves, pages already turning as they flew to Jamie's desk. One Rhaegynne in the back yelped when one of her books got yanked out of her pile. When she saw it fly over to Jamie, she waved, only slightly shocked to see us so bloody and ragged. But then again, when were we *not* these days?

Jason and I took our seats next to Jamie and frantically poured through the books while I filled him in.

Page after page of dark and grotesque magic passed through my fingers, but none of them matched the one on Jamie.

I glanced nervously at her. The effects of the sustaining

spell from earlier had almost worn off completely. Her eyelids drooped, and sweat beaded on her brow.

"How is it now?" I asked.

She lifted her shirt in answer.

The spiraling tendrils had almost disappeared.

Her gaze met mine, and my stomach dropped. The brown swirls now ringed the whites of her eyes.

"Never mind. Maybe . . . maybe you should go lie down." I called one of the other Rhaegynne over, and he helped guide Jaime to a recliner in the corner.

Jason's face mirrored my own concern.

He shook himself and turned back to the books. "No, no," he whispered, opening another book. "A curse like a . . . bloody spiderweb." A few more books joined our table.

The other resistance members in the library joined our hunt while Jason and I buried ourselves under reference books, our search becoming more desperate the weaker Jamie became.

Jason jumped, straightening up and pointing at a page in his book. "It's called the Assassin's Leech," he said, reading from the book. "It kills slowly, parasitizing itself on the magic of the victim and shutting down all bodily functions."

I know how that feels, I thought, bitterly watching a small blue line on my own hand disappear. "How do we stop it? What's the counter?"

He paused to read a little further down the page. "The counter seems simple enough as long as the leech is still visible. It takes about an hour to burrow under the skin. Once it has, there's no known magic that can stop it. The victim has about two to three weeks to live. A little longer if modern medicine can keep the body from shutting down."

My blood ran cold. I snatched the book from him and sprinted over to Jamie.

Her eyes shifted between human and dragon again, but the whites of her eyes were clear.

"Jamie, can I lift your shirt again, please?"

She weakly lifted it herself.

Nothing.

"No," I said, trying to move her to check her back. "No, no, no..."

The leech was gone.

I read the counter from the book anyway. "*Ta'is isoperé, sanare corporus!*" I shouted. A blue-tinged green magic poured from my hands, but Jamie didn't look any better. "*Ta'is isoperé, sanare corporus!*" I shouted. Again and again, I cast the spell. The pain in my chest nearly threatened to overwhelm me with each casting, but I couldn't let Balaskad win. The pain of using magic was nothing compared to the pain of losing Jamie. "*Ta'is isoper—*"

Jason's warm hand grabbed my icy, magic-depleted one.

I looked at him, my vision clouded with a misty blue. *When did I fall to my knees?*

His eyes swam with tears. "You won't do the resistance any good if you're dead too."

I turned to Jamie, and she smiled sadly. "It doesn't hurt so much now, darling."

"No. Don't... don't lie, please." *How long have I been crying?* My chest ached. Whether from extending too far or from grief, I couldn't tell.

"I know a Rhaegynne doctor who's said she'd take care of me if something like this ever happened. She's under King Aurakbahor," Jaime added, referencing the other tyrannical dragon king — the one whose curse I was stuck under.

I shook my head slowly so I could try to avoid aggravating the vertigo that had set in. "You can't trust any of us if you're dying. If any of us slip up and change into a dragon, Balaskad or Aurakbahor will know where you are." The curse we fought so hard against gave us our minds and our freedom, but only if we stayed human. The second any of us — except Jamie — took dragon form, our king could control our bodies and read our minds, leaving us no better than oversized puppets.

It was a risk we all knew, but one we could take because we could defend ourselves. I swallowed down my fear. "If your location is revealed, you won't be able to fight back."

She smiled, a real smile this time. The kind that made her eyes glint with mischief. "I'll take my chances."

"No. We can't lose you," I said, clenching my teeth to stop the tears. "If you're gone, there's no fight left!" I wanted to feel the heat of anger, but the ice of fear quenched it.

"Do you remember the prophecy, Coleman?"

I nodded.

"Until salvation soars on *willing* wings," Jaime repeated. "There's no chosen one or any of this nonsense that ties our freedom to me."

I wanted to scream, but my voice came out in a hoarse whisper. "But what about the free dragon? That's you! You're the only one left who isn't magically tied to the kings!"

"My lineage does not die with me—"

"Your daughter refused!" Jason protested.

"Yes," Jamie said, her voice sad, "but *she* has a daughter. My granddaughter only knows about Rhaegynne dragons from bedtime stories, but she has a strong magical affinity. I can almost guarantee she'd be free if she chooses this life. Or maybe the curse will fail to take hold on a new dragon. There is no specified chosen one. It's every one of us who stands up against the kings, their curse, and their senseless war."

Jason held up a hand. "I swear, if you say the chosen one is the friends we made along the way . . ."

She let out a soft laugh. "No, but when the time comes, my

granddaughter's name is Katherine Lance. If she chooses this path, I need you to train her, Jason. Keep her alive for me, please."

He bowed his head. "I'll do my best, but you know my magic isn't—"

"It's enough, Jason. It's always enough."

"What about me?" I asked. "Won't she need my help too?"

"Of course," Jaime said, "but I have something else planned for you."

I sniffed and tilted my head. "Like what?"

"Jason, could you leave us alone for a moment?"

He flinched but turned to leave. "Would you like me to call that doctor for you?"

"Yes, please. You'll find her number in my medicine cabinet with a list of all my other doctors. I'm an old lady. I have many of them."

Jason's lip twitched as he left.

I nearly called him back. I didn't want to face Jamie dying alone.

But she *wasn't* dying. Not yet.

"Coleman, I have a difficult task to ask of you. You can say no. I'll understand."

"I've just learned a whole arsenal of curses to use against Balaskad. I'm ready to resume my old role as an assassin." I tucked my hands behind my back, hoping Jamie hadn't seen the way they trembled. But I *would* go back to a job I abhorred if it would help a woman I respected so dearly.

She smiled. "Actually, I have something else in mind for you."

Truths Revealed

Kat

Grandma's face was gray against the white hospital pillowcase. I held her fevered and fragile hand in mine while she took labored, rattling breaths.

"Will you tell me a story again, Grandma?" I asked. I avoided looking at the IV port in her hand and focused on pulling a thread in the thin, crinkly sheet.

This infection had struck so hard and so fast. Less than a week ago, she'd been healthy and full of life, and now... now, I glanced up at her, scared to see how weak she was, but my heart lifted when her mouth curled into one of her easy smiles.

"You've heard them all by now, Kat," she said, patting my hand.

I smiled at her words and glanced at the old, weathered book on the hospital nightstand. I had begged her to read that book to me every time she came over. My mom hated it, yet Grandma would sit on the edge of my bed long past bedtime, reading stories of magic, adventure, dragons, monsters, and so many mystical creatures. "Are you sure there's not a chapter you skipped?"

Her laugh caught in her throat and turned into deep, hacking coughs. I helped her sit up and passed her a paper cup from the side table. She sipped slowly, taking deep breaths until the cough subsided.

"What would you like to hear?" Grandma asked finally.

I rubbed my thumb over the interlocking V's on my small necklace. She'd given it to me years ago when she had first told me the stories of the cursed dragon shapeshifters. She told me it would help me control my magic. My mom had scoffed and reminded her magic wasn't real. But I never took the necklace off. It *felt* magical to me, and that was good enough.

I smiled at the memory. "Tell me about the Rhaegynne again. Please?"

Her yellowed eyes no longer glittered the way they used to. *How could so much change in so little time?* But somehow, that old spark in her eyes flared to life like it did when I would beg for one more story. "Are you sure?" she asked. "The Rhaegynne are only a very small part of those stories."

I grinned. "Absolutely."

"What do you want to know?"

"Well," I said, crossing my legs and propping my head up on my hand, "last we left off, they were still waiting for someone to break their curse, free them from their kings, find the lost heirs, and end the war. So . . . has anyone saved them yet?" If I could pretend this was just story time again . . .

Her eyes darkened, and the spark died. Grandma pulled her hand away from mine, gripping the place on her side where the infection had started. "No," she whispered, looking away. "I tried, though."

She *tried?* "What do you mean?" I asked.

A knock on the door interrupted her.

The door cracked open, and a nurse in powder blue scrubs walked in. "Jamie? You have another visitor," he said, hesitating in the doorway. "Can he see you? He says he's a friend."

"Of course!" she said. "Come in!"

The door opened the rest of the way, and a man in a long, black suit coat walked into the room. His dark hair and neatly trimmed beard had a few strands of white along the sides, and the slight wrinkles on his forehead and around his light brown eyes betrayed his age but gave him an imposing edge. He wore a royal blue scarf around his neck and held a dark wooden cane sideways so it dangled nearly horizontally by his hip.

The nurse shut the door behind him.

I turned back to Grandma. Her welcoming smile had turned stale.

"Is everything—" I asked.

"Would you mind going to get me some water, please?" she interrupted. Her smile brightened again. "And a cup for this old friend?"

I eyed the half-full water pitcher on the small table. "Are you—"

"And ask that nurse for something to eat, please?"

Picking up the pitcher, I skeptically crossed the room, stealing a glance backward. Grandma and the man watched me, so I left, pulling the door closed behind me.

"You've gotten old," I heard the man comment, his voice muffled through the door.

"You haven't." Grandma's voice carried a sharpness I had never heard before.

I froze and pressed my ear against the door.

"So, Balaskad finally caught you?" he asked.

"I assume you're here to finish what she started," Grandma

said, her voice strong. "That somehow, you'll get credit for finally putting an end to the resistance once and for all. That you'll finally get the edge on Balaskad. You are nothing, Aurakbahor. The resistance will rise again, and you and Balaskad will find yourself buried in the same earth. Coward."

A slap sounded from the room, followed by Grandma's gasp of pain.

Anger turned my blood to fire. The water pitcher fell from my hand, splashing ice and water up my legs. I threw the door open. "Get out," I hissed.

Aurakbahor turned to face me. His once-brown eyes were pitch black. His hand contorted with rage as electricity crackled around it.

Fear held me in place, but Grandma pushed herself out of bed, staggered to her feet, and shoved him off-balance. The lightning fizzled out with a *pop* when her frail body slammed into his, and they tumbled to the ground, nearly bringing her IV pole with them. She turned toward me with strange, glittering blue eyes and black slits for pupils.

"Run," she cried as the man shoved her back against the bed.

Aurakbahor grabbed Grandma, and something in me snapped. I ran toward him and wrapped my arms around his neck, trying to pull him away with my weight.

"Stay away from her!" I screamed, hoping I was loud enough that someone would hear.

He stumbled backward, slamming me into the wall. A gasp escaped me, and my arms lost their grip. He wheeled around and pinned me by my throat against the wall. His hands burned like fire.

My fingers raked across his hands and face, my feet dangling beneath me as I fought to breathe. The necklace Grandma gave me tangled between our fingers and snapped.

He glared back at Grandma, reaching his free hand out toward her. Black mist coiled around his fingers, and the hatred in his eyes told me the distance between him and my grandmother meant nothing.

Fury boiled in my chest with a heat that took my breath away. I leaned into the wall, braced my back, and slammed my knee into his crotch. A thunderous boom shook the windows. His grip around my neck broke, and he slid backward across the white tile floor.

I stumbled toward him, coughing and rubbing my throbbing throat. I shivered, strangely cold despite the effort of the fight. I kicked at his side, but he caught my foot and pulled me to the ground. I tried to scream, but my throat was still tight from his stranglehold. I could only muster a pathetic gasp.

He stood, laughing, and dragged me across the floor.

I locked eyes with my dying grandma. "Please," I whispered.

Her eyes opened, revealing those strange, catlike irises. She rose to her feet with a strength I didn't think she had left. "Leave us," she snarled. Light flashed through her fingers and flew directly at Aurakbahor.

The man grunted in pain, let go of my legs, and turned toward her. His gloves glowed with a dark mist.

I growled, pushing myself to my feet.

He glanced at me with a dangerous smile, hissing out words I didn't understand. The dark mist around his hands rippled out to surround him. I lunged. Grandma rushed toward me with a shout, knocking me aside.

A strangled gasp escaped her lips as her arm passed through the strange mist.

Her knees buckled, and she collapsed into my arms.

The mist evaporated. The man cursed and fled from the room.

Moments of silence passed between us before I spoke. "What just happened?" I fought to lift Grandma back into her bed. "Who was that?" Her hand bled from where the IV had been ripped out.

Her skin was ice cold. She croaked a word, but I couldn't make it out. I leaned closer, my ear inches from her mouth. She whispered my name.

"I'm right here."

She squeezed my hand and spoke again. "Katherine" — she sucked in a breath — "I need to tell you something."

I reached for the help button on the side of the bed, but she placed a weak hand on my arm. Her blue slitted eyes made me shiver. They matched the dragon eyes in her book.

Grandma struggled to catch her breath. "I should have told you the truth a long time ago." Her breathing became labored and raspy. "I was afraid . . . you would act as your mother had. She refused . . . to believe. Katherine, the stories . . . are true." She fumbled for the necklace around her neck. "I was . . . I was going to teach you. I was supposed to have . . . a little more time." Her hands trembled, reaching for the clasp.

"Don't say that like a goodbye!" I cried. "You have time!"

She shook her head and pressed her locket into my hand. "To replace the old one."

I tried to find the broken necklace, but I couldn't. I'd worn it every day for twelve years, and my heart broke to lose it, but replacing it with this locket somehow felt . . . right.

"The dragon's blood is in you," she said after gasping for air. "Keep . . . the book."

Grandma turned her head to the side, and I followed her gaze to the nightstand. I picked up the old leather book of bedtime stories with a dragon and compass on the front. My eyes blurred. I'd never read it myself, only listened to her read it. I ran my hand across the leather cover.

"The stories . . . are true. Save them. Please."

A tear slid down my face. "What are you talking about? Who? The *Rhaegynne?* How do I . . ." This couldn't be real!

"You must . . . become a Rhaegynne." Her voice cut off, her body once again wracked with violent coughs.

I looked at the spilled water in the doorway. Guilt cut into my heart, leeching at whatever warmth remained in me. "How?" I whispered, blinking back helpless tears.

Finally, her coughing ended. "I've told you before. You must be very special to a dragon to be gifted with their powers." Tears brimmed in her strange eyes. "And, darling, you are so, so special to me." She let out a long sigh and went still. Her eerie eyes dulled, turning back to her normal blue.

"Grandma?" I flung my body across the bed, slamming the call button and cursing my hesitation. I shouted for help and began chest compressions. I'd had to learn it during a first-aid course a year ago, but I never thought I'd actually need it.

"Please don't go! Please!" The compressions moved in time with my rapid chanting.

Ten, eleven, twelve compressions. "Help!" *Is it constant compressions? Do I give breaths? I don't remember!*

Twenty-eight, twenty-nine, thirty.

I tilted Grandma's head back, blocked her nose, and gave her two breaths before hastily returning to my compressions, chanting, and calling for help. I tried not to think about the way her old bones — *Don't think. Just bring her back.*

Someone's arms wrapped around me. "No! No!" I screamed, fighting against their grip.

"Let us do our job!" a voice said, and I finally allowed myself to be pulled away.

"What happened?" a nurse in white scrubs asked, gesturing toward the cracked pitcher in the doorway while she guided me into the hall.

Words failed me. How was I supposed to explain the fight? How was I supposed to explain the strange man or the magic?

"A nurse brought someone," I croaked. Tears dripped down my face. "I didn't know the visitor or the nurse," I croaked. I described them both the best I could, but I hadn't noticed much. I hadn't caught the nurse's name. *Did he even have a name tag?* I trailed off, trying to peer into the room.

"Did he do anything to her? Did he do anything to you?"

I tried to cover my neck, hoping his fingers hadn't left a mark. "I don't know!" I cried, wiping at the tears on my face. More replaced them in seconds.

From inside the room, I heard the team stop.

Someone called time of death.

I rushed past the nurse and into the room. "No!"

The doctor standing over my grandma turned to me with pity in her eyes.

"Please," I begged, my legs wobbling beneath me.

"I'm so sorry for your loss," she said, her voice breaking. "I'll go call your family."

The nurse I'd abandoned touched my shoulders and guided me back into the hall. I clutched at the heart-shaped locket in my hand, wishing I could trade this heart for Grandma's still beating one.

I didn't notice when my family arrived, but at some point, Dad sat next to me on the bench, rubbing my back while I watched my mom weep over her mother. I wanted to stay on that bench forever, becoming a fixture next to the fern and IV poles. But a nurse convinced my parents we needed to leave. Someone pulled me to my feet and out to the car.

Dad handed me Grandma's book when we got home. "Kat?" he said. He said something else, but I couldn't process his words. I took the book from him and stumbled down to my room, closing the door behind me.

I crawled into bed, trying to commit Grandma's last words to memory. Trying to forget the way the man's hands squeezed my throat. Trying not to think of the mist that drained whatever life remained in her. Trying not to think of dragons.

But when I did finally sleep, I dreamed of dragons.

A Feast Fit for a King

Coleman

I lounged at the head of a familiar long wooden table in a chamber carved from red stone. I propped my feet up on the table and picked apart a dinner roll to keep my hands from shaking.

The door behind me closed, and someone let out a heavy sigh.

"You did it," I said, not turning around but raising a glass with a clear, bubbly liquid inside.

Footsteps filled my heart with dread. King Aurakbahor slammed his hands against the table beside me. I did my best to hide my flinch. "What are you doing?" he demanded, his voice a deep growl, his rage and exasperation barely contained.

I gestured at the table covered in food. "Throwing myself a feast! Isn't that what you're supposed to do when your best rebellious assassin returns home?" My voice carried a confidence I didn't feel.

His fingers twitched toward the knife mere inches from his hand, but he stopped before grabbing it. "I should kill you."

But something stayed his hand. Curiosity? Nostalgia? More likely he just wanted to make it hurt when he killed me and didn't want to deal with the mess in his dining room.

I speared a large portion of spiral cut ham with my fork, ripped off a chunk with my teeth, and waved the rest of the floppy slice at him. "But you won't." *Oh, Tasalgré, I hope you don't...*

"Why are you here?" Aurakbahor spat through clenched teeth, his hands curling and uncurling into white-knuckled fists. A vein bulged along his hair line.

I shrugged, but my heart pounded against my ribs. "You won, didn't you? Jamie's dead. The rest of the resistance has scattered and given up. I'd like to ally myself with the strongest contender for the throne. Better you than Balaskad anyway." I took another bite, but the meat tasted like ash around my grief and fear.

I nodded toward the lonely feast. "Help yourself. It's as much your celebration as it is mine."

"Sa'hranet."

I winced at the use of my dragon name.

"This is my food. On my table. In my *personal chambers.*" His eyes flashed black, and I struggled to hide my terror. "*Why are you here?*" he screamed, swiping his arm across the table and sending plates and fruit and the roast pig flying.

I took a slow sip from his surviving cider glass. "To re-swear my allegiance to you, *sire.*"

He took in a breath, his nostrils flaring.

I pointed at the door with the glass. "You should really think about getting some guards for your doors," I said and took a bite of sweet roll.

The hard set to his shoulders softened. "You *really* think I'd welcome you back?"

I spread my arms wide. "With open arms, sire." The bread tasted sour.

A smirk danced along the corner of his mouth. "It's beneath you to behave like a stupid child. I won't trust you again."

"First of all, rude. Second, stupid is an ableist word, and you shouldn't use it. Especially to me, your favorite disabled assassin. Third, what would you have me do to prove my loyalty? I'll rejoin your knights if I have to." I had to choke back some bile at that. The Knights of the Raven's Vigil were Aurakbahor's private group of elite assassins, specializing in espionage, murder, and torture.

I hated them. And I hated that I was supposed to have *been* one. And I hated them even more after being on the receiving end of their torture more than once.

He leaned in close enough for me to smell his smoky, hateful breath. "First of all," he mocked, "treat your king with respect. Second—" He kicked my cane out from behind my chair.

I fought to keep the rage off my face as I watched my mobility aid clatter against the floor. *One day he'll pay for that.*

"Third, if you're serious about this, I need a spy. Jamie's dead, but I need to ensure no one else will try to challenge my throne. Give me reliable information, and I'll consider reinstating your position in my court."

"Done," I said, clapping my hands together and making a show of brushing off the crumbs. *Anything but the Knights.* "I'll book a flight to Croatia in the morning. Balaskad won't even—"

"I don't need a spy for Balaskad, you fool."

My stomach clenched. *Why will no one let me kill Balaskad?* "Who else then. Your subjects are loyal. The resistance is dead."

Aurakbahor grinned a sly, wicked smile. "Jamie had an heir. I need to know if the resistance will rise again." He waved a dismissive hand. "Go back to your *friends*. Let them believe whatever you want them to. But I need accurate information."

"Easy." *Might have preferred the Knights.*

"Coleman," he said, eyes dragon-dark. "Betray your friends, and I'll return your seat in my Court."

I bowed my head low over the table, using it as an excuse to hide my warring emotions. "This is most generous, Your Majesty. Consider it done." I straightened and lifted my glass again. "Dust off my robes, sire. It won't be long."

I took a long drink from the glass.

"Get out of my room, Sa'hranet. I suspect your friends will try to find Jamie's heir in the Dream Realms soon." He eyed me through draconic eyes. "Defy me again, and I won't be so merciful."

I stood, squeezing my eyes shut against a wave of blue-ish stars swarming my vision. I grabbed my cane where it lay in the center of the floor — a cane I only needed due to Aurakbahor's *mercy* — and bowed toward the king. "Thank you, sire." I stared at the cane strapped to his side and swallowed my disgust that, in his hands, the mobility aid was only ever used as a weapon.

"Get out."

I didn't need to be told again.

Dreams of Dragons

Kat

I dreamed I was a child again.

Mom tucked me under the blankets with my stuffed tiger. "Goodnight, baby." She kissed me on the nose and walked to the door.

Grandma squeezed my knee, kissed my messy blonde hair, and stood to leave.

"Wait. Can't you read me a goodnight story, please?" I begged.

Mom held up a disapproving finger. "No dragons tonight, Mom."

"Wouldn't dream of it." Grandma's eyes twinkled with mischief.

Mom left, closing the door softly behind her.

"What kind of goodnight story do you want?" Grandma asked, lifting a large leather book from my dresser.

"The one about the dragon!" I said.

Grandma's blue eyes crinkled. "I had a feeling you would say that." She sat next to me on the bed and cleared her throat.

"Once upon a time . . . That makes it sound like a fairy tale, doesn't it? But this one isn't entirely make-believe. How about 'a long time ago?'"

I giggled, snuggling in close to her.

"A long time ago, in a tall mountain overlooking a tiny village in a beautiful valley, there lived a dragon."

I turned my head to grin up at Grandma, but instead found myself cuddled up against a massive, crystalline dragon. Her white scales glittered like diamonds. When she noticed me looking, her lips curled into a soft smile. Her gentle eyes were pale blue with slitted pupils and sparkled like the sea.

I knew those eyes . . .

There is a difference, Katherine, between a dragon to be slain and a dragon to be saved. The dragon spoke to me in my grandma's voice, but her voice rang out in my head.

Even though the dragon felt deeply familiar, I recoiled and fell, tumbling backward and down, down, *down*.

I landed on my feet, wearing heavy plate armor. A band of equally armored fighters marched past, hiking up a mountain on a stony trail. The men sang while they walked, a deep, rhythmic chant that urged them onward. They sang of treasure and slaying dragons. My stomach curled in disgust.

"Rhaegynne? Are you okay?" a man with shoulder-length blond hair asked, turning back to check on me. He carried his helmet under his arm, his face suntanned and streaked with sweat, but he wore an easy smile when he spoke.

"I'm fine, Evren." The words came from my body, but they weren't mine. My voice was firm but feminine. Recognition shot through me.

Rhaegynne was a character in Grandma's stories. She was the first of the Rhaegynne dragons. And Evren . . .

My feet — Rhaegynne's feet — quickened beneath me to rejoin the knights.

"The cave of the beast is ahead!" Evren said enthusiastically. "Our quest is nearly over!"

I smiled and pressed on, but my stomach continued to twist with nerves.

As promised, the cave was not much farther, but the yawning maw of the mountain stank of rot and decay. I prayed the others would slow their march, but Evren continued on, undeterred.

Inside, a massive red dragon slept on a pile of bones and gold.

One of the armored men behind me grinned and rushed forward, drawing his sword and preparing to strike while the beast slept. The dragon's eyes opened, widening in fear. In a blink, the dragon changed to the same diamond dragon from before, and my heart lurched in my throat.

"No!" I leaped forward and threw my own body between the blade and the dragon.

Just before the blade hit, I found myself in a much cleaner version of the dragon's cave, sitting in a rocking chair by a stone hearth crackling with flames. I held an infant in my arms, and I knew intuitively the dragon was safe. A man with blond hair pulled back in a bun and tied with a strip of leather played with a toddler on the ground in front of me.

"What are the chances this one has your power, too?" the man asked, turning his face to me.

I gasped, recognizing Evren from before. His eyebrows crinkled with concern.

"Are you all right, Rhaegynne?"

I searched the face of the infant in my arms and nodded. "Our children and their children and their children still, will all share my dragon's blood," I said confidently. "Perhaps one day, they'll learn to share their gifts with others, and they will share my power too."

Something needled at me. A sense of déjà vu — a dream within the dream.

I knew this story...

Rhaegynne had nearly died saving that dragon. The dragon had tried to save her in turn, but granted her the ability to become a dragon, a gift that would follow through Rhaegynne's bloodline for generations. But something had happened...

"*Save them, Katherine.*" Grandma's voice echoed around the cave. "*Save them all.*"

The cave dissolved around me, throwing me onto the middle of a battlefield. Humans and dragons alike fought and bled and died around me. I ran between clashing bodies, dodging blades and flashing magic alike.

"*Save them!*"

In the distance, a giant, smoky gray dragon wrestled with a copper red dragon. Someone beside me screamed before transforming into a dragon and taking flight with wings that didn't move quite right, as though she didn't have complete control over her own body.

"*Save them!*"

I ducked under a bright curse, covered my head, and crouched low on the battlefield. A corpse stared at me, its mouth lolling open. I screamed.

"*Katherine,*" a quiet, masculine voice said.

The battle faded around me, and I found myself in a meadow amid a vast mountain range. Soft grass and wildflowers cushioned my bare feet.

This was still a dream, but I felt like *me*.

A huge bird circled overhead. It spiraled lower, and I could make out jet-black scales, a long neck and tail, and four legs.

Not a bird. A dragon.

The dragon landed in front of me, stretching his massive, batlike wings toward the sky before folding them against his sides. Two large horns curled ram-like around his face, and two more stretched back from his temples. "Hello, Katherine." His voice — the one that chased away the nightmare of the battle — sounded in my head. *"My name is Aerolan. I was a friend of Jamie's."*

I stepped backward, my heart pounding as questions flooded my mind.

He leaned his massive head toward me, and I took another involuntary step back.

"I'm not going to hurt you." His mouth didn't move when he spoke. He shifted his massive head closer to me, reached out a claw, and tapped Grandma's locket around my neck.

When I reached up to snatch it away from him, the world suddenly snapped into focus, as if a dirty lens had been removed from my eyes. Every inch of my body itched and trembled, but the itch was nothing — *nothing* — compared to the energy that filled my body. Every fiber of my being thrummed with a power both exhilarating and terrifying.

A shiver ran down my spine. My muscles bunched. My hands fell to the ground, replaced with talons that bit into the earth. Wings unfurled from my back, reaching for the sky. Confidence replaced my fear, and I threw back my head and roared. Warmth bubbled up in my chest, and fire chased after the jubilant noise. I pushed my wings down and lifted myself off the ground, flying straight up, lost in my power.

My grief lingered, sharp and fresh, but somehow, I felt closer to Grandma than I'd ever been.

I knew this was only a dream. I remembered I was human. But that awareness faded quickly, replaced by the power and *joy* of being a dragon. My wings and tail moved as though they had always been a part of me. The muscles across my back and chest worked effortlessly with my wings to send me into the heavens.

I was *born* to fly.

Aerolan flew up next to me with some draconic semblance of a grin on his face. Beneath us, even the mountains seemed small from here.

I tried to speak, but another exuberant roar came out.

His grin turned into deep, rumbling laughter. "*We communicate through thought.*"

"*This is incredible,*" I said, imagining my words projecting out to him.

"*It is!*" he said, tucking his wings to roll and turn away.

I pulled my wings in and dropped into a free fall.

The ground rushed up to greet me, but at the last second, my wings opened, and I shot up again — spiraling, corkscrewing, and looping as I did. This was more than power. More than joy or pleasure. This was *freedom*.

I circled the meadow while Aerolan landed and watched me. I dove and spiraled, basking in the sensation.

"*Time to land,*" Aerolan said.

Anger sparked. I wasn't done. What right did he think he had to command *me?*

I shook myself. That wasn't like me. Besides, there was a gravity to his voice that drew me back, so I let myself fall until the ground grew dangerously close. I threw out my wings and caught myself just before landing.

As I touched the ground, everything felt wrong. I was tiny, weak, and dizzy. I tried to spread my wings to steady myself, but nothing happened. My eyesight turned fuzzy. Grief crashed over me like a wave.

I refused to look down, afraid to see what remained. Instead, I opened my mouth to roar and spew flames at

Aerolan, but instead of fire and a thunderous roar, words came. "What have you done to me?" I screamed.

I was human again. A weak human enslaved by gravity and the crushing weight of reality.

I crumpled to my knees and buried my face in my hands.

"I'm sorry," a kind voice said.

I jerked my head up. A boy about my age, maybe seventeen or eighteen, with messy, black hair hanging in layers around his blue eyes and a tawny face stood in front of me. He wore a long-sleeved black shirt advertising The Band Chaos. A white scar poked out the top of his collar.

"Who are you?" I asked.

"I am Aerolan." He gave me an apologetic smile. "I couldn't keep the magic going. You've not accepted your grandma's gift and changed into a dragon in real life, so I had to use my magic to sustain it here."

"You're talking about Rhaegynne?" The waves of grief tried to suck me under as the events at the hospital came back to me.

Flashes of my earlier dreams. Of Rhaegynne, the first dragon shapeshifter, and of her optimistic hope for the future for her descendants. Of Rhaegynne calling her powers a gift. But I knew the stories. The dragons would be cursed and plunged into war for over a century. And if the stories *were* true, the Rhaegynne were still cursed. The prophecy had never been fulfilled, and those who dared to spend any time as a dragon would be forced to fight for their king.

The power wasn't a gift. It was a death sentence.

Terror built up inside me. "No. I don't . . . I know the stories! The dragons are cursed! I don't want this."

"Your grandma was free. When she died, she opened the way for you to take her place. If you accept, you'll inherit her protection. And if you're willing, you could free the rest of us."

Save them, Grandma's voice had begged.

A movement like a meteor blazing through the sky broke through my astonishment. A massive red dragon crashed into the meadow. He hit the ground as a human, rolled to deflect the impact, and stumbled into a run. "Time to go!"

"Sa'hranet?" Aerolan said, looking shocked and terrified at the young man's appearance. "What—"

"He knows!" Sa'hranet said, his face pale under his dark red hair. He kept glancing over his shoulder. His hands trembled as he fidgeted with a bracelet on his wrist. "He's coming! We have to leave. I'll explain later. Go!" His whole body rippled like a mirage before he disappeared.

Aerolan looked beyond me, his eyes widening in fear. "Kat, you have to wake up!"

A smoky gray dragon, the same from the battle in my dream and larger than Aerolan and Sa'hranet combined, darted through the sky.

"Who is the unclaimed?" The dragon's powerful voice shook through my head so hard it rattled my bones and made my teeth click together.

I knew his voice.

"Leave!" Aerolan begged. "If you die here, you won't wake up! Go!" He shoved his hands against my chest.

As I fell backward, the new dragon roared. His throat glowed white hot, and fire reached out for me.

I JERKED awake in my own room, still feeling the heat of the flames on my skin.

I clutched something close to my chest, and for a moment, I thought it was my old stuffed tiger. But it was too large.

Realizing what I held, I hugged Grandma's book tighter and sat up. My clothes stuck to my skin with sweat, and I struggled to catch my breath. I wiped the sweat off my face with a shaking hand.

She was gone.

Why couldn't the hospital have been a horrible nightmare too?

Though, maybe it was. The fight was probably some bizarre way for my mind to cope with seeing Grandma struggle and die. Shock could do wild things. The parts where I relived Grandma's old fairy tales and flew as a dragon were definitely dreams, though. Dreams born from my sorrow.

Tears pricked my eyes. I *wanted* it to be real. The magic. The dragons. I had found a connection to Grandma there. She had felt so *close*.

I swallowed hard and took a shaky breath, trying to think of something else.

I wasn't about to be eaten by an angry dragon, so there was that, at least.

What time was it? I fished around until I found my phone in my pocket. The bright light made me wince. It wasn't even six yet. I had a series of notifications from Aaron. First a series of texts about our homework. When I hadn't responded, his messages turned to ones of concern.

Homework. School. Aaron.

Grandma.

I sent a message back to Aaron, telling him I was calling out sick, then set the phone face down on the nightstand and turned on the light. I carefully turned Grandma's book over in my hands and traced the embossed dragon and compass on the front with my fingers. A tear broke free and ran down my face.

Hoping to find her in the pages, I opened the book.

The artwork stood out first. It was nothing like what I remembered from when I was a kid. All the pen strokes and colors combined to create abstract pictures. Dragons from all different mythologies, a sword, and a crown. The more I stared, the more it changed. I scanned the page, drinking in every brush stroke. I could have stared at the intricate details for the rest of my life, but when I reached the edge of the page, I froze.

The words weren't written in any language I'd ever seen before. I flipped through the pages, trying to find a place I *could* read. I begged the next page to be legible. I needed to have this so I could still have a part of her.

I checked the front and back for a key or some sort of note I might recognize. Nothing but runes and artwork. Why did Grandma give me a book I couldn't even read? How did she read it? Did she make it up?

The memory of the hospital came rushing back. The beeping machines. The man. The fight. The smell—

I could still smell it.

I threw off my covers. I hadn't changed my clothes before getting into bed.

Desperate to get away from the stench of antiseptic, I scrambled out of bed and pulled off my clothes.

I threw on running clothes, laced up my shoes, grabbed my phone, and raced to the car. I had to get out of the house, lose myself in the mountain trails, and calm my mind.

I drove faster than I should have, trying to outrun the anguish building inside me. My hands burned as I clenched the steering wheel like it might fend off the pain.

Once parked in the trailhead's empty parking lot, I jumped out of the car and sprinted up the path, barely remembering to lock the doors.

And I ran.

My legs cramped and my lungs ached, but I pushed on

through the overgrown trails. The short bushes licked at my exposed ankles with morning dew. Far-reaching tree branches clawed at my arms and snagged in my hair, but I kept running.

A thin creek flowed beside me in the opposite direction. I pushed over a steep incline to a rocky ridge and silently begged the river to roar loud enough to drown out my thoughts.

Grandma is dead.

My feet stumbled, and I sprawled out on the dirt. I pulled myself to my knees, trying to catch my breath, but my throat, still bruised from the man's grip, tightened, and the sorrow I had outpaced engulfed me.

The locket around my throat was heavy. I gripped it in my hand, tears blurring my view of the rising sun along the horizon. I took short, gasping breaths, trying to get in control, but my sobs came out in hitches, and my body shook.

"Why did you leave me?" I shouted at the sky.

I probed at the raw, ragged edges of my heart and tried to make sense of the tragedy.

It might have been childish, but I wanted to believe her stories. Because believing her stories was the only way I could keep her with me.

She'd asked me to save the dragons — to *become* one. So, I would. I'd break the curse, defeat the kings. Free the dragons.

I squeezed her locket until it dug into my skin.

I would accept the gift of Rhaegynne.

Like in my dream, there was a surge of energy, a rush of power. My left shoulder itched. My already good vision got even better. The necklace I still cradled like a talisman burned.

A cry of pain escaped my lips but was cut short by a thrill of energy across my body.

My body shifted instantaneously. My cry turned into a roar.

I froze and looked down at myself.

I was a *dragon*.

Each scale was a perfectly polished silvery mirror, weaving seamlessly into the next. They reflected the early autumn leaves around me and my own draconic face. From the faintly distorted reflection, my snout was long and square through the jaw and nose. A dramatic crest of horns wreathed my head like a crown. Even my eyes were mirrors, and reflections bounced into eternity between my scales and irises.

The dream was only a shadow of what it was really like.

I leaned over the cliff wall, eyeing the drop below. I didn't even bother to think about whether I could fly. I knew I would.

I launched myself off the edge.

My wings flared out and caught the wind beneath me, catching an updraft and sending me spiraling into the sky. I pushed toward the clouds for miles, as high as I could go. The Montana town nestled in the Rockies where I'd spent my whole life sprawled beneath me, and the miles of farms, forests, and houses shrank into minuscule versions of themselves.

I couldn't tell if it was instinct or luck, but flying came as naturally as breathing. My body rejoiced at the thrill of it all.

But my wings burned, and my lungs ached. I had no endurance for actual flight.

I dipped my wing and pivoted back to the cliffs. I landed at the edge of the tree line, panting hard. I fell to the ground and shrank back into a human.

My legs collapsed beneath me, and my stomach roiled. On trembling arms, I dragged myself to the nearest bush and spat bile into the dirt.

I wiped my mouth, slumped onto the ground again, and ran a finger over the small pendant Grandma gave me. My thumbnail got caught in the clasp, and the locket popped open.

A small piece of paper fell into my hand.

I uncurled it curiously and smiled when Grandma's tight, curly handwriting greeted me.

"Trust Coleman and Jason. Save the dragons, darling. I love you." A phone number was written on the back.

Save them.

I dug my fingernails into the palm of my hand. The sharp sting of reality bit back. My heart sped up, responding to the fear mounting inside me.

What was happening to me?

Save them.

With one last glance at the deep gouges my claws left in the earth, I ran back to my car, sliding on the damp earth and slick rocks. I couldn't outrun my grief. I couldn't outrun the fear threatening to overcome me when I considered for even a moment that any of this was real.

But I could try.

I slid to a stop beside my car and fumbled to unlock the door. I yanked open the glove box and pulled out my phone. With shaking fingers, I dialed the number on Grandma's note.

The phone rang twice and went to voicemail. The tone beeped in my ear, and a half-choked sob escaped me.

"My name is Katherine Lance. Jamie told me to call you before she . . . died. Help me."

The New Guy

Aaron

I tapped my foot impatiently and scrolled through various apps on my phone while I waited at the library's desk for the printer to finish making a copy of my notes for Kat.

A breaking news headline caught my attention while I scrolled: A gas leak caused an explosion a few hours from here. I frowned. There'd been other reports like this lately. Usually with some insistence that it was a construction failure.

Before I could get too conspiratorial, the red-haired librarian passed me the stack of warm paper. I thanked her as I took them, then rushed to go find Kat.

I walked into the school's common area, already heading to where I knew I'd find her sitting with Miranda and Lily. I scanned our section until I caught sight of them. Lily sat on the edge of the bench with her dark skin and perfectly styled curls. Miranda leaned close to Lily, with her short, straight strawberry blonde hair, and pale, freckled skin. Her nose ring flashed in the light.

Kat sat beside them, gaze unfocused, and twisted a lock of her long, wavy, dark blonde hair.

She had missed school yesterday, and I was glad to see her today, but she didn't look ready to be back yet. I jogged over to them and set my backpack down, waving to Lily and Miranda. Kat didn't even blink. I took a seat next to her and touched her shoulder.

She jumped, startled out of her haze. "Oh, hey, Aaron." She sounded exhausted.

Lily gave me a pointed look, gesturing her head at Kat like I was supposed to do something.

Miranda took Kat's hand, but Kat didn't seem to notice.

"Are you okay?" I asked, taking a closer look at Kat. Her eyes were puffy and red, but the rest of her face was pale as a sheet. She dropped the lock of hair she'd been playing with and let it hang limply in front of her face. *Oh no.* "What's going on?"

"Huh?" Kat said, blinking back to the present. "Oh. I . . ." She sniffed.

"It's your grandma, isn't it? Did she get worse?" It had been so sudden, but we'd all hoped she'd recover.

"Yeah . . ." Her face stiffened to stone, trying to hide her emotions.

Oh, Kat . . . "What happened?"

She finally looked at me, her brown eyes bloodshot and full of a haunted hollowness. She clenched her jaw. "She's gone." Her voice cracked, but she kept her eyes locked with mine, as if daring me to ask if she was okay. Begging.

I didn't know what to say. "I'm here for you."

She didn't respond, just leaned her head on my shoulder. I wrapped my arm around her and prayed she couldn't hear the way my heart pounded. Miranda and Lily joined in to hug Kat.

We sat like that for a time until Kat shifted away.

"What are you *doing* here today? Go home," I said.

She shook her head. "Missing more class means falling behind, which means adding even more stress to this mess."

I swallowed and glanced around the room as though I might find some words of comfort written on the walls.

"Aaron?" Kat asked. "Have you ever seen something you couldn't explain?"

"Like the creepy child I swear I saw in the window of that abandoned house across the street or like everything I've ever seen in a calculus textbook?"

Miranda gave me a death glare, but Kat let out a half-hearted laugh. "More like the creepy kid, I guess. Do you believe in stuff like that? Ghosts and magic or whatever?"

I raised an eyebrow. "In some ways, sure. Why?"

"What about you two?" Kat asked our friends, pulling away from me to sit up again.

"I think there's more than we can see," Lily responded, clearly avoiding an answer.

Miranda twisted one of the many earrings decorating her ears. "I don't *believe* in it, but I won't mess with it."

Kat chewed her lip, her eyes wandering around the room — looking anywhere but at us. "Listen, something horrible happened when I was at the hospital before she . . . I don't know what to make of—" Her face paled.

I tried to follow her gaze across the common room. "What's wrong?"

Her face turned pink again. "Nothing."

She pointed across the room at a boy standing awkwardly near a girl with light brown hair who I was pretty sure was our senior class president. The new guy wore a long-sleeved blue T-shirt and had dark, messy hair that came down to his chin in places and tan skin.

Kat wiped her eyes, somehow erasing all evidence of her

sudden fear. She picked up her bag and started to make her way through the rest of the students between us and the stranger.

"Where are you going?" I asked, rushing to catch up with her.

She only hesitated a moment. "To introduce myself."

I glanced back at Lily and Miranda, who shrugged and stood to follow us. I trailed behind Kat, baffled. We didn't get many new students, but Kat wasn't usually one to go out of her way to introduce herself to strangers.

"Hey! You're new, right?" she asked when we reached him, an odd edge to her voice.

He raised an eyebrow at her. "Yeah, my name's Jason. I just moved in from out of state." He adjusted his shirt collar to cover a thick scar on his collarbone.

"Well, welcome to Montana," she said without any actual *welcome* in her tone. "I'm Kat. This is Aaron, Lily, and Miranda."

I awkwardly waved next to her. Why was Kat being so . . . cold?

"Think you four could show me around?" He gestured to the class president. "Amanda has to help out in the office this morning."

"Oh, I'm happy to help," the class president insisted. "But, if you could . . ."

"Of course," Kat said before I had the chance.

Amanda waved and ran off, her brown hair bouncing behind her.

"What's your schedule?" Kat asked, reaching for the printed schedule in his hand.

Jason passed her the paper.

She scanned through it. "You have first period with me and third with Aaron and me."

"It'll be nice to have some familiar faces!" he said with a smile.

The bell rang, and Kat jumped again. She nervously laughed, trying to brush off my worry with a wave of her hand.

It didn't work. "Are you sure you'll be okay, Kat?" I whispered under my breath, hoping Jason wouldn't hear.

"I'm *fine*," she said in the most unassuring way possible. "I'll walk you to class, Jason!" She waved over her shoulder and led Jason to their shared first period.

They were just going to class, but I couldn't shake the feeling something had happened between them without a single word spoken.

Mitosis and Dragons

Kat

My hands shook as I walked with "Jason" to class.

Definitely some random new kid named Jason.

Definitely not Aerolan from my dream. Only a coincidence they look the same.

Yet that scar...

We turned the corner, leaving Aaron behind. Jason pulled us to the side and leaned in close, his voice barely above a whisper. "I'm sorry I couldn't explain more in the Dream Realms the other night. We have more freedom there, but he still found us."

My palms started to sweat. I glanced past him, scared someone had overheard. Most stared at their phones, oblivious to the way the world fell to pieces around me.

"What?" I squeaked.

"Sorry. The Dream Realms is a place Rhaegynne can go in their sleep and won't end up as giant dragon puppets," he explained, moving his arms up and down like a marionette.

I rubbed my hands into my eyes. "This is still a dream, isn't it?"

"It's not, Kat." Jason looked away. "I'm sorry."

I wanted to believe it. I *chose* to believe it.

But my mind was reeling. "It was real? All of it?" My knees wobbled with relief. "I was *actually* a dragon yesterday?"

His attention snapped back to me. "Wait. By yourself?"

"Yes! That's why I called. That was you, right?"

Jason frowned. "How . . . do you feel?"

My chest burned with an energy I couldn't shake. My back itched. "My grandma is dead, dragons might be real, and I might be one. What do you *expect* me to feel?"

"Lost. Scared. Sad." He rubbed his arm. "I feel it too. Especially now that Jamie . . ."

My stomach clenched. I wanted this — the gift and the curse — so I could be close to Grandma. I *was* scared, lost, confused, and sad.

But a *rightness* had resonated in my bones since yesterday.

As much as it scared me, I needed this. And, selfishly, I wanted to succumb to that primal instinct and *fly* again.

"My grandma said I could trust you," I said. "But I need answers first."

"I'll explain as much as I can, but we should get to class."

The hallway was deserted. I led him to our class, walking in with our heads down as though that would keep Mr. Moyes from noticing our tardiness.

Mr. Moyes rubbed at his short blond beard in irritation, but he rarely stopped his lessons for anything, never mind a couple tardy students.

Jason took his seat next to me at the empty lab table at the back of the class.

I leaned in close and whispered. "All right. Start talking."

"You know the stories. What do you want to know?"

"Who are you?"

Jason eyed Mr. Moyes at the front of the classroom before continuing. "I'm Jason right now, but call me Aerolan as a dragon—"

"Why is there any difference?" I snapped louder than I meant to.

Several heads turned toward us.

Mr. Moyes glared at us across the classroom. "Question, Miss Lance?" Everyone turned around, curiosity and confusion etched on their faces.

"Uh . . ." I read the slide projected onto the whiteboard, trying to find a valid question to ask. "I wanted to ask . . . what is the difference between . . . meiosis and mitosis?" I cringed. The slide literally explained the difference. And we'd gone over this material already.

"Miss Lance?"

"I'm sorry. I see it now. I got a little lost."

He pulled at the short ends of his beard like he wanted to rip them out. "Please pay attention, Katherine," he said before continuing his lesson.

I considered ripping out my own hair.

Jason and I sat still, trying to act as innocent as possible until everyone turned back toward the teacher.

Jason whispered under his breath, pretending to take notes. "Until the curse is broken, every Rhaegynne that isn't you, your grandma, or the kings are essentially two separate creatures — the rational human and the hive mind dragon. When I take dragon form, my mind is one of *many* swarming in my skull, with my king at the center of it all. But if we can convince ourselves we're *different* as a dragon — if I can convince myself I'm *Aerolan* — I can keep my free self — *Jason* — away from the king's influence. It protects us and those around us.

"Aerolan is a prison." He turned the page in his notebook. "Jason? Jason is just trying to understand the phases of meiosis."

I fought back a smile at that. I could see why Grandma liked him.

"Even in the Dream Realms where it's safe, if I'm a dragon, I'm Aerolan." A smile twitched at his lips. "I'll do my best to make sure you don't meet Aerolan anywhere else."

I scratched at someone's initials carved into the black lab desk. "How can you stay human? I want — *need* — to be a dragon again."

His smile turned sad. "It's amazing, isn't it? It's why the puppetry even works, especially at first. Being a giant puppet is almost worth it to have the chance to fly again. Until your king needs you to fight for them or change someone else into a Rhaegynne. Then nothing's worth taking that risk willingly."

I remembered from the stories that Rhaegynne could share the gift with others. The gift could follow bloodlines, and if a human got Rhaegynne blood mixed with their own, they could change that way too. There was something about giving tokens — items enchanted with magic — that could share the gift. And I remembered how even biting a human could change them — assuming they survived, of course. But I didn't realize the kings could force their dragons to change others.

"When were you . . ." I trailed off, unsure if I could ask what I wanted to know.

"When was I changed?" Jason brushed his hair out of his face. "Over a decade ago. I was ten." My face must have betrayed my shock because he quickly added, "Rhaegynne age slower than humans. I'm seventeen. I think. I've been alive for twenty-two, but the magic slows things down. Jamie looked — *was* — a lot younger than her age. Until the curse . . ." His face fell.

I hadn't thought much of it, but growing up, people always asked if my mom and grandma were sisters. Only after she got sick — *cursed?* — did she begin to show her age. "What happened?"

"Balaskad — one of the dragon kings — hit her with a curse we couldn't stop."

My stomach seized into knots at the name. Blood drained from my face. "Someone came to the hospital." We'd already been whispering, but my voice came out so soft, I couldn't be sure Jason heard. "He and my grandma both mentioned Balaskad." I hadn't told anyone what I had heard. Or seen. I still wasn't sure if it had even happened.

"Who was it?" Jason asked, worry and confusion creasing his eyebrows together.

I shook my head. "I don't know. Aurak-something or other, but—"

"Aurakbahor?" Jason's face paled. "*King* Aurakbahor?" He looked torn between anger and terror as he struggled to keep his voice down. "He found her?"

"If that's who it was," I answered.

"Does anyone else know he was there?"

"I told the nurses someone came, but I don't think they took me seriously," I admitted. "I couldn't explain what he had done. He doesn't know who I am, right?"

He shook his head, and fear sent a shock through my body. "He knows. Coleman — he's Sa'hranet — told me. Aurakbahor knows, but he's terrified of you."

"*Me?*" I was somewhat athletic, but besides the hospital, I'd never been in a fight before, and if that was anything to go off of, I wasn't exactly intimidating.

"He and Balaskad have been at war for decades. Jamie was the only one strong enough to pose a threat to them. He assumes you'll end up like her."

"Why'd he let me go?"

"I don't know. But I know Jamie held on for you."

"How did you know her?" I asked.

"I met Jamie about a decade ago. I'd been taken prisoner after an accidental change. My king caught my rebellious thoughts, and I suspect he didn't like that much." He shot me a wry grin. "Sa'hranet was the one who found me and helped Jamie plan the prison break. They rescued almost a dozen prisoners that day. I've been close with them both ever since."

I turned my head to pretend to listen to Mr. Moyes's lesson about gametogenesis. I bit my lip, begging the tears not to come. Grandma must have fought her whole life to try to free the dragons, only to be killed by the kings who cursed them in the first place. Now, she wanted me to finish what she couldn't. The only thing keeping me together was the thought of carrying on her legacy.

I missed her so much.

"Kat," Jason whispered.

"What?" I answered, wiping away a tear.

"You're a Rhaegynne now."

"So?" Even as tears filled my eyes, my vision sharpened instead of blurred.

"I know this is a lot to take in, but I need you to take a couple deep breaths. Rhaegynne are prone to changing when they experience strong emotions."

My anger flared at his words. "So, I can't grieve?"

"No. Please grieve; I'm grieving too. But we can't let it consume us. Stay in control of your emotions, especially when you're in a classroom filled with people who don't know dragons exist."

"How do I control *emotions?*"

He was silent for a second, rubbing at his right arm. "Most Rhaegynne will find something we call a tether. It's a small object or a texture or a song or whatever you can keep with you to help you ground yourself when the emotions start to take over."

I immediately reached for grandma's locket at my throat.

Jason caught the motion and nodded. "That would be perfect."

But grounding myself when reality sucked so much only made my heart quicken and my breath hitch. I buried my face in my shaking hands.

Jason put a hand on my shoulder. "If you'll let me, I can teach you how to be a dragon. How to control all of this. Your grandma sent me to find you, but it's your choice."

He was taking a risk just being here. Risking what little freedom he had in hopes of getting more. Grandma told me to trust him.

So, I did.

I took a ragged breath. "Did she ever talk about me?"

"All the time." I lifted my head from my arms. He gave me a sad smile. "When she was injured, most of the resistance fled. Coleman and I were the only ones who stayed, so she told us how to find you. She wanted you to know she was sorry she never told you the truth. She was sorry to leave you this huge responsibility. She also wanted you to know she loved you and is so proud of you."

I lifted my head and found him watching me with a startling intensity.

His blue eyes swam with tears under his shaggy hair. "I'm sorry," he said. "I know we're strangers, but we need your help to stop the kings who killed her."

A spark of determination ignited in my soul, numbing the grief that consumed me. I grew up hearing how horrible the kings were. They both had a hand in Grandma's death. And they couldn't control me.

If I had the power to help in any way, I *should*.

I could accept this responsibility, but this fight had taken everything out of my grandma. It *killed* her.

I clenched my jaw, gathering courage I didn't know I had. "What do I need to do?"

"Let's go to the mountains after school. I'll teach you what I know."

Oh, heavens help me.

A Crash Course in Being a Dragon

Kat

The final bell rang, and I jumped up and ran to the hallway before anyone else had even left their seat. Jason and I had agreed to meet at the exit closest to my car.

I wanted to sprint through the parking lot, but Jason kept us at a leisurely pace.

"I will go without you," I hissed.

"Do you want people to stare?"

I didn't care, but I slowed to a walk and pulled out my phone to tell my mom I'd be home late. I climbed into my car and sighed.

His door had barely closed before I drove off and navigated around the cars and pedestrians also trying to escape. The car's tires squealed when I finally pulled out onto the road.

"Whoa! Kat, I am a strict believer in speed limits and *not dying*," he said sarcastically, reaching for the car's ceiling handle.

I rolled my eyes, fighting the urge to drive even faster. My stomach fluttered, and my blood burned. "Everything feels weird. I *have* to change again."

He leaned back in his seat. "So, what's our cover story when someone asks what we're doing all the time?"

"Why do we need one?"

"The kings have literal task forces to cover up dragon sightings. You'd put anyone you told in danger."

I shivered. "Th-that makes sense. What do you have in mind?"

"We could say we're dating," he said with a wink.

I blushed and looked away. *What would Aaron think of that?* It wasn't like Jason and I would actually be together. And Aaron and I were just friends, but I couldn't help but wonder what he'd think if I started dating some guy I literally just met.

I laughed to try to soften the rejection. "That would raise more questions than answers. Besides, pretty much everyone knows I'm demiromantic and ace so it wouldn't be realistic."

"Oh, nice! I'm bi! I was mostly kidding anyway."

"Any other ideas?"

He didn't answer at first. "We could say you're helping me catch up with my classes."

"What if I start gaining muscle? How would I explain that with studying?" I turned onto the dirt road toward the trail head.

"We're taking a body building class together?" he suggested.

I pulled into the narrow parking lot and put the car in park. "Do you play any sports?"

"Yes, let's definitely put a Rhaegynne — prone to changing with strong emotions — into a competitive environment that's bound to cause an adrenaline rush and force a change." His voice was playfully sarcastic. "Nah, I don't. Do you?"

"Not really," I said, getting out of the car. "I know how to play lacrosse a bit. We could say I'm helping you train for spring."

He closed the car door behind him. "Would that be suspicious, though? Is lacrosse co-ed? I know nothing about it."

I let out a short laugh. "No. Girl's and boy's lacrosse have different rules and equipment, but I've only ever played by boy's lacrosse rules. Aaron used to come back from practice when we were kids and show me things so we could practice together. We've played for years."

"Deal. Now, let's go learn to be a dragon!"

"Do we have to worry about people seeing me when I'm a dragon?" I asked, the sudden anxiety of getting caught twisting with the anticipation of flying again.

"I'll put up an enchantment to keep you hidden. Try not to fly too far, but human brains, at a subconscious level, are *very* good at trying to explain away magical things with mundane justifications, so you'll probably be fine."

"Okay," I said. He wasn't wrong. Hadn't I done just that after the hospital?

The distraction of our conversation had kept me focused enough to drive, but now excitement rushed like adrenaline in my limbs, and I wasn't sure if I'd be able to stay human much longer. I sprinted ahead of Jason, hardly paying attention to my footing on the rocky dirt.

I made it to the tree cover at the top of the hill before I decided I couldn't wait any longer. I flipped around to face Jason, panting.

"Here?" he asked.

I nodded, and his blue eyes darkened to a solid black, and I took an involuntary step back, horrified at the similarity between his dragon eyes and those of Aurakbahor's.

He stretched his arms out. "*Contra mortabalis ally!*"

Blue light flashed from his palms and set a circle of blue

flames dancing around us. His eyes returned to their normal blue.

"Are you ready?"

"I . . . don't know." Something twisted inside me. The urge to shift waited eagerly for me to give in, but now I was here . . . "If my grandma really did fight for this, if she really did *die* for this—" My voice cracked, but I managed to push on. "Then I *have* to do *something*." My knees shook, but I tried to contain my roiling emotions. I grasped my locket, feeling the smooth edges press into my hand. "But I'm scared."

Jason's face softened.

"I *want* this," I pressed on. "I used to beg Grandma to tell me stories about Rhaegynne dragons every time she was over. I used to dream of being a dragon."

"Then change, Kat."

My body itched from the power coursing through my veins. I shuddered, shaking off the limitations of my human body and transformed.

I stretched my back, loving the way the muscles bunched in my wings and shoulders. I spread my wings as wide as I could and turned my head to the sky, basking in the sun's blissful heat. I closed my eyes, enjoying how this body felt so alien, yet so natural. I relished the tingling magic in my blood.

It was real.

I turned my head to Jason, curious to see his reaction. I don't know what I expected to see, but I certainly wasn't expecting envy and . . . sorrow?

Jason swallowed hard and smiled. "That was all you needed to do."

"*What's wrong?*"

"Nothing." His eyes softened. "You look a little like Jamie."

"*I—*" My heart lurched at his words.

"Kat, you look awesome. *Go*."

I glanced down at the disorienting mirrorlike scales across my body reflecting his concerned face. My dragoness pride found it hard to disagree with him. I did look awesome with my sleek scales, curving crest of horns, and long, dangerous spines down my back. But my scales caught the reflection of the other emotions Jason tried to hide.

I blew steam out of my nose and glared at Jason. *"Don't change the subject! Something else is wrong."* I bared my fangs.

He stumbled backward, holding up his hands. "It's just that you can change whenever you want, and you don't have a dozen dragons hunting you for treason and a thousand more in your head telling you to do a million things you don't want to do. Not to mention Aurakbahor himself yanking on your soul. But you can change that!"

I stared at my feet. *"I want to fix this."*

"We'll get there. Now, go fly. I'll wait here."

I hesitated, wanting to help, but the rest of me begged to fly. The look on his face said staying wouldn't do any good anyway, so I extended my wings and pressed down hard.

I still had no idea how flying came so naturally, but it did. I soared over the mountain just to feel the power in my wings and taste the sweet air. The changing leaves were even more vibrant through the eyes of a dragon. The burning of my magic within kept me warm even in the icy, thin air amidst the clouds I tried to use for cover in case I'd flown too far away from Jason's spell. At best, I wouldn't be seen at all. At worst, people would think I was a bird or a plane. Hopefully.

At the very least, I was smooth, so I didn't glitter, but I'd blind anyone unfortunate enough to catch the sunlight bouncing off my side.

No words could describe the freedom of leaving gravity behind. But my joy was marred by the reminder of Jason's inability to do the same.

I circled back to him after a few short loops. Guilt ate at my stomach for doing that much.

"Back already?" he asked.

"*Yes. How do I change back?*" I was so exhausted last time that I didn't have to think to shift.

"Will it."

I closed my eyes and focused. Next thing I knew, I felt small and like I had run a marathon without training while having the flu.

I opened my eyes to find Jason's above mine again. I grinned. "I did it!"

He stepped toward me. "Good job." My knees buckled under me, but thankfully, Jason caught me. "The drop in power is *brutal*. Sorry."

"I'm gonna barf." I covered my mouth and clutched my stomach.

He helped me toward a bush and held my hair back. "The first few times are the worst," he admitted as I heaved. "It gets easier the more you do it."

I wiped my mouth and spat into the bush before collapsing against him, shaking. "Sorry."

"Don't worry about it. It happens to most of us."

I squeezed my eyes shut. "Why does something so amazing make you feel like death when it's over?"

"It makes you feel *normal* when it's over."

"Ugh, I hate normal. Why don't I get superpowers as a human, too?" Realizing how much of my weight I left on this near-stranger, I awkwardly pushed myself away, opting to rest against a nearby boulder instead. At least I felt strong enough to stay upright on my own.

"You do though. You don't age as quickly. You're stronger now. Your hearing and sense of smell are better."

I leaned back against the boulder, trying to take it all in.

"So, what's the plan? How do we break the curse and save the dragons?"

"Just like that?" he asked with a laugh. "You're already willing to go to war for us?"

Save them.

I paused. "When I heard the stories, I wanted someone to save the dragons. I could *be* that someone."

A smile twitched at the corners of his lips. "My plan is to train you while Coleman looks for resistance survivors and gathers intel on how to infiltrate Aurakbahor's and Balaskad's lairs. Once we know more — and you're stronger — we're going to assassinate the kings."

I recoiled. "Will that break the curse?"

Jason shrugged. "How could we still be puppets if there are no puppet masters?"

"Won't there still be puppet strings?"

He hesitated. "Only one way to find out. Are you in?"

Was I? I wanted to be a dragon, not an assassin. But if this was what it took . . . I swallowed and nodded. "What do I need to do?"

"Training," Jason said. "We'll use the Dream Realms at night so we can practice fighting as a dragon. In person, we'll build your stamina as a dragon, and I can teach you how to fight as a human and use magic. This is, unfortunately, something we'll need to do every day and every night."

"This seems like a lot," I said with a nervous laugh. I don't know what I expected, though. I was picking up the mantle Grandma had left for me. I had to be ready.

"It is." He helped me to my feet. "How do you feel now?"

"Significantly less wobbly."

"Good! Let's start tomorrow?"

My mood soured with fresh grief. "I . . . can't. We're busy

until the funeral on Saturday. Can we wait until after? Monday?"

"Monday works for me. Coleman should be in town for the funeral. Are you still okay to train in the Dream Realms?" he asked.

"Please? Spending time as a dragon might be the best way to honor her memory."

"Deal. Let's—" He cut himself off and pulled me behind a bush.

"What are you—"

"*Sh!*" he answered telepathically. "*I think there's another dragon.*"

The residual fatigue disappeared, replaced by a hot flash of fear. "How—"

He clamped his hand over my mouth. "*Talk to me telepathically. It's the same way you do it as a dragon.*"

"*Are you telling me,*" I said slowly; telepathy was harder as a human, "*we could have had the entire discussion in biology in our heads?*"

Jason shot me a panicked look. "*I think we have more pressing things right now. Listen.*" He glanced to the sky.

I held my breath, straining my ears. A low, rhythmic drumming came from above. "*Wings?*"

He nodded.

"*How did they find me already? I thought you put up some kind of spell!*"

"*I did, but it's against mortal eyes!*" He grasped my shoulders. "*Get out of here. I can distract them.*"

"*No,*" I said firmly. I couldn't risk losing him. And if he had to fight alone, I didn't want him to accidentally change and risk everything he and my grandma had worked for. "*What do I need to do?*"

"*Kat,*" he protested with a silent groan.

"*Give me the crash course on dragon fighting.*" I hoped he couldn't tell how terrified I was.

He gave me a rueful smile. "*You really are Jamie's granddaughter.*"

My pride at his words mingled with the fear of the imminent fight.

A massive shadow rolled across the ground, cast by a slender, burnt-orange dragon circling beneath the sun. The dragon dove and slammed into the clearing in front of me. I let my emotions — the pride and the fear — rush through me.

I shifted, and the dragon turned to look at me, baring her fangs. I regretted my stubborn insistence that I could do this. I tried to reach for my confidence again, but all I got was the horrifying realization that I was going to fight an actual dragon.

The dragon almost smiled as she approached.

Instinct insisted I get as large as possible. I reared back on my hind legs, opening my wings wide. A monstrous growl bubbled out of my throat as I swiped my claws across her face.

She reared back in surprise, her snarling lips breaking way to a burning, open mouth.

"*Watch out!*" Jason warned.

I jumped into the air, dodging the fire as my wings lifted me higher.

The dragon turned back toward Jason, distracted by the easier prey, but I swung my barbed tail at her head. She roared and jumped into the air, seeking vengeance.

"*Don't let her get above you!*" Jason shouted in my head. "*Whoever her king is will know you're not linked to them, and they'll force her to fight you anyway. She likely doesn't have any control here.*"

"Can't you use magic?" I tried to climb upward as fast as

possible, but she shot up like a bullet, knocked into me, and kept going. She arced above me and dove.

"*Jamie would haunt me if I hit you!*" he answered.

I dodged, twisted, and pulled up.

"*What do I do?*" I hoped telepathy carried the right volume and desperation I intended.

"*Keep your enemy in front of you at all times. Preferably below you.*"

I took advantage of the time it took her to correct her course.

"*Watch for lapses in her defenses,*" he instructed.

The orange dragon pulled out of her dive, and I pushed higher, trying to stay away.

"*Aim for the neck and underbelly. Avoid her fire, but don't forget your own. Use your talons and fangs. Your whole body is a heavily armored weapon, but so is hers. Your opponent may not be in control of themselves, but they have the insight of other dragons at their disposal. Think fast and move faster. Go for stunning blows; a mind-controlled dragon will not — cannot — back down on their own.*"

I turned and dove at her, but she continued upward, slamming her spiny back into my stomach. Our bodies colliding rang out like cannon fire, and I hoped Jason's enchantment worked for noise. I gasped and tried to reverse my dive and get above her again, but my wings kept flapping against hers beneath me.

"*You're a dragon, Kat. Let your instincts take over!*" Jason instructed unhelpfully.

I pulled my wings in tight and rolled off to the side, over her wing. I knocked her off-balance and sent her spinning. She righted far too quickly, and I pushed myself higher, trying to keep my advantage.

Her teeth sank into my tail, yanking me out of my ascent.

Howling, I turned and thrashed at her body, but my claws glanced off her scales.

"I take back what I said about seeking the higher ground. Seek any ground where you find an advantage." Jason had the audacity to sound apologetic.

"Now is not the best time to second-guess things!" I growled.

The dragon whipped her head to the side, flipping my body. She let go, and I spiraled out of control.

I caught myself and turned toward her, fire bubbling up my throat. I managed to produce an embarrassingly small jet of flame. She dodged easily.

"Your fire won't burn you. Do it again!"

I followed after her, trying my best to predict her path. I exhaled. My fire ignited again and raced toward the dragon. She dropped out of the way, disappearing behind the smoke and flames, but as the smoke cleared, she slammed into me and grabbed my shoulders with her talons. I dug my talons into her limbs, piercing through her scales. She roared, and I snarled back.

She tucked in her wings and leaned back, forcing me to support her weight. We plummeted. My stomach flipped in fear. I tried to break free, but she held on tighter. My wings strained under her dead weight.

"Don't be the first to break out of this. It's a battle of wills. If you let go first, she'll see it as a sign of weakness."

I snarled. Not being able to support the weight of two dragons felt like the real sign of weakness. But the dragon inside me knew this game, so I let her play it out. I folded my wings, and we plummeted through the sky.

We picked up speed and spun. The dragon thrashed, trying to force me to let go, but I dug my talons in deeper and growled.

We hissed, bit, and thrashed, but neither yielded. The

ground drew close, but I couldn't lose. I forced myself back into human form with the hope that I could slip out of her grasp. Her orange eyes widened in surprise, and I fell from her slack grip, screaming in pain.

Every injury I'd sustained as a dragon showed on my human body. Blood smeared down my arms from her talons. Involuntarily, the dragon took over, and I shifted back.

I had won our contest, but our fight wasn't over yet. I chased her into the sky.

"*Fire! Now!*" Jason commanded.

Warmth built in my throat, and I released it. The fire engulfed her, and she screamed a haunting, chilling scream. She dropped out of my range, spinning in the air to extinguish the flames. She snarled but then darted off into the distance.

My dragon roar trumpeted, triumphant, chasing after her fleeing form. I landed beside Jason and changed back, collapsing to my knees. My body trembled from the pain, and my hands didn't move quite right.

Jason ran up to me with awe across his face, but his eyes widened when he saw me.

"Wh-what do I tell the ER?"

He crouched next to me and took my arms in his, applying firm pressure to the wounds. "You don't." His eyes turned black again, and I realized his dragon eyes were nothing like Aurakbahor's. Jason's still had softness in them. He whispered something I couldn't understand, and his hands glowed light green over my bleeding arms.

Warmth flooded my arms until it burned, but the bleeding slowed, then stopped. Then not even a scar was left from the deep gashes.

"Where else are you hurt?" he asked.

My back. My chest. Everything was one radiating blob of pain. "Everywhere."

"Narrow it down. I need to know what to prioritize now that you're not bleeding out on me."

"Breathing hurts."

"Broke your ribs?" he asked.

I lifted up the side of my shirt, horrified to see the splotchy discoloration running from my hip and disappearing up my shirt. Touching it sent pain flaring through the shaky fog in my head. "Yeah. I think I broke my ribs."

"Let's start there," he said. "I'd rather not heal a collapsed lung if I can avoid it. Is it okay if I touch your side?"

"Yes."

His eyes turned black, and his hand glowed light green again, and this time, I caught the words. "*Sanare ossa.*"

Like with my arms, my ribs burned as the magic worked to knit my bones back together, but the relief when it ended could have brought me to tears.

"Magic," I breathed in awe, but my stomach churned. "Well, at least the attack at the hospital wasn't entirely a shock-induced hallucination," I muttered. "Though, admittedly, this could be one too."

Jason snorted a laugh. "You were literally just a dragon. Why is this shocking to you now?"

"In my defense," I said through chattering teeth, "I'm *in* shock. Everything is shocking."

His eyebrows creased together in concern, scanning me like he could see my pain.

I shrank, uncomfortable with the scrutiny. "You have to draw the real/not-real line *somewhere*."

"Well, draw it way beyond what you think is possible. What's next?"

I twisted to let him reach whatever was causing the throbbing pain between my shoulder blades. He began to work, muttering words I didn't understand under his breath, and again I caught that strange green glow from the corner of my eye.

"Maybe," he added, once the healing burn had subsided, "witches, werewolves, Santa Claus, and the boogeyman are real, too."

"I'll suspend my disbelief until proven otherwise, I guess." I stretched out my back in awe. "How does magic work?" I asked, my head clearing a little with each healed wound.

"It's similar to changing. There's this well of power in you — your dragon fire. You tap into it, say a few words, and direct it. The language — and the magic itself — is called Tasalgré. It's kind of a mix of everything. Some words were definitely stolen from Latin. I think I've recognized Spanish and Russian. But it's mostly a matter of memorizing the spells. Anywhere else hurt?"

I pointed out the bruising across my stomach.

"The words to heal cuts and bruises are *sanare cutis*," he said.

"*Sanare cutis*," I repeated, just to try it. Even without power behind them, the words tasted *zappy*. Like I had licked a battery but more pleasant. "Whoa."

He grinned. "It's cool, isn't it?" His face turned more serious while he reached to heal a bleeding gash on my face. "Congrats on surviving your first fight, but how did you *do* that?"

"Do what?" I asked. "Win?"

"No, not that," he said, moving to another set of injuries. "You changed back and forth in battle."

"Am I not supposed to be able to do that?"

He shook his head. "The adrenaline in a fight would keep most people stuck as a dragon until it was over. Where else needs healing?"

One by one, he healed my various wounds until everything

life-threatening or hard to hide was healed. My muscles still ached, and a few bruises remained, but I sighed in relief as Jason taught me the phrase to get blood out of my clothes — *safisha sanguis* — and helped me to my feet. His fingers were ice cold.

"Thank you," I said.

"Don't mention it," Jason said with a wave, but his lips were blue and shivering. It was getting a little cold now, but not *that* cold. "You'll return the favor eventually. Sorry I can't do more. I'm about tapped out. Mind if we stop for food? I'll pay. I'm starving."

"Are you okay?" I asked.

"You know the power drop after you shift back to a human? It's like that but worse. The magic draws on the dragon fire within you. If you burn too much, not only will you get tired, you'll get cold. If the fire goes out, so do you. I've seen magicians develop hypothermia and frostbite from overspending their flame."

I brushed the dirt off my pants. "Is there anything else I should know about magic?"

Jason started back toward the car. "Don't try to use it as a dragon. It's all locked in keeping you that way. There are plenty of other rules, but I'll teach them as we go."

As we reached the start of the trail, I could see the blue flames from Jason's ward again. "A cool thing about Tasalgré: Sometimes, it's not spoken." He held out a hand and closed his eyes. The blue fire around us extinguished itself, leaving no trace behind.

"Show-off." I laughed, relieved it didn't hurt now. "Is there anything magic *can't* do?"

Jason tugged at his shirt's collar, his scar slipping from view. "Old scars don't disappear. Some magical damage needs specific counter curses, or you can't undo it. And you can't make something out of nothing."

When we got to the car, I cranked the heater up for Jason. He gratefully hunched over the tiny vents while we drove to find food.

"Hey, Jason?" I asked a little later, eating a french fry while I drove. "Did you ever see Grandma's old leather book?"

"Book?" he said. "I think I know what you're talking about. Why?"

"She gave it to me at the hospital. It's . . . not in English."

He didn't reply until we pulled up to the school. "Bring it to our next practice," he said. He pointed at one of the only cars left in the parking lot. "That's my car over there."

I drove home with the radio off. My life had shattered, and I wasn't sure where all the pieces would land.

I parked in my driveway, but halfway to my front door, I heard a car coming around the corner. I looked back, surprised to see Aaron's car pull to a stop in front of my house.

Confused, I walked down to meet Aaron on the curb. "What are you doing here?" My stomach clenched. If there was anyone I wanted to tell about Rhaegynne, it was him. He'd been my best friend, my confidant, for as long as I could remember. How was I supposed to keep this from him?

Aaron stepped out of the car and leaned up against the passenger side. His giant dog, Prince, sat in the back seat with his tongue hanging out and his tail wagging. He rubbed his black nose on the foggy window.

"I know you said you were fine," he said, shyly running his fingers through his messy blond hair, "but you're clearly not fine, and you're not supposed to be fine. But I figured you can be at least a little fine. Prince can pretend to be a service dog. I have ice cream and a movie, and I found this cool leaf when I was leaving." He proudly held up a bright red leaf from a maple tree.

A rush of fondness and guilt filled me, but I accepted the leaf. "Thank you."

"It's nothing."

Prince managed to climb over the middle console and push his way out the driver's door Aaron had left ajar. He barreled out to me, tail wagging furiously as he sat beside me.

I rubbed his ears. "Good boy." He leaned his body into my leg, and I turned back to Aaron. "Want to come inside?"

"Only if you share the ice cream with me," he replied, already grabbing the ice cream tub and movie from the passenger side.

"You mean you came all this way, pretending to be worried about me, all so you could eat the ice cream you gave me?" I teased.

"I mean . . . why else would I get ice cream?"

Livin' that Double Agent Life

Coleman

He's late, I thought, irritably shoving my phone back in my pocket. I checked down the alley's entryway, which was lit only by a flickering streetlamp, trying not to seem like an easy mugging target. I sighed and leaned back against the brick wall behind me.

Except the brick wall wasn't a brick wall at all. It wasn't even there.

I fell backward through the illusion, ever so gracefully landing flat on my butt. My cane bounced on the ground next to me.

At least I didn't scream.

With the illusory wall gone, my senses were met with a chorus of conversation and the stench of incense and cheap alcohol. I stood with my cane, brushed off my pants, and looked around the tavern. I smiled awkwardly at the dark-haired hostess. "You, uh, moved the door, I see."

She seemed unamused and uninterested at first, but as she studied me, her mouth opened.

I looked down to make sure nothing was on my shirt. "Is something wrong?"

"By the Ancients. You're *back*." She had a faint southern accent.

"Ah, yes. Well—"

She leaned over the counter conspiratorially. "I heard you ran away with that resistance boy and Aurakbahor killed you himself."

I shrugged, trying to figure out if I'd ever met her before. "Um, yeah. Well, ta-da..."

"You come back from the dead and decide the best use of your time is to cause trouble like the old days?" She placed a hand on her chest. "Well, bless your heart. Come on now, honey. Let's get you seated. What can I get for you?" She led me through a crowded and smoky dining room to an empty table. Vines hung down from the walls, liquors and potions filled the racks behind the bar, and illusionary finches flitted about the room.

"Does the bird sing today?" I asked.

She scowled. "What is someone like — well, excuse me, but someone like you doing with someone like..."

Ah. So, she recognized me from the Court. "Do not make me ask again."

Her face paled. "Yes, but we keep it in the back to not disturb the other guests."

I passed her a handful of cash. "No one needs to know I was here. Got it?"

"Of course, of course," she said, bowing and retreating to her hostess stand.

I sure didn't miss any of this. I glanced around the room, hoping no one else noticed her attention and complete disregard for thieves' cant. Luckily, everyone seemed either too absorbed in their food and conversation or knew better than to acknowledge what they had heard.

I sighed and made my way through the room to a side door. I didn't bother to knock.

"You're late, boy," a gruff voice greeted me in the dark room.

"You were supposed to meet me in the alley, Jinx." I turned on a light, revealing a short and balding man with large tufts of curly gray hair on either side of his ruddy, round face.

He squinted. "And be seen with you?" He barked out a laugh.

I spilled a pouch of gold on the table. His eyes went wide, and he began separating and counting. He pinched a ruby ring between his filthy fingernails and held it up to the light.

"So, I hear you're trying to get back into the Court." He set the ring back on the table, and I watched him palm a small gold chain. "After what you did?" He gave me a scathing look. "They say snitches get stitches. What'd they give you?"

Schooling my rage, I sat in front of him and casually inspected my knife. "Less than you deserve."

"You were supposed to be searched," he said through squinted eyes.

I stabbed the knife into the table. "Whoops."

He flinched. "Listen, kid—"

"I'm not a kid." I said it calmly, but I let my eyes flash dragon-red.

He eyed me. "How old are you then?"

"Thirty, fifty, two hundred. What does it matter when you're practically immortal? I lost track."

He sniffed. "All right, oh Ancient One."

I forced a smile. "Much better. Now, what can you tell me about the rest of the resistance?"

He poked the gold and jewels on the table before replying. "You'd know better than me. Besides, this barely covers your debt."

"*My debt?*" A cold hatred burned in my chest. I struggled to keep it off my face.

"From the last time, kid. You paid me half—"

The tight, burning frost built up in my chest. I rose and slammed his face into the table, making the gold bounce and clatter. I let the frost pour down my arms and felt blue tendrils crawl up my face. My vision turned faintly blue, and I pulled him up by his hair to watch the color drain from his face. "I paid the other half in Aurakbahor's dungeons after *you* sold me out."

His jaw dropped. "How are you not dead?"

"Who says I'm not?" I snarled. I grabbed his arms and let the blue lines slide down my hands and up his arms.

He screamed at the burning pain I had come to live with. "I don't know anything about the resistance! But I know a guy who might! Take it away! Take it away!"

I pulled the cursed poison back into myself — the transfer was only temporary anyway — and sat back in the chair. "Tell me who it is, and I'll consider *your* debt paid."

He panted in his seat, looking at the gold on the table like it might be as cursed as me. "You'll want to go to the Talisman Casino. Ask for Kroll. They'll know more than I do."

I scooped the gold back into the pouch and stood.

"Wait! That's—"

It hurt, but I let my eyes burn blue again. "Keep the chain you stole. That should at least cover the damage for the table." I ripped the knife out of the wood and stormed out.

Man, I forgot how much I hate espionage. I waved to the hostess and left to catch the bus. I had a training session to get to.

"I've been trying to pull Kat into the Dream Realm for ages now, but she's late," Jason said once I joined him in something vaguely resembling a rodeo pit. He leaned up against a wooden post with his long legs crossed and his hands in his pockets.

Seems to be a recurring theme for me today. "That's fine. I wanted to talk to you anyway."

"What's up?" He watched me out of the corner of his eye, seeming too relaxed at his post to bother turning all the way.

"Jamie's plan worked a little too well. Aurakbahor wants me spying on the resistance like she assumed he would, but he wants to follow up on everything I tell him and make sure I'm telling the truth — or at least most of it. If I'm right, he'll let me back into the Court. If I'm wrong, he'll kill me, and our whole plan will fail."

Jason shrugged like he didn't care, but he chewed his lip. "We'll have to plant some real stories along with fake intel and staged evidence then. But I'm not too worried. Kat's . . . well, I know Jamie said she's been accidentally using magic for years, but holy cow. She switched back and forth in a fight today."

I laughed, but when he didn't join me, I froze. "You're serious? She's been a full-fledged Rhaegynne for *two* days, and you already got her into a fight?"

His cheeks turned pink. "Kat fought brilliantly though. They had a free fall challenge, and she forced the other dragon to let go by changing mid-fall, and—" His shoulders fell. "This sucks, Coleman. I hate that Aurakbahor knows about her. I had hoped we could have an edge on him."

I placed a hand on his shoulder. "We have so many edges. We're practically a throwing star."

He laughed, a real laugh like I hadn't heard from him in months. "A throwing star?"

"Yeah! We've got me on the inside, ready to rip out his throat and regather the resistance. We've got Kat, who's both free and can do the impossible. We've got you training Kat to be a deadly weapon! And Aurakbahor's more worried about Balaskad than what a couple kids can do. That's at least four edges."

Kat materialized in the middle of the arena, and Jason's face lit up. He grabbed my arm and dragged me over to her, bouncing all the way. "Show him!" he demanded.

"You're going to have to be more specific," she said.

"Show him how you can switch back and forth in the middle of a fight!" he said, hardly controlling his excitement.

I put a restraining hand on his shoulder. "Or I could actually introduce myself this time? Since there wasn't really time before." I reached a hand to her. "I'm Coleman."

"Jason's been telling me about you," she said, shaking my hand.

"Only good things, I hope?" I asked, glancing at Jason and praying I wasn't blushing.

"Only the worst," Jason said proudly. "I told her you snore and you—"

I playfully slugged his arm. "I'm sorry for Jason, Kat. He's lying, of course. *He* snores."

Kat snorted, but Jason rolled his eyes. "Okay, okay," Jason said. "Can we *please* get back to Kat being able to switch mid-fight?"

I turned more toward her, trying to speak softer. Our joking seemed to have put her at ease a little, but she still looked overwhelmed. "Has he taught you any magic yet?"

She shook her head. "Not really."

"We won't bother with that, then. Let's fight and try to figure out the dynamics before we figure out combatant flairs." I took a step away from them, enjoying the painless Dream Realms transformation, the magic running freely through my veins before changing.

Her shoulders relaxed and shifted. I fought back a pang of familiarity at her silver scales. She didn't have Jamie's diamond scales, but it was close enough.

I pounced and slammed into her. My talons pierced into the muscles of her upper arms, and I shoved her to the ground, sending us rolling and throwing her off-balance even further. I growled and pinned her shoulders and wings to the ground.

"Bit rough there, buddy," Jason chastised.

"Just making sure the adrenaline is real," I answered.

Kat struggled beneath me. Only her tail could move, and even that only thrashed a few feet to either side.

"Switch, Kat," Jason instructed.

Moments passed with her squirming and panting beneath me. *Do I . . . give up?*

Kat's massive dragon body disappeared, and I found myself falling. We made eye contact, and her tiny human frame screamed, rolled onto her stomach, and started to push herself up, at which point she changed back into a dragon with even less room than before.

Her nasty back spikes slammed into my stomach, and we both grunted in surprise and pain. I tried to pry myself off her, but her arms buckled, and I fell on top of her again.

Groaning, I rolled to the side, landed on my back, and

dropped my dragon form. "That sucked," I muttered. Blood dripped down my chin and soaked my shirt. I clutched my chest.

Kat changed back, lying face-first in the dirt. "No kidding."

Jason's laughter drifted over to us. Kat and I managed to sit up enough to glare at him. He also laid on the ground, but he was laughing so hard sound barely came out.

"Ha, ha. Very funny," I said without a hint of humor. I pushed myself to my feet, wiped the blood off my chin, and walked over to him. "I'm glad we could entertain you."

He wiped at his tears. "Oh, that was good!" He gasped through his laughter, trying to sit up. "Kat's face was all *Ah! Big dragon!* And yours was all *Ah! Little human!* And then you both bounced off each other like *Ah! Big dragon!* It was beautiful."

I kicked his arm out from under him, making him fall to the ground again and laugh even harder. A small smile of my own tried to break free.

Kat stood and limped over to us. "Next time, can we have a plan before you tackle me and we both die?" she asked, her lips twitching like she was fighting to remain immune to his infectious laughter.

"Oh, no!" Jason succumbed to another fit of giggles. "I would prefer to watch another game of dragon pinball!"

Kat and I exchanged glances, fighting back laughter. "I guess we did look ridiculous, didn't we?" I asked.

Jason couldn't even make words come out through his laughter.

Abruptly, my blood ran cold. I froze, trying to figure out why my hair stood on end.

Wings.

I dropped to the ground, throwing a hand over Jason's mouth. Kat turned her face to the sky.

"How did he find us again?" Jason whispered, annoyance barely covering the fear in his voice.

"It doesn't matter. Go! Wake up!" I hissed and snapped my fingers under Kat's nose.

She disappeared. I barely had time to wave goodbye to Jason before we followed suit.

Kat Thinks I'm Family!

Aaron

I understood grief could do weird things to people, but Kat seemed extra off during our movie night last night. She seemed jumpy but also overly cheery like she was trying to hide her sadness from me. And I could have sworn she was *limping*. Not heavily, but with the other things, it was enough that I couldn't shake the feeling that something wasn't right.

I *tried* to give her space and ignore the weird vibe, but my mind turned it over and over again like pebbles in a rock tumbler all night and still rattled in the back of my mind when I got to school Friday morning. I found Lily and Miranda, but before I could even ask where Kat was, Miranda pointed across the common area to where Kat and Jason sat next to each other. They had their heads close together, talking intensely.

I nodded in thanks to Miranda and headed over to Kat.

They cut off their conversation as I arrived. Kat smiled, her face lighting up.

"Hey, Aaron!" She stretched her arm across her chest like her shoulder was tight.

"What's up?" I asked, giving Jason a fist bump and trying to ignore the rattling rock tumbler of anxiety. Even now, something was . . . different. I searched her face, her clothes, and her hair, trying to pinpoint what was causing my brain to fixate on it so much.

All I could decide for sure was that Kat moved with a certain stiffness this morning, and the grief still lingered in her eyes, but she also held herself with a confidence I hadn't seen in her before. It wasn't a bad thing, but it *was* new.

"You okay, Aaron?" she asked.

My face warmed when I realized she'd asked a question I hadn't responded to. I gulped. "Yeah, sorry. I'm tired. What did you ask?"

She laughed. "I asked how you're doing."

My face burned even warmer. "Yeah, tired is a good answer."

"Me too," Jason said, stifling a yawn.

"It should be illegal to start school this early," I said.

Kat slammed her fist into her hand. "I say we protest!"

Unfortunately, the bell rang before any of us could mount an adequate revolution.

Jason jumped up, panicked. "I was supposed to meet up with my English teacher ten minutes ago! Tell Mr. Moyes I'll be late!" He dashed away, waving over his shoulder.

Kat held out an arm for me. I pulled her upright, startled by how warm — almost fevered — her skin was. She stretched when she stood, twisting her torso back and forth to pop her back before she picked up her backpack and walked with me to class.

"I got you something, by the way," Kat said fishing in her pocket while we walked.

"You . . . got me something?" I asked.

She reached out her hand, proudly presenting a small, flat dark gray rock that glittered slightly under the lights. "As thanks for the leaf from last night."

"This is the highest honor," I said, accepting the gift. It was smooth and fit nicely in my palm.

Her smile faltered as we reached my classroom. "Grandma's funeral is tomorrow. Can you come with me?" she asked, her voice soft.

I hesitated. "Am I allowed? Isn't it supposed to be a family thing?"

"There will be plenty of non-family people there. No one will mind. Besides, you're basically family."

I pulled on my backpack straps, trying not to grin. "I'll have to check with my parents, but sure."

"I can give you a ride," she added.

"Cool."

She stopped outside her class and waved. "See you later."

"Have fun in bio," I replied, walking away.

Then my stomach sank. *Cool, Aaron? Cool? It's a funeral. You can't say that about a funeral!* I buried my face in my hands, trying to wipe the embarrassment from my memory.

Kat caught up to me in the hallway after school. "Did you walk here today?"

"Yeah. It was a nice morning."

"Want a ride?" she asked, guiding me around a group of students who were taking up most of the hallway.

"Sure." I'd never say no to a ride home.

We walked in silence until we reached her car. I cleared my

throat, trying to think of something to say. "Did you hear the end of year raffle assembly got canceled?"

She shook her head, climbing into the car. "No. What happened? That's the one with like, free parking passes and scholarships, right?"

"That's the one. I guess some juniors were running a ticket black market, and a fight broke out, so the sponsors dropped out."

"Weird that they'd punish the whole school for that."

I shrugged. "Guess they wanted to set an example."

She fell silent for several minutes while she drove. "How were classes?"

I blinked. She wasn't usually one for small talk. "Okay, I guess. I think I'm going to fail calculus."

Kat scoffed and pulled into my driveway. "Same . . ."

"Oh, whatever. Didn't you get the highest grade on the last exam?"

"Ha! I missed the extra credit questions." She grinned at me, but it felt forced. Was she . . . mad at me?

I shook my head and unbuckled my seatbelt. "You'll do fine, trust me." I climbed out of the car but crouched a little under the doorframe to keep talking. "Want to come in?"

She frowned. "I have to get home. We have that big family dinner tonight."

Oh. Right. That would explain why she was acting so strangely. "Well, see you tomorrow!" I jogged up to the front porch, cringing at my insensitivity, and opened the door. In the living room, Prince perked up next to my dad who was reading a book on the dark leather couch. *Odd.*

"Hey, Dad. What are you doing here?"

"Oh, we got sent home. There was an explosion a couple buildings down. I think it was a gas leak, but someone said it was a bomb." His voice was steady and calm, but his hands shook.

"A bomb! Is everyone okay?" My own hands trembled a little. He was so close to the explosion. I moved over to sit by him on the couch. Prince shoved himself under my arm, and I buried my hands in his thick fur.

"Yeah. One woman was reported missing, but she showed up eventually. She didn't even know she was missing. Said she'd left for lunch and forgot to sign out."

"Isn't this the fourth weird explosion this month?" I asked, remembering the news report from just yesterday morning. My stomach tangled into knots. The others were in other states. This one was a few miles away.

"The fifth," Dad said softly.

"Do you think they're linked at all?"

He shrugged. "How could they be? Almost all of them have been accidents. But I hope not. It would make all of this more terrifying than it already is."

"No kidding."

He reached an arm around me and pulled me closer to him in an uncharacteristic display of affection. I leaned against him, and we sat in silence for a few minutes.

"Hey, Dad?"

"Yes?"

"Kat's grandma died a few days ago, and the funeral is tomorrow morning. She asked me to go with her. Is that okay?"

"Kind of a weird place for a first date," he said with a teasing tone.

"Ugh, Dad! It's a *funeral!*" I complained, blushing and wiggling out from under his arm. "Who in their right mind would ask someone on a date to a funeral?"

"You're the one that got asked. Ask her."

I sighed and rolled my eyes. "Anyway, am I okay to go?"

"Sure."

"Cool. Thanks." *There I go again, saying cool about going to a funeral.*

Kat's family gathered under a pop-up pavilion around a closed casket suspended over the six-foot-deep hole. Flowers lined the chair aisles and were arranged in large, beautiful bouquets on top of and around the casket. Kat had flowers woven into her hair.

She leaned against me, and I wrapped my arm around her shoulders. She smelled like the flowers in her hair and something warmer. Maybe cinnamon?

Kat's mom leaned over. "Thank you for coming. She loved you, you know."

I smiled sadly, unsure how to respond. Jamie was almost always around when Kat and I were kids. I remembered her as a remarkably kind lady, quick with a joke but even quicker to offer comfort. I could tell she and Kat had a strong bond, and I was surprised Kat was doing as well as she was. Tears pricked my eyes. I wasn't expecting it to be so hard to say goodbye.

Kat's mom gave a nice eulogy, sharing memories of the joy she brought others, and how, even in death, she was still trying to help others by donating her house to a charity group. She ended with the hope that she was finally reunited with her late husband after over twenty years apart. One of Jamie's old friends got up after her. I barely paid attention. Instead, I watched Kat. She kept taking deep breaths and fidgeting with her necklace. I gently squeezed her knee, letting her know I was there.

"Thank you," she whispered.

Jamie's friend took her seat, and Kat's dad leaned over to Kat. "I think you'll really like what your grandma requested for the casket," he whispered.

She gave him a quizzical look. But he pointed up to the front where someone from the funeral home removed the large flower display over the casket, revealing an elaborate carving of a dragon wrapped around a compass. It'd been years since I'd been with Kat during story time with Jamie, but I still recognized the symbol from the cover of Kat's favorite storybook.

Kat stifled a sob, and I pulled her close again. She felt feverish. She turned and rested her head against my shoulder, shaking.

But then she stiffened and pulled back, turning away. "I'll be right back. I have to . . . go." Her voice sounded hoarse. "To the bathroom," she added when I moved to stand up. She stood and dashed away toward the parking lot.

I doubted she actually had to go to the bathroom, but I *did* know she didn't want me to follow. Her dad watched her leave, a pained expression on his face.

"I think the book design was sweet," I whispered.

"I should go after her," he said, rising from his seat.

Kat's mom caught his hand and urged him to sit back down. "It's a lot for her right now, dear. She needs some space." A sad smile adorned her face, yet there was a discontentment to her, a quiet anger that I couldn't quite place as she watched the funeral workers lower her mother's casket into the ground.

Chivalry Doesn't Matter if You're Dead

Kat

Crying in front of people was embarrassing. But changing into a dragon in front of your potentially anti-dragon family at your dragon grandma's funeral would be devastating. So, I ran.

Despite *being* there when Grandma died, it hadn't felt *real* until I saw the casket with her dragon and compass on it.

With her inside it.

My hands trembled but with rage instead of grief.

The kings did this to her.

They took her from me.

I would take their puppets from them. Even if that meant they had to die.

I stumbled, shocked by the ferocity of my thoughts. I shouldn't be thinking about revenge at a funeral.

I shouldn't be thinking about revenge *at all*. What was the *matter* with me?

The itching in my shoulder spread down my lower back

and down my arms. I put on a burst of speed, hoping to make it to the tree line at the end of the cemetery.

I glanced backward to see if anyone had noticed I'd left, but with my focus directed elsewhere, I collided into something warm and solid.

Jason's hands caught me before I could fall, steadying us both. "Where are you going?"

"Changing," I gasped.

He held onto one of my arms, dragging me behind a large headstone. "You have to control it."

I sucked in a shaking breath, trying to calm down. I tried to reach for my necklace, but my hand trembled too much to grab it. A tear slid down my cheek and sizzled. I flinched at the noise. "What is that?"

"A dragon is a *fire-breathing* reptile. Fire needs heat, and that heat comes from inside. We run *hot*. As a Rhaegynne, the fire doesn't disappear when you change. It stays in here." He pointed to the center of his chest. "Luckily, instead of normal fever symptoms with chills, it feels more like sitting by a nice campfire. A normal human would probably be dead at your body temperature."

My stomach sank, and tears sprang to my eyes from painful memories of Grandma's temperature spiking and dropping into impossible ranges at the hospital. My vision sharpened again.

"Your eyes are really cool, you know," Jason continued. "I've never seen mirror dragon eyes before. They're like little silver coins with slits in them."

I remembered Grandma's eyes, slitted and crystalline, and how Aurakbahor's and Jason's eyes both shifted to black when they used magic.

"Your eyes changed back to brown when we were talking

about temperatures, but they keep little flecks of silvery mirror stuff even when they're human. Look!"

I managed a shaky laugh. "I can't look at my own eyes."

"I know," he said. "But are you in control again?"

I paused. The itching was gone, and I didn't feel quite so warm anymore. "For now, yeah. This is *so* much more than I signed on for," I complained.

"You'll get better at it. Come on. Let's go back."

COLEMAN SAT cross-legged in the dirt in front of me, instructing me on how to draw from my dragon fire to use magic. The Dream Realms muddied details, so sitting in front of him in real life, I was surprised to find that, unlike most redheads, he was almost tan. Though that might have been an illusion from the vast number of freckles across his body. A dragon pendant rested against his chest. "Close your eyes and try to find your fire," he said.

We sat together in the trees off the side of a new trail today. Jason's blue shield flickered around us, hiding us from view. I glanced at Jason for support.

He looked up from where he studied Grandma's book and gave an encouraging thumbs-up.

I took a deep breath and searched for the fire Coleman promised. With a thrill, I found it. Chills ran through my body, and my vision sharpened. I gasped and pulled away, reaching for my tether.

Coleman put his hand on my knee. "It's okay. You're safe."

"I almost changed! I could have crushed you!"

"But you didn't! And you weren't going to. As long as you

say the incantation fast enough, you'll be fine." He sat back and grinned, eyeing my necklace. "Is that your tether?"

I nodded.

"Good. This is mine." He held up his arm to show a bracelet with round stone beads. "I count the beads when I can't control it with anything else, though I usually resort to burning off some magic first since you can't change when you're using magic."

"What do you use?" I asked Jason.

"Oh, uh." He rubbed at his right sleeve. "I need to remind myself I'm human and want to stay that way. So, I just . . . rub my arm."

Coleman gave him a strange look like Jason hadn't explained his well enough, but I figured a tether could be personal, so I didn't want to pry. Coleman must have decided the same because he didn't press and turned back to me.

"Magic," Coleman continued, "is a lot about manipulating elements, energies, and objects that already exist around you. The easiest to manipulate are the simplest elements: fire, water, earth, and air. They're all either around you or within you.

"With that said, this is difficult. These are new muscles your mind has never used before, so we'll go slowly. If you think you can't carry a spell all the way through, pull back before you're committed, and don't be afraid to say you're tired or cold while we're training. This is dangerous."

"Got it. What's first?"

"Let's start with fire. It should be easiest. The word for fire is *eathia*. Say it."

I repeated after him, dragging out the *th* sound the way he did.

"Very good. Now, your human body isn't used to fire

coming from it, so you have to convince yourself you want it outside more than inside. Watch me."

He held out his hand, and his eyes changed to red. "*Eathia!*" he hissed. A small flame sprang to life in his palm.

I jerked backward from the almost-blue flame threatening to singe my eyebrows.

"*Gasić*," he said, making a fist over the extinguished fire. "That will put it out. When you get stronger, you can add words before and after each of these to make them larger or more precise. For example, adding *ally* after a word will create a wall. Before the word, it means all. For example, *ally eathia* could release all the heat from your body, or it could summon all the heat around you to be directed somewhere else. *Eathia ally* would create a wall of fire. You try."

The energy was easier to find this time. My vision sharpened. I called for the fire, scared I would change if I didn't release the magic. It pooled in my hand like lava before erupting into a ball of flame that flickered harmlessly around my fingers. I stared, mesmerized.

I made that.

"Go ahead and extinguish it."

"*Gasić.*" The fire and the energy it had taken to sustain it went out. The whole mountain spun, and I must have swayed because Coleman caught me just before hitting the ground and propped me back up.

I pushed my head between my knees and moaned. "Why is all this magic stuff so painful?" I shivered from the cold in my veins.

"It won't always be this rough, I promise."

I glowered, but since my head was still between my knees, no one saw but the dirt.

Jason passed me a water bottle and a protein bar. "You'll want it if you're going to beat me today."

95

I looked up to see him doing that annoying grin of his again.

"Beat you?" I asked, taking a bite of the bar.

"Sure! I'm planning to teach you sword fighting as soon as Coleman is done."

I shuddered. "I don't know if I'll be able to even stand after this."

Coleman took off his jacket, revealing lean muscle wrapped around his arms like he spent most of his life fighting. Which, he probably did. He placed his jacket over my shoulders. "Here."

I caught a flash of a tattoo on the inside of his now-bare forearm, and my stomach flipped. "That's the same dragon and compass symbol on Grandma's casket and on her book."

He extended his arm to show me. It was much simpler than the version on the casket. "It's a symbol of the resistance. We've charmed it, so it will turn gold if someone is still loyal to the cause." He clenched his hand into a fist, and the symbol glowed with a warm golden light.

"Will I get one?" I asked, a little apprehensive about trying to hide a tattoo from my parents. Didn't mean I didn't *want* one though.

"If you want," Jason said with a shrug. "It's not required though."

"Does it hurt?"

"A little," Coleman answered. "But we use magic, so it's over pretty quickly."

"Can we do it now?" I asked. Maybe it was exhaustion or grief, but if it was important enough for Grandma to be buried with it, I wanted it too.

Coleman and Jason exchanged a look with each other before coming to a wordless agreement. "Sure," Jason said.

I didn't want to lose the comfort of the jacket, but I shrugged it off and lifted my shirt to show the left side of my rib cage. "Put it here, so I don't have to explain it to my parents."

Jason placed a warm hand on my ribs. His eyes flashed black as he whispered unfamiliar words in Tasalgré. My side burned with a sharp heat that made me suck in my breath, my own eyes shifting to dragon eyes from the pain. I clutched my tether hard enough to hurt.

As promised though, it was over in a few seconds. Jason moved his hand, and I twisted to try to look at it. My head spun from the pain and the earlier magic use. "Too bad I *am* the mirror," I said. "Looks cool upside down though."

"I'll take a picture if you finish your protein bar," Coleman said, taking out his phone.

"Oh right." I did as I was told, but my stomach still growled. I frowned. "Do you have another?" I asked, showing them the empty wrapper. "I'm still hungry. Actually, I'm always hungry now."

"Welcome to my world!" Jason laughed. "The fire inside needs fuel."

"I am not a huge fan of being this hungry. Or cold." I blew on my freezing fingers and huddled into the jacket.

Coleman smiled sympathetically. "You should start feeling warmer again soon."

Even as he said it, my core warmed, slowly radiating out to my fingers and toes.

"Your face has color again," Jason said. "Feeling better?"

"A little."

Coleman grinned. "Brilliant. Try summoning fire again!"

I huffed but did it anyway. My head spun before the fire formed. I called to extinguish it within seconds and buried my head in my knees again.

Another protein bar slid into view under my legs, and I devoured it.

"Can we be done with magic for today?" I begged, teeth chattering from the freezing cold.

Jason coughed several times before responding. I think I heard the word *wimp* in there at some point, but they agreed I could be done for now. Coleman passed me more water and a blanket, instructing me to lie down and recover for a few minutes.

While I lay in the dirt and watched the sun sink in the sky, Coleman and Jason chatted nearby. "This book is weird, Cole," Jason said, passing the book over to Coleman. "It's like I almost understand it — more like I almost recognize it — but then I look directly at the words, and they scramble and change again."

Coleman frowned and flipped through the pages. "I'll take a shot at it."

I managed to push myself upright without the world spinning.

Jason smiled. "Ready? Want to sword fight or do some mixed martial arts first?"

I eyed his small black duffle bag leaning against a tree. There was no *way* a sword could fit in there. "Do you actually have a sword hidden in those bushes? If you do, I want to start there."

His eyes sparkled mischievously. "Forty sit-ups first. Then we'll start."

"*Forty?*" I gasped.

"Remember that extra dragon strength I told you about? You'll need *at least* forty for it to even do anything."

I grumbled but obeyed. It *was* easier than I expected it to be for the first twenty or so. But it burned by forty.

Once finished, he sat next to me on a small boulder. "We

summon our practice swords. *Adamas chalybs haerent!*" His eyes flashed black while a blade materialized in his hand. He passed it to me.

I wrapped my hand around the hilt and almost dropped it in shock. It was solid enough to hold, with some heft to it, but it somehow still had the same consistency I imagined a cloud might.

"Whoa." I swung the blade a little to get a sense of the weight.

Jason smiled and summoned a second sword for himself. "The first thing you'll need to do is make sure you're holding it correctly." He passed his sword to his less dominant hand to help me with my grip. He moved my fingers around and told me to squeeze in some parts of my hand and lighten up in others. I followed as best as I could. He then adjusted my form, kicking my feet apart and lifting my arm. Satisfied, he stood in front of me with his sword drawn.

"Tell you what. You beat me today, and I'll give you some dragon time. Begin!"

He swept his sword toward me, and I scrambled backward.

"What are you doing?" I shouted, jumping away from another swipe. "Shouldn't you teach me something first? Aren't there rules to this?"

"Chivalry doesn't matter if you're dead." Jason jabbed his sword at me again.

I awkwardly grasped my sword with both hands and swiped to block him. The blades met partway with a clang before he pulled his off and attacked again.

"You just need one hand." He caught the flat of my blade against the palm of his hands when our swords met a second later. "Keep the sharp parts pointed at me. But block with the flat of the blade to not blunt it." He continued to attack, breaking through my pathetic defenses over and over.

"You're swinging too wildly," Jason continued, poking me in the side. "It'll never work like it does in the movies." He made a small flourish to knock my sword out of the way, and in his flourish, I found an opening and rushed for an offensive move. He knocked my attack aside, and my sword slid past his shoulder. The flat of his blade rested against my neck.

"How did you do that?" I asked, dancing away from the cold magic steel.

"Keep your weapon pointed at your opponent. You don't seem very determined to get dragon time today," he added, knocking my defense away again.

A flash of heat burned through my body at his words. My vision shifted to my dragon eyes, but I could control it. I found I could predict where Jason was going before his sword even moved. I caught his attack with the clang of magic steel against magic steel.

He met my eyes and smiled. His blue slipped into black. "That's cheating."

"I thought you said chivalry wouldn't matter if I was dead," I said smugly, blocking his next shot. I ducked and lunged, but he parried and returned, faster than before.

"Get 'im, Kat!" Coleman cheered, still studying the book.

I blocked, jabbed, parried, and then jumped back. Our dragon instincts took over, and we picked up speed. We danced around the clearing, our swords nothing more than blurs. The only sounds were metal on metal and our breathing as we moved faster and faster.

This is almost easy!

His sword slammed into me, passing harmlessly through my chest with a chill. My sword clattered to the ground before disappearing.

"What happened?" Jason asked, puffing. Sweat shimmered under his hairline.

"I got cocky..."

"Glad to keep you humble then." He walked over to his bag and pulled out his water bottle before passing another to me.

With our sword fight over, Jason shifted to teaching me hand-to-hand techniques, and, just as before, he seemed to prefer the reckless teachings of chaos over the gentle instruction of *logic*. He immediately threw us into a fight with nothing more than a quick correction to make sure I didn't break my hand when I punched him.

Coleman interrupted our fight some time later. "Wait — guys!"

I breathed a sigh of relief as Jason released me from a headlock and ran over to where Coleman sat under a tree, Grandma's book in hand. I followed close behind.

"Did you find something?" Jason asked.

"I'm not sure." His brow furrowed. "It's hard to make out, and the text changes while you read it, so I'm only getting part of an answer here. Maybe it's not worth—"

"What is it?"

He had a bright, hopeful gleam in his eyes. "I think I just learned how the kings have been controlling us. And ... I think Kat might be able to take dragons from Aurakbahor or Balaskad."

My stomach sank. "I don't want to have dragon puppets!"

Jason's jaw hung open for a moment before responding. "You don't understand, Kat! I've never heard of Rhaegynne switching which king they're tied to. If you could take even a few of us under you ... Do you know how much of an advantage we could have?"

"It wouldn't be a final solution," Coleman added. "But being under an ally instead of an enemy would give us an edge when we're ready to overthrow the kings!"

I felt colder than I did after using magic. "I . . . I don't want that."

He frowned. "Do you have a better idea?"

I fought to remain human. "N-no . . ."

Jason glanced at the setting sun. "Let's research it a little more. Kat, let's train at the rec center tomorrow. I know you didn't beat me, but if you want dragon time, go now, so you can get home on time."

"Wait! Before you go . . ." Coleman said. He pulled a ring out of his pocket and passed it to me.

I turned it around in my fingers, studying it. A thin line of blue ran through the middle of the metal band.

"I've enchanted it to carry the anti-human shield. If you're wearing it, you'll be essentially invisible as a dragon. It'll probably even keep your normal magic hidden too, but we'll still use the barriers when we practice. Be careful. It's not perfect."

The ring only fit on my thumb, but it was snug enough. "Thanks," I said and set off at a run toward the clearing in the trees. I leaped into the air, changing mid-jump.

I flew as high as I could, trying to sort out the emotions warring inside me. How did Coleman even decipher that much from the book? Could I really be responsible for other Rhaegynne? I would give them freedom, but how free were they really if I could take over? Was there another option?

Did I have a *choice*?

Question after question chased themselves in my head during my flight. But I couldn't fly for long. My body ached, and my wings were fatigued.

"I'll do it," I said to Coleman and Jason when I landed. My stomach twisted with nerves. I didn't like it, but we had to try. "How does it work?"

Coleman frowned. "The book claims there's a link in the soul of a dragon that allows them to connect mentally with others, but it can be pinned in place. In theory, this means we could find the link and readjust the pin."

"How would I find it?" I asked, squirming at the thought. "Better question — how did the kings find it?"

Coleman and Jason exchanged glances.

"I was told a disaster caused the war," Coleman said. "The dragons on either side swore themselves to their kings in exchange for extra strength and wisdom. Instead, the four kings ended up with complete control over their subjects. Unfortunately, even after two of the kings were killed, the war didn't end, and somehow, the link between subject and king is inherited by any new Rhaegynne.

"Jamie never explained how she remained free. Whatever it is, you inherited *her* protection from the curse instead."

"We're all enlisted in a war we never signed up for," Jason said. "We came up with some ideas we can try."

"Not tonight though," Coleman said. "It's late, we're all tired, and I need to go back to work, but I'll try to find out what I can about this book and our theory. I'll let you know what I find."

I drove home alone, still nervous about my decision but confident it was the best option. We had to do something.

"Where were you?" Mom demanded when I walked into the house. Her face looked so much like Grandma's — so much like mine — was torn between worry and fury. But despite her frustration, she still passed me a plate of lasagna.

"I told you I was going to help Jason train for the lacrosse season," I responded.

"I thought that was last week."

"No, we're still training," I replied, shoveling lasagna in my mouth. "This is really good."

She sniffed. "Thank you. There's more on the stove but be sure to save some for your dad's lunch tomorrow!"

I scooped half onto my plate and put the rest into a container. Then I cleaned the kitchen while I ate to try to make up for my tardiness.

"I am so ready for bed," I announced once I scraped my plate clean.

"Do you have homework?" Mom asked.

I froze. "Ugh, yes." I grabbed my backpack, trudged to my room, plopped down on my bed, and opened my textbooks.

My dad knocked on my half-open door a few minutes later and poked his head in. "How are you feeling?" he asked.

For one horrifying moment, I thought he meant how I felt after practice. But then I realized he was probably asking about *Grandma*.

I didn't know how to talk about her either. My grief was too closely entwined with Rhaegynne and my magic, and I didn't know how to talk about any of it. I swallowed hard. "I wish . . . I actually had time to grieve," I confessed. "I have so much homework, and it's not slowing down."

He gave me a sad smile and sat on the edge of my bed. "I'm here, whatever you need."

I fidgeted uncomfortably, then looked at the rather intimidating set of derivatives I'd have to figure out for calculus before I could finally sleep. "Think you could help me with my homework?" I asked.

He hesitated but then nodded. "Yeah, of course. Let's do it."

It was well past midnight by the time we finished, and I wasn't in bed until after one.

The Talisman Casino

Coleman

The best part of espionage was, under Official Kingly Business™, I could be a dragon.

I tucked my cane into my belt next to my sword since I didn't really need it today; I was less dizzy, and my pain was low. I didn't even bring it to see Kat and Jason. But I might need it later and didn't want to be stuck without it.

I took a deep breath, trying to fill my head with thoughts of loyalty and subservience — a habit I learned as a child. Aurakbahor usually ignored his "children" when they played by the rules. So long as good ol' Aurak wasn't in the mood to build his army by forcing me to change humans along the way, I'd be okay. I needed to check in with the dude anyway.

My chest tightened painfully for a moment but released when I transformed. I sighed, basking in the strength of my dragon body, temporarily able to ignore the other Rhaegynne voices in my head.

I missed this, I thought as I launched myself into the star-filled sky.

"*Do you have a report for me?*" Aurakbahor's voice boomed in my skull.

I tried not to jump but failed. *I didn't miss* — I stopped the thought before he could notice it. "Not yet, but I have a lead at the Talisman Casino."

"*Come to me afterward.*"

He faded from my mind, and I braced myself for the surge of other voices. A small whimper cut through them, and I tried not to flinch at how young they sounded.

I hummed a little song to try to tune them out. Then I laughed to whomever was paying attention. "Get it? Tune them out? Cause it's a song?"

Someone groaned.

It's not talking to yourself when there are a dozen other voices in your head.

I pushed onward, angling myself southwest and fell into the rhythm of my wings. I flew for almost an hour, lost in the novelty of being uncontested in my dragon form. So much so that I nearly missed my destination.

I looped back around and landed on the hard dirt just outside the small desert town. It was little more than a convenience store connected to a gas station, a small church building, and a couple of ranch houses. I pulled out my cane and walked the rest of the way.

The bell above the gas station door chimed, announcing my entrance. A teenager stood behind the counter. He glanced up from his phone and gave me an uninterested nod. I waved and wandered over to the slot machines in the back corner of the room.

A bright flashing machine against the wall caught my eye — The Dragon's Hoard. *Subtle.* Fishing in my pocket, I pulled out a couple quarters and pushed them into the game. A small pool of magic filled my hand as I pulled the lever. The slot machine whistled and flashed as the rollers spun, landing on three dragons. The machine clicked and popped forward.

Glancing back to make sure the attendant was still distracted, I pulled the whole thing toward me, revealing a narrow doorway covered by a red curtain. I ducked inside. The slot machine slid into place behind me, and I found myself somewhere that definitely didn't fit inside the rural gas station.

Bright colors, music, a dozen card tables, roulette wheels, and slot machines filled the room. Tall red velvet curtains lined almost every wall, hiding other rooms and exits. Waiters carrying platters of champagne and potions wandered among the patrons.

One paused to offer me something from her platter. I grabbed a luck potion and replaced it with a gold ring.

I leaned in and whispered, "I'm looking for Kroll.'

She smiled and nodded to a set of curtains in the back of the room. I slipped her a gold bracelet from my bag in thanks and worked my way over while taking the shot of luck. The potion was more of a cheap party trick than anything useful, but it tasted like strawberries and warmed my insides. The tight coldness in my chest receded.

The curtains were heavier than I expected, but Kroll was even more of a surprise.

They sat at a roulette table under a crystal chandelier, shrouded in a gray hooded robe. Their torso was abnormally long and skinny. Their arms seemed too short for their body. White gloves hid their hands, and a white, featureless mask hid their face. Even their eyes were veiled with a strange mesh.

"Kroll?"

"What can I do for you, honey?" they asked in a gravelly voice.

I set my pouch of gold in the center of the roulette table

and propped my cane against a chair. "Jinx told me you knew about the resistance."

Their masked head cocked. "Who are you asking for?"

I pulled up my sleeve to show my glowing dragon and compass tattoo. "This wouldn't work if I wasn't still loyal to Jamie."

They hummed, satisfied. "My answers must be won, dear boy." Their short arms gestured at the table.

When in a magical casino, do as the . . . magical casino-ians do . . . "How do I play?"

Kroll's laugh sounded like it came through a voice distorter — like several different people laughed at once. They pointed a gloved finger at the table. "Place your bets on either a range of numbers or a single number. If you win, I'll tell you what you want to know. If you lose, I take your gamble and keep my secrets."

"All right. Well, I'll gamble that pouch from Aurakbahor's personal hoard and place my bets on . . . black?" I picked up the pouch and dropped it on the table's black square.

That strange laugh came from behind Kroll's mask again. "My dear child," their voice said softer than before with a higher timbre, "my answers do not come that cheaply. I want important things . . . your most treasured memory, an hour of your powers, or perhaps a secret you've never told. I will allow you three bets — increasing accuracy with increasing value. I will provide information I deem appropriate to the value of the win."

I swallowed hard, trying to think of the least expensive bets that could still give me the information I needed. I reached for a chip at the side of the table, my heart pounding. "I bet a single secret on black." The chip glowed and made my fingers tingle.

Kroll spun the wheel and flicked the ball.

I chewed my lip while it spun. *Which secret? I have too many . . . I didn't specify what kind of secret. It could be anything they don't know. Like my favorite color is—*

The ball fell and bounced, landing on black. I breathed a sigh of relief.

"Very well." The voice changed timbre again. "The resistance has scattered. There are no remaining cells of the resistance besides the one with your friends and another two children in England. Though they do not band together to resist, only to survive. All the others have given up or were left to rot in the kings' dungeons. The resistance is on life support, dear boy."

"Who are the kids? Where are they?"

Kroll leaned over the table. Their body was so long that I worried they might topple over. "Place your next bet. I already gave you more than your bet was worth."

Trying not to glare, I picked up another chip. "I offer a memory from Aurakbahor's torture on the first dozen."

Kroll sat back in their seat and crossed their arms. "That memory is of no worth to me. I want the memory of your first kiss."

I flushed. "There wasn't much time for kissing in prison."

"Fine. Then I want a memory of a warm moment with your friend. Jason, right?"

My heart fluttered. It was just a memory. I'd forget it eventually. Why was I so reluctant? "Have the memory of the time Jason and I sat outside the burning prison the first time we met. On the first dozen." The chip glowed again, and I set it on the table.

The wheel whirred while I replayed the memory as many times as I could. It was old and full of tragedy, and we had better ones since, but still . . . I had been the one to notice him. It was the first time I had found a Rhaegynne as young as myself, and I hatched a plan with Jamie to rescue him from Aurakbahor. We tried to free as many prisoners as possible, but Jason stood out. Half dead and bloodied, he still had hope in his eyes.

I had broken my ankle in a fight with one of the guards on the way out. I thought I would be taken prisoner again. But Jason came back for me. What little fight he had left he used to save me instead of himself. Together, we'd managed to escape. We collapsed on each other on a nearby hill while we watched the whole fortress burn.

I remember feeling his heartbeat against my cheek. It felt like resistance. It felt like *hope*. And for that moment, I could believe we could actually save the Rhaegynne.

"Seven," Kroll said, interrupting my thoughts. "You get to keep your memory, though I do wish I could taste even a hint. Your face suggests it would be... *delicious*."

My cheeks burned, and I tried to look anywhere besides Kroll's featureless mask.

"One's named Tythan, the other is Hope."

Anger coursed through my body. My eyes shifted and ringed my vision in blue. My chest tightened with that unrelenting cold burn. The table shook as energy rumbled out from my feet. "That is the information you offer in exchange for my memory? *I already know Tythan and Hope!*" The room rattled, and a string of crystals fell from the chandelier and crashed into Kroll's mask.

Their hands flashed up to the mask, covering a crack in the porcelain. "This is the risk you take. Control yourself."

"At least tell me where I can find them."

They hissed. "You break my mask, disrupt my guests, yet still demand more than the bet was worth?"

"My memory is worth more than information I already

have! You gave me more on a one-to-one gamble than on a two-to-one. Where are they?"

Kroll sighed. "They move often to protect their location. But they tend to visit homeless shelters for supplies. Start there."

I ground my teeth but picked up another chip. I held it up to Kroll's broken mask, still held in place by a gloved hand. "I offer you a favor."

"This one is the high-stakes bet, dear one. I can tell you of the spies still hidden in Aurakbahor's own walls — ones you wouldn't even dream of. I can tell you where Balaskad sleeps and all the unguarded passageways into her room. I can provide a list of every surviving ex-member of the resistance with their last known location. I see all . . . I *know* all. But I'll only *tell* all with a high enough price. A single favor will not suffice. I want an hour of your power starting immediately after the game."

I shook my head. "I need to leave after this game. I can't go unprotected that long. I'll offer you sixty *seconds* of my power, free for you to take at any time. It's yours to take without warning, but it reverts back to me at the end of those sixty seconds."

Kroll hummed. "I accept."

The chip between my fingers flared, and I set it on eighteen.

They spun the wheel and flicked the ball. My heart pounded faster as the ball dropped from the track and bounced onto the wheel. *I hope that luck potion was worth the ring.*

The ball clacked around the wheel more than it had on the previous spins. My head spun with anxiety, and I gripped the edge of the table for support.

Bounce.

Bounce.

Bounce-bounce-bounce.
Stop.
Six.
Just my luck.

Kroll chuckled. "You got more than you should have already. I will hold you to your debt. If you have more to offer, come back. Otherwise, I look forward to using your strength one day."

I clenched my cane and walked out of the room. *At least I could tell Aurakbahor I didn't learn anything new.* I passed the waitress who still had my ring on her platter, and I patted at my hip for my gold pouch. It wasn't there.

"Oh, Tasalgré," I swore, turning back to Kroll. I pushed the curtain aside. "I left my—" My cane fell from my fingers.

Kroll's robes lay in a pile on the ground, their mask in two pieces on the table. Three short, blue-gray *creatures* with white hair, large fangs, delicate wings, large bellies, and thin limbs picked through my gold pouch, placing rings on their fingers, and fighting over necklaces.

They froze, turned toward me, and then scrambled to hide. One leaped for the mask, knocking half off the table but tried to cover their face with the rest. Another struggled to untangle the robes while the third jumped on their shoulders, knocking them both over.

"*What are you doing here?*" the one with the mask hissed. Their voice matched the higher pitched one I had heard a couple times.

I stood with my mouth open in the entryway. My heart pounded as my curse's burning-cold tendrils snaked up my neck. I struggled to push them back down before they noticed. "What *are* you? Only Rhaegynne are left. I—"

One of them cackled and jumped onto the roulette table. "You were told wrong, kiddo."

"Why are you — *How* are you here?"

"If anyone asks, we aren't!" the last one cried while the others laughed like hyenas.

The one on the table tossed my mostly empty bag at me. I fumbled but caught it.

"Now, scram!"

I stumbled backward, and the curtain closed, cutting off my view.

I wanted to laugh. I was just tricked by three imp things in a trench coat. But I couldn't. Aurakbahor told me all the other mythical creatures had been wiped out by humans.

Admittedly, he wasn't the end-all be-all of reliable information, but . . . I'd traveled the world over. I'd been in some shady parts of the magical underground. I'd only met Rhaegynne. I'd only *seen* Rhaegynne.

And yet three imps in a trench coat robbed me in a Rhaegynne casino.

I glanced around with new eyes at the casino's patrons and staff. How do I know those weren't elves in the corner with the pinball machine? Maybe that was a werewolf at the bar.

I lurched through the casino, trying to find the transport doors I knew would lead to Aurakbahor's Court. I pushed my way through the crowd until I found the right set of curtains, pushed through them, and stepped into the cool caverns of Aurakbahor's palace.

I wandered through the halls, still clutching my bag to my chest. Halfway down the hall, I swore. I'd left my cane at the casino. I'd never get it back.

RIP, Cecil. You were a good cane. I relied on muscle memory to get me to Aurakbahor's chambers, and I entered without knocking.

Aurakbahor glanced up from his dinner. A look almost like

concern crossed his face as he saw me. "What happened? What did you lose?" He stood and rushed toward me.

I shook my head. "Nothing important. I didn't learn anything, but—" I cut myself short. Why had I come groveling to Aurakbahor like an injured child?

"But what?" His concern was gone, replaced with impatience.

"How certain are you that everything mythological besides Rhaegynne are extinct?"

His face paled. Somehow, his fear was more terrifying than his rage. "What did you see?"

Make him trust you, or he'll kill you and your friends. "I'm not sure, but unless the luck potion I took was actually a hallucinogen, there were these blue guys with wings in that casino."

"What?" he whispered.

"They shouldn't exist, right?"

He frowned, and something almost like pity replaced his fear. "Coleman . . . I'd apologize, but you can't know about them. You can't know about the Council—" He cut himself off.

"About the what?"

Aurakbahor flinched. "You can't know, and I really don't want to kill you."

I stepped back, but he grabbed my arm with a burning hand. Blue magic filled his hand as he reached for my head. I tried to jerk away, but a hex froze me in place.

The blue light from his free hand pressed against my temple, and I couldn't even scream.

I pushed against the attack the best I could. His voice filled my head. *"It never happened. It was a dream fueled by a cheap potion."*

Aurakbahor's power retreated, and he smiled and cupped my cheek. "You can't come back to the Court if you're going to drink any odd potion at strange casinos, child."

I furrowed my eyebrows. I could still remember it all — the roulette game, the creatures, the waitress with the luck potion.

The luck potion! I struggled to keep the realization off my face and tried to play along. "You're right, sire. I'll . . . have to be more careful."

"I'm sorry you were drugged too heavily to have gained any useful information. I'll need genuine intel before I can let you in. You are excused."

I bowed and left the room, unwilling to even breathe.

What was he so afraid of?

I'M NOT JEALOUS. YOU'RE JEALOUS.

Aaron

"Think she'll ever remember us?" Lily sighed as she stared at Jason and Kat walking together to the cafeteria. They didn't even glance our way as we sat in our normal spot under the stairway.

I frowned. Kat still talked to me, but she'd distanced herself in the couple weeks since the funeral. At first, I figured it was grief, but as she'd gotten further and further away, I wasn't so sure anymore.

She'd spent almost every afternoon with Jason since the funeral.

Something was different. *Wrong.* But I couldn't put my finger on it.

"I don't know," I answered. "She's been acting weird lately."

"She somehow seems both exhausted *and* full of energy? Like at the same time?" Miranda said, her voice pitching up like a question.

"*And* she seems like she's always sore," Lily added. "And stressed."

I paled. "Do you think . . . I don't know. Do you think she's in trouble?"

Miranda chewed her lip. "Maybe."

Lily's eyes brightened. "You like Kat, don't you? Like, *like-like*, right?"

My cheeks burned. "What makes you say that?" My voice was too high.

Both girls burst out laughing.

"It's *obvious*!" Lily managed to say through her laughter.

My whole body flushed. "She's my best friend, and I'm more than happy to *keep* it that way! I mean, yeah, I have a crush. Can you blame me? She's a beautiful person. And funny. And smells nice . . . But I don't need us to be anything else! Being her friend means too much to me! Besides, she's demiromantic and ace. I don't need her to feel the same way back." I sometimes wondered if I was asexual too, but we didn't need to get into *that* right now.

Miranda leaned forward on the bench. "I've seen the way she looks at you. Maybe it's not romantic attraction, but she cares about you. Ask her to homecoming!"

I nearly choked. "*What?*"

"Okay, hear me out. Go as friends, no pressure. You'll both have fun, and she'll remember how awesome you are, and *maybe* she'll tell you if she joined the Mafia."

"At the very least, bring her home by like, seven-thirty and tell her to go to bed," Lily added. "She looks like she hasn't actually slept in weeks."

"Jason's probably going to ask her — assuming he hasn't already," I protested. But a plan was beginning to form in my head. Just a fun, no pressure night. *As friends*.

"Better act fast then," Miranda said.

"Hey, guys!" Lily said, waving past my shoulder.

I turned to see Kat and Jason walking over to us.

"What did you two do to poor Aaron?" Kat asked. "He's as red as a tomato!"

I hadn't realized I was still blushing, but I certainly was now.

Miranda laughed. "We were just having some fun! What are you guys doing?"

"I was helping Kat with something," Jason said.

"And I was wondering if anyone wanted to go out for lunch," Kat said. "It's meatloaf today, and it doesn't look . . . safe."

Jason gazed longingly at the food court, but his nose crinkled in disgust as someone walked by with an oddly gray pile of meat. "I'd love to eat literally anything else."

"I brought lunch today, but you guys have fun!" Lily said.

"Me too," Miranda said.

"Are you coming, Aaron?" Kat asked.

I hid my lunch bag in my backpack. "Of course!"

"I can drive. Beat you to the car!" Kat said, taking off to the exit.

It was good to see Kat laughing again as we raced after her. Normally, even with a head start, I would have passed her by now. But I couldn't even get close.

She made it to her car and turned to face us. Her smile turned into a frown. "You let me win!" she said, breathing hard.

Jason's face was pale. "Nope," he puffed, climbing into the car. "I can't race on an empty stomach."

Kat cringed as she exchanged glances with him like they were in on some secret I wasn't.

Jealousy snaked its way through my gut, but I beat it back.

"Sorry, Jason." She turned and glared at me. "But that doesn't explain how I beat *you*."

"You're extra fast today or something. You won fair and square."

"Sure . . ." She unlocked the car, sliding into the driver's seat. "What's for lunch?"

"I dunno. What sounds good?" I asked, taking the passenger's seat before Jason could.

Kat and I both turned to Jason as he buckled himself into the middle seat in the back.

He held his hands up. "Whoa! Don't look at me. I'm new! I don't know what's around here!"

"We could head over to my house and raid the fridge," she suggested.

"Sounds good to me," he said.

I offered a little I-don't-have-a-strong-opinion-whatever-works-for-me shrug.

Kat dumped a pocketful of loose change into the cup holder and turned on the car.

"Where did all this come from?" I asked, poking at the pennies and making them jingle.

She stared at the pile like she hadn't noticed how much change she had. "I don't know. There were a lot of coins on the ground today."

Jason laughed from the back seat. "Like shiny things, Kat?"

She blushed. "I mean . . . doesn't everyone?"

She pulled out of the parking lot, and we drove in relative silence, broken only by Kat's staticky radio and Jason's gurgling stomach.

Once we arrived, Kat led the way inside. "Mom! We've come to steal your food!"

"Hey, sweetie," her mom said, folding clothes while watching the news in the kitchen.

"Do we have anything worth stealing?" she asked, already opening the fridge.

"We should have some bagels in the pantry, and I bought some chicken nuggets at the store today. Who's this?"

"Oh, this is Jason!" Kat said. "He's the one I've been practicing lacrosse with!"

He waved.

"Hi, Jason," Kat's mom replied. "You're welcome to practice with Kat, but I do need her home earlier. Where are you—" A news report caught her attention. "*Another* explosion?"

The TV showed a breaking news session about a small explosion in southern Washington.

"Gas leaks, they say!" She scoffed. "Either someone's behind these or we have an epidemic of bad contractors!"

"You think they're connected?" I asked.

She folded a shirt angrily. "Seems like more than a coincidence."

Kat turned to Jason, exchanging another one of those looks like they knew something I didn't. I knew Kat enough to know she was asking a question. But I couldn't guess Jason's answer.

"I hope they can be stopped soon," Jason said, maintaining eye contact with Kat.

Her shoulders stiffened. "I'm sure whoever can do that is trying their best," she replied, a strange edge to her voice. "Anyway, who wants bagels, and who wants nuggets?"

I went for the chicken. Jason and Kat went for both. And seconds of both. In the same amount of time it took me to eat ten chicken nuggets. I stared. I'd never seen her eat that much. She just downed fifteen chicken nuggets and still seemed hungry.

She glanced at me over her bagel. "What?"

"Nothing. We should leave soon."

She checked the clock on the stove. "Oh. Right!" She threw

her plate in the dishwasher and kissed her mom on the cheek. "Bye, Mom!"

"Bye. Be safe! I love you!" she called after us.

We made it back to school with time to spare, so we found our bench under the stairs. Lily and Miranda were gone, but Kat plopped down on the ground, propped herself against the wall, and closed her eyes. Within seconds, her breathing slowed, and she let out a soft snore.

I laughed and reached out to wake her, but Jason stopped me. "If she's asleep, let her rest."

I nodded and sat down against the wall too. Jason tugged at the end of his sleeve and sat sideways on the bench, kicking his legs across the rest of it.

"So," I said, trying to break the silence. "You guys have been practicing lacrosse?"

"Yep, almost every day," he said, glancing at Kat.

"Can I join you guys? I took the summer off, but I need to get ready for spring tryouts."

"Oh, yeah. Sure. Anytime! Fair warning: I'm not very good — hence practicing daily."

"No worries. I taught Kat, so I'm sure you're better than you think! I'll get my stick after school and meet you guys at the park later."

Jason shot a look at Kat again. "Sure! That sounds fun! Let's plan on it!"

Sword-Fighting Dragon Assassins

Kat

I didn't mean to fall asleep, but I was *so* tired.

Almost immediately after closing my eyes, I found myself in a foggy field, standing right in front of Aurakbahor. I'd know his face anywhere. How could I forget?

He smiled a forced, cold smile, like he hadn't done such a thing in years.

I took a step backward, begging myself to wake from this nightmare.

Aurakbahor caught my arm and pulled me closer. He smelled like smoke and too much cologne. "Katherine *Victoria* Lance." He said my name like a dessert he couldn't wait to taste. "Welcome." He spread his arms wide, gesturing toward the fog.

I glowered at him, thinking of all the ways I wanted to strangle him with his scarf. My rage muted the fear shaking my legs but not enough to send me into action.

"Do you know who I am, Katherine?"

"What do you want?" I hissed. I was hoping for a regular

dream, but it seemed Jason wasn't the only one who could invite me here.

"What do I want?" he parroted. "You get right to the point, don't you, Kitty?" He smiled unnervingly. "I like that."

I snorted. Definitely a politician, talking in circles like that.

"I've come to offer you a deal," he said. "Balaskad doesn't know you exist. You and I both have quarrels with her. She's the one who caused your grandmother to suffer, after all."

My lip pulled up into a sneer.

"No, no. I *helped* her. Remember? It was simply euthanasia — Greek for good death. Balaskad's methods are sadistic. She thought killing your grandmother would end the free dragons. She feared Jamie; she'll fear you. Join me. You can overthrow her with the strength of my entire army behind you. Join me, and I'll let your friends have their freedom."

His voice was as smooth as silk, and I wanted to believe him. I could save my friends . . .

I shook my head. I needed to save more than a couple Rhaegynne. I needed to save them all. Besides, he killed Grandma. "Never."

He smiled and turned to leave. "Think about it, Kat. We could be powerful allies and prevent excess bloodshed."

"*Eathia!*" I screamed, pushing my hands out. Fire blazed from my palms.

Aurakbahor's hand shot up and caught the flames. His honeyed smile faded, and his voice dripped with venom. "There are rumors Jamie has an heir who has recently come into their power. It's giving everyone a sense of hope." He studied the fire crackling in his hand and cocked his head to the side. "We can't have that."

His eyes flashed dragon-black, and fear curdled in my stomach. But despite my best efforts, I couldn't wake up.

He shimmered, but instead of changing into a dragon, his

hands — still burning with my fire — appeared around my throat. I fought to shove him away, but his grip only tightened.

"No wall to brace off this time, Kitty. No magic to throw me off."

He smiled the more I struggled. Black spots danced across my vision. I tried to change, but I couldn't figure out how. My lungs burned for air, and my neck felt like an anvil had been dropped on it. The world swayed.

"Bye, bye, Kitty."

My vision turned gray . . .

A loud ringing jerked me out of the Dream Realms. I could still feel his fire — his hands — around my neck. But the hands touching me now were softer. My vision cleared, and I found Jason not Aurakbakor shaking my shoulders, his mouth twisted with concern.

"Kat wake up!"

I gasped for air, but adrenaline still coursed through my body. My vision sharpened.

No! The itching spread across my back. *Not here!* I managed a couple of deep breaths, forcing my vision back to normal. My hand was already at my throat so I clenched my tether until I could assure Aaron and Jason I was fine, though my hands trembled.

"Just a bad dream," I lied.

Aaron helped me to my feet. I impulsively pulled him into a tight hug, nearly bursting into tears. I wanted to tell him everything, but I didn't dare. Aurakbahor knew my name and where to find me. I couldn't defend myself against him. What would happen if he found *Aaron*?

I pulled away from the hug, clenching my hands into fists. I couldn't lose him. Not Aaron.

The final bell rang, and my heart pounded in anticipation. I rushed to the hallways, trying to find Jason. I needed to train, and I needed to train *now*.

Jason found me when I reached the parking lot and fell into step beside me. *"Do you have any lacrosse sticks?"*

I raised an eyebrow. *"I have one. Why are you talking telepathically?"*

"I need a stick. I told Aaron he could practice with us today."

The sudden range of emotion from shock to disappointment to horror made my head spin. *"What?"*

"I'm sorry! I figured it was good for our cover!"

I rubbed my eyes in frustration. *"Okay. Let's get you a stick."* I needed to train. I needed to free my friends and avenge my grandma. I needed to be *ready* for the next time I met one of the kings.

Jason waited by the passenger door for me to unlock the car, then slid in and reached for the coins in my cupholder. "You're hoarding," he said with a laugh.

"What?" I asked, starting the car and pulling out of the spot.

"You're hoarding." He dropped a nickel into the pile. "Ever heard of a dragon's hoard?"

My eyes widened. "That's real?"

"Dragons like shiny things," he said, slipping a dime into his pocket with a wink.

"Thief!" I narrowed my eyes while still trying to keep them on the road.

"Hey, I'm a dragon, too!"

I pulled out onto the street, heading toward the small

sports shop a few blocks away. "Do Rhaegynnes hoard other things?" I asked.

"Oh, sure. All sorts of things. We make excellent librarians and museum curators."

After a few minutes of silence I asked, "Did Grandma have a hoard?" She'd collected pictures and scrapbooks over the years, but I hadn't ever noticed anything unusual.

"There's a magically hidden portion of her house," Jason answered. I shot him a glance, trying to gauge if he was joking or not. But he looked . . . nostalgic. "There's an incredible magical library in there. I'll show you sometime."

I pulled into the store lot and parked. "I can't wait to see it," I said, turning the car off.

Jason stretched as he got out of the car. "But first, let's go get a stick and practice lacrosse! We're sword-fighting dragon assassins! How hard could it be?"

So . . . Not Lacrosse

Aaron

"Kat! Over here!" I called, dodging Jason in our makeshift lacrosse field in the park behind the school. I lifted my stick above my head.

Kat jogged to the side, awkwardly cradling the orange ball in the net, and launched it toward me. It fell short and bounced straight to Jason.

He seemed startled to see it coming and bent to try to scoop it into his net but somehow ended up knocking it back to me. I caught it and sent it into the goal.

"That's Kat-Aaron: Seven, Jason: Zero," I said. The euphoria of a clean shot had long since worn off. "Do we want to switch it up a little?"

"Want to lead us through some drills?" Kat asked, running to retrieve the ball and toss it back to me.

I cradled it in my net out of habit, enjoying the satisfying sensation of keeping the ball nested inside while the stick spun. "That seems like a good idea. Let's toss it back and forth while I think of something that works for three."

We formed a giant triangle in the park's soccer field. I threw the ball to Kat, who fumbled it and had to scoop it off the ground. She spun her net around a couple times and passed it to Jason.

He kept his shoulders tight and his hands too close together, restricting his mobility. He didn't even get close to the catch and had to chase after the ball. But he ran so smoothly, and his stance was so fluid. Why was he so awkward with a stick?

The ball slipped from his net twice before he passed it back to me. His cheeks flushed.

His toss was good, though. I caught it and sent it to Kat, who yelped and ducked.

"Sorry!" she shouted, running to catch the bouncing ball. "I wasn't paying attention."

"It's fine," I called back. "Let's . . . take a break for a minute."

I jogged over to our water. While I was happy Kat offered our friendship to Jason — he was the new kid after all — I felt weird about it now. It wasn't even jealousy. I felt . . . betrayed?

I could give Kat space. I had no problem with Kat having other friends. I had no problem with her keeping secrets. I knew she'd tell me if she wanted to.

I *was* okay with her spending every afternoon with Jason "practicing lacrosse."

But I wasn't oblivious. Whatever their four-hour practices for the past several weeks actually were, they were not lacrosse practice. Kat dropped more balls than she ever had before. Jason acted like he'd never even *seen* a stick.

I just wanted to spend time with them.

But Kat was lying to me.

Why?

They *did* still hang out with me at school and over the

weekends, so maybe I wasn't being replaced. But *something* was happening, and it hurt.

Kat pulled off her baggy hoodie, revealing a loose purple tank top underneath. She lifted her water bottle to her mouth, and I couldn't help but stare at the lean muscle through her arms and shoulders. *Those weren't there before.*

Maybe they were only conditioning, and that was why they weren't good at lacrosse...

I took a long gulp of water from my bottle, trying to avoid staring at both of them.

Conditioning didn't fit what I was seeing either. Something more was going on. She'd fall asleep in classes, and she was falling so far behind that she couldn't *afford* to sleep through them. Dark circles that got darker every day grew under her eyes.

"Should we switch to strength or cardio?" Jason suggested after finishing some trail mix.

Kat's shoulders visibly relaxed when I agreed.

She stretched her arms while running, and her shirt lifted slightly. I almost tripped when I noticed dark bruises along her back. Sometimes, she'd walk into school with a limp or would wince when she'd lift her arms. I figured it was soreness from practice, but what was *that?*

I pushed forward, trying to drown out the suspicions mounting in my head. I didn't have any real evidence pointing to any conclusion. For all I knew, they really had been practicing lacrosse and were having a bad day. Maybe she'd miss a catch — which was far from uncommon for any player — and the ball would leave a bruise.

Whatever it was, she was fine before Jason showed up. And I felt certain he was the reason she was getting hurt.

Was he hitting her?

Okay, that's probably jumping to conclusions. Maybe I am a little jealous. Beyond the exhaustion and the bruises, there were no other signs of abuse. Besides, Jason was equally battered.

I called an end to practice when Kat seemed to deflect all of my attempts to get back to lacrosse. I drove home alone, trying to push down mounting suspicion and panic.

LIE, LIE, LIE

KAT

I watched Aaron drive away from the park with a pit of guilt threatening to swallow me whole. I hated lying to him. But how could I keep him safe if he knew the truth?

Jason rubbed at a welt on his arm and walked over to the car with his practice bag and stick slung over his shoulder. "Well, I think we have about thirty minutes before you need to get home. We should try to work on freeing us from the kings."

I stared. "Right here?" *Right now?* We hadn't even tried since Coleman left, so *why now?*

"Why not? Coleman and I came up with some ideas to try." He tossed his stuff in the back of my car and set up a shield around us. Sitting on the grass, he patted the ground next to him. I joined him, my heart heavy.

"Okay, close your eyes and focus. You're going to do the same thing you do when you speak telepathically, but instead of speaking, you're going to keep pushing to get inside. No matter how willing your subject is, it's going to be hard. The mind doesn't want to be invaded. I don't know what you'll find."

"*Um, hi,*" I said telepathically. As soon as I reached him, I tried to keep pushing, but he yelped, and I jumped. My eyes flung open, and my hands covered my mouth. "I'm so sorry!"

"Don't worry about it. And you don't need to say anything beforehand. Try again."

I did, but his mind pressed against me harder than I could figure out how to push back.

"I can't," I said.

"Well, not with that attitude! Try again!" He kept an easy smile but sweat glistened on his forehead.

How could he be so cheery? Reluctantly, I closed my eyes, reaching out to his mind only to be met with even more resistance. Pushing in was different from communicating telepathically. Telepathy felt like sending a text or leaving a voicemail. This felt like searching through his personal possessions.

I flinched under the bombardment of his thoughts and memories. He whimpered again, but I kept my eyes closed. I didn't want to see how much this affected him.

Instinctively, Jason's mind built up walls around his thoughts, but I pushed back. Somewhere in there was a link to Aurakbahor.

Jason panted under the search, and my stomach churned. This was *hurting* him.

Am I expected to do this to everyone to steal them away from the kings?

My whole body recoiled at the thought, and I lost my grip. "I'm so sorry, Jason!"

His black hair stuck to his sweaty forehead. He almost looked angry. "You can't be sorry. This is the best chance we have right now! We have to keep trying."

I shook my head. "This is hurting you!"

"Our freedom depends on it."

"I need more time," I said.

He shook his head. "We don't *have* more time. Coleman's back to spying on Aurakbahor. He says he's growing impatient with the war. We think he's planning something."

I flinched. "He's planning an attack against Balaskad but wants *me* out of the way."

"How do you . . ." His voice trailed off, and his eyes widened. "Your nightmare at lunch."

I pulled away from him. "He wanted me to join him. When I refused, he tried to kill me."

"I'll have Coleman try to get more information. But let's try at least one more time."

My stomach dropped. Fear rose in my throat, and the fire inside me grew to meet the occasion. My vision shifted, and I struggled to stay human.

"Kat, please," he begged.

"I want him gone as much as you," I said, my voice shaking. "He *killed* my grandma! He tried to kill me *twice*. I'm terrified of him. I want to free you. But I can't do it. Not tonight. Your mind pushes me out, and it's impossible to fight back. It hurts me too."

His frown deepened. "Please?"

"Not today, Jason. I can't do it today."

"Let's work on some combat then."

"I want to go home." I stood and walked to the car.

"We have to practice! You have to be ready!"

I spun on my heel, fire rising inside me. "You're right. I *need* to practice. I need to take down the kings and break the curse. But we practice every *single* day. I can't even *sleep* anymore because I'm either training with you or being attacked by Aurakbahor himself! I'm *exhausted*. I feel sick because invading your mind hurts and feels pointless. And I feel awful because

I've told Aaron for weeks now that I've been practicing lacrosse, and now he knows that's a lie."

Jason stared at me, mouth agape.

"So, no. I don't need to practice anymore today. I need to go apologize to Aaron."

I got in my car and slammed the door, the heightened magic in my blood causing me to pull harder than I meant to, and the handle inside the car cracked from the pressure. I drove away, rubbing tears off my face, feeling even more guilty than before.

Unsolved Mysteries: Kat, Abducted by Aliens?

Aaron

I dejectedly flopped down at my desk to attempt to get some homework done despite the betrayal raging inside me.

Why is Kat lying to me?

I pressed my head into the desk with a groan, nearly knocking my head against the little gray rock Kat had given me a few weeks ago, and stared at the sliver of ground between the edge of the desk and my knees. My backpack sat open beneath me, reminding me of the mountains of homework left to finish — complete betrayal from my best friend or not.

Reluctantly, I pulled my notebook out of the bag, and a loose sheet of paper floated to the ground. It landed front side up with the words "Least Awkward Ways to Ask Kat to Homecoming."

I'd started the list after lunch instead of paying attention in chemistry. Back when I didn't know Kat was lying. I snatched the paper off the ground to wad it up and throw it away.

Lily and Miranda thought it would give her the chance to talk.

I hesitated, the paper half-crumbled in my fingers. Despite the heartache, I still cared. And I still wanted to ask her to homecoming.

The doorbell rang, and I got up to answer it, grateful for the excuse to ignore my feelings and homework. Prince barked incessantly at the door, and I had to fight my massive dog away to open it.

I froze.

Kat's eyes were rimmed red, but she smiled. She still stood like she held the world on her shoulders, but she rolled her shoulders back a little.

"Aren't you supposed to be with Jason?" I hoped I didn't sound as bitter as I felt.

"No. Can I come in?"

No. "Sure." I stepped out of the way. "Are you okay?"

"Yeah," Kat said as she entered and closed the door behind her. Prince jumped on her, forgetting his manners, but she scratched his ears anyway.

Ask her now! I wished the little voice in my head would make up its mind.

"Hey—" I said, just as Kat said the same thing.

"No, you first," we both said in unison.

"Okay, here — Stop that!" Again, we spoke at the same time. We made eye contact and burst into laughter. The pain of the last several hours eased slightly in my chest.

"You first," Kat insisted.

"Well, I, um . . ." *Keep going.* "I was wondering if you'd dance to the go with me?"

She cocked her head to the side, eyebrows furrowed.

So much for the list . . .

I took a deep breath. "Kat. Will you go to the dance with me?"

"Oh! I—"

"You don't have to if you don't want to! Or if Jason's already asked you—"

"Jason's going with Lily," she interrupted.

"What? Since when?"

"She asked him during class this afternoon."

I owe Lily my life. "Oh, well, I mean, if you haven't been—"

She flung her arms around my neck. "I would love to go with you!"

I hugged her back and grinned in spite of the way my ears burned.

My phone buzzed, and Kat broke off the hug, checking her own phone. "Crap. Mom's mad, and dinner's ready. I have to go," she said, showing me the text.

I checked my phone and realized it was hers that had buzzed, not mine. "Oh, okay. See you tomorrow then?"

"Yep! And in a few weeks?" she asked with a smile.

"I don't know. I'm kind of committed to go to a school dance with one of the coolest people I know."

She blushed, twisting a ring around her thumb. "Well, whoever you're going with is really lucky." She pulled her keys out of her pocket and opened the door. "See ya."

"Bye."

I waited to hear her car pull out before doing a victory dance.

Wait.

She had tried to say something! But I was so focused on asking her to the dance that I didn't let her finish! What if she wanted to tell me what was going on? She even seemed upset!

What if she was in danger? What if I blew it, and she'll never tell me again?

I dropped my arms in dismay. But my right arm fell faster than I meant it to, and it slammed into the corner of a potted plant's box. I cried out and sucked at my bleeding knuckles, cursing my unending thoughtlessness.

"WHAT DID YOU DO?" Kat asked the next morning, catching my scabbed hand in hers when I sat beside her. She muttered something but stopped.

"I could ask you the same thing," I replied, brushing a bruise on her forearm.

She dropped my hand to tug her sleeve over it. "One of my missed catches yesterday."

I wanted to remind her she could tell me anything. I wanted to blame Jason, but I didn't want to see that look of betrayal she always gave when I said things like that. I cleared my throat and tried a question instead. "Are you okay?"

"I . . ." She paused for a second. "Yeah. I'm okay."

"I'm glad." I pulled my hand away, but she caught it again and pulled me toward her, wrapping me in a hug. I held her back, letting her hug me as hard as she needed. *What is going on?*

When the hug broke, she turned away, trying to hide her pink cheeks behind her hair.

The bell rang, and she helped me to my feet. We walked in silence, and I watched her take her seat in her classroom before heading to my own class, frustrated that there was something she wouldn't — *couldn't* — tell me. Frustrated that something was hurting her and that her lies were easy to see through but not so easy that I could see the truth.

I turned the corner and bumped into Jason. Anger bubbled up in my chest, boiling over. "What is your *problem*?"

He laughed, obviously assuming I was joking about our collision. "Whoops. My bad."

"No. What's going on with Kat? What did you *do* to her?"

His smile melted. "I—"

"You need to leave her alone. She hasn't been the same since you showed up!" My voice rose, and people stared, but I didn't care. "I don't know what you've done, but it needs to stop."

"I haven't done anything! She's helping me train."

"For what? It's not lacrosse."

"What?"

"Lacrosse. The thing we were supposed to be doing last night. You both suck! There's no *way* that's what you've been doing!"

His eyes darkened beneath his glare. "We *have* been training."

"Where do her bruises come from?" I stepped closer to him. He mirrored, leaving mere inches between us.

"Practice," he snarled, his voice low.

"You're lying."

He shook with his anger. "I am trying to *help* her!"

A group of students formed a ring around us, expecting a fight. Some had their cell phones out.

Jason glanced to the spectators and rubbed his right arm. "Please don't do this," he hissed, but he glared at me with piercing black eyes. "Don't push me."

"Is that a threat?" I asked, clenching my fists.

"Stop it. Both of you." It wasn't a shout. But it was quiet, disappointed, commanding, and *dangerous*.

I turned to find Kat, furious and clutching a hall pass. The crowd had parted for her, and a hushed silence fell around us.

I stepped away from Jason, toward Kat. "Kat—"

She didn't look at me. "Jason, get some air. I'll deal with you later."

He broke off at a run, pushing through the crowd and disappearing down the hall.

She turned and stalked away.

I followed, reaching for her hand. "Kat! I'm sorry! I'm worried and—"

She yanked her arm away and spun on her heels, eyes burning with anger. "I don't care! I can fight my own battles." She crossed her arms and let out a frustrated huff. "That was so *reckless* of you!"

"I hate seeing you fall behind in class and show up to school covered in bruises! He—"

She threw up her arms and stomped a foot. "It's not him!"

I stopped and stared, struggling for words. "What's going on, then? If you don't trust me, at least go talk to a counselor or—"

"I don't need that kind of help. I appreciate the concern, but stop jumping to conclusions."

"I'm not jumping, Kat."

"You're interpreting things wrong!"

"What's actually happening then?"

"Nothing!" She paused to take a breath. When she spoke again, her voice was eerily calm. "We condition. I'm a klutz. I'm tired. That's it." She met my eyes with a steely glare. There was no way she'd back down and tell me the truth now.

I stared at my shoes. "I'm sorry," I muttered.

"Go to class before you get in any more trouble," she replied coolly.

My hands shook. "Do you still want to go to the dance with me, or did I ruin that?"

"I already said yes, didn't I?" And with that, she left to, I assume, go chew out — or maybe sympathize with — Jason.

I watched her leave, emotions warring inside me. My traitorous eyes stung with tears I didn't deserve.

What have I done?

Pockets!

Kat

I fumed all the way back to class. I *understood* why Aaron was angry. He just wanted to make sure I was okay. But his concerns were misplaced, and he shouldn't have cornered Jason.

I took a detour into the bathroom, trying to steady my breathing before I went back to class. Cool water ran over my shaking hands, and I wiped them across my face, trying to get the fire under my skin to calm down.

Aaron *did* have reason to worry. Bruises covered my body, and my face was gaunt with deep, puffy bags under my eyes. As I got better at fighting, our blows got worse. We'd spend an hour of practice healing each other most days. We'd try to fix everything, but bigger injuries — like broken bones — took priority, while the easier-to-hide bruises had to wait.

I shuddered. I'd broken nearly every bone in my body. And I'd broken at least as many of Jason's.

We were getting stronger magically, too. We could heal more, and I could perform more difficult magic than summoning a flame. I could build magical walls, send out attacks, and create my own spells. I was only limited in what I could do by my knowledge of Tasalgré, my imagination, and my magic store. And those were expanding every day.

But I barely recognized myself in the mirror.

I squeezed my eyes shut and took a deep breath. I scrubbed my face in the water, trying to wash away my frustration and exhaustion. I had been worried about my classes and keeping up with my family and not dying, but I didn't realize how close I was to losing Aaron. I didn't think keeping him away from danger meant keeping him away from *me*.

I shook the water from my hands and shut off the faucet. The paper towel tore as I ripped it out of the dispenser.

I am not *going to cry about torn pieces of paper.*

But I felt trapped. Torn in too many directions. Jason made it clear I could die at any moment. A spell could go wrong and kill me. He could lose control and be forced to kill me. Another dragon could come and kill me. The possibilities were endless, really.

I didn't know if I'd survive to graduation, let alone college.

But lying to Aaron was putting him in danger too. Jason could have accidentally changed when he confronted him like that. Then Aurakbahor could have forced Jason to attack Aaron.

I shook my head and grabbed a new paper towel to dry my hands and my face. *Whatever. It happened. It's over now. I'll keep taking it one day at a time. And pray that Aaron doesn't get caught in the crosshairs along the way.*

I headed back to class, checking my phone as I walked.

There was a text from Jason. I almost didn't want to open it. But I did anyway. "He has a point. We look awful. Let's shorten practice for the next couple weeks."

"What about the curse?" I responded.

"We have to find a balance between saving the world and saving ourselves. We're of no use to anyone if we're too exhausted to fight back. Half practices and full Realms training from now until the dance."

Two weeks later, I walked out of the changing room in a black floor-length dress with a hoop skirt.

Miranda gasped when she saw me, turning from where she held a green satin dress suit against her chest in front of a mirror. "Oh! I love that one!"

Lily, her dark brown skin absolutely glowing against the purple and silver ballgown she had on, nodded next to her. "Me too!"

"You've liked *every* dress I've tried on," I said. "I can't breathe in this."

"Breathing's for peasants, and" — Miranda dramatically swept herself into a deep bow — "my queen, you are no peasant! You can crush your enemies beneath your ridiculously impressive biceps!" She straightened and rolled her eyes. "But find another if you want."

"Why aren't you bowing to Lily? I'm dressed for a funeral, but she's over there looking like a goddess!" I hadn't hung out with just them in ages, and it felt nice to joke around again.

"Miranda already paid her proper respects to me," Lily answered, mockingly regal as she tossed her curls over her shoulder. "I'll pardon you for not bowing to me. One queen to another."

I tried to laugh, but the tight bodice restricted my breathing, so it came out as a wheeze.

With practices shortened, I could finally think about things besides training. I'd caught up on sleep and homework. I forgave Aaron. And the closer the dance got, the more excited I became. Weird butterflies filled my stomach when I thought about going with him, and I — *Oh no. Was this a crush? Is this what alloromantics feel all the time?*

I'm doomed.

But the actual dress shopping sucked. I hated shopping. Regardless of how giddy I had been about the dance, the thought of trying on yet another dress made me consider calling off the whole thing. Everything was so expensive. None of the ballgowns allowed the movement I wanted and most showed way more skin than I felt comfortable with — too many bruises to hide. Though we'd been careful to avoid sparring too much the last week or so.

I slumped to the floor, the tulle of my dress poofing up to my chest. I shoved it back down. "I hate this," I grumbled.

Miranda rolled her eyes again. "Fine. I'll go pick one." She returned a few minutes later with a short, golden dress.

"That's going to look awful on me," I said, staring at the sparkles on the bodice and the accent sequins on the skirt.

"It'll bring out the color in your eyes! And look so good with your tan! Please?"

I heaved myself off the floor, struggling with the excessive fabric, and grabbed the dress.

She plopped down in the chair in front of the changing rooms. "I'm so ready for this."

After stepping into the changing room, I struggled into the dress and changed my eyes to my mirror eyes just to laugh at my own joke. Anything brings out the color of my eyes now.

The dress fit perfectly.

I stared. I thought Miranda was exaggerating, but my body *had* changed. I'd been so focused on the bruises that I hadn't even noticed the other changes. There were muscles in places that used to be soft. I *was* tan from training outside so much, and the dress did look nice with it, even if the tan lines on my shoulders were a little uneven.

Surprisingly, it did bring out the color in my eyes — not just the mirror flecks but even my human brown-turned-gold. I spun in a tight circle, and the skirt flared out.

I reached my arms out and found the beaded cap sleeves still offered a full range of motion. I threw a test jab into the air, followed by a changing-room-sized kick. I could move! I could defend myself if needed. I turned slightly, trying to see it from other angles. A fold in the fabric stood out near my hip. Were those...

Pockets!

Was this a dream?

I walked out, and Miranda gasped. "I know I've said I loved every dress, but this one is amazing! Please take this one!"

Lily poked her head out from behind her changing room's curtains. "You look amazing!"

"Dude," I said reverently. "It has pockets."

Miranda jumped off her chair. "Done! Sold! Take it and run before someone hears you!"

I laughed. "Okay, I will. The sooner I decide, the sooner I can be done."

She gave me another eye roll and shooed me back into the changing room.

Aaron picked me up the afternoon of the dance. He'd told me to wear athletic clothes and good shoes, but he didn't say why. When I got in his car, he shot me a mischievous smile. "Ever played laser tag before?"

"Nope," I said.

"Seriously? Never?"

"Never ever."

A wicked gleam flashed in his eye. "Then we're going to play laser tag."

A little later, we found ourselves in the parking lot of an ancient arcade. A plastic banner over the doors read "Laser Tag Now Open!" Aaron excitedly guided me to the counter inside. He handed cash to the worker and led me to the laser tag doors.

He put on a vest with an attached laser blaster, before helping me into mine. "Prepare to be destroyed."

"Destroyed?" I scoffed while he handed me the last strap I fumbled for behind my back. "Oh, my dear, sweet Aaron. You are horribly mistaken. You cannot destroy me."

"Nice accent there, Shakespeare."

I sighted down the blaster's barrel. "Pew! Pew!"

He fought back a smile while a worker ushered us into a room lit with spinning laser lights. My shoes and Aaron's shirt lit up under the black lights. The worker signaled for us to wait a few minutes, but no one else arrived.

"It looks like it's just you two," the worker said in a bored voice. He droned through some basic instructions. "Game ends in fifteen minutes or until one of the bases is destroyed. Don't climb the walls. Don't die. Have fun."

He stepped out of the way, and we entered the arena.

A robotic voice spoke over the intercom, and Aaron darted off to hide. "Game beginning in three, two, one. Go."

Music started over the speakers, a laser sound came from my blaster, and both my vest and blaster lit up blue.

I crept forward, peering around the padded obstacles and walls, trying to find Aaron.

A flash of movement behind me caught my attention. I

jumped out of the way, tucked, and rolled. His blaster fired, so I came up shooting, everything I'd learned in training coming almost instinctively.

An electronic voice came from my vest. "Your point."

Aaron yelped and ran up a ramp to the second level before ducking behind a wall. I slunk into the shadows, using the pulsing lights to disguise my glowing vest. Somewhere in the darkness, his vest beeped as it reset. I heard him move before he peeked over the guardrails.

I ran out of the shadows, jumped, pushed off the wall opposite of him, and hurdled over the ramp onto the second floor. I pulled the trigger, and my vest announced my victory again.

He just stared at me.

I backflipped off the second floor and set off to hide again.

"I think that counts as climbing the walls!" he shouted. "Since when can you do *backflips*?"

I ducked into a corner with a cackle and backtracked to follow behind him. When I found him again, I cleared my throat. He jumped and spun, pulling the trigger, but I'd already fired.

"How are you *doing* this?" he asked.

"I'm secretly an assassin," I told him, then darted away.

"This is what you're doing with Jason, isn't it?" he called. "Playing laser tag?"

I climbed the stairs and stalked him from above while he looked for me. "Maybe. Maybe not." I shot him again as soon as his vest flared back to life.

"Oh, come on!"

"I'll give you ten seconds! I'll close my eyes. You hide."

I waited out the time before creeping out into the open again. But he'd either stopped moving, or he was better at hiding than I gave him credit for.

I wandered through the empty arena, wondering if he'd just left entirely.

Movement flashed, and I spun, pulling my trigger.

But my vest went dead.

"Wha—"

"Base destroyed," the electronic voice in my vest declared. "Red team wins."

Aaron sheepishly poked his head from behind my forgotten base. "Couldn't face an assassin directly," he muttered.

We stared at each other in baffled silence before bursting into laughter.

"Rematch?" I asked, my heart filling with pride for him. But my chest hurt. We'd make a good team . . . if I could just tell him the truth.

Homecoming

Kat

My mouth went dry when Aaron knocked on the door a little later to pick me up for the dance.

I'd been so excited to go with *Aaron* — my best friend — that I'd forgotten dances always made my skin crawl. The idea of being that close to *one* person under what was expected to be romantic circumstances had never seemed very appealing to me.

I froze outside my bedroom as Mom welcomed Aaron inside and called for me.

What am I doing?

It was *Aaron* though. And he was waiting for me. Regardless of whatever feelings I may or may not have started feeling for him recently, this didn't have to *mean* anything.

Unless... I wanted it to.

I took a deep breath and took the steps back up two at a time.

"Wow," Aaron said as I reached the landing. He held a little plastic container with a corsage inside.

"Good wow or bad wow?" I asked, smoothing out the gold dress. My cheeks warmed slightly.

"Good wow. *Definitely* good wow."

"Thanks," I said, unable to make eye contact. My face burned. "It has pockets..."

Mom passed me the boutonniere we'd ordered for Aaron, and I'd never been so grateful for the opportunity to focus on something else for a second. My hands shook slightly as I tried to pin it to his admittedly very flattering suit coat.

He smelled nice.

My back itched. *Am I about to turn into a dragon from embarrassment?*

But I smiled and let Aaron put the corsage on me. His fingers gently brushed across the inside of my wrist as he adjusted the beaded bracelet, and I had to pretend to be extremely interested in the white roses sprayed with gold glitter.

Mom forced us to pose for at least a million photos before finally letting us leave for the car where Lily, Jason, and Miranda were already waiting for us, smooshed together in the back seat.

Miranda rolled down the window and let out a piercing wolf whistle as we approached. "Kat, you look *hot!*"

"No, you!" I said, laughing.

Aaron opened the front passenger door for me and carefully made sure my skirts were safely inside before closing the door.

Then we were off, and there was no turning back.

And I found... I didn't want to.

Once at the dance though, I realized for all my anxiety about the dancing being too intimate of an occasion, I shouldn't have panicked.

The school's gymnasium was decorated with butcher

paper posters, crêpe paper streamers, and silver Mylar balloons. The lights had been turned low, replaced with colorful LED light strips and spinning lights. The music was loud enough I could barely hear anyone, and most of the school had crammed themselves onto the dance floor. No one was slow dancing; the song playing was too high energy.

The five of us formed a little circle on the dance floor. Miranda hadn't brought a date, but that didn't stop her from dancing with each of us individually for the next several songs while we laughed and joked, the party already passing in a blur.

Until the DJ broke in at the end of one song and announced the next was a slow dance, and Aaron shyly held out a hand for me.

"Only if you want," he said, his face sincere.

I took his hand, my heart pounding, and he gently lifted my hand and placed his other hand on my back.

"Do you know how to waltz?" he asked as the gentle music started.

I swallowed hard, my heart in my throat. "No," I admitted.

He smiled, and the dancing lights made his green eyes light up. "Can I teach you?"

I nodded and let him pull me closer.

"Step back with your left foot when I step forward," he murmured, gently guiding me through the first steps. He kept moving, holding me close enough he could lead my feet with his. He counted softly under his breath while I clumsily followed him, barely able to look up from my feet.

It was awkward at first, and I stepped on his feet at least twice, but soon, I found myself understanding the rhythm and began to feel confident — graceful even.

And for as nervous as I'd been for this exact moment, dancing with Aaron was . . . *safe*. Under his patient tutelage, it was even fun. And soon, I found myself grinning as we practically floated around the dance floor.

I dared to look at him instead of my feet. My heart skipped a beat, and I stumbled as I found him earnestly watching me, his eyes painfully soft.

His cheeks pinked, and he looked away quickly, helping me get back on beat.

"I never noticed how you have little flecks of color in your eyes," Aaron whispered.

My lips parted in surprise, and I met his gaze again. "What?" I asked.

"Your eyes," he said, but his eyes flashed down to my lips and then away.

I blushed, but I couldn't keep from looking at his lips either. They were full, a soft pink with a light bow on the top lip. I'd never noticed before. I'd never kissed anyone before. Never really thought about it. But he was only inches away, and my heart was pounding, and . . . I *wanted* to kiss him.

The world snapped into focus, and my cheeks burned with a surprising heat with the revelation. I bit my lip, glancing away.

Aaron pulled back slightly, his face pale. "Are you okay?"

Something clicked. My vision was *too* sharp now. Even happiness could be a strong emotion. Strong enough to bring on an involuntary change.

It wasn't an emotion I had trained with.

Happiness turned into ice-cold fear as I recognized a change only seconds away. It was far too late to reach for my tether.

"What's wrong?" he asked. "Kat, your eyes . . ."

"It's . . . nothing." Now would be a great time to not be such a horrible liar. "I . . . have to go."

I did the only reasonable thing: I pulled away from him, his fingers still reaching for mine and the waltz still playing. I ran out of the school, kicking off my painful heels as I went. I headed toward the old football field, the only place I could think of for a safe — hopefully unnoticed — transformation.

"*Kat, what happened? Where are you going?*" Jason asked.

"*I'm going to change. No time to explain. I need you to distract everyone else so nobody realizes I'm gone.*" I realized too late the ring on my thumb was missing, but I couldn't hold back anymore.

"*Where did you go? I'll get a ward up and come find you.*"

I changed mid-stride and unfurled my wings, preparing to launch into the air as I tried not to glance back. Trying not to cry as I realized I'd probably just offended the only boy I'd ever wanted to kiss. But he couldn't find out. I had to keep him safe. "*No, Jason. Listen to me. No matter what you do, do not let Aaron follow!*"

"*Yeah, about that...*"

"Holy—" a painfully familiar voice yelped behind me.

I froze.

I squeezed my eyes shut. I couldn't turn around. I couldn't face Aaron like this.

Like a monster.

Conflicting emotions — fear, regret, *relief* — turned my stomach to acid. At least I wouldn't have to lie to him anymore... But I wouldn't ever be able to look at him again. I couldn't bear to see the fear and hate I knew I'd see on his face.

But, of course, I looked back.

As expected, I saw the fear. Aaron's eyes were wide with it, his face devoid of color. But there was something else there that wasn't hate... awe?

I shook myself and took off into the sky, trying to get high enough my dragon eyes wouldn't be able to see the details on his face. He wasn't in *awe* of me. I was a dragon. A thing of myth and legend, always portrayed as the bad guy.

Aaron's shoulders fell, and he turned back to the school, head held low.

"Don't let him get away!" Jason cried.

"Get out of my head!" I snapped back. It wasn't his fault. I knew it wasn't.

But I also knew he was right.

I reluctantly went back, but as I did, Aaron's eyes widened, and he pointed behind me.

I twisted around to see what scared him, relieved it wasn't me.

The stars were moving.

I squinted, making out a long, snake-like dragon with night-blue scales.

"Kat, look out!" Jason cried. I turned and saw he'd made his way out to the field after all, ready for a fight, hands blazing with magic.

The new dragon turned her long ribbon-like body and dove — but not at me.

Not at Jason.

At Aaron.

In what was only the latest in a long stream of poor decisions, I flew straight at Aaron and landed in front of him, cutting off the dragon. I reared up to face her, shielding Aaron with my body and my wings outstretched.

He let out a terrified shout that made my heart clench.

Jason sent a curse straight into the dragon's side, and she whipped her head toward him.

I dropped back to all fours and turned to face Aaron.

"I'm so sorry Aaron," I told him.

He cowered beneath me. His face was pale in the dark.

"You can *talk?*" he yelped.

"*Telepathically. Let me take you somewhere safe!*" I reached for him with a taloned paw, but he recoiled.

"If that's really you, Kat, let me on your back," he said.

"*What?*" I gasped, but behind me, the dragon shrieked, and Jason shouted out in pain.

"Kat! I need help!" Jason cried.

Aaron stepped toward me on shaking knees. "I can ride a horse. I can do this."

I gulped but stretched out a wing, helping him climb up. I could do this. I could get him away and get back to help Jason.

"Kat! *What are you doing?*" Jason screamed. "*Just send him back inside!*"

But it was too late. Aaron was on my back, and I was in the air. He let out a shout of fear, but once I leveled out, he quieted, his grip shifting to something more secure. I took off toward the far end of the football field where I hoped Aaron could hide behind the bleachers, but the dragon abandoned her efforts in attacking Jason and turned and gave pursuit.

"*Hold on!*" I tucked my wings and dove, hoping to get him to the ground before she could get to me.

The dragon caught up to us. I pulled up from my dive, but she did as well and jammed her horned head into my chest.

I spun around, whipping my tail across her face. The crack echoed through the night.

The dragon breathed fire. I tucked my wings to drop but remembered Aaron was on my back and doubted I could fall fast enough. Frantic, I tried to shoot up out of the way, taking the full impact of the flames on the lower portion of my body. I screamed in pain and frustration.

I raked my talons across her neck. She reared and tried to bite, but I dodged.

Her missed strike threw her off target. Instead, she

smashed into one of the spikes on my neck and ripped it out at the base.

I screamed again — putting all my faith in Jason's wards to shield us — and writhed in my instinct to protect an injury I couldn't reach. I sent fire chasing after her, but she ducked and moved like she wanted to fly over me. For a moment, I hoped she was leaving, but then I realized she wasn't flying past me. She was aiming for Aaron.

I tried to weave out of the way but was too late. I felt Aaron slide and watched him fall alongside a young woman whom I assumed was the dragon. But why had she changed back? I dove, caught them both in my talons, and then carefully set them down behind the bleachers before turning back into a human. Blood dripped down my back and chest, staining my golden dress. I crouched next to Aaron, who fortunately was still conscious. He leaned over the unconscious girl, worry written across his face.

"What happened?" I asked. I pushed her jet-black, chin-length hair back and checked for a pulse along her neck.

"I caught your spike and used it like a bat when she attacked me." He showed me the broken spike before turning back toward the woman. "I didn't kill her, did I?"

"She's still alive. Just a nice knock on the head." I motioned to the cut arcing from her jaw to her forehead.

"What are you going to do?"

I inspected the wound and then whispered healing spells, green light pouring out of my hands. The swelling subsided, and the gash stitched itself back together.

"Wow," Aaron whispered, watching over my shoulder.

The woman woke and sat up, pushing me away. I moved to shield Aaron from her, but instead of attacking us, she *cried.* "I-I'm so sorry! I didn't mean to! They made me do it!" I put a hesitant hand on her shoulder, trying to soothe her.

"I know," I said. "It's okay. Can you find your way home from here?"

She took off running without another word. We watched her disappear around the corner, just as Jason appeared from the other direction.

"Are you okay?" Jason asked, panting as he reached us.

I looked at Aaron, who looked *far* from okay. "Could you... give us a minute?" I asked Jason.

He looked between the both of us. "Yeah, I'll go check on Lily and Miranda. And apologize for ditching my homecoming date." He looked at me sympathetically. "*Good luck*," he added privately, and he set off back to the school.

I took a deep breath. "Aaron, I—"

He held up a hand. "This is what you've been keeping from me, isn't it?"

I nodded and sat on the grass beside him. "I... didn't want you to get hurt. I didn't want you to find out like this. Can... I explain?"

He looked away but nodded, and everything came gushing out. I told him of the stories Grandma used to read to me about the first dragon shifter, Rhaegynne, and the four dragon clans that descended from her, the power that was named after her and how her power could be shared though things like blood, tokens, or inheritance. I told him about the war, the curse, and the kings. I told him about how we were pretty sure the explosions around the country were because of the war, not gas leaks. I told him how Aurakbahor killed my grandma. I explained that Jason and I had been training to fight back, but because he was cursed, the fight came down to me. I told him about the prophecy that should have been about Grandma, but she died before she could fulfill it, and how I'm trying to take her place, but her shoes are too massive to fill.

I spilled everything I'd kept from him since Grandma died

nearly two months ago, and he let me speak for however long it took to tell my story.

"I wanted to do this differently, Aaron. I'm . . . I'm so sorry. You shouldn't have ever had to learn about it like this, but we sometimes change with strong emotions like fear, pain, or grief. But I just found out strong *positive* emotions can do it too . . ." I flushed, remembering what triggered it in the first place. "I realized that I . . . well, I really like you. We use grounding techniques to help prevent changes, but I wasn't prepared, and I was scared you'd get hurt. I have a ring that's supposed to hide me when I'm a dragon, but I lost it, and we couldn't get other wards up in time, and I'm so sorry." I knew I was rambling, but I hoped maybe if I said the right combination of words, he'd understand, and I could fix what I'd done.

"I think I have your ring." He reached into his pocket and handed it to me. "It fell off in my hand when you . . . left. But Kat, you're *hurt*." He touched my arm, just below a narrow trail of blood.

"I'll fix it later." I wiped a streak of blood tickling my neck before sliding the ring back into place. "I'm . . . sure you have questions . . ."

His lips twitched into a smile. "You're a Rhaegynne dragon. Is it Raegan? Like the name?"

"Pronounced the same, spelled differently."

"So, you're basically a werewolf but a dragon?"

The dragon in me wanted to protest, but the human part of me realized I had made the same connection ages ago. "Yeah. Except I'm not limited to a forced change at a full moon, and I don't think I'm allergic to silver or whatever."

He smiled for a second. "Man. You're a *dragon*. What am I supposed to tell Lily and Miranda? They've been worried sick about you!"

"We can't tell them!" I said, my stomach twisting into knots at the thought.

"Why not?"

"I don't want them getting hurt..."

"They literally have a board with little strings attached to pushpins, trying to figure out what's going on with you. I think they're leaning toward alien abduction."

I laughed. "They do not!"

"Being a dragon almost makes more sense. I'll have to suggest it next time I see the board."

I sighed. "No... I'll figure something out later..."

We fell silent for a moment until Aaron gasped. I jumped and turned, preparing for another attack, but saw nothing. I turned back to him. "What?" I asked.

"So, you *were* cheating at laser tag?"

"What? No!" My face felt hot, but I couldn't help but laugh.

"Yeah, but *you're a dragon*. I'm not. Unfair advantage. Next time, you need to be blindfolded or something."

"I'll still kick your butt," I said, laughing. Our eyes met, and my cheeks flushed. I must look like such a disaster right now. I tried to push a tangled piece of hair back into my destroyed updo. "Do you have any other questions?" I asked.

"So, you said positive emotions is what..." He ran a hand through his own windswept hair. *How can he still look so put together after a fight?* He shook his head like he was trying to clear the thought. "I'm sorry. Never mind."

"What is it?" I asked.

His cheeks bloomed crimson. "Well... I just..." He put a hand on my knee, and I suddenly realized how close we were under the bleachers. I leaned toward him, and he leaned closer.

"Can I kiss you?" I whispered. My stomach fluttered at the question I hadn't planned to ask.

To my relief, Aaron nodded, and his lips brushed mine

hesitantly, like a question. I kissed him back harder, like a promise.

I savored the way my magic tingled in my blood at the contact, but I was prepared this time and able to control the rising emotions. *Thank goodness.*

My dress was blood-stained, my updo was half undone, and my back really did hurt, but Aaron wrapped his arm around me and pulled me closer, and none of that even mattered because his lips were against mine. And he knew I was a dragon.

And he wasn't scared of me.

My demi heart chose well.

We broke apart, basking in each other's warmth as the night grew cold.

But when my eyes opened again, they widened at the blood across his suit. "Is that a rental?" I gasped. "I can fix it!" I quickly wove the spell Jason had taught me that first day and watched the blood disappear.

Aaron let out a low whistle. "Well, that's useful."

I grinned but shivered. I still had plenty of magic, but between the cold night air and the come-down from the fight, my dragon fire wasn't quite enough to fight back the chill.

"Here," Aaron said, shrugging off his suit coat.

"Wai—" I started to protest, but he had it around my shoulders before I could form a coherent sentence. "Thanks," I said, rubbing the silk hemming.

"Don't worry about it."

"We should get back . . ." I muttered, climbing to my feet.

"Kat?" He caught my hand in his, preventing me from standing all the way.

I turned, not able to fight the smile rising to my lips. "Yeah?"

"You said you'd have to fight the other dragons alone."

My smile faded. "Yeah . . ."

"Well . . . what if I fought with you?"

I shook my head. "I don't think I can give the gift to anyone until the curse is broken. I don't know what would happen, but I don't dare risk it."

"I don't mean as a dragon."

I blinked. "What?"

"I could fight like I did tonight. From your back."

That pesky smile tried to surface again, but I hesitated, glancing back toward the school. No one had come out, and with my ring back . . .

"Before you agree . . . can I show you?" I asked. "Properly this time?"

He smiled. "I would love that."

Welcome Home

Coleman

Aurakbahor had summoned me to his court.

I checked my new watch, paranoid to lose my powers in his presence. I already had a splitting migraine; if he was mad, I didn't need any other hurdles keeping me from staying alive. I wasn't sure what I did, but I was fairly certain I hadn't proven myself enough yet.

I entered the white marble courtroom, flinching at the bright lights. After blinking a few times to adjust my vision, my blood froze. A young woman with black, chin length hair cowered on the ground, her shoulders shaking.

"You had her!" Aurakbahor screamed, pacing in front of her, his dark cane clipped to his side like the concealed sword I knew it was.

She sobbed. "I'm sorry! She was supposed to be alone!" The woman wiped her eyes with the back of her hand. "If we—"

"We?" he interrupted.

"I can try agai—"

Aurakbahor spun, and a blade of white magic flashed from

his hand, slicing her throat. She fell to the ground, blood pooling on the white stone beneath her body.

I tried to hide my disgust. "Who was she?"

He turned to me, blood splattered across his face, and smiled. "An assassin I sent for Katherine. Thanks for the tip about the dance."

I clenched my fist, feeling the warmth of my glowing resistance tattoo under my sleeve. *I'm doing this for them.* "Of course, sire. Is that why you sent for me?"

He took a seat on his throne and gestured for me to take the seat to the right of him. My stomach fluttered as I obeyed. He placed a fatherly hand on mine and met my eyes.

I tried not to stare at the blood on his face.

"It's unfortunate that she failed, but you gave good intel. It was brave of you to betray your friend. I'm willing to put you back in my Court."

I bowed my head to hide my face. "Thank you, sire."

A servant entered with a platter of food and drinks. He sidestepped the body in the middle of the floor and set up a small table for the tray. "Your Majesty." He bowed.

While the man hurried out of the room, Aurakbahor turned back to me. He picked up a glass with a sludgy appearance and passed the other with clear, bubbly liquid inside to me. I glanced at my watch. Kroll hadn't cashed in on our deal yet, so I should still have magic if he tries to poison me . . . again.

"To your success," Aurakbahor said as he raised his glass.

"Long live the king," I said, clicking our glasses together. *Or not . . .* I tipped my glass back. It had a pleasant, fruity flavor.

He drank, wiped his mouth, and grimaced. "Helps keep my mind sharp in my old age."

I eyed him. He probably hadn't aged in a century at this point.

He smiled and gestured at the food. "Eat! It's our own

private feast! And you didn't even have to break in for it this time. I'll hold a full one when I've announced your return!"

My appetite had already been weak from this awful migraine, but it was gone now.

I ignored the corpse in the center of the room, aware of the implied threat he'd left for me. Picking up a plate of roast beef from the tray, I smiled, trying to ignore the nausea building in my throat. "Thank you, sire. I won't let you down."

Well ... This is my First Rodeo

Aaron

Kat's a dragon.
Either that or I need to see a doctor.
My pride wanted to claim I'd known all along, but of course I didn't.

Holy crap, I kissed a dragon.

Importantly, I kissed *Kat*. And she wasn't a dragon for any of those, but *she's a dragon*.

When did myth and legend enter my world?

I fought a dragon! On a dragon!

Maybe there was something wrong with me because my first instinct was to sign up to help Kat. My subconscious must have a death wish. Her blood had run in small streams down her back, and if a giant dragon couldn't walk away from a fight like that unscathed, how was I — a powerless human — expecting to join the fight and survive?

But how could I not try? Kat needed my help, and there was an entire group of *people* who needed saving.

Part of me wanted to run away and hide, to try to go back

to being ignorant of it all. But the rest of me buzzed with excitement at the thought of training with Kat.

I barely slept all weekend, counting down the hours until I could join her. And I spent all day at school on Monday watching the clock and ignoring the teachers.

No wonder Kat's always so far behind in her classes...

When the final bell rang, I raced into the hallway to find Jason and Kat waiting for me.

Kat grinned when she saw me, reaching out her hand to hold mine.

On the other side of the commons, I noticed Miranda grin and give me a thumbs-up before running off, probably to go find Lily.

I smiled, taking Kat's hand. "How's your back?" She'd healed it before we'd gone back into the dance, but I struggled to believe the damage was *truly* gone.

"All better!" She turned and lifted her hair to show perfectly healed skin.

The skin didn't even hold a scar. I reached out to touch the spot in awe.

Jason cleared his throat.

"Oh, right! Training," Kat said. "To . . . my car!" She grabbed my hand and pulled me along to the parking lot.

For once, I didn't wonder where all her strength came from.

Magic.

Kat drove us to the base of a trailhead and grabbed a bag from the back. She disappeared behind a thick knot of trees and reemerged a little later in exercise shorts and a t-shirt.

"Aren't you freezing in that?" I asked. It was late October, but the first snow of the season had left a thin blanket on the mountains.

She pressed her burning hand against my face. "Nah. I'm a

fire-breathing beast. Besides, I'll want to be wearing this once we get started."

"Did you bring a change of clothes?" Jason asked me.

"I didn't even think to," I admitted, staring down at my jeans and thinking of how uncomfortable they would be to run in.

"Here." He tossed a wad of clothes to me. "Sorry, they're long-sleeved." He grabbed a change of clothes for himself and also ducked behind the trees.

I followed suit and found my own bush. Jason was several inches taller than me, but the clothes still fit okay.

By the time I finished, Kat and Jason were already trying to murder each other with swords and magic. Their swords were nothing but blurs and ringing metal as they danced around each other. She flung a ball of fire at him, and he redirected it back at her. She dissipated the flames with a wave. Neither missed a beat in their swordplay.

Jason threw a punch when he stepped into her reach. She ducked and snuck her sword under his, laying it against his collarbone. He dropped his sword and stepped back. Both were panting as they turned to me. Blood dripped from Jason's nose, and Kat had a bruise forming over her eyebrow, and both had unnervingly inhuman eyes. His eyes were black. Kat's were silver with catlike slits in them.

I shuddered and sucked in a breath.

Their eyes shifted back to normal, and Kat smiled like she didn't even know how terrifyingly awesome she was.

"Aaron," Jason said, still breathing hard. "Let's get you started on swordsmanship. Kat, will you get him a sword, please?"

"Of course!" she said, handing her sword to him. Instead of turning back to the car to get one, her eyes turned silver. She held her hands out and said something I didn't understand.

The air blurred between her hands before solidifying into a sword. She passed it to me, her eyes once again shifting back to her normal golden brown.

"Okay, that eye thing is weird — and so is this sword!" It was solid but somehow not.

"Magic," Jason and Kat said at the same time.

"Magic," I repeated, hearing the awe in my own voice.

"How are you going to teach him?" she asked Jason. "He's not Rhaegynne."

"What does me being human have to do with it?" I asked, feeling a spike of defensiveness.

"It's instinctive for us. Not so much for humans."

"So, why do you have to train so much?"

"Instinct is sloppy?" Jason said.

Kat shoved him a good two feet at the jab. "I almost beat you in my first fight!"

"Wasn't trying as hard back then . . ." he mumbled.

"Oh yeah? Then how come I can I beat you now?" she asked, stepping in close to him.

Jason rolled his eyes but ignored her. "Let's get you started, Aaron."

"You're bleeding," I pointed out.

He wiped at his nose and examined the blood on the back of his hand as though he hadn't noticed it before. He picked up a clump of snow and wiped his hands off. "Eh, I'll fix it later."

"What if your nose is broken? You need a doctor!"

They exchanged glances and burst out laughing.

"A doctor?" Kat asked. "We've got something better!"

I rolled my eyes. "Magic?"

"Magic!" she replied in a singsong voice.

Jason cleared his throat. "Let's get started for real this time," he said as he took a step forward. He bent his front knee slightly and raised his sword.

I awkwardly mimicked him. Kat stepped up behind me and corrected my posture. My stomach flip-flopped at the contact.

"Keep your eyes on Jason, and keep your sword pointed at your target." She backed away and waved her hand. "Begin!"

He pounced, and I stumbled back, blocking wildly. With a blur of silver, his sword slammed into my chest, and I landed on my back in the snow.

She pulled me back up and glared at Jason. "Dude, he's human. You can be a little less aggressive with him to start!"

"I *know* he's human," Jason said. "I'm *intimately aware* he's human. But he needs to be able to fight *dragons* if he's going to join us." His face softened. "I don't want him to get hurt, but I especially don't want him to get killed, and I don't want *you* to get killed trying to protect him because he can't hold his own yet. You literally put yourself in danger and abandoned me to protect him at the dance! So, no. I'm not going to pull my punches."

Kat looked at me like I was something fragile.

"It's all right," I said, resetting my stance. "I can handle it."

She clenched her jaw but nodded and made a few adjustments to my form.

Again and again, I found myself in the snow with Jason's sword tip on my chest or my back or my neck or any number of other places he counted as a kill. I struggled not to feel too frustrated, but if I couldn't figure this out, I would be worse than useless in a fight.

"Jason: Nine. Aaron: Zero," Kat said, pulling me out of the snow again. "One more point, and Jason'll make you do horrible, awful things. Like burpees."

"Speaking of which, you owe me twenty, Kat," he said.

Her face turned white. "I thought you forgot about that."

"I never forget. I'll start charging interest if you wait any longer."

Her eyes turned silver, and she muttered something under her breath.

"*Gasić ally!*" he cried out as he blocked a small fireball from Kat. "That's ten more!"

Her eyes continued to reflect her surroundings, but she started paying off her debt.

Jason and I resumed sparring. This time, he went slower, instructing as we fought, but like the nine times before, I ended up with a sword on my chest in the snow. I groaned, climbing to my feet again. My clothes were wet with snow and sweat.

Kat walked over, panting and trying to warm her hands. "Ha! Your turn to suffer!"

"I did get to ten first. Do as many push-ups as you can while Kat and I practice," he said.

She looked like I'd been issued a death sentence. I stepped out of the way and returned to the snow.

She and Jason tapped blades before starting into a dance of steel and magic.

I reluctantly turned away from the fight and began the push-ups. Only a few in, my arms shook, but I pushed through, determined to prove myself. I chanced a look at the fight. Neither had the advantage yet, so I went back to the push-ups.

Kat's scream interrupted my concentration, and I jumped out of my plank, running toward her before I had gained my footing. She lay on the ground, shaking and curled around her arm that was bent the wrong way.

"Kat!" I rushed to her, but Jason held me back.

Kat cried out a spell. "*Key Ally!*"

Snow shot up between us, creating a cylindrical, transparent wall around her. Her frame was distorted through the wall of ice, but I could still see her place her hand over her broken arm. A green light cast an eerie glow on her face.

"She has to practice protecting and healing herself in a fight," he explained. His eyes widened, and he shoved me out of the way.

Kat yelled over the sound of shattering ice as she came out swinging her sword. He met it, and they launched into their deadly duet. I stared, mesmerized.

"Push-ups!" he reminded me while they spun past.

I started again, my arms trembling from the effort and adrenaline.

The fight ended with Jason sneaking in a cheap shot, which allowed him to get behind her and hold his blade against her neck. Her sword tip touched the snow, and he let her go. I slumped to the ground, relishing the cold snow against my hot and aching muscles.

Jason stretched and looked at the sky. "It's not dark yet. Might as well get in some fly time."

"Yes!" she shouted, jumping in the air. She shimmered at the top of her jump and landed as a dragon, shaking the ground and sending up a plume of powdery snow.

"All right, Aaron. You get on. I'll throw obstacles, and Kat, you're going to dodge them. Aaron, stay on, and when you get the chance, cut it down."

I climbed up onto Kat's back and accepted a sword from Jason.

"Ready?" she asked.

"Of course," I said, swallowing a sudden lump in my throat.

She shot into the air, and I clung to her neck. She circled above Jason while she waited for our first obstacle. A giant snowball came barreling up at us, and she swerved around it, allowing me to slash it. It smashed into little bits and coated me in snow.

I gathered a ball of snow and chucked it at Jason. He

dodged and hurdled another snowball. Kat dodged again, and again, I made it snow around us.

My streak was perfect. Kat would dodge, and I would destroy the snowball.

"I'm going to throw other obstacles now! Get ready!"

With that, he flung a fireball at us. It came in at just the wrong angle to force Kat to rear up and flip away. Despite my best efforts, my hands lost their grip. At the peak of her flip, I flopped.

Kat shrieked, but I couldn't scream. I think I left my voice with my stomach in the flip.

The wind ripped my breath from my lungs. Kat pressed her wings hard and raced for me, her draconic face terrifying in her desperation. Her claws reached for me but closed around open air.

I was going to die.

What would Kat tell my parents? "Sorry. He fell off a dragon."

Something pushed against me, slowing my fall enough for massive dragon claws to wrap around me before I hit the ground. My body jarred at the disruption, but I was alive.

Kat set us back on the too-close ground and shifted back. She grabbed my shoulder. I assumed it was out of relief that I was okay, but then I noticed her face drained of color.

"Are you okay?" I asked, putting a shaking hand out to keep her upright.

"I'm fine," she said, waving me off while Jason came running. "Are *you* okay?"

"You're both fine!" Jason said, his voice shaking with fury, his eyes black. Kat stepped in front of me, trying to shield me from his anger. "You're both fine, but it's because *I* was there. What are you going to do in an actual fight, Kat?"

Kat crossed her arms. "I can hold my own now, Jason."

He raised an eyebrow. "Are you really going to turn your back on an enemy because your human boyfriend can't hang on? *This* is what I was talking about earlier! Aaron would have *died!*"

"I caught him at homecoming," Kat said defiantly.

Jason rubbed his temples and let out a slow, measured breath. "This isn't working. Aaron, if you're going to be a dragon rider, we *have* to figure out how to keep you on her back. We'll . . . craft a saddle or something."

"A *saddle?*" Kat hissed. "I'm not a *horse!*"

He scoffed. "Of course you're not! But how else are we—"

"How *exactly* do you expect me to keep a dragon saddle on my person?"

He shrugged. "You want to keep a human on your back as a dragon. You can figure out how to keep a dragon saddle on your person. Your human clothes are still there when you shift back to human. Maybe it works for dragon saddles."

She glowered.

He held up his hands. "Do you have a better idea?"

She crossed her arms, a pout furrowing her brow. "No. But I'm not going to wear a *saddle!*"

Jason glanced at me, his anger softening. "Fine. I've got another idea anyway."

"This," I said, shocked as Jason guided us into a reserved practice room at the rec center, "is your idea?"

Jason looked proud of himself. Kat looked like she might explode from holding in laughter.

The mechanical bull in the center of the room looked very beat up.

"Well, it's safer than practicing from dragonback, but it should give you the same kind of practice *without* a saddle." He stared at Kat.

She stopped laughing and glared at him.

"It'll at least improve your ability to stay on, but we can test out new ideas here."

"Can't I be tied on? We could hide a big coil of rope, right?"

Kat gave me a skeptical look. "How? Looped through your belt loop like a lasso? People will still think that's weird."

"Well, what if I wore it like a belt?"

Jason rolled his eyes. "Stop stalling and get on the bull."

"This is bull," I grumbled, wading across the thick, blue landing pads, and climbing onto its back.

I lasted longer on the dragon.

Kat couldn't contain her laughter as she helped me out of the landing pads.

"I think I preferred the whiplash from falling yesterday," I complained.

"This is safer," she said.

"I'm not so sure about that," I said as I massaged my newly aching shoulder. "Isn't there some kind of safety harness we could magic up instead?"

"We'd have to test them out on this, assuming we could even make one," Jason said.

With that, my fate was sealed. I went from being a dragon rider training for battle to a dragon rider training for the rodeo until my whole body *hurt*, and Jason blessedly called an end to my humiliation.

"You did good today, Aaron," he said, helping me once again. "Kat, we can talk more in the Dream Realms tonight."

"Dream Realms?" I asked.

"It's a place Rhaegynne can go when we're sleeping to

meet with other Rhaegynne. We train there every night," he answered.

"Should I train there too?"

"I don't know if we could call a human there," Jason said, trailing off as if calculating a way to get me there. "But we can try."

I'm a Real Cowboy Now!

Aaron

I lay in bed, too anxious to sleep. I fell off that obnoxious bull too many times to count. I was frustrated and scared. There was a lot more to this than I expected, and I was beginning to doubt I'd be able to help Kat after all.

To top off the nerves, I hoped I'd be able to join them in the Dream Realms tonight. But to *get* there, I had to be *asleep*.

I sighed, and Prince shifted like I had offended him. He huffed and slipped off the bed.

"Oh, okay. Bye, Prince," I muttered, turning over and pulling the pillow over my eyes.

Prince shoved his nose into my face, and I yelped.

"Well, hello again," I said, scooting over to let him and all his seventy pounds of fluff back onto bed. "Were you not comfortable before?"

He curled up next to me. I hoped it was his head by my face, but it was dark, and it was Prince, so I was pretty sure it was his butt.

I don't remember falling asleep, but I woke up the next

morning without any Dream Realms adventures. I thought I heard Kat say something to me, but she wasn't there. Just me and a fluffy dog butt in my face. Turning off my alarm, I sat up and rubbed my eyes.

My phone buzzed on the desk.

Prince got off the bed, stretching and yawning, when I reached for it.

"We couldn't find you," the text from Kat read. My stomach clenched. I wasn't surprised, just disappointed.

It's fine. I'm human. They're not.

Things could've been worse. Being a dragon these days wasn't all it was cracked up to be. Unless you're Kat, of course. At least I wasn't a mind-controlled dragon puppet.

But if I couldn't pull myself together, I wasn't going to be able to help the dragons *or* Kat.

My legs cried as I stiffly got ready for school. I had ridden a horse before, but these were saddle sores on steroids. Not to mention the chafing I still had on the insides of my thighs from dragon scales. I would never dare think about asking Kat to wear a saddle — or letting her know riding bareback hurt — but some padding would be nice.

KAT RAN up to me as soon as I limped into school almost half an hour later. "I caught up on homework!" she exclaimed, waving a handful of papers under my nose.

"That's awesome! How?"

"I don't know. I cranked it out after dinner. I went to bed really late, and Jason was pretty upset with me, but I did it!"

"I'm so proud of you," I said.

She hugged me, bouncing with joy. Her eyes had the

faintest hint of silver, like she could hardly control her excitement. "I need to run and go get this turned in before school starts. I'll see you later!" She kissed me and bolted off.

I watched her bound away with a spring in her step I hadn't seen in months.

"I'm glad she told you," Jason said from beside me.

I turned, startled. "I thought you didn't approve."

"I don't. But she's happier, and I know it's only been a few days, but she's been more focused in training. Admittedly, I think half of that focus is trying to impress you, but if it works, it works."

I shifted on my feet. "I don't think it has anything to do with me."

"Maybe. All I know is you joined us, and now she's catching up on homework and training better." His eyes shifted to black.

I stepped back, my blood running cold. "Jason?"

"Just know, if you hurt her, and she stops training this hard, I'll curse you to stub your left pinky toe every day at 3:57."

"A.m. or p.m.?" I squeaked.

"Both."

"Promise," I whispered.

His eyes flashed back to blue, and he smiled. "Dude, I'm messing with you!"

"No, you're not. You need her."

"I do. But I'd be more scared of Kat than me. And I can't actually curse someone with that. Not yet anyway . . ." he added.

"I won't hurt her."

"Stay on a little longer, and we can take this to dragonback!" Jason called while my brain jiggled in my skull from the mechanical bull getting progressively angrier beneath me. Two weeks of daily training on this death machine was finally paying off.

Jason's stopwatch beeped, and the bull came to a slow stop. I slid off and onto the landing mats, trying to catch my breath. I was elated at beating the bull but also so sore.

Kat pulled me out of the mats, grinning. "Dragon time!"

"No backflips, please," I begged.

"No promises."

Her smiles had come easier the past several weeks. She joked, laughed, and stayed caught up on her homework. She still wouldn't talk about college, but she was happy, so no one bothered her about it. Besides, I understood why she didn't want to apply. I didn't either.

We ran out to the car together. Kat was nearly glowing with excitement. We'd been focusing so much on training me that Kat's dragon practice had been limited.

Once at the trailhead, Kat ran on ahead, leaving Jason to make a wall against onlookers. Using a boulder on the edge of the trail, she propelled herself into the sky. In a heartbeat, her wings pushed her higher, and she flew off. She circled and spun and dove like a dancer above us.

She always had a careful beauty about her, but now, she held herself with the poise of a fighter: confident, strong, and beautiful. Watching her soar and tumble through the air as a dragon took my breath away.

She landed ahead of me, breathing hard. Her impressive crest of horns around her face curved gracefully upward, and her tail flicked lazily behind her. *"Ready?"* She extended her leg and wing out for me.

I ran and climbed up to her back. "Please don't drop me."

Her body shook with laughter beneath me. "*I promise to catch you if I do.*"

"Good enough."

She launched off the ground, sailing into the sky. I held onto one of the stubby ridges in front of me and gripped her sides with my knees, surprised to find new strength in my legs.

"*Comfortable?*" she asked.

"Yeah. Is it okay?"

"*Yep. Are you holding on tight?*"

My knuckles whitened on her back, and I avoided my nervous reflection in her scales. "Yes."

She pointed her nose up, and we climbed steeply upward. I leaned toward her as the wing muscles in her back bunched. She twisted. We corkscrewed higher, and I held on tighter. She arced and spiraled downward.

"I'm getting dizzy!" I complained, but the wind on my face felt amazing.

"*Is this better?*" Her wings folded against her side, brushing the backs of my legs, and we plummeted. My stomach twisting in fear and excitement.

I screamed and cheered. We free-fell for what felt like hours, enjoying the feeling of the crisp November air rushing past knowing gravity had no power over us.

She landed eventually. I slid from her back, and my legs wobbled. I reached back to steady myself against Kat but caught her hand trying to steady herself on me. We both had expected the lacking support, so we tumbled to the ground, landing in a heap of laughter.

Jason came over, arms folded across his chest. "All right, lovebirds. Had enough?"

Kat reached her arm up for his help. "No, but I guess so," she replied as he pulled her to her feet. She helped me up in turn.

As I stood, a young man with red hair wandered off the trail toward us. "Your wall's still up, right?"

Concern flickered across Jason's face. "Yeah, of course."

"Coleman!" Kat shouted, rushing forward and embracing him. "What are you doing here?"

"Just checking in. I saw you flying and figured I could find you here," he answered.

Jason walked over to them and clapped Coleman on the shoulder. "Welcome back!" He gestured to me. "This is Kat's boyfriend, Aaron. He's human, but he's training with us."

Coleman reached out and shook my hand. "It's good to meet you, Aaron. It's nice to finally be building our numbers again." He grimaced at Jason. "I've not made much progress on rebuilding the resistance on my end. Not since getting confirmation that Tythan and Hope are still in the UK. Tythan's been mostly ignoring me, but maybe once we can prove that Kat's ready, they'll be more willing to come out here."

Jason shrugged. "At least we know where to find them when we're ready."

Coleman didn't seem to love that answer, but he shrugged. "Have I missed all of practice?"

"You could help Kat with trying to break the mind control," Jason suggested. "We haven't been able to make any progress."

A few small flakes of snow landed around us. Kat looked up at the falling snow, trying to catch one on her outstretched hand. "We can try," she said, "but it hurts, and I don't think I can make much progress with you as a human since your connection is when you're a dragon."

I made eye contact with Kat, hoping she'd give some hint of what they were talking about.

"*I'll tell you later,*" she answered telepathically.

"That's a good point," Coleman said, "and one of the reasons I came . . . I was thinking about the whole puppet-curse issue and about how it must be overwhelming for the kings to keep up with all of us. Aurakbahor let me back into his Court, so I've been close to him. He's using a potion to help him. We could try to recreate that potion and see if it helps you."

Kat perked up. "We can make potions?"

"Potions require bizarre, rare, or expensive — or bizarre, rare, *and* expensive — materials and a great deal of skill. So, the answer is *maybe*."

"What's in this potion?" Kat asked.

"This one seems relatively straightforward. It's got a bunch of random herbs and spices I could buy at the store, water, chocolate, and, um, mud from a very specific hot spring in Yellowstone National Park."

Kat's face fell. "How on earth are we supposed to get that?"

"I was hoping you guys could help me come up with a plan."

Jason sat on a rock and rested his head in his hand. "Well, the North Gate is still open. Please tell me the spring's there so we don't have to break too many laws for it."

Coleman grimaced.

Kat sighed. "Where is it?" The snow fell in large flakes now. One landed on her eyelash, and she blinked it away.

"You know that colorful hot spring you see on all the postcards?"

"Coleman, don't tell me I have to deface one of the most beautiful hot springs on Earth to save the dragons."

He winced. "Well... that's why we need a plan."

She rubbed her temples. "Is there anywhere else?"

"What do you think causes the pretty colors?"

"Thermophilic bacteria!"

"And... magic..."

"We are *not* going to ruin a nationally protected and

universally loved landmark just so I can maybe get an edge on Aurakbahor. How does Aurakbahor get his? Can we steal from him?"

Coleman shook his head. "He's running low. He'll need to go in the next week or so. I can go with him and take notes on what he does. We'll make a plan as soon as I have more details."

The wind picked up with a howl, sending snow spiraling through the air.

"Great. Let's go home," Jason said, already running down the trail.

Heists and Betrayal

Kat

"Hey, Kat?" Dad called from the kitchen.

I grabbed my cleaning supplies and left the bathroom. "What's up?"

"Could you help me chop more potatoes when you're done with the bathroom?"

I showed him the cleaning bucket. "I just finished. Give me a minute." I put the cleaning stuff away, washed my hands at the kitchen sink, and grabbed the bag of potatoes.

We worked in silence for a few minutes, falling into the mindless rhythm of preparing potatoes for Thanksgiving dinner.

"How have you been?" Dad asked. "You've been so busy this semester. I hardly see you."

A potato slipped, and I nearly cut my own finger. "Oh, uh, just busy is all." *Thanksgiving is not the time to tell my dad I'm a dragon...*

"I—"

Mom came bustling into the room, looking stressed. "Mrs. Johnson called. Her family will be here any minute! Kat, can you grab the plates? I didn't realize how late it was!"

With Grandma gone, Thanksgiving threatened to be a very lonely holiday with just my parents and me. So, we invited Lily's, Miranda's, and Aaron's families to fend off the loneliness. I told my parents Jason's dad was out of town and got him invited too.

I turned to grab the plates, passed them back to Mom, and returned to the potatoes with Dad. "What were you saying?" I asked.

He shook his head. "Nothing. I think we should have enough potatoes now."

The dinner table was surrounded with friends and full of food. The only ones missing . . . were Coleman and Grandma. When the doorbell rang at the end of dinner, Jason's face lit up with hope, but my stomach sank.

It *could* be Coleman.

It wouldn't be Grandma.

I got up to answer the door. To my surprise, it *was* Coleman.

"You're back!" I said, genuinely delighted at least one of my missing people could make it. "We just finished dinner, but there's still food."

He shook his head. "I ate, but I have news."

I stepped aside and let him in.

Jason jumped up to greet him. "You made it!"

"I did," he said, his voice low. "Is there somewhere private we can meet?"

Jason and I exchanged worried glances. "Meet us downstairs," I said. "We'll be down in a bit."

Jason followed Coleman down the stairs. I returned to the table and leaned in close to Aaron. "Coleman's here."

He nodded but didn't react.

"Who was that?" Dad asked.

"A friend. He needed a place to go for the evening," I lied.

"Does he want food?" Mom asked.

"I already offered. I'm going to go down and make sure he's okay."

"Can we help?" Lily asked.

I looked to Aaron, but he shrugged, leaving me to find something to say. "Oh, no. It's okay! I won't be long."

Aaron got up to join me, and Miranda shot me a quizzical look but didn't say anything.

We hurried downstairs and closed the door behind us. "They deserve to know the truth," Aaron whispered.

I sighed. "Everyone does, but I don't know how to keep them safe if they know."

"They think we're up to something," he added.

"That's because we *are* up to something," Coleman said. "Who are we talking about?"

"Lily and Miranda," I answered.

"Okay, I'll try to keep this short." He gestured for us to sit at the small card table and laid a map across it. "I came here as soon as I could get away. Aurakbahor just left Yellowstone with a vial of the mud. It actually came from the Excelsior Geyser Crater." He pointed out a spot on the map. "It's next to the Grand Prismatic Spring — the one I thought was the source."

I asked. "How did he get the clay without damaging himself or the geyser?"

"He flew in and used magic to dunk a vial into the geyser."

"Most of the park is closed and snowed in now. How are *we* going to get in there?" Aaron asked. "Only one of us can fly."

Coleman glanced at me. "How many people do you think you can carry as a dragon?"

"No clue. I hardly feel Aaron. But I don't know how much room there is. What kind of magic did he use to—"

Jason held up a hand. "Someone's outside the door."

I stood and hesitated by the door. How much did they hear?

Lily and Miranda stumbled backward as I opened the door. Miranda replaced her look of embarrassment with a smile and walked into the room. Lily followed behind, seeming chagrined.

My heart pounded. I hated that my eyes shifted, and when I glanced at the others, Jason's and Coleman's eyes had changed too.

"So," Miranda said in an accusatory voice, "you guys have been playing some nerdy tabletop role playing game."

Well, that would have been a good lie.

Lily pouted behind her. "And you didn't even invite us!"

"I've always wanted to play as a mysterious half elf sorcerer with a tragic backstory!" Miranda declared.

I forced a laugh. "I'm sorry. I didn't know."

Lily took a startled step backward. "Kat, what's up with your eyes?"

I squeezed them shut, trying to decide whether forcing the fire inside me to die down and make my eyes switch back would be worse than just letting them remain mirrored. I could lie. I could keep lying. They'd given me a perfect cover story. It would be easy. Safe.

But I didn't *want* to.

I left them mirrored and opened my eyes. "You were right,

Aaron." I sighed. "They should know. Maybe they can help cover for us."

Aaron inclined his head and touched my arm for reassurance.

Jason's black eyes widened, but he nodded in understanding and gestured to the couch. "Let's take a seat."

Lily and Miranda hesitantly took a seat. Jason and Aaron sat next to them, Coleman remained back by the table, and I walked up in front of them.

"Okay, you're kind of freaking me out," Lily confessed.

I let out a nervous laugh. "Yeah, it's freaking me out too. I'm not . . . I've not done this before. Aaron found out when I accidentally showed him, but I can't really do that here. I guess there's not really a good way to say this, but, um . . . I'm a dragon."

Miranda rolled her eyes. "Yes, we established that you are playing a game."

Lily put a hand on Miranda's leg. "I don't think she's talking about a game . . ."

I held out my hands and summoned a little flicker of fire shaped like a dragon. I watched it flit between my fingers for a moment before dismissing it. Miranda's mouth opened in shock. "It's not a game," I said.

"Here I was thinking you'd been replaced by aliens . . ." Lily whispered.

I turned to Aaron. "You weren't lying about that?"

"Why would I lie about that?"

Miranda swore softly.

"So . . . you believe me?" I asked.

"Dude," she said. "Either you're all experiencing some group psychosis that you've pulled us into, or you have magic. And I guess I'd rather believe that."

"Jason and Coleman are dragons, too," Aaron added. "I'm not. I'm just training with them."

Lily's eyes darted between us like she wanted us to be lying. "Right . . ."

I sat on the ground and started from the beginning. I liked to believe it came out less ramble-y than it did with Aaron, but it was probably just as incoherent. Jason and Coleman helped fill in the gaps. The girls sat in silence until the end.

Miranda chewed her lip. "So, when are we leaving for Yellowstone?"

"We?" I asked. "No, I can't let you get hurt."

She gave me one of her famous eye rolls. "We don't have to go all the way with you, but we can tell our parents we want to go on little road trip before the roads get too bad. It'll seem a lot less suspicious if we all go. We'll drive with you to the North Gate, and you can do your cool dragon thing. When you come back, we'll buy a few souvenirs, and no one will question us. We can *totally* be your alibi."

"The North Gate is just over two hours away," Coleman said thoughtfully. "I figured if we left around six tomorrow morning, we'd have plenty of time to get there and back. Does anyone have a bigger car we can drive?"

Lily nodded. "I can take my mom's minivan. She won't mind." She laughed. "This is going to be so much fun! We should get to bed. We have a huge heist in the morning!"

COLEMAN SANG in the passenger seat while Lily drove.

His confidence and skill were too infectious, and soon we were all singing along. The song ended, and Coleman hit a perfect high note.

"I didn't know you could sing, Cole," I said before the next song started.

He shrugged. "I don't get the opportunity much."

"What else don't I know about you?" I asked, smiling.

He laughed. "Considering we've only known each other for a few months, a lot."

"Okay, but did Jason know you can sing?" Aaron asked.

"This is not our first road trip together!" Jason said.

"Sure, he's good," Miranda said, "but can we talk about how amazing Lily sounded?"

Lily flushed behind the steering wheel, and Jason knocked her shoulder. "You sounded amazing."

Her blush deepened. "I took lessons as a kid."

"Well, you're incredible!" Miranda said.

"It looks like the main road into the park is closed up head," Lily said, changing the subject and pointing to a road closure sign. "I think this is as far as I can get you. I'll let you out here. Be careful."

"We'll be quick," Aaron promised as Lily found a parking spot.

Lily motioned to the darkening sky. "You better I think a storm's coming in."

"If it gets bad," Jason said, "get out of here. We have our own transportation."

We got out of the car and wandered through the narrow paths in the knee-high snow. Lily and Miranda followed close behind. There were only a handful of people brave enough to face the cold, but even a few were too many to change in front of, so we followed a trail into the tree cover as far as we could. Then, Coleman covered our tracks as we blazed our own path.

Finally out of sight, I turned toward Lily and Miranda. "I need you to be careful. I don't know what kind of attention we're going to draw, but if anything seems weird at all, don't wait for us."

They nodded somberly.

"Good. Coleman? I have my ring, but can you keep a shield up. Just to be safe?"

"Of course," he answered.

I took a deep breath and shifted.

Lily and Miranda gasped, and Lily stepped forward. I lowered my head to her, and she tentatively touched one of my horns.

"You're beautiful, Kat," she said.

"*You're seeing your own reflection.*"

She jumped at my voice in her head but scoffed. "Whatever. Go steal some mud."

Aaron climbed on first. Then Jason and Coleman shuffled into place behind him.

"Is this okay?" Aaron called.

"*You guys hardly weigh anything. I'm fine.*"

"You two should back up," Jason called down, and the girls shuffled backward.

"*We'll be back soon!*" I said and launched into the sky.

I had been to Yellowstone over the summer before and was stunned at the beauty. But the snow-covered park from above was breathtaking. I flew above the forests and rivers, catching glimpses of wildlife and steaming thermal features below. I tried to hurry, but I just wanted to stop and enjoy the wonders below me.

Gorgeous fields and snaking rivers passed beneath us, the distance disappearing beneath my wings as I pressed southward. Steam made the air foggy as we approached our destination.

"*It's to your left, Kat,*" Coleman instructed.

I turned to see a massive cloud of steam billowing out of a pool of rainbow colors. *"It's beautiful."*

"We're going to want to go to the crater in front of the colorful spring."

I circled to the ground, trying to watch for wildlife or park rangers, and set us near the wooden walkways. The heat from the springs left the planks mostly clear of snow.

"You have the jar, right?" I asked Jason as soon as I had turned back into a human.

He pulled the glass jar out of his backpack and gave it to me while we walked up the ramp to the top of the crater.

"Okay, Kat," Coleman said, sounding like a coach before a big game. "I can either help you fly out over the crater, or we could enchant the jar to go in."

Water boiled and steamed across the entire crater. "Let's try to send the jar."

"I'll watch from the other side and make sure you're not going too far." He hurried across the slick walkways.

"What kind of spell do I use?" I asked Jason.

He thought for a moment. "Close your eyes."

I did as he instructed.

"Reach out with your mind. What do you feel?"

"You, Aaron, me—"

"No. What objects do you feel?"

I tried to focus on *things* until my mind bumped against an object in Jason's hand. "Found it."

"Try to pull it out of my hand. I have a hold on it too, so you don't need to worry about dropping it."

I tugged, and it moved toward me. I opened my eyes, startled to see it floating between us.

"Brilliant! I'll stabilize the jar; you direct it out into the crater."

I pushed the jar over the steaming pool below.

"Good, Kat!" Coleman called. "Now, drop it in about there and push it down as far as you can. You won't be able to see it, but you should still feel it. You can have it scoop at the mud on the bottom and bring it back up."

I lowered the jar into the muddy water. The dormant geyser roiled around it, but it remained intact. As it slid beneath the water, I felt around at the rest of the crater, trying to find the bottom.

As the jar dipped into the boiling earth, I felt a massive presence come up behind Coleman on the boardwalk. It was heavy... imposing.

Familiar.

I ripped the jar upward and opened my eyes. "Coleman, watch out!"

Aurakbahor walked up to Coleman with a sly smile. His words somehow carried across the chasm with chilling clarity. "Excellent job, *my prince*. Stop them."

Coleman froze and my stomach dropped. But he didn't run. He didn't fight back. He *bowed*. "Yes . . . Father." He raised his hand and the ground beneath us rumbled. The old geyser spat and gurgled, and a dull roar filled the air.

"*No!*" I screamed. The jar tumbled into the mud, and I tried to run to Coleman.

Aaron grabbed my arm. "We have to go!" he yelled.

I struggled against him but slipped on the slick and shaking ground. I scrambled on my hands and knees, trying to reach Coleman. "No! We have to stop him!"

"We can't win this fight. Run!" Jason pulled me to my feet and yanked me away, but he kept glancing over his shoulder.

Coleman watched with cold, unfeeling eyes while Aurakbahor backed away. Aaron stared in horror.

"You *traitor!*" I screamed so hard my throat burned.

The old geyser erupted.

Jason snatched Aaron and me away as boiling water erupted in a massive pillar.

Steam blocked our view of Coleman and Aurakbahor as we tried to escape the explosion. Water, somewhat cooled by the cold air but still scalding, poured around us. I grabbed Aaron's arm with my free hand and ran.

The fire inside me burned hotter than the water around us. I clung to the boys on either side of me as I let the transformation overtake me.

I gripped them in my talons and took to the sky, trying to get us away from the eruption. I landed in the snow a short distance away and turned to hunt down the traitor, but he and *his father* had disappeared in the steam.

I snarled at the sky and fell to the earth, letting the snow cool my burns.

"He's gone," Jason croaked.

In the distance, the unstable walls around the geyser crumbled, collapsing in before being shot into the sky and splattered burning mud into the white snow.

"He destroyed the geyser," Aaron said, staring at the ongoing explosion.

Jason scooped up some of the mud that had fallen nearby. "We'll need to hurry back to Lily and Miranda before Coleman can lead Aurakbahor to them," he said numbly.

"*You might as well leave the mud, Jason,*" I said. "He probably lied about that too."

BANE

KAT

J ason and I trained alone in the Dream Realms for the first time in over three weeks since Coleman's betrayal. We'd barely even talked since then. Everything was a reminder of him.

We sat facing each other, the mountains of the Dream Realms echoing the Montana mountains we usually trained in.

"I've been thinking," he said. "The mind link might be a lie."

I hesitated. "We both saw the same things he did." I wasn't going to say his name if I didn't have to. "There's something there."

"I thought about that, too. Are you still willing to try?"

"It's the best hope we have right now."

"Then let's try again. After, we can try to get Aaron in here." Jason tried for a smile, but it seemed painful.

I tried to smile back. He patted my knee before he closed his eyes.

Pushing into his brain felt different this time. There was

hardly any resistance. The walls didn't come up as fast, and I didn't lose more ground than I gained. I couldn't tell if it was because we were in the Dream Realms or if he just didn't have the energy to fight back anymore.

I searched through his mind and slipped deeper.

And then suddenly I was sliding, being pulled down like a leaf in a whirlpool, drawn to some overwhelming *force*.

I recognized it, that force. That *presence*. It was the same power I had felt at the geyser. And it sat in the center of Jason's head. Hesitantly, I reached out to it.

Aurakbahor's face — turned to the side as though talking to someone else — appeared as clearly as the day he killed Grandma. I gasped, and he stiffened.

My body recoiled, and I yanked myself out of Jason's mind, physically scrambling away from him before Aurakbahor could know it was me.

My thoughts raced. Jason wasn't a dragon right now. He wasn't even *awake*. Did Aurakbahor sense me enter Jason's mind? Did that mean he could hear Jason *all* the time?

My heart pounded. If Aurakbahor could sense our communication, then we weren't safe *anywhere*. It wouldn't have mattered if Coleman told Aurakbahor everything he knew about us or not. Aurakbahor *would know*. Then he'd know our plans. Which meant he knew our names, where we lived, our families, our friends. He *knew everything*.

But there was a chance he didn't know that *I* knew.

"What happened?" Jason asked, worry creasing his brow. "That didn't hurt that time!"

I shook my head, trying to organize my thoughts. If the king could hear everything I told Jason, then I couldn't tell him *anything* unless I was okay with the king hearing.

Which meant I couldn't tell Jason I knew.

Which meant I would have to plan everything twice. Once with Jason and once by myself.

I swallowed my guilt. "I couldn't even get in."

It felt dramatic to say I was alone sitting across from a friend, but the honest, awful, gut-wrenching truth was that I was.

I couldn't find Aaron before school the next day, and I didn't see him in third period either. I figured he ditched the last day of class to start his winter break early — heaven knows I'd considered it myself — until I spotted him near the front of the cafeteria line at lunch. Eagerly, I butted in line next to him.

"Sorry we couldn't get you in last night," I told him, grabbing a tray and accepting an extra-large portion of enchiladas from the lunch lady.

"It's okay. Is that why you're always so tired?" Aaron asked as I reached over his arm to grab an applesauce cup and a banana.

I scooped out a generous pile of salsa and sour cream and led Aaron around the salad bar, and toward our table. "Yeah, I sleep, but it's not resting. If that makes any sens—' I yelped as someone knocked into my elbow, spilling my applesauce all over the tray and across the floor.

"Sorry! Sorry!" a girl said, grabbing a napkin and trying to clean up the spill.

"It's fine," I said. "I'll go back for mo—"

"I can do that!" She stood and ran back to the salad bar, throwing the soiled napkin in the trash on the way. She paused for a moment, checking each cup before picking one. She wiped her sticky hand against the top of her jeans and rushed back. "I am *so* sorry about that."

"It's fine. Thanks for getting a new one!"

"Was the least I could do," she said and turned, running off to catch up with some friends waiting by the cafeteria exit.

"Who was that?" Aaron asked.

"I dunno, some freshman?" I said as we joined Jason, Miranda, and Lily at our table.

Jason was already wolfing down the slightly questionable enchiladas. He barely came up for air to greet us when we sat. None of us spoke. We just ate, filling our stomachs — even if the food did taste a little expired.

Aaron watched Jason and I eat our dragon-sized portions and smiled. He'd long since given up on trying to keep up.

I finished my banana and started on the applesauce. "I think they put cinnamon or something on it today. It tastes different. Bad."

"It's bad, but you're still eating it?" Aaron questioned, laughing. It felt nice to hear him laugh. It almost made me forget the danger I was in sitting next to Jason.

"Like everything else in this cafeteria! Besides, I'm hungry." I swallowed wrong and coughed.

"Are you okay?"

"Wrong tube," I choked out, my eyes watering from the pain.

Jason stared at me in horror.

"What?" I asked, finally catching my breath. Pain shot through my stomach, and I doubled over like I had been punched, letting out a grunt. My throat tightened, and I started hacking.

Aaron patted my back while I gasped for breath. My throat burned with an icy heat.

"Are you allergic to anything?" Aaron wrapped his arm around me for support.

I tried to speak but could only shake my head. The edges of my vision blurred as I struggled to get enough oxygen. Instinct demanded I shift to open my airways a little more. I managed to take a breath, concentrating on the fire within me, ignoring the witnesses.

I needed to *breathe*.

Seconds passed. Panic fluttered in my chest.

I couldn't change.

I'd changed over little things! Why couldn't I change now when my body screamed for air? My stomach twisted, and my breath hitched and caught. Aaron thumped my back, trying to dislodge whatever was stuck, but it only sent pain burning through my body.

I tried to scream, but nothing came out.

"Kat, open your mouth," Jason demanded.

I managed to open my mouth for a moment before my throat spasmed, sending me into another coughing fit — at least a little air got in between coughs.

Jason swore.

"What's going on?" Aaron asked, a note of panic in his voice.

"Dragonstongue. The applesauce was spiked with Dragonstongue!" He cursed, grabbed our food, and threw it in the trash.

"What—"

"We have to get her out of here!" he said, helping Aaron lift me up.

Aaron draped my arm over his neck and laced his arm around my back, holding me so my feet barely touched the ground. I could barely even feel my feet.

"Cover for us!" Jason begged Lily and Miranda, but his

voice sounded like it came from the bottom of a swimming pool.

I was vaguely aware of Jason handing Aaron his car keys. Jason and the girls ran over to an administrator as Aaron dragged me to the exit. I swear Jason's eyes turned black for a moment before the teacher nodded, and they disappeared around the corner.

Or Aaron dragged me around the corner.

Was there a corner?

Jason reappeared a few moments later, out of breath, and helped Aaron get me to the car.

"What's Dragonstongue?" Aaron asked, his voice low as though he didn't want me to hear.

"Ever heard of Dragon's Bane?" Jason asked, helping to maneuver my useless, freezing, and burning limbs into the car.

I knew that word. Didn't I? It alarmed me at least, but I didn't know *why*.

All I knew was pain. Nothing existed but the pounding drums of my pulse in my ears and the icy fire of pain cutting through me with every heartbeat. My muscles cramped across my body, and I tried to scream, but I couldn't get enough air, and my jaw was locked shut. Everything from the fire in my veins to the way my lungs struggled for breath *burned*. Something was wrong with my magic. My *own* fire was out cold.

Then, like striking a match at a gas station, everything got worse.

My insides felt like someone had replaced my blood with boiling acid and dunked me in a vat of liquid nitrogen. I might have screamed. I couldn't tell.

Aaron pulled me toward him, resting my head on his lap. His eyes looked funny, and a weird, rapid whooshing noise came from somewhere. Was that my heart?

The car swerved, and I tried to gag, nauseous from the

movement. But I couldn't move. Thick pins of pain held my limbs in place, and each movement sent shocks through my burning blood.

I couldn't see out the window, but smoke and fire rose, and I heard screaming.

The car smelled like burnt rubber. The car was burning! We needed to get out!

I couldn't move! I burned. I couldn't scream. Surely, Jason or Aaron had noticed the smoke around us. Why hadn't they pulled over? Were they trying to kill me? Trying to kill *us*?

I thrashed or thought I thrashed, trying to get their attention. Aaron's face twisted with worry. My vision swam as smoke stung my eyes. He reached out to touch my face.

He's worried that his plot to kill you won't work.
What? No! He's my friend! He's my boyfriend!

But then Aaron and Jason laughed. Somehow, Aaron circled around me, pointing and laughing, as I writhed in agony.

The pain, the burning, the freezing, the suffocation — I would take it a hundred times before facing his betrayal.

Smoke entered my mouth as fire embraced me. I thrashed and screamed and arched my back, but did I? I couldn't move. I couldn't breathe! It didn't matter. Aaron didn't care. I didn't care. I was going to die. Like this. In the fire. Alone.

Cold.

I tried to close my eyes and accept my fate, but they couldn't move either. Something soft brushed against my forehead, sending agony through my body.

Aaron.

The illusion of him mocking me shattered, and my head was simply resting in his lap with his fingers stroking my hair while the fire raged around us.

He was trying to help. I wished I could tell him not to. It

hurt. But I didn't *want* him to stop. If I could speak, I would tell him how much I liked him. But maybe I wouldn't. Too many people said that while dying in the movies.

But right now, I meant it. Losing him in this warped reality brought that into perspective. It was the only thought capable of warding off the pain and the fear. Even the fire and ice.

Aaron.

Pain blocked out the rest of my vision, and the suffocating smoke stopped up my lungs.

Crap Crap Crap Crap Crap – A Poem by Aaron

Aaron

Kat's tongue was blue — bright electric blue.

Her eyes were silver and slitted, but she didn't change. Instead, they rolled in their sockets. She lay stiff in my lap, her face turning a darker and darker red as Jason sped through traffic. The veins in her forehead and neck bulged, slowly turning the same blue as her tongue. Her breaths came in sharp gasps.

She didn't move. She didn't scream.

She just shook.

The needle on the speedometer maxed out while Jason drove down the freeway with white-knuckled fists and black eyes. The cars around us swerved out of their lanes to make way. For a minute, it seemed like there was a blue net around the car, but it might have been the way the street lamps hit the falling snow.

"What's happening?" I asked, my voice thick with unshed tears.

"Dragonstongue is a plant with magical properties and a

toxin lethal to dragons. But it doesn't make a fast, clean kill. It's more than poison; it's a *curse*. It warps the victim's reality, inducing hallucinations to make them *want* to die. Depending on the dose, it can kill in a few hours or drag the torture out for days."

My mouth was dry. "W-why are her eyes like that? Is she going to change?"

"She can't. The toxin binds to magic."

"Can *you* do something?" *Please do something.*

"No. I'm not skilled enough. But I know someone who is."

"Who?"

He looked at me in the rearview mirror with pain in his draconic eyes. "Coleman."

"*What?*" Had he lost his *mind?*

"We don't have a choice!"

"He's the prince!"

"He's our only chance!"

"He tried to kill us!" I yelled.

"If he wanted us dead, we'd be dead. Jamie gave him that mission for a reason."

"Jason, be realistic."

He chewed his lip for a minute. "He's the only person I know who can cure this. Either we risk Coleman killing us or Kat dies in your lap."

The worry in his eyes made me believe him, and I sighed. "Fine."

Jason had to have used magic to get us there because it normally took a lot longer than an hour and a half to get to Canada. Kat's breathing had become thin and irregular, only managing a few rasping breaths a minute. The blue tracks had crept under her collar and down her arms.

She'd stopped shaking.

She made eye contact with me, but she seemed to be seeing something that wasn't there. Her face didn't move, but her eyes betrayed incomprehensible pain.

"Jason... hurry," I managed.

"We're almost there," he replied, sounding more like he wanted to reassure himself as he turned down a forested road.

"Hear that, Kat? You're going to be okay," I said, brushing her bangs off her forehead for the hundredth time. Her cold skin was slick with sweat. Goosebumps rose up her arms. "Stay with me."

Her eyes flinched at my touch, but they didn't show as much pain. They looked almost appreciative. Was she back in her own mind? Or was this another trick of the Dragon-stongue?

I swear, whoever did this will suffer more than she is.

Her eyes unfocused again, and she let out a small gasp.

I would give anything to not have to watch her suffer like this. If I could even take just a little of her pain, I would.

Jason screeched to a stop outside a cabin off the side of a dirt road. "Help me get her inside."

I lifted her, and he took her limp body from me and carried her toward the house. I pounded on the front door, but he hissed out a spell like a curse, and the door swung open.

"Coleman!" he shouted into the house. He dropped his voice to a growl. "He better be home, or I'll kill him."

"I might kill him anyway," I muttered.

Coleman ran into the living room and froze. His mouth fell, but he took one look at Kat and jumped into action. "Bring her here. Quickly." He shoved a coffee table out of the way, accidentally tipping it and sending books, coffee, and piles of loose paper to the ground with a crash.

Jason laid her on the ground.

Coleman checked for a pulse along her neck.

Sorrow twisted his face. He met Jason's eyes and shook his head.

Anger flashed white-hot in my stomach. "What's that supposed to mean?"

"It's too late." He sounded dejected.

"What do you mean? *Too late*?" I yelled. "For all we know, this is your fault! *Fix it!*"

His eyes swam with tears. "I cannot help a corpse."

It took me half a second to process what he said. "No. Kat! No!" I shoved him aside to kneel beside her. I lifted her by the shoulders.

Her head lolled, and her eyes, dull and gray but shot through with blue, rolled back. I set her back down and closed her eyes, unnerved by the sight.

Desperation seized me. "No!" I screamed. "Don't leave *me!* Kat . . ." I pressed my mouth to hers, hoping against all reason that among the myths and magics that were real, a kiss to break a curse might be too.

It wasn't.

I turned to Coleman, still protectively holding her. "She was alive when we pulled up to your house!"

He just looked at me with sorrow in his traitorous eyes.

"Your magic is *useless*," I growled and started doing CPR. If magic couldn't save her, I'd do it the human way. "Come on. Breathe!" I begged under my breath.

After a few harrowing moments, Kat gasped, and her eyes shot open — still mirror, still bloodshot with blue. But open.

"She's alive! *Save* her!" I barked, yanking Coleman back toward her.

He blinked at me, looked between Kat and me, and nodded. Eyes closed, he took several deep breaths. I clenched my fists, resisting the urge to shake him.

When he opened his eyes again, his irises were bright red. He put one hand on the side of Kat's face, and his other hand covered her heart. "*Agnrot as alla nognocar!*" he cried.

Green light wrapped down his arms, covered her like a blanket, and filled the room. The magic seeped into her skin and down her throat, illuminating her eyes for a brief moment.

The light faded, and for a heartbeat that stretched into eternity, nothing happened.

Blue light exploded from Kat, filling the room. Coleman shouted the spell again, except he sounded like he struggled under thousands of pounds of pressure. He inhaled, gasping in pain as he absorbed the blue light. His irises turned electric blue, and he cupped his hands. The light pooled into a ball in his palms. He pressed his hands together and slid them apart roughly.

The blue light disappeared. Kat arched her back and gasped. Her beautiful, human brown eyes darted around the room in a frenzied panic. When they landed on me, her body relaxed. She smiled, closed her eyes, and fell limp. Coleman collapsed on top of her.

"Kat!" I cried, reaching for her.

Jason yanked me back. "She's okay. It's over. She needs rest." He gently shook Coleman awake and helped him off the ground and onto the couch. Jason then pulled Kat into his arms.

"There's a guest room down the hall," Coleman muttered. He sounded a thousand years old. For just a second, I could have sworn I saw those same blue tracks from Kat's body slither across his cheek. But I blinked, and they were gone.

"Thank you," Jason said, already carrying Kat down the hall.

I turned to Coleman. I wasn't sure if I should thank him or murder him, but he cut me off before I could decide.

"Thank you," he said. "I owe you a great deal for that. She's the only hope we have left. Losing her would mean the end of the resistance. I lost hope, Aaron. But . . . sometimes our only hope is the hope we forge ourselves. She's very lucky to have someone like you."

"That's a lot of talk from the heir to the puppet master himself."

He looked at his hands. "I may be an heir, but I'm still his puppet . . . and he thinks I'm his spy, not the other way around. I don't know how he knew about the geyser. I did what I could to save you. I'm sorry."

"You should be." I stalked away to find Jason.

I walked down a dark, wood paneled hallway to where a door stood ajar, leaking light into the hall. Inside, I found Kat on the bed. Her head was turned slightly, an arm lay across her stomach, and her hair flared across the pillow. Jason glanced at me, his eyes rimmed red like he had been crying.

"This is my fault," he said, his voice thick. He rubbed at his arm through his sleeve.

"How?"

"I thought I had recognized the girl with the applesauce from school. But the more I replay that scene, the more I realize I was wrong. I don't know her from school. She works for Aurakbahor."

"She's Rhaegynne?"

"Does that surprise you?"

"No. I just thought you were all free as humans."

"Freedom doesn't mean we all choose to be good."

I pulled a chair from by the wall next to the bed and took

Kat's hand in my own. I brushed her hair out of her face again. She felt warm. Alive. But shivering. I grabbed the blanket at the foot of the bed and covered her with it.

Her shivering slowly stopped.

I didn't dare look away from her. "So, who is she?"

"Morgan," Jason said. "I was captured by Aurakbahor as a kid, and she . . . tortured me." My stomach dropped. "I never saw her dragon form."

"How . . . did you escape?"

He looked at the ceiling. "Do you want the short answer or the long one?"

I gestured at Kat who hadn't moved other than the gentle rise and fall of her chest. "I think we've got some time."

He sighed. "I was changed twelve years ago. I was ten. I ended up with a token that was meant for someone else. The change was . . . terrifying. I had no control as a dragon and even less control staying human. My mom freaked out — thought I was some demon spawn who had replaced her perfect son. She tried to kick me out so I wouldn't destroy the house and her pure soul or whatever." He laughed darkly. "Would have hated to see how she'd react finding out I'm *bi*.

"Dad stayed with me and tried to help me control my power, though he was probably more scared than I was. We moved a lot. Things were tough for a while. Dragons tend to hoard things, but with the war, a lot of hoards ended up abandoned. I had a talent for sniffing them out. So, we usually had enough to move as often as we needed to. But it wasn't easy. There weren't always funds. But we did what we had to, to survive. Some things . . . weren't good, but I don't regret it."

He clenched his jaw, seemingly lost in the memory for a moment. "Dad was always angry at the dragons for doing this to me. He told me to fight back, to do something. After a while, his encouragement ignited me. I *wanted* to be free. But my rebellious thoughts attracted attention, and as soon as we realized someone had noticed, we hid. I hadn't known much about Rhaegynne politics, but I understood my rebellion would get me killed.

"We made it about four months before they captured me. I have no idea what happened to my dad..." He trailed off, a deep sadness in his eyes.

"Back then," Jason continued, "if you were captured, they tortured you until you changed. Once you did, they could make you...well...they can make you do whatever they want you to. But Aurakbahor has changed tactics over the last couple years. He had converted and magically hidden parts of Zion National Park into his underground headquarters years ago, but he's made some changes recently. The crown jewel of his new renovations is his coliseum. Instead of making traitors kill themselves, he now enjoys making them fight each other. Balaskad won't even fight for her own dragons if they're taken. She lets them die in those caves."

My stomach churned with horror. If I had any doubt that helping Kat was the right thing to do, it was gone now.

"Luckily for me," Jason said, "good ol' Aurak wasn't the only one who noticed my hopes for freedom. The resistance did too. *Coleman* did. We couldn't manage a prison break now. We're too scattered and too many of us are dead...but back then, we had the numbers. They rescued me and dozens of others...

"Coleman saved me."

I kept my eyes pinned on Kat. I couldn't look at him. I hated that Coleman had betrayed us, but I didn't have the history with him that Jason did, and I felt *sick*.

"There were ten of them," he continued. "Each came as humans, but they were heroes — warriors with the strength of dragons. The guards all shifted to fight" — a small, sad smile flashed across his face — "but even as dragons, they never stood a chance. The resistance burned the whole prison to the ground.

"Coleman and I kind of adopted each other. Though Jamie unofficially took us in. We lived at Jamie's house in secret for a long time."

"Was that weird?" I asked.

He shrugged. "There were others too. There's a lot of secret rooms in the house. After Jamie was cursed, she told us about Kat, but most of the resistance felt like Kat was too much of a gamble. They gave up and lost hope. Some surrendered to the kings and joined their armies. We're back to ground zero.

"But Kat accepted her gift. And holy *Tasalgré*, she's strong. And now Aurakbahor knows that. Everyone knows. We just have to prove she can save us, and hopefully, others will have hope again." His eyes turned black. "If we have hope, we have an army."

I squeezed Kat's hand in my own.

Jason dragged a hand down his face. "It's been a long day. Your parents will wonder where we are soon."

My heart skipped a beat. "My parents! We have to get back, but we can't leave without Kat. What if she's out for days?"

He thought for a few seconds. "I think Coleman should come back with us. We'll need him to help Kat. Besides, he's better at magic than I am."

"No way," I said, crossing my arms. "He's done enough damage."

"He saved Kat."

"He'll run right back to his father as soon as he has enough information."

Jason rubbed his arm. "Do you trust me?"

"If you trust him? No."

"He deserves a chance to tell his side of the story. Something about Yellowstone . . . doesn't make sense to me."

"Do what you want," I said, turning back to Kat. "I need to get home."

"I'll talk to your parents and tell them something to cover for school today, so you don't get in too much trouble. I can be very . . . persuasive." His eyes flashed black with his suggestion of magic, but he spoke with a sadness darker than his eyes and turned away from me.

"I have some calls to make," he said, standing and pulling out his phone. "Will you go make sure Coleman is awake enough to make it to the car for an interrogation?"

I hesitated long enough to hear someone on the other end pick up. Jason spoke rapidly in Tasalgré.

He hung up and hung his head. "Magic . . . was not *meant* to manipulate people."

I wasn't sure what he had done, but I decided he needed a moment. I squeezed Kat's hand and left to go check on Coleman, closing the door behind me.

Twinning with a Traitor

Kat

I woke in an old, musty room. Strange vials, bottles, and books sat on every horizontal surface. The only light came from a window shrouded by a thick yellow curtain and hanging plants. Aaron slept in a chair to my left, but he jerked awake when I moved.

"Aaron," I croaked. I tried to sit up, but my head spun, and my arms were weak and heavy. A moan escaped my sore throat, and I sank back into the pillows.

"Kat!" Aaron jumped out of the chair and embraced me. I groaned, so he tried to pull back, but I managed to find enough strength to wrap my arms around him. He let out a weak laugh, carefully extracting himself. "Sorry."

"Don't leave..." I begged.

"He hasn't left your side," a familiar voice said. Fear and rage sparked to life as Coleman wheeled his wheelchair around a tall shelf. A small vial of leaves sat in his lap, and his face was pale with dark bags under his eyes.

A traitorous part of me felt concern for him, even as fear made it hard to think. I couldn't protect Aaron from Coleman.

"Glad to see you're awake," Coleman said.

"Sorry to see you're here," I huffed.

He winced. "I know. I'm sorry. I didn't tell Aurakbahor anything. I don't know what happened, but I had to play along to make sure you'd be able to get out."

Liar, I thought. But he spoke with a sincerity that made me want to trust him. And if he was telling the truth, it was proof my theory was right; Aurakbahor *could* hear his followers, even when they weren't dragons.

"You're his son," I whispered, not ready to trust him yet.

He sighed. "I was born to a dead mother and a nonexistent father. Or at least that's what the social worker told me. Aurakbahor *reclaimed*" — he put the word in air quotes — "me when I was still little and made me Rhaegynne. He told me I was his biological son, and I guess there's enough evidence that I should believe him. But regardless of bloodline, he raised me — though, until Yellowstone, he never claimed me as his heir. He kept me a secret, and the fact he has now formally announced me as his son is . . . concerning. But he taught me to be strong. He taught me how to kill and how to rule. I was as free as you . . . for a time." He paused and rubbed his chest, looking pained. "As I grew, I learned of his evils — the tortures and the killings and the curses — and I rebelled in secret the best I could. I was sold out by an informant named Jinx and captured, and then . . . I don't know how Aurakbahor did it, but he cursed me, too."

He stared at his knees for a moment. "I'm certain if he were to ever capture you, Kat, he would try to do the same to you."

I clenched my jaw, not willing to show how much that scared me. Aaron squeezed my hand. His face was pale.

"When I was in his prisons," Coleman continued, "I met a

dying man. He told me about Jamie and the resistance. He had been sent as a spy and seemed so broken to have failed. But to know others hated my father . . . I decided to take the man's place as a spy. And I became Aurakbahor's 'perfect' little prince and assassin.

"I figured I could help Jamie from behind the scenes. I saved Jason and dozens of others. I fed Aurakbahor lies for years until he found out, and then I ran. But I went back after Jamie died. Because she asked."

He played with the beads on his bracelet for a moment, but neither Aaron nor I spoke.

"I didn't tell him about Yellowstone. I said we were going to New York to recruit an assassin. I don't know how he knew." He finally looked up from the ground. Tears brimmed his eyes. "Kat, please believe me."

Part of me wanted to fight him, but I wanted my friend back. I turned to Aaron. "You believe this?"

He chewed his lip for a moment. "Jason does."

"Where is Jason?" I asked, looking around the room like he might also be hidden among the shelves and potions.

"Sleeping," Coleman answered. "We've been taking shifts watching you."

We sat in silence for a moment, and I played with my locket, running it along my lips and thinking about the message Grandma had hidden inside. She trusted Coleman. He'd saved me. But he betrayed us, lied to us, and nearly killed us.

But maybe I didn't have to decide to trust him . . . not yet. If he wanted to come back, he could regain our trust the hard way.

"What did he do to you?" I asked, breaking the silence.

Coleman shifted forward in his chair. His jaw muscles clenched and unclenched. Slowly, he lifted his shirt, revealing a sprawling web of bright blue veins. Aaron's eyes bulged.

"He did the same thing to me that he did to you," Coleman said. "Except he did it for months. Maybe years. He'd send me to the brink of death and then bring in his strongest magicians to heal me enough to see if they'd broken me yet. It, uh, left a lot of scars. The poison's still in me. They never bothered to get it all out." He pulled his shirt back down and looked at the floor.

"How are you still alive?" Aaron asked, horrified.

"Aurakbahor makes it out as some Sign — capital *S* — that I truly am a son of Rhaegynne herself or whatever. I think the universe just hates me."

"Does it hurt?" Aaron asked.

"Yeah. Especially when I use magic."

"But you always use magic," I pointed out.

He scoffed. "Guess that's why I always hurt. But the amount of magic I use makes a difference. Like what it took to save you can leave me bedridden for days. Other spells are fine. Sometimes I need a mobility aid, like good ol' Gertrude here." He patted one of the wheels of his wheelchair. "I get super dizzy, I get migraine attacks, my chest almost always hurts, my heart beats too fast, and I'm *always* exhausted."

He shrugged. "Sometimes, I'm fine. Like it never happened. Sometimes, just for fun, it likes to flare up for no reason. I used to take a potion to treat it, but the side effects sucked more than the potion helped. There's magic I can't do anymore, but I shouldn't complain. I know I can still do more than most Rhaegynne." He rolled back and forth in his chair, avoiding eye contact. "Still sucks to remember the things I could do before, but I guess I should be grateful I'm not dead."

He could still be lying, but the anger and hurt in his eyes made me *want* to believe him.

"You can be grateful for the things you can do, but that doesn't mean you can't still be furious about what happened to you," I said, offering an olive branch.

Coleman opened his mouth to reply, but Jason threw open the door, running into the room. "You're up! Welcome back to the land of the living!"

I smiled, forcing myself to sit up. Aaron tried to stop me, but when I glared, he supported me with one hand and arranged my pillows with the other. "Thanks?" I said, unsure if that was the correct response.

Aaron looked upset. "Seriously, Kat. You were dead."

"I-I what?"

"But that was only the first day," Coleman said. "Aaron brought you back."

"First day? Aaron?"

"You've been out for three days. Aaron did some fast thinking and performed CPR."

My chest throbbed. I assumed they would have healed my ribs, so I didn't understand why that hurt so — oh.

Grandma.

Why did CPR not bring *her* back? Did I do it wrong? "Th-three days?" I gasped, trying to ignore my newfound guilt.

"Yeah. Lucky it's winter break now, right?" Jason asked, knocking my foot.

"What about my parents? Where do they think I am? Where *am* I?"

"We brought you up to Coleman's safe house in Canada," Jason answered. "I told your parents I wanted you to come with me to visit my sick grandpa a few hours away. Only, I told them with magic, so they wouldn't think twice about it. Once you stabilized, we brought you back to Montana. You're at resistance HQ right now, but you might also recognize the not-magically hidden parts as your grandma's house. I've been living here awhile."

At the mention of Grandma, my chest ached like I'd been shot.

Something must have shown on my face because he changed topics. "Hey, you know what? You've been through a lot. We should let you rest."

"I've had three days of rest," I argued. "I don't need more. What happened?"

The three of them exchanged glances before Coleman wheeled across the room to an overflowing bookshelf. He selected a book and thumbed through it before bringing it over to me. He flipped it around, pointing out a hand-drawn picture of a plant with blue flowers.

"In Tasalgré, this is called *racongon alla sa tornga*, but it's known as Dragonstongue or Dragon's Bane. It's said to be the most effective way to kill a dragon. Jason recognized the girl who got your applesauce — Morgan. She works for Aurakbahor."

I shivered as my memories of those pain-filled hallucinations returned. "So, if it's the most effective way to kill a dragon, how am I still alive?"

"Well . . . Coleman," Jason said, motioning to him.

"How did you know Coleman would be at his safe house?"

"I took a gamble on what I knew about the person I thought was my best friend."

Coleman flinched.

"And how on earth did you get to Canada?"

"Um . . . magic," Jason answered.

I sat thinking for a moment before replying quietly. "Thank you."

"You've got to remember it was more for us really. I mean,

you are our only hope. It was entirely self-serving." But he said it with a teasing shove I was proud of myself for withstanding.

I rolled my eyes. "Naturally. When can I go home?"

"When you can walk," he said.

"Might as well try."

Aaron reached his arm out, which I accepted as I carefully put my bare feet on the cold wooden floor. My legs shook, and I leaned against him, but I managed to remain upright.

Jason and Coleman applauded, encouraging me to walk. I took two wobbly steps, but my knees buckled on the third. Aaron held onto me, swept me into his arms, and put me back on the bed. I growled at my failure, but nausea twisted my gut, and I tasted bile.

I took several deep breaths, trying not to vomit. "You said this is resistance HQ?"

Jason nodded.

"So, where is everyone else? I had the impression there would be more than three of us."

"Well, it's not like this place is swarming with rebellious Rhaegynne. That would draw unwanted attention. Besides, I've told you there aren't many of us left."

"You said this is the magically hidden portion of my grandma's house. How big is this place?"

"I mean, we could show you around, but you can't even make it to the door, so . . ." Jason teased.

"Oh, *eathia*," I sent at him, but nothing happened. "Wh-what's wrong with me?"

"You'll be okay," Coleman answered. "Dragonstongue blocks your magic, but it *does* come back. It just takes time."

I stared down at my hands. "I swear, whoever did this to me will pay."

"Get in line," Aaron said darkly.

We sat in silence for a minute before Jason broke it. "Who's hungry?" All hands went up, and he left the room.

I caught Coleman watching me.

"What?" I asked.

"You're stronger than me." It wasn't said as a compliment or with any emotion. He said it plainly, as if a fact.

"What do you mean?"

"You are. Your magic will be back in a few hours. Trust me."

"What if it doesn't?"

"*Trust* me. I'm going to go help Jason." He wheeled himself out without another word.

Aaron and I sat in silence while I tried to get my emotions under control. I was poisoned, killed, and brought back. I couldn't get my magic to work, and despite Coleman's assurances otherwise, I was terrified my magic was gone for good. The warm ball of fire in my chest had gone cold, leaving a pit more distracting than a newly missing tooth.

If my magic was gone . . . all hope was lost.

"What's the matter?" Aaron asked, interrupting my thoughts.

"Why do you ask?"

"You always play with your necklace when you're worried about something."

I glanced down, realizing I was running the locket against my lips again. I dropped the locket and propped myself up higher. "Sorry. It's a lot to process."

"It's going to be okay. You're already improving. Half an hour ago, you couldn't even lift your arms."

"I was *dead!*"

Aaron leaned forward, putting one hand on top of mine. I turned to him. "Well, you're not anymore. Coleman was right about at least one thing."

"What?"

"You're strong. You're the strongest person I know, Kat. You'll be okay. You'll recover, and then we'll break the curse and free the dragons."

The pit was so empty. Not even an ember remained. "How can you be so sure?"

"Because you're a dragon, and I'm awesome with a sword."

A smile cracked my dry lips. "I bet you still can't beat me."

Aaron pulled his hand away. "You can't even stand right now."

"Finally, a fair fight then!"

He held up his hands with a laugh. "Whoa, too far!"

"Bring it!" I pulled myself out of bed and lunged at him, immediately toppling forward.

He reached out to catch me, but we both ended up going down, turning his chair over on top of us as we fell. He groaned, pushing it off and holding onto me. "You okay?" he asked, trying to sit us up.

"I will be once I win!" I declared, struggling to pin him with my weak noodle arms.

He effortlessly — *embarrassingly* — lifted me off him. "This is a bad idea."

My pounding heart made the hole less noticeable. "It's a great idea!"

He gently pulled me to my feet. "You're going to hurt yourself."

I protested, but my head spun, and I fell back onto the edge of the bed, cradling my head in my hands.

Coleman and Jason burst through the door, Jason pushing Coleman.

"What happened?" Coleman asked, taking in the tipped over chair. "Is everyone okay?"

"Kat would rather fight me than fight to recover," Aaron said.

"That *was* me fighting to recover!" I defended.

"Okay, well, lunch is ready. Try not to fight the pickles or whatever," Coleman responded while Jason jogged back out of the room.

"Hold on," I said, stomach churning. "If I've been out for three days... that makes today..."

"Christmas Eve," Coleman said.

My stomach dropped. "I have to get home!"

"We can have you home soon."

"I need to be home *now*!" No amount of manipulative magic from Jason could save me from my mother's wrath. "Aaron! What about you?" I attempted to stand again, but he held me back.

"There is a way to help your recovery, but it's not *pleasant*," Coleman said.

"What is it?" I asked, already deciding to try it.

"The potion I mentioned. You've been force-fed it for the past three days, but it tastes like sewage."

I grimaced. "Can't wait."

He rummaged around a counter filled with odd-looking flasks and come back with a glass of a foul smelling, sludgy, green liquid.

"Don't smell it before you drink it."

I gagged. It smelled like *rot*. "Too late."

"You don't have to drink it. Now that you're awake, you'll get stronger on your own."

"Does it hurt?"

"It's an assault to your taste buds, but it doesn't hurt at this dose."

"Bottoms up." I downed it before I could think twice. I gagged and tried not to wretch as the chunky liquid went down. I shuddered, wiping my tongue on my shirt. It burned all the way down, but then the heat extended out to my arms and legs, making my fingers and toes tingle with a pleasant warmth. My head buzzed, but the world snapped back into focus. "Whoa."

"I can't give you much," Coleman said, taking the glass from me. "Give it a minute, and you can try to stand again."

Jason came into the room, carrying a tray loaded with sandwiches. My stomach growled *loudly* at the sight.

I blushed and covered my stomach while the others laughed. Jason handed me a sandwich. It was just ham and cheese with pickles and a tomato, but it was the best sandwich I had ever had. "Besides being force-fed potions, did I eat at all while I was out? Were any of those potions meal replacement shakes or anything?" I asked between bites.

"Just potions," Aaron answered, glaring at Coleman.

"I guess that's why the food Jason prepared actually tastes good!"

"Whoa! Hey, my cooking's only been completely inedible *a couple* times, okay? I'm a good cook!" Jason replied, taking a bite of his peanut butter and jelly sandwich.

I scoffed but focused on my sandwich, savoring every bite.

Finally satisfied, I set my plate off to the side. I made eye contact with Aaron and gave my best attempt at puppy dog eyes. "Can I try to walk again? *Please?*"

He hesitated. "Let's do it."

Much to my delight, I managed it. I even made a full lap around the room, weaving around the shelves and plants, without falling over. Strength had tenuously returned to my legs, but there was still nothing to fill the pit in my chest.

I got back to my starting point and threw my hands up in the air like a gymnast completing a complicated floor routine. "Can I go home now?"

We walked through my front door — Coleman leaning heavily on Jason — and were immediately enveloped by the scent of pine and cinnamon. I inhaled deeply, entranced by the smell of Christmas.

Alerted by the opening door, my mom poked her head around the kitchen corner, her short blonde hair pulled back into a ponytail. Her brown eyes looked tired, and flour covered her green apron.

I gasped, struck by how much I had missed her. "Mom!" I'd pushed her away so much these past few months, but now, I needed her.

She stuffed a washcloth in her apron pocket and rushed forward to embrace me.

I hugged her back, and for just a moment, I was a kid again, willing to believe that Mom's hugs could fix anything.

Maybe I should tell her the truth. My heart pounded, and my throat went dry. Grandma said she refused to believe, but maybe now that *I* needed her, she'd believe me.

Enough lies. I've already told my friends.

But when I opened my mouth, I couldn't do it. "I missed you," I managed instead. It was true. But it wasn't enough.

"I missed you too." She pulled away from me and examined my face. "I was worried about you. Jason called, but he didn't explain very well . . . but you're home now! Will you and your friends help me get ready for dinner? Dad's sister and her family will be here soon, and I invited Miranda's and Lily's families again. Your friends are welcome to join, of course."

"We'd be happy to help, Mrs. Lance!" Coleman said. He'd moved away from Jason, but he leaned against the counter and looked a little pale still.

"Thank you. I know you came by at Thanksgiving, but I don't think I've met you officially."

"Oh, I'm Coleman."

Dad wandered into the kitchen, dragging the vacuum with him. He nearly dropped it when he saw us. "You're back!"

I rushed forward and hugged him. "I missed you!" *Maybe I could tell him?*

"I'm glad you're home safe. Do you have a minute?"

"Actually," Mom said, "would you mind showing the kids where the tables and chairs are? And Kat? Could you help me in the kitchen?"

Aaron shot me a look of concern, but I waved him off.

Mom handed me a wooden spoon and set me to stirring some onions and aromatics while she measured the broth. But once the others had disappeared downstairs, she sighed and turned to me. "I think I know what's going on."

I swallowed. "You do?" *Does she know about Rhaegynne?*

"I know your grandma and I didn't always get along," she said, wiping her hands on a towel. "I had my reasons, but I need you to know I loved her. The last few months have been hard, and I'm sorry if you felt like you couldn't talk to me about her. I'm grieving her too, Kat."

Tears sprang unbidden to my eyes. I hadn't realized how much I needed to know I wasn't the only one. "I miss her so much," I confessed.

Mom pulled me into her arms. "I do, too. I hope you know you don't have to avoid me."

"No! I'm not avoiding you!" But I pulled away. I couldn't deny that I had kept my distance, but it wasn't because I thought she wasn't grieving.

She kept a hand on my shoulder and smiled sadly. "She was a wonderful, strong woman."

I nodded. Maybe this wasn't going toward the reveal I'd thought. "She had the best stories," I said cautiously.

Mom's face stiffened, but she tried to soften it with a laugh. "She also had some really awful stories."

My stomach churned.

I knew which ones she meant.

Rhaegynne.

"Some of them were better than others," I managed, forcing a laugh.

She let out a sad sigh and stood up. "She'd want us to enjoy Christmas..."

"You're right," I said and opened the door to leave.

"Kat?"

Despite everything, hope curled in my chest as I turned back to her.

"You can tell me anything. You know that right?"

I smiled. "Of course."

Anything but the truth.

SNOWBALL FIGHT!

COLEMAN

Aaron left to be with his family, and Kat had to run errands with her parents. That left Jason and I alone in Kat's room.

He kept his distance like my lineage and betrayal were contagious, and he watched me with a mixture of pity and disgust.

I didn't blame him.

I fiddled with the knickknacks on Kat's desk, trying to avoid turning when he moved to sit on her bed. He trusted me with her, and he *seemed* to believe that I was on his side. But I should have told him the truth from the beginning, and we both knew it.

"So, what now?" Jason asked.

I shrugged, lining up Kat's pencils. "I told my father I was going to continue spying, but I've been hiding in Canada. He shouldn't know I helped Kat. So, I'll finish what I started. Jamie called it Operation Prodigal Son. I'll swear my loyalty to him and tear him down from the inside. I'll let you guys know what I find out, but I'll leave."

Jason put his hand on my shoulder, and I jumped. I hadn't heard him get up. "I want you to stay."

I continued to play with the pencils. "I'll put you in danger."

"If you're with us, *nothing* can touch us."

"I hurt you. I hurt all of you."

"I *want* to trust you, Coleman," Jason whispered from behind, close enough I could feel his breath against my neck.

I gulped, my throat dry, and reached for my sleeve, rolling it up to reveal the dragon and compass on my forearm. I hadn't dared to test it after Yellowstone, afraid that I'd pushed things beyond all hope of redemption, but I'd do it now, with him.

But he reached around me and put a hand over it. "No, Coleman. I don't need to see it to trust you. Do what you need to do but come back."

I had a thousand things I wanted to say, but before I could find the right words, Kat came back.

"Do you want to stay for dinner?" she asked. She was still pale, but the blue veins had faded entirely, and she seemed much more comfortable than before.

Jason grinned. "Can your parents feed three starving Rhaegynne?"

"We could feed an army tonight."

"I'll come help set up. Coleman, are you coming?"

I didn't really have an appetite, but I stood to follow them — and promptly had to lean against the wall as the world spun for a moment. *Curse my curse.*

Kat stepped forward, but I waved her off. "I'm okay. Can you get me some water?"

"Do you need anything else?"

I shook my head, still leaning against the wall. She hurried back up the stairs.

"Can I help?" Jason asked gently, reaching out a hand.

I hesitated, trying to decide if I could get up myself, but I nodded.

He wrapped a warm arm around me. "Should I run home and get your chair?"

I shook my head and straightened, supported by his body. He smelled nice. Like pine trees. "I'm okay. Besides, Kat's house isn't exactly wheelchair accessible."

"Want me to get your cane at least?"

"I lost Cecil on a mission a while ago. I haven't gotten another yet."

"Cecil? When did you name your cane?"

"Literally right after I lost him. I miss him. I *will* accept help up the stairs, though."

He smiled and tightened his arm around me.

Kat hadn't lied. They had food for everyone and leftovers.

While cleaning up dinner after everyone had left, Kat checked her phone and grinned mischievously, motioning for us to follow her.

"Aaron just got here," she said as we snuck through the back door into the cool night air and armed ourselves with snowballs.

Kat peered through the back gate and signaled the all clear. She and Jason jumped the fence and ran out into the front yard, snowballs flying. One hit Aaron square in the back, announcing their surprise attack. He barely managed to dodge the next two as he scrambled for a snowball of his own, taking advantage of the lull in their attacks while they rushed to rearm. I pushed my way through the gate and chucked my snowball. It slammed into Aaron's side.

He turned and threw one at me, but I dodged.

"Gentle!" I warned. My legs wobbled, and I let myself fall into the snow — all the better to fling massive piles of snow at them. I hadn't realized how bad my head hurt until I plunked it in a snow drift. I enjoyed the brief respite from the pain.

Kat let her new snowball fly at Aaron, but another icy ball hit her.

Jason's smile melted, replaced by fear as she turned to see which of us had turned on her.

He ran as she lobbed a snowball at him, nailing him in the back of his head. But I had seen a look in Jason's eyes as he ran, so I flung my snowball at her.

Then Aaron's smacked me in the side.

The air erupted with snowballs, laughter, and death threats. After several minutes of free-for-all, Aaron, Jason, and I formed an alliance against Kat. Jason helped me up, and we turned toward her. I couldn't help but smile as we opened fire.

She threw up her arms. *"Key ally!"*

My stomach sank in anticipation of her dismay, but the snow in front of her exploded upward into a crystal-clear shield, stopping the snowballs. We stared at each other in shock behind the warped ice.

Her wall shattered, and she threw her arms in the air. "I have magic again!"

I grinned and lobbed another snowball. She yelped, dodging behind a new ice wall.

Jason and Aaron chased after her, throwing snowball after snowball while she ran, erecting ice walls and using magic to send more snow at us. Unfortunately for her, Jason and I also had magic, and we returned fire, slowly forcing her to retreat.

Kat backed up until she knocked into the front porch's steps. The three of us exchanged glances, trying to decide whether we should accept her surrender or bury her in snow.

Aaron slowly raised a snowball. Jason grinned, and I prepared to fire.

Kat smiled weakly as if hoping for mercy, but we showed none.

She seemed panicked as the snow rushed at her, but at the last second, she took a deep breath and spewed fire, melting the snowy ballistics before they could find their target. The flame lit up the night, giving an eerie cast to the winter fog.

But it also lit up her father's stunned face as he opened the front door.

This was not the best way to realize we hadn't put up any wards besides Kat's ring...

"Dad! I—"

He grimaced and held up a hand. "Well . . . alright." He sighed. "Everyone, inside."

The four of us exchanged looks of dread but followed him inside.

My hands shook, and magic burned in my chest, pushing me closer to an involuntary change than I'd had in *months*.

Aaron and Jason each took one of Kat's hands, and I followed close behind, trying not to panic. I flicked at the beads on my bracelet.

Aurakbahor would kill me if he caught me doing something like this.

Kat gave me a distrustful glance as I reached out to touch her shoulder.

Her father led us to the downstairs living room and told us to sit. He studied all of us before turning to Kat. He stood in front of her, arms folded.

"Dad—"

"That was very irresponsible of you."

Her eyes were mirrors. "What?"

Couldn't have said it better myself...

"You used magic in the front yard without wards. We both know how your mother would react if she found out. And what would we tell the neighbors if they saw?"

"You know?" she asked, her voice a little higher than usual. I was impressed she could talk at all. I think my jaw had forgotten how to close.

Well, that would explain why Kat's ring wasn't enough to hide her magic from him...

He shook his head and sat on the ottoman in front of Kat. "Could one of you ward the door?"

Jason nodded and did so wordlessly.

Once in place, Kat's dad started talking, words tumbling out of his mouth like he'd been practicing this conversation for months. "Your Rhaegynne blood comes from both sides of the family, Kat. My grandfather — your great-grandfather — was Rhaegynne. He fought alongside Jamie in the war and was free too. I was young when he died. Balaskad killed him... Some of my earliest memories are of him carrying me while he flew..." His face turned soft at the distant memory, but my mind was reeling.

I'd long suspected Jamie might have been an heir to one of the clan thrones that were lost in the war. As Aurakbahor's heir, I was free until he decided to curse me too, so it made sense that she might have similar protections if she also had a claim to one of the four thrones, but she never confirmed my suspicions.

But if Kat's great grandpa was free during the war too...

"Why didn't you tell me?" Kat asked, interrupting my thoughts.

His face fell. "I tried, Kat. Your grandma told me she was going to tell you when she was in the hospital, but she didn't get a chance to finish. I wanted to talk to you after, and at the funeral, and dozens of other times since, but . . . it never worked out."

She kneaded her forehead with her hands. "Why didn't *anyone* tell me before she died?"

He sighed. "It's not a secret that your mom and grandma didn't see eye to eye. Jamie left you hints and stories because that's all she *could* do, out of respect to your mom. There was a time when even meeting your grandma would have been out of the question. It took them *years* to repair their relationship. They loved each other, but this was like a bone that was improperly set. It healed, but it was never the same. I—" He paused, seeming deep in thought.

"None of my grandpa's children were Rhaegynne. I'm not, and neither is my sister. I thought my line had died off. But when I met your mom, I recognized Jamie. I tried to talk to her — and to your mom — about it, but when Jaime found out I was dating her daughter, she told me to stop. Your mom wanted nothing to do with this world. She denied her own magic and refused her inheritance. When you were born, Jamie hoped you'd inherit her powers — and your great-grandpa's powers. But she'd hoped you would inherit it *after* the war ended. But you manifested magic when you were a toddler, and Jamie wanted to keep it hidden for as long as possible. If she was going to risk her relationship with your mom again, Jamie wanted to be sure the prophecy was fulfilled and the war was over first. She wasn't going to risk losing both of you."

Oh, Tasalgré! The prophecy! "With two left and all to remain . . ." I knew it was about the kings; Balaskad and Aurakbahor were the only two left. But I'd always wondered how the "all to remain" part worked. But if Balaskad and Aurakbahor hadn't killed the heirs when they killed the other two kings . . .

"When it became clear she wouldn't survive," Kat's dad

continued, "we agreed it was time for you to know the truth, about the stories and about your family."

"Was Jamie a king?" I blurted out. "Or at least an heir? And was your grandpa a king, too? Is that why they were free? Is that why Kat's free?"

He eyed me appreciatively. "This one's smart. I like him."

"He's Aurakbahor's son," Kat said bitterly, but her face flushed like she didn't mean to say it out loud.

Her dad looked less impressed. "Well then..."

"Jamie told her to trust him," Jason said, butting in. He grabbed my arm and rolled up my sleeve, showing my dragon and compass. "Besides, this still works."

My cheeks burned. I didn't know that for sure, so he *certainly* didn't either. But his confidence gave me the strength to try. I flexed my wrist and the tattoo flared to life. Relief flooded through me.

It still worked.

Kat's dad pulled up his pant leg, then pushed down his sock. A tiny dragon and compass tattoo shone gold on his ankle. "That's good enough for me," he said with a shrug.

Kat's jaw dropped. Aaron looked even more lost.

"I know a lot's going on, but *what is going on?*" Aaron asked.

Kat lifted her shirt and showed her resistance tattoo on her ribs. It glowed softly. "It's the symbol of the resistance. The magic only works if we are still loyal to the cause." She pulled her shirt back down. "But that's also what Coleman told me, so it could be a lie, too."

"It's not," her dad said.

Kat shuffled uncomfortably in her seat, avoiding eye contact with me. "When did you get yours? Does Mom know?"

"Jamie gave it to me. Your mom *does* know, and it nearly ended our relationship. It wasn't the *only* reason, but it was a contributing factor to why they stopped talking to each other at the time."

My eyes tracked between them. When it was clear Kat wasn't going to ask any more questions, her dad nodded toward me. "Coleman's right. Kat, you combine the sole remaining bloodlines of the last two dragon clans. As such, you are considered a daughter of Rhaegynne herself and have a claim to two thrones. Not that there'd be much *to* rule, of course. Balaskad absorbed my grandpa's clan into her own, and Aurakbahor did the same after he killed Jamie's mom. Jamie was only spared since she was an heir in hiding. Your grandma made it very clear that other than through family inheritance, she wouldn't be able to change anyone. Though, maybe once we overthrow Aurakbahor and Balaskad, you could take the throne and—"

Kat held up her hands. "Hold up. Take the *throne*? And be like the kings? No!"

"Once the curse is broken, the dragons will be free, but they'll need a leader."

"That's part of the prophecy, too," I added. "All of this. 'With two left and all to remain' is about *you*. The lines weren't destroyed. They were *combined*. And the final line — "A free dragon, one to break the chains, will free them from the snare, and take their place as rightful heir" — *that* has to be about you!"

Kat stood and paced up and down the room. "So, I not only have to kill Balaskad and Aurakbahor, but I also have to take over for them? I have to rule two kingdoms that have been warring for years. And somehow succeed in unifying them?

"If I can't create more Rhaegynne until I take the throne, what happens to one clan when I kill its leader, and the other king remains? Are they free? Do I take the place of the fallen king and control them until the other is dead? Or do I end up doing the dirty work for the other, and they get all the dragons themselves, doubling their army?

"Grandma failed to fulfill the prophecy. How do we know it was even about her — or me? The kings are free, too! Are they sitting there on their thrones, thinking they're doing the right thing as much as we're thinking we're doing the right thing? What if I make things worse?"

I opened my mouth, but I didn't have a good answer. Looking around the room, no one else seemed to know what to say either.

We were messing with forces we didn't understand, up against two incredibly powerful Rhaegynne who very much wanted Kat dead. And if they ever found out about Kat's heritage...

Well, they wouldn't send assassins with poison again.

They'd make sure she suffered before they killed her themselves.

I was Promised a Feast

Coleman

I finished off the last knot in a set of transport beads. It was a complicated process of tying strands of beads into intricate patterns and weaving magic into every knot. They were time consuming to produce and burned themselves up during the spell, so we didn't use them often, but when done correctly, the transport beads could take someone anywhere they needed to go.

My body still hurt from saving Kat, but I needed to get to Aurakbahor, and I couldn't fly there as a dragon and risk Aurakbahor finding out about Kat.

Jason smiled and handed me the set of beads he'd made for my return. "Do you have everything?"

"I'm the prince. Aurakbahor would never let me go without while acting as such." But my stomach had more knots than the mess of beads bundled in my hand.

This was my idea, I reminded myself. *I'm doing this for Jamie.*

"Just . . . be careful, okay?" Jason begged.

I chuckled. "You knew I was a spy in Aurak's Courts before! Why are you nervous now?"

"Because *you're* nervous now. He's made you do things you didn't want to, and he's declared you as his heir. That carries a lot of weight."

I gulped but tried to smile. "I guess when you put it that way..."

He gave a sad smile. "Get out of here, Your Majesty."

"Actually, that title is used for a king. I'm a prince, so the correct term is Your Highness. Though I would accept Your Eminence or Your Greatness."

He rolled his eyes and gave me a shove. "Whatever, Your *Highness*."

For some reason, my cheeks felt warm. But it was time to go.

I checked my watch — it had become a habit since Kroll — before tossing out a set of beads on the ground. The tangled net of beads flared out like a disc and landed on the ground. The knotted beads glowed a light blue and shuffled around, untangling itself. "Kat should be referred to as majesty, though. I think she's technically a king now." I stepped into the large ring and disappeared before Jason could respond.

I reappeared in a cleaning closet with my foot in a mop bucket.

After extracting myself from the bucket, I brushed dust off my clothes. I straightened my shirt and walked down the hallway to his courtroom.

My stomach dropped when I caught sight of six guards stationed outside the doors with their distinctive dark cloaks and birdlike masks to obscure their identities.

Knights of the Raven's Vigil.

What are they doing here?

I only hesitated for a heartbeat before nodding to the

assassins and passing between the first four. The last two stepped aside from the door, but I only opened it a crack. If the Knights were outside, I wasn't sure I wanted to know what was *inside*.

A woman leaned against a marble pillar, staring Aurakbahor down. My breath caught, remembering the last time I had come here and found a woman in front of the king.

She wore a black leather jacket and combat boots over black skinny jeans. Her curled blonde hair was in a messy bun. A dozen knives were strapped to her belt and across her chest. She bit into an apple, totally at ease in front of the most malicious man I knew.

Morgan.

I stared, almost more scared of her than I was of my father.

And certainly more scared of her than of the assassins behind me.

Aurakbahor paced in front of her, squeezing his cane between his hands like he might snap it, and grumbled something I couldn't make out.

She groaned. "What does it matter if it didn't work? The dragons are still under your control. Balaskad is losing ground."

"What does it *matter?*" He stopped pacing and threw his hands against the pillar on either side of her head.

She didn't flinch, but my heart roared in my ears.

"The sooner Jamie's heir is gone, the faster we can crush the Council-Rebellion, and the sooner I can focus all my efforts on Balaskad."

The Council-Rebellion? Is that related to the Council he mentioned after Kroll?

"The rebellion is an inconvenience to Balaskad, too. They're nothing more than a thorn in your side." She pushed him away and took a chunk out of her apple.

He returned to his pacing, fuming. "My resources are split between them and Balaskad. You were supposed to kill Katherine, but you couldn't even do that! And now Balaskad is trying to escalate with the rebellion. I need her gone so I can finally be rid of this curse!"

She rolled her eyes. "Whatever."

He lunged at her, but she flicked her wrist, and he slammed into a translucent barrier.

"What are you doing? You have no control over me."

He seethed against the barrier. "You and I won't always be on equal footing, Morgan."

She dropped the barrier, and he staggered forward. She handed him the half-eaten apple. "I look forward to the day when you make good on these threats, darling."

She swept across the courtroom, leaving through one of the side doors.

He screamed and threw the apple in her wake.

I started to back away, but Aurakbahor's sigh echoed in the now empty courtroom. "I know you're there, Sa'hranet."

I checked my watch, sent up a prayer that Kroll wouldn't collect on my debt yet, and entered the room.

"Why did you come back?" he asked.

I frowned. "What do you mean? Why are you working with Morgan again? You hate her."

He turned his black eyes toward me. "Sa'hranet." He paused, clenching his teeth. "I know you. I know *everything* about you. I knew you were a liar. I knew you were a spy. But I wanted to give *my own son* a chance." His hands curled into fists and electricity arced up his forearms.

I took a step backward, wincing when I bumped into one of the Knights. "You knew?"

"Always," he spat.

"You set me up," I whispered. Yellowstone, Dragonstongue — it was his plan all along.

"I don't want to murder my only blood, but if you do not leave this room *immediately*" — he paused as lightning arced up his arms — "I will."

The lightning slammed into the marble by my feet. I ran, sprinting past the assassins guarding the door, and away from the king and my failure. I threw the second set of beads ahead of me as fire chased me down the hall. I leaped, landing back in Jason's front room.

Jason jumped, his mouth forming a small O. "What are you—"

I pulled him into a hug, breathing heavily. "He knows. He knows, and I've failed everyone." Tears streamed down my face.

He wrapped his arms around me, enveloping me in that stubbornly hopeful rhythm of his heart. "No, you've done plenty. You're home now."

AH, SO WE WERE DOOMED FROM THE START. COOL.

AARON

Slipping under Jason's right cross, I grabbed hold of his shoulder and pulled his chest into my knee. He wrapped his arms around my leg, trying to throw me off balance. I jumped and swung my other leg up behind his neck and rolled, throwing us both onto the ground. Before he could recover, I pinned him down.

Jason pushed his entire body up and threw me forward a few inches. My hands landed in the snow on either side of his head. He pushed me off him, and I ended up face-first in the snow with my arm twisted up my back, his other hand pressing my head deeper into the snow.

I managed to break free, and we scrambled to our feet. He threw another jab. I caught his wrist and spun underneath. Pulling his arm over my shoulder, I sent his whole body flipping over my back.

Jason clung to me, dragging me to the ground with him. He rolled over me and pressed a practice knife to my throat.

"Dead," he declared.

"I'll be in good company," I whispered, my own knife against his chest.

"W-what? How?" he stammered, standing.

"I have my secrets," I replied, accepting his hand and slipping the practice knife back up my sleeve.

"You, Aaron, are a terrifying man," Jason said, slapping me on the back. He puffed out his chest and wiped imaginary dirt off his nose. "All thanks to me and my phenomenal teaching abilities."

"If by teaching you mean trying to murder me until I could fight back, then *sure*." I hopped onto the pasture fence next to Kat.

After her dad had come clean about his knowledge of Rhaegynne two days ago — a terrifying fact that still made me a little nauseous — he showed us this bit of property his family owned a few miles out of town. He said his grandfather had practiced here. It was an old crop and livestock field, away from other people and without needing to hike up a mountain.

Kat slid off the wooden fence and walked to the center of the field, burning a path through the snow. She held her arms out to the sides, and the air shimmered around her hands, solidifying into two long, thin blades.

Coleman jumped the fence — coming from the barn house — and met her at the center, his dual weapons drawn as well.

They fell into a deadly dance of metal and magic. Until today, I believed Kat to be good at magic, but his experience and skill far exceeded hers.

She attacked with large sprays of snow and fire, like the scatter of shotgun pellets. His attacks were small, perfectly executed to block or attack in exact spots.

He sent them both airborne with a powerful gust of wind. He flew gracefully on the wind as she got tossed aimlessly through the air. Her form warped, and he slammed his body into hers, sending them both crashing to the ground.

"That's cheating!" Coleman shouted. The crash of metal drowned out Kat's reply.

They continued their battle. She lost one and then both of her blades. Coleman cast his aside, letting them disappear into the air, and their fight continued to rage on with magic as their only weapon. Coleman's magic was tinged blue, and I had a suspicion it was the Dragonstongue.

A wind with the strength of a hurricane picked up behind Kat. She directed it into a carefully controlled funnel and sent it crashing into Coleman. He pushed back with winds of his own, and the sound of the two currents meeting shook the ground. The winds didn't reach me, but the fence rattled from the sound wave.

Lightning flashed as the winds twisted into a swirling tornado of snow and debris. They both stood their ground, each pressing against each other until Kat staggered and got thrown backward. Coleman's storm cut off, and he fell to his knees.

Jason stood and applauded while I ran to help Kat. "That was brilliant!" he shouted. "I've never seen anyone stand up to Coleman for so long. Let alone make him tired."

"That's a lie," Coleman said. "I'm always tired. I just don't show it."

Kat's forehead was slick with sweat. Her hair had slid out of its ponytail and tangled in the wind. She panted as she combed her hair with shaking fingers. "I thought you said you're the weapons guy, and Coleman's the magician," she told Jason. "He's better at both than you."

"He's not better than me." Jason huffed. "You're sloppy with dual blades, and you confused your lack of skill for mine."

Coleman stood to join us. He was as disheveled as Kat, but

his eyes danced. "We're going to do that again. But not today. Today, I want a nice, long nap."

"A nap sounds amazing." She staggered over to the fence and glared at the snow. "It's too cold for this nonsense." She held out her hand and melted a patch of snow large enough for her to collapse into, the heat evaporating the moisture and leaving her a patch of dry ground to rest on.

Coleman didn't even bother clearing the snow before collapsing next to her.

"Oh, this is so much colder than I expected!" he yelped, but he made no effort to leave.

Jason shook his head and pointed next to Coleman. "*Ally eathia.*" A large fire erupted in the snow and crackled despite its lack of fuel. "You're welcome, oh, powerful one."

Coleman muttered something unintelligible.

Jason laughed. "Shut up and sleep."

Coleman grunted something else, but Jason didn't react.

"Now," Jason said, turning to me, "it's your turn with dual blades."

He summoned two swords, one much shorter than the other, and passed them off to me. But then he flinched and reached into his pocket. Smiling sheepishly, he checked his phone. "Lily's inviting us to go to a New Year's Eve party on Monday. But for now, let's fight!"

He summoned his swords and then set me to drill work until Kat and Coleman recovered from their fight. By that point, the sun hung low in the darkening sky, and the temperature had plummeted.

I dropped my swords and helped Kat stand up. "You okay?"

She nodded, but she kept most of her weight against me as I helped her cross the field to the car. Jason busied himself with supporting Coleman, who tried to walk by himself but stumbled like a drunkard.

I had unofficially become the dragons' designated driver. I might get tired, but I didn't exhaust myself like them. At least Jason was coherent. I hated dragging all of them to the car.

"Does anyone need healing today?" Jason asked, following Coleman into the back seat.

Kat glanced at her bruised and quivering limbs and shrugged. "I'll wear long sleeves."

Everyone else voiced similar thoughts, so I started down the road. We drove in silence for several minutes until Jason spoke. "So, New Year's Eve party Monday? Who's coming? We can carpool."

Kat and Coleman gave half-conscious votes of approval before falling into silence. I dropped Jason and Coleman off at Jamie's old house. As soon as they were gone, Kat let out a long, heavy groan.

"What's wrong?" I asked as I backed out of the driveway.

"A lot of things. Can we go to your house? I don't want my mom to overhear us."

"Sure," I said, switching my blinker's direction from right to left. "Want to talk about it now?"

She shook her head. "I need a moment to gather my thoughts."

A few minutes later, she followed me inside and into the game room, barely giving Prince more than a pat on the head.

Sitting on the couch, she put her head in her hands. "We can't trust Coleman *or* Jason."

My heart rate spiked. "I understand Coleman, but why Jason? What did he do?"

She shook her head and stared at the ground. "Nothing that he knows of. And I believe Coleman's story. But we can't trust them."

"Why?"

"You know how I've been trying to find the link to Aurakbahor in their minds?"

"Yes?"

"Yeah, well, Jason and I decided to try it in the Dream Realms right before I was poisoned, and . . . well . . . I found the link. There's no way I can break it. It's more of a" — she paused as she struggled for words, moving her hands in a circle — "it's more of a continuation between Jason's mind and Aurakbahor's."

"Okay, so what's wrong?"

"Rhaegynne are supposed to have their minds to themselves when they're human."

"Right," I said.

"I don't think that's accurate. Jason was human when I found the connection, and . . . I had the strongest sense that Aurakbahor could still see and hear us."

My blood ran cold, and I shook my head. "No, that doesn't make any sense. Why would he need Coleman as a spy then? Why doesn't he just track down and kill resistance members?"

She shook her head. "I wondered that same thing, but Aurakbahor knew where I was the first time I changed with Jason and sent a dragon after me. Aurakbahor came to me in the Dream Realms once when I was taking a nap at school. He knew about Yellowstone. Coleman didn't tell him about any of those things. I wouldn't be surprised if he let Coleman be his spy so he could feed us false intel through Coleman. But I don't think either of the kings want us to know the extent of their powers. I don't think they want this public."

Blood rushed in my ears so loudly that I could hardly hear her. If he knows everything, none of us are safe. My family isn't safe — not even *Prince* is safe. "Have you told them this?"

She shook her head. "I'm fairly confident Aurakbahor doesn't know that I know, and I need it to stay that way."

"What do we do?"

"I can't break the link like we'd planned. We're going to have to kill the kings directly. But whatever I plan with Jason and Coleman, I'll have to change privately. Can I plan with you?"

My head nodded before my brain could even sort through the risk. "Of course. But what about *you*? Jason and Coleman were both there when your dad told us about your grandparents! Aurakbahor will know."

She set her jaw. "He might. And he'll know I'm coming for him."

"That—"

"And I want him to be scared of me when I do."

The Broken

Coleman

Flying in an airplane was significantly more uncomfortable than flying as a dragon — annoying hive mind and puppetry included. At least I could safely store a mobility aid as a dragon. Couldn't really count on ever seeing Gertrude again if I brought her on the plane. But Aurakbahor would drive my body off a cliff if I turned into a dragon now. And flying internationally with my own wings sounded exhausting. Not to mention the seagulls and geese. They were always a pain.

But if I was a *dragon*, I wouldn't have a smelly dude falling asleep on my shoulder or a kid kicking the back of my seat. *Father has to ruin everything, doesn't he?*

In his defense, my body still hurt.

Though I suppose that was his fault, too.

Kat, Jason, and I only had time to make two sets of transport beads. I needed two for the return trip. So, no dragon wings and no transport beads. Just me and eight hundred of my closest friends crammed into a metal tube in the sky.

After the fifteen-hour torture of discount air travel ended, I found myself lost, sore, and missing Cecil on the cold and foggy London streets. New buildings stood next to ancient ones on narrow, winding streets. I kept my eyes down, trying to prevent the history nerd in me from gawking at every major landmark. I could come back when Aurakbahor was dead.

I found the red brick homeless shelter I was searching for a couple blocks from the Tower of London, but even though Kroll had suggested I start looking for Hope and Tythan here, it didn't *feel* right, so I kept walking.

Kroll said they were seen collecting supplies from homeless shelters in the area. Not that they were *staying* there.

But they had to be *close*, right? Kroll might be three imps in a trench coat, but they *did* know more than they should. If they said to *start* with homeless shelters, then maybe they meant it as a clue.

I walked past the entrance of the shelter and continued around the block and turned down the backside of a nearby building and into a narrow alleyway.

It wasn't every day that instinct drove me to wander down back alleys, but I guess there was a first time for everything.

Heading down the narrow street, I tried to act like I belonged there and tried to figure out why something seemed to be pulling me there in the first place.

I nearly reached the end of the road, following the twists and turns of the alley as it led farther from the shelter, and began wondering if it actually wasn't instinct that urged me down this way when a spot of graffiti stuck out to me.

A gold compass.

I pressed a hand against the design, and the dragon and compass on my wrist glowed to life. Light spread out beneath my fingers and along the points of the compass, and then spilled out to form a narrow door in the brick wall. I pushed, and the door creaked open.

I entered a dimly lit gymnasium-style room. At least a dozen sleeping bags lined the walls. Several people with scared and hollow eyes turned to face me. I swallowed but kept walking. The door sealed behind me.

A woman with pale, freckled skin and a tiny baby in her arms eyed me apprehensively, passed the baby to another woman, and approached. "Who are you?"

"I'm Tythan and Hope's friend." I rolled up my sleeve to show my still-glowing tattoo.

She relaxed and pointed to the back of the room. I noticed Tythan's familiar black hair with red tips and cool, beige skin and breathed a sigh of relief. I hurried across the hallway, passing young and old alike. I had never seen any of them before, but the room had a certain smell I associated with magic — like cinnamon, pine trees, and freshly fallen rain.

Tythan watched me with expressionless eyes, but the tiny, curly haired girl with dark skin behind them grinned and ran out to hug me.

"Coleman!" she squealed as I lifted her off the ground.

I was surprised she remembered me; it had been at least a year since I'd seen her. She had only been about four or five at the time.

Tythan stood, the chains connected to their belt loops clinking against their black jeans. They crossed their leather-clad arms and glared. "What do you think you're *doing*?"

"Looking for you," I said. "What is this place?"

"A refuge for people who have been ruined by *your* father and his petty war with my king."

Ah. Word about my unfortunate relation travels fast, I suppose. I flashed my tattoo again. "I can't control who I'm related to."

Tythan gave me a distrustful glare but visibly relaxed.

I glanced around the poorly lit room, taking in the small tables, the sleeping bags, and the little samples of burnt wood paintings I knew Tythan sold. But my mouth dropped at the sheer number of destitute Rhaegynne huddled together for warmth. "They're resistance?"

"No. They're the Broken."

"The Broken?"

"Their *condition*,"— they spat out the word like it was something dirty — "has left them unable to work or live a normal life. They don't like what the kings stand for, but they don't have the energy to fight. They hide and survive. That's it."

"And you? Have you and Hope become Broken?" I asked.

They looked at the small girl still in my arms. "I've been Broken for years, Sa'hranet. But Hope fights, and I want to see Balaskad dead, so I do what I can to help various groups of the Broken around the country."

"There are more?" I asked, my jaw hanging open.

They glared at me with disdainful indifference. "Not everyone is in the pocket of the kings or actively plotting their demise. Most of us are just trying to survive to tomorrow."

"I thought people gave up and spread out or were dead or in prison!"

"They *have* given up."

I looked around the room, my heart sinking. We could have an army with even a few groups this large. "Jamie's granddaughter is free," I whispered. "There's hope."

"Not everyone wants to fight anymore."

"Will *you*?" I was practically begging. "Will you come back and fight with us?"

Tythan sighed, but Hope answered. "Yes! I want to go!"

Tythan pursed their lips and frowned. "Aurakbahor claiming you as his heir hasn't granted you much good will.

Not with me at least." Then they eyed the tattoo on my arm and sighed. "But fine." They gave Hope a somber look. "I'd have to make arrangements here. I can't leave these people like this."

I glanced back at the Broken and unzipped my backpack to pull out a bag of gold from inside. "This is the last of what I stole from Aurakbahor. I don't think anything would infuriate him more than his own money going to make sure these people have a better life. How far do you think this would go?"

Tythan almost smiled — which for them was practically a grin — and accepted the pouch. "It'll get heat, food, and new clothing for us and a couple other groups. It'll take a few weeks at least before we can leave, but we'll go."

Hope let out a quiet cheer.

"Take this for when you're ready then," I said, setting down Hope and fishing out a set of beads.

They took them and walked past me to speak with the woman who had greeted me, Hope by their side. The woman peered inside and covered her mouth. After a moment, she embraced Tythan and called others over, an excited buzz filling the solemn room.

I quietly left but glanced back at the Broken behind me and hoped my tiny offering would be enough until they were free.

Coleman Brings Swords to Parties

Kat

Aaron and I picked up Coleman and Jason at my grandma's old house. Coleman climbed into the car with several long, thin boxes.

"What's that?" I asked as we drove away.

"Swords," Coleman replied. "I always forget to bring them to training. It's time you tried the real thing, so I figured I'd grab them while I was thinking about it."

"Leave it to Coleman to bring swords to a party," Jason teased.

"They'll just be in the car tonight. We'll hide them in the barn at practice tomorrow. But besides swords, I have good news! I found Tythan and Hope — the two Rhaegyrne in the UK I've been trying to reach. I had to go physically find them, but I convinced Tythan to come help us. It'll be a few weeks before they can, but we're getting the resistance back together!"

I turned around in my seat. "When did you even have *time* to go to England?"

He shrugged. "I flew out right after practice and got back yesterday. Please do not ask me how jet lagged I am because I am being held upright by lethal amounts of caffeine right now."

Lily and her family had rented out the rec center for the party and invited what felt like the entire town. Inside, balloons and streamers lined the walls, and the smell of popcorn and chlorine from the pool filled the air. Colored lights flashed from the upstairs gymnasium, pop music blared, children squealed, and the adults laughed among themselves.

"It's so festive!" Jason exclaimed. "You'd never guess a bunch of teenage dragons came here to train for a war!"

"Wait. You train here?" Coleman asked, sounding almost scandalized. "In a place with so many humans?"

"Embarrassing, isn't it?" Aaron said sarcastically.

Before he could say anything else, Miranda caught sight of us. "You all came! It's good to see you alive, Kat!" she exclaimed and embraced me. She hugged Aaron, then Jason, and reached for Coleman but froze. Her face hardened, and she backhanded him across the face with a *smack*. "Why is *he* here?"

He clutched his face, where a welt already rose. "I had to trick the king," he groaned. "I'm still on your side."

She turned to me. "Really?"

"As far as I can tell, he's told us the truth," I said.

"And you didn't bother to tell us?"

I flushed. "It's a recent update. I survived being poisoned, Coleman saved me, and my dad's known about dragons the entire time."

She leaned back in surprise. "That's . . . a lot. Coleman, I'd apologize, but I think you still deserve that, regardless of your motivations."

"It's fine," he replied, his face pink from embarrassment.

"Well, I'll have to find Lily and let her know. Are you here to stay then? Are you going to go to school with us?"

"No—"

"Yes," Jason said over him, staring him down while Coleman shook his head.

"Um, okay." Miranda cleared her throat and stood a little straighter. "Well, anyway, everything's open. Skate rentals are covered tonight for the ice rink outside. There's food in the party room, and we're going to meet back here to watch the ball drop. Happy New Year! I'll see you later." She waved over her shoulder as she left to help Lily with welcoming guests.

We started down the hall, but as soon as Miranda was out of earshot, Coleman turned to Jason, his fiery red hair looking more like fire than hair. His eyes shone a bright red. "I am *not* going back to school."

Jason sighed. "Please? For me?"

"No! I dropped out years ago! Even Jamie allowed that!"

"You're still seventeen."

"On a technicality!"

"It's a better cover story than sitting at home!"

"We'll talk about this later." His hair died down, and his eyes returned to their normal shade of brown, but he still radiated heat.

"Cool down, Cole. You'll set off the fire alarms," I warned.

He rubbed the handprint on his cheek. "Let's dance and find some food."

The four of us hurried down the hall to the basketball court, where lights flashed and bass shook the ground. The room was packed with kids from school. Most pressed together in a jumping and dancing mass around the DJ. On the outskirts of the room, the social dance club practiced lifts and friends socialized.

A song by The Band Chaos came on, and Aaron grabbed my

hand, pulling me into the mosh pit. Jason and Coleman followed behind.

Once inside, it was all elbows, jumping, loud bass, and bad singing. The crowd closed in around us, separating our group, but none of us cared, losing ourselves in the music.

After a few minutes, I muscled my way out of the crowd, searching for the boys to try to find something to eat.

As I pushed my way through the room, I froze, my senses on high alert. Something was *wrong*. I scanned the room again, trying to figure out what had caused this spike in adrenaline and did a double take.

Morgan.

A familiar itching filled my body as my vision sharpened. The rational part of me reminded myself that changing in the middle of a crowded gym was an awful idea. Yet my dragon side wanted to rip out her throat and leave her cold corpse behind.

The violent thought made me flinch.

A hand touched my shoulder, and I spun around, my arm shooting up to grip Aaron's throat. My hand recoiled like I had been burned. "Sorry!"

"What's wrong?" he asked. "You may want to turn your eyes off."

"We're going to need Coleman's swords. Morgan is here."

His hands balled into fists at his side, and the muscle in his jaw jumped. "Let's lure her outside and finish this."

"You go outside and get yourself a sword. I'll look for the others."

He pushed his way through the crowd while I scanned the room for Coleman's distinctive red hair. Hopefully, Jason's shaggy black hair would be close by.

Someone grunted as I pushed past them. I muttered a

distracted apology and tried to keep going, but a strong hand caught my wrist.

"Just where do you think you're going, Kitty?"

I turned and came face-to-face with the assassin. With proximity came clarity, and I realized this woman was several years older than me.

I let my arm heat up, hoping to burn her hand. She smiled, squeezing harder, and sent a sensation through my arm like it had been submerged in shards of ice.

I tried not to scream.

"Lost something, Kitty? Your little boyfriend, perhaps?"

I opened my mind, hoping to find Aaron or to call for help, but instead, I was met with a mental assault of shooting pain.

Gasping, I recoiled and closed my mind to shield myself from the onslaught. "What are you doing?" I hissed. "You can't hurt me here. Everyone will see."

She scoffed. "Oh, I'm not here to *kill* you." I yanked my hand away, and she tsked. "My plans are so much more *fun*." She then dissolved into thin air.

Aaron.

Somehow, I still couldn't reach out telepathically. I sprinted out of the room, running into Coleman on the way. "They have Aaron!" I grabbed him and continued running.

"What?"

"Morgan said she kidnapped him! I told him to go get the swords from the car after I saw her. He left. Then she found me."

"Where's Jason?" He searched the crowd as we rushed down the hall, navigating between partygoers with drinks and food.

"I have no idea! I thought he was with you."

Miranda noticed us passing through the lobby and ran to catch up. "What's wrong?"

"There's going to be a fight. I'll do my best to ward the area, but keep people inside!"

"On it!" she said and hurried away.

We sprinted outside, and I almost crashed straight into... Aaron.

"You're okay?" I asked. Relief and confusion made my knees weak. I threw my arms around his neck and pulled him close, the sword boxes pressed into me uncomfortably, but I was too relieved to care. "How did you get away?"

"I went to the car," he said, sounding mystified. "I thought you said you were going to lure her out here."

"She said she had my boyfriend and then disappeared. But you're safe!"

He paused. "Kat, where's Jason?"

"Probably still in the mosh pit. We couldn't find him."

"Did she think Jason was your boyfriend? You two do spend a lot of time together. Alone."

My stomach jumped into my throat, and my body hummed with power. I snarled, stepping away from the boys and the nearby cars, knowing I couldn't stop the change.

I didn't want to stop it.

"*Get on!*" I said once I had finished my transformation.

"I'll provide ground support," Coleman answered, paler than usual.

"*What? All powerful dragon is afraid of flying?*"

"I have no issue with *my* flying. You fly like a drunk chicken."

"*Remind me to squash you when I get back.*"

Aaron seated himself between my shoulders, and I took off.

"*Watch out for Jason or another dragon anywhere.*"

He traced an arrow on my back. "There!"

I turned to see a bronze dragon flying toward me. As soon as he was in range, I opened my mouth and spewed fire.

My flames parted harmlessly around the dragon. Morgan stood on the dragon's back with her hand extended, palm facing out, creating magic barriers around her ride.

"Oh, do be careful, Kitty. You wouldn't want to harm your boy." She kicked what I thought was a traveling bag in front of her. It groaned.

"Coleman, I could use your support up here."

"Working on it!" he said.

Bright blue currents of electricity coursed through the air around the bronze dragon. Morgan yelped and yanked her hand back.

A flash of red formed around Jason, so I sucked in air and breathed out fire again. This time, my flames got close enough to singe them before she could block them. She screamed and made a motion of throwing something at me.

Her spell hit Coleman's shield with a crash that made my ears ring. Even with the protection, I was flung backward before regaining control.

"Ready to commandeer a dragon?" I asked Aaron.

"Bring it on."

I shot over the dragon, feeling Aaron jump as I swept past. My stomach seemed to fall with him, terrified until he landed on the enemy. I heard the clang of metal on metal as they fought below.

Thank heavens Coleman brought real swords to the party.

The dragon gave chase. Our powerful wings slapped together, sending us plummeting before we could break and come back together. He dropped under me and rammed into my chest hard enough to make the wind rush out of my lungs in a pathetic jet of flames.

I dropped briefly as my chest muscles spasmed from the pain, but my wings caught the air, and I was back in the fight. I flew straight up, crashed into the dragon, and kept going higher, arching above the bronze dragon.

A scream and high-pitched profanity rang through the night, signaling a partial end to Aaron's fight. I dove under the dragon, trying to slow myself enough to ensure a safe fall. Two bodies landed on my back with a soft groan and the closest Aaron ever got to swearing.

"*You okay?*" I asked, speeding away from Morgan.

"Yeah." His voice was higher than normal.

"*How's Jason?*"

He took a few breaths before responding. "Unconscious but alive."

I coasted back to the ground, paused to let Coleman pull Jason off, and took to the air again.

I met the dragon and rider halfway through their dive and flew close enough for Aaron to get a good swipe at the dragon's side. The dragon roared, and Morgan sent a blood-red curse at us.

Time seemed to slow as my senses went into overdrive. I saw Coleman down on the ground, trying to help Jason sit up and unable to aid us magically. Her spell vibrated through the air like a shockwave, coming closer to us with every heartbeat.

Acting fast, I jerked my back up, catapulting Aaron into the air, and turned into a human. "*Bri ally!*" I cried. The air in front of me shimmered for a moment, looking like a brick wall, before the assassin's curse slammed into it.

Time snapped back to normal as a *boom* split the night, shattering the windows below us and setting off car alarms.

I turned on my stomach and changed back into a dragon, catching Aaron in my claws. I set him on the ground by Coleman and returned to the air.

Morgan waited for me on the bronze dragon. I should have taken that as a warning, but instead, it enraged me. I charged.

I slammed into her wall so hard I recoiled almost half a block.

They followed me, keeping her magical buffer between us. "Oh no," she said in a sickly sweet tone. "This fight is over. It was fun, though. And it's so sweet to see the loyalty you show your friends. I wonder what would have happened if that really was your boyfriend."

They disappeared into thin air.

I landed and turned back toward my friends, fuming. My vision still maintained the hawklike clarity of my dragon form. My whole body hummed with anger, and electricity flickered across my fingers, lifting my hair off my back. "How dare she—"

"Kat, calm down," Aaron said, reaching for me, but recoiled as a small electric arc jumped off my arm and shocked him. "Kat!"

The only thing keeping me human was the expenditure of power. "No! How dare she come here! To my territory! How dare she hurt my friends! How dare she poison me! How dare she endanger the lives of my friends and family! Whole families are in that building." I pointed. A flash of lightning jumped off my finger and shorted out the streetlamp. "She has the nerve to show up here, kidnap Jason, and disappear when the fight gets fair?"

"Kat, I'm fine," Jason said, but his face was pale, and he used Coleman for support.

"I'm not!"

"That's clear enough," Coleman said. "Kat, stop. You'll burn yourself out!"

"Good!"

"You're not mad at us."

I stared at them, trying to plead for help through my rage.

"I know." I tried to shut off the light show coming from my hands, but I couldn't. My heart raced faster. "I can't."

Aaron took hold of Jason, and Coleman stepped forward to help, but lightning jumped out for him.

His hand flashed up and caught the jagged streak, creating a current between us. "I'm really, *really* sorry about this." The lightning flared out on either side, forming a wall of hissing blue and purple electrical currents around me.

The gaps between the bolts filled, and the entire wall became a translucent red.

Coleman's eyes betrayed the strain of whatever magic he was working. Aaron tried to step forward, but Jason's leaning weight caused him to stumble.

The wall's edges rolled in, encompassing me. It fed off my own magic, and I stumbled to my knees. I reached out, inexplicitly drawn to the wall, and touched it.

"*Katherine!*" Aaron's muffled cry sounded as I lost consciousness.

T IS FOR TRAITOR

KAT

Someone brushed my hair off my face, and the air smelled like rain.

I opened my eyes to find Aaron's blurry, worried face above me.

"Rise and shine..." he muttered.

"How long was I out?" I asked, groaning as I sat up. My whole body felt like a glacier pressed into me, heavy and cold.

"Not long."

Coleman came over and held his hand out to me. I took it and pulled myself up.

A pang of guilt turned my stomach as I saw the parking lot filled with shattered windshields and flashing hazard lights. A lamp post had been knocked over.

"Why has no one come out yet?" I asked, looking at the deserted parking lot.

"Miranda did her job," he said. "But I also made a shield before the fight started. I'm working on cleaning up the mess before I pull the wall down."

"Want help?" I asked.

Coleman snorted. "Can you even change into a dragon right now?"

He was right, but I opened my mouth to protest.

"That wasn't a challenge," he interrupted. "You need rest." He shared a look with Aaron, who nodded. "I'll be fine." He turned and walked toward the center of the parking lot, already chanting incantations. Glass shards lifted off the asphalt and reassembled into windows. I chose to ignore the fact I was being babysat.

I looked at Aaron. "Are you okay?"

"A little bruised but fine."

"Where's Jason?"

"Over there. He'll live, but he's hurt." He led me to the side of the rec center where Jason leaned against the wall.

"You okay?" I asked, kneeling next to Jason.

He sucked in a shaky breath. "Yeah. I'm all right. A few broken ribs, a nasty headache — the normal stuff."

"What did she do to you?"

"Well, Morgan caught me from behind and used a dirty trick to knock out my magic for a while. Then she knocked *me* out, and I ended up in a sack on a dragon."

"Knocked out your magic? How?" I asked, stunned at the thought.

Jason winced as he turned and lifted his shaggy hair off his neck. A blue, runelike symbol of two wide *V*s interlocked at the base of his skull. Three dots danced around the main symbol.

Recognition shot through me like a bolt of lightning. I'd recognize the symbol anywhere. It had been engraved in the pendant Grandma had given me when I was little. The one Aurakbahor broke.

"What is that? What does it mean?" I asked, brushing my fingers across it.

"It's old magic. The paint's made of Dragonstongue's non-lethal roots. It prevents magic usage until the paint fades."

I gasped. "Can you wash it off?" But my mind was reliving a moment from twelve years ago when Grandma had first given me that old pendant. Hadn't she promised it would control my magic? My stomach clenched, and my heart pounded.

"No, but it'll fade in a few days," Jason said. "I'll be okay."

He leaned against the wall and let out a small hiss, clutching his stomach.

"Let me see," I said, trying to distract myself. "I'm as useless as you with magic right now, but I at least know some first aid."

"I'm fine," he insisted, but he panted from his pain.

"Jason, let me help you! Are you embarrassed you got hurt?"

"No! It's not that. It's just . . . fine." He pulled his hoodie and long-sleeved shirt off.

I gasped when I saw the new and old damage on his body. A dark, veiny, twisting mass spread across his torso from his right side. The curse writhed and crawled up his chest, leading to a mess of scars and bruising. A dragon had been carved into his arm long ago, the scar tissue wrapping from his forearm to his collarbone. From the dragon's mouth, old, angry burn scars reached across his entire torso.

"Jason . . ." I whispered, unable to take my eyes away.

"The burn scars are from dragon fire . . ." He looked everywhere but at me. He rubbed at his arm, his fingers tracing the raised scar there. "It happened when I was little. It's nothing."

I watched his fingers nervously run along the tail of the dragon on his arm and remembered with dawning horror that his tether was *that* arm. He'd told me it was to remind him he was human, but I wondered if it was more than that. "This is your actual tether, isn't it?" I asked.

He only nodded in response.

"Who did this to you?"

"It doesn't matter."

"Yes, it does."

He sighed. "I kind of explained it to Aaron while you were recovering from Dragonstongue. I got this and this" — he turned, showing me a thick calligraphy *T* etched into his back in scar tissue — "in Aurakbahor's prisons. The *T* is for traitor. That's what Morgan told me each time she carved and recarved it anyway."

I reached out to touch the scarring without thinking. He flinched as I brushed against the tendrils on his chest. "What's the web?"

He looked down. "Morgan hit me with it first. It hurts, but it's not too bad." I decided against calling him on his bluff.

The cars' hazard lights turned off, and a screeching filled the air as Coleman straightened the lamp post. He walked over to us, sweat beaded on his forehead.

"Would you look at this?" I asked, gesturing to the strange curse spreading across Jason's stomach. "I assume it's bad, but he doesn't—"

Coleman's eyes widened, and his face went white. He checked his watch and knelt next to Jason. "It's bad, but I know the counter. It's still visible, so we can get rid of it. If it burrows under the skin, it's fatal. We have about an hour."

He reached his hand out, a dark green energy already forming in his hands.

But it dispersed before it reached Jason.

Coleman frowned and tried again. The magic stopped inches away from the wound. He checked his watch again. "What's going on?"

Jason flinched. "Does the, ah, Tasalgric Deflection rune also prevent magic from being used on the victim?"

Coleman buried his face in his hands. "This is bad. This is so bad."

"Fantastic bedside manner, Cole," Jason said, wincing.

"I know, I know. I'm sorry." He hesitated. "This killed Jamie."

"*What?*" I gasped.

Jason nodded. "Yeah, I know . . ." he said, placing a hand on the curse.

I stared at him. "Why didn't you say anything?"

"I didn't know the rune stopped magic." He was sweaty and pale.

"But you figured out the cure, right?" I pried, my heart pounding.

"Yes. Too late for Jamie, though," Coleman answered.

"What do we do?" Aaron whispered. "He has other injuries too."

Coleman frowned. "Let's get him home. I have a couple ideas, but I don't want to be out in the open for it." He tried to pull Jason to his feet.

Jason bit his lip and whimpered, hugging his side. "No, no. I can't." Tears sprang to his eyes as he sank to the ground. "I'm sorry."

"I'll get the car," Aaron said, jogging off with a slight limp.

Coleman filled Jason's discarded shirt with snow and gently held it to his bruised ribs.

My hands shook, and my mind reeled from fear and renewed grief for my grandma. The curse wriggled beneath his skin, and I couldn't look away.

Aaron drove the car as close to Jason as possible.

"We need to get up just enough to make it into the car. Do you think you can do that?" Coleman asked, wiping a tear off Jason's cheek. "I'm sorry I can't use anything to dull the pain." His voice trembled with tears of his own.

"Quit crying, Cole," Jason chastised, reaching up to wipe Coleman's tears. "I'll be okay."

He sniffed and held out his hand. "On three, then?"

"Three," Jason said, trying to push off Coleman. He cried out but managed to get up enough to transfer to the car.

Coleman climbed into the back seat with him, and I took the front passenger seat. Aaron pulled out of the parking lot as gently as possible, but Jason still whimpered.

"We just have to get you home," Coleman whispered. "I'll fix this."

Assassin's Leech...
Again

Coleman

Some spells can gently send someone into unconsciousness or numb pain when healing spells fall short. But Jason's rune wouldn't even allow that kind of mercy.

I checked my watch again, anxious that Kroll's deal could still happen at any minute. I was still wiped out from curing Kat's Dragonstongue and worn out from my transatlantic flight. I *really* did not need one more thing making this any harder than it already was.

Jason kept his eyes squeezed shut, his head resting in my lap, and he winced every time we hit a bump in the road. I looked away and watched Aaron as he navigated the snowy roads home with white-knuckled fists, silently praying for him to go faster.

As we drove, I could only think about Jamie.

I watched Jason, and my eyes stung again. *No. You're not going to lose him.*

I'd stayed up so many nights, wondering if I could have

done anything to save Jamie. I'd considered everything and had one *possible* idea on what I could have done — what I might be able to do now. I just wasn't certain it would work. And I wasn't sure if I was strong enough.

Aaron hit the edge of a pothole, and Jason gasped and grabbed my hand. He squeezed it as tears leaked out the sides of his eyes. I gave him a light squeeze and held on. *Why were my cheeks burning?*

We pulled into the driveway of Jamie's old house and somehow managed to lay Jason on the couch in the front room. I sat on the floor, still holding his hand. He squeezed my hand so tightly that my fingers lost feeling.

I didn't know if my plan would work. But I had to try.

"Kat, is your magic back?" I asked.

"Most of it, I think. But—"

"Repeat after me: *ta'is isoperé, sanare corporus.*" I wanted to be surprised I still remembered the counter, but how could I forget?

She did so but frowned. "Why? Magic won't work on him."

I tried to smile. "But it will work on me."

"What?"

I placed my hands on the writing mass across his chest and reached out mentally to the curse tangled under his skin. I'd manipulated poisons and curses before, like when I controlled the Dragonstongue in my body to intimidate Jinx or when I pulled the poison out of Kat's body. I just had to hope this worked the same way.

I closed my eyes and mentally grabbed hold of the curse and *pulled*.

The curse resisted, unwilling to leave. It needed a place to go, a body to parasitize itself on.

I offered it mine.

I opened my eyes and watched the tendrils seep away from

Jason's body, crawling up my fingers and twisting up my arms. It burned as it tangled with the blue tendrils of Dragonstongue, and I bit back a scream.

"Cole?" Jason asked, trying to bury himself in the couch to pull away from me.

"Shut up," I grunted through clenched teeth as our combined curses crawled up my neck. The last of the strands disappeared from his stomach as they reached across my chest and face.

I took several deep breaths, trying to control the toxic magics mixing in my body. "Kat . . ." I gasped, unable to say anything else.

"*Ta'is isoperé, sanare corporus!*" Green magic poured off her hand, bringing soothing relief until the leech was gone.

I collapsed against the couch, panting and cold.

Without the curse, the dark bruising and thick scarring across Jason's chest were a lot more noticeable.

"How did you—" Jason said.

"I can do something similar with the residual Dragonstongue in my body. I figured I might be able to do the same with yours."

"How did you know that would work?" Kat asked.

"I didn't."

Aaron's face was pale. "What are we going to do about his physical injuries? It's New Year's, and the ER is probably full of people with fireworks injuries, but I don't think we can convince them that firecrackers did that."

"I'll be okay tonight," Jason said. "We can try to scrub the rune off in the morning. The paint will stain, but maybe we can break the rune enough to let some magic through. I just . . . want to sleep." He still held onto my hand.

Kat rubbed her locket across her lips. "Cole, I believe you

now. While I'm thinking about it, I actually need something from you, if you have the strength for it."

"What do you want me to do?"

"I need to know how to find and kill Aurakbahor. Tell me everything you can. Give me books or maps or anything that will help me get these kings out of the way."

Aaron shifted behind her, giving her a strange look.

"You're the prince," Kat said. "You're going to know more than any of us."

A small smile danced at the corner of my lips. "I'd love to."

We are, All of Us, the Succumbing Senior

Aaron

We left the house with an armful of hand-drawn maps and old books from Jamie's magical hidden library. Kat insisted we get to work immediately on alternative plans to fight the kings, so I drove us to her house despite the late hour.

She led me to her basement and unrolled the sprawling maps on the table. I sat beside her and studied the mess of maps in front of me. This wasn't exactly how I expected to spend my New Year's Eve. I picked one up and shuddered. The twisting labyrinth in front of me was labeled "coliseum," and I remembered Jason's stories of his own torture and Aurakbahor's recent changes. Hundreds of prison cells and cages lined the walls of the winding corridors. It would be nearly impossible to get in or out without a map. Almost every hall led to the arena at the center. One wrong turn would put us in the coliseum.

Kat lifted a map that Coleman claimed was a layout of

Aurakbahor's private quarters. She frowned. "Do you think this shows all the secret passages?"

"What makes you think it has *any* secret passages?"

She pointed. "This one's marked here, and the walls don't quite match here."

I chewed the inside of my lip. "The man has managed to stay alive this whole time. No matter how good Coleman is, that map isn't complete."

"Are any of these trustworthy?"

"They're the best we have. So, if you were an assassin — which I'm assuming you're planning to become — where would you go to kill a king?"

"There have been times," Coleman started as he stared down the school hallway on the first day back from the break, "that I truly disliked people. But currently, I hate everyone and their dog."

He looked as tired as I felt. His red hair stuck up all over the place, his jacket buttons didn't line up, and his backpack hung open with papers dangling out. He leaned against Jason, who was still pale and bruised with dark bags under his eyes.

We'd managed to get the rune to fade enough that Coleman could help with the pain and his broken ribs but not much else yet. Besides, Kat and Coleman were still too exhausted from the attack two nights ago to do much healing.

"Hey, leave the dogs out of it!" Kat protested, trying to fix his backpack and jacket.

"Fine. Not the dogs," Coleman said, combing his fingers through his hair. "I still hate everyone."

"How are you guys feeling today?" she asked. "Besides annoyed."

"I can barely walk," I admitted. "But I knew what I signed up for." Bruises ran all the way up my inner thighs.

"I can't wait until I'm strong enough to heal us and still have magic in case of a fight. Everything hurts," Coleman complained.

"Are you expecting a fight?" I asked.

"I've learned to."

"Can we even fight in this condition?"

"If I'm clever with a few cheap tricks, maybe." Coleman seemed confident, but he eyed Jason with visible concern.

"Well, let's hope there isn't a fight then."

Coleman sighed. "Well, if I'm expected to participate in this school stuff, can someone at least show me around?"

"Well, to your left," Kat said, "you'll see a senior succumbing to existential dread, and to the right is our first period class!"

Coleman stepped to the left. "Is the succumbing senior me?"

"You haven't even been to class yet!" Jason protested, barely above a whisper. "But no. The succumbing senior is all of us."

We wandered the halls for a few minutes, showing Coleman to his classes.

Just a few minutes before the bell, Kat pulled us to a stop by the bulletin board outside our first period class. "Wait a moment. I want to see what that poster says."

"'Back and bigger and better than ever before,'" Jason read aloud. "What's the end-of-year raffle assembly?"

Kat's eyebrows creased in confusion. "It's an assembly to try to convince students to keep their grades up and behave, with options to buy tickets for charity. But they canceled it right after you came. I wonder how they convinced the sponsors to do it again."

I stepped up to the poster and scanned the rest. "Because they got new sponsors," I said, pointing at a picture of the various prizes. "They're raffling off a *car* as the grand prize."

Coleman whistled appreciatively. "You guys have some sweet sponsors here."

I shook my head. "Not usually..."

"This isn't even the end-of-the-year," I noted, pointing out the date. "They're doing it in a *month*."

"Guess the sponsors didn't want to give us time to cause problems again. Anyone going to try to win?" Kat asked.

"I'm not paying for tickets, but I'll have a few entries from my grades."

Coleman and Jason seemed too exhausted to answer.

"Well," Kat said, "we should go. Coleman, you'll want to talk to the teacher and prepare for your introductions today."

"I would rather die," he answered but allowed himself to be dragged to class.

I showed up twenty minutes late to the field we'd been practicing at for our first training session after Morgan's attack. We weren't all the way recovered yet, but we needed to start training again.

When I arrived, Jason's car was in the farm's driveway, but they weren't in the field.

I wandered through the old farmland, crunching through the snow, heading toward the barn, and hoping they were inside. As I got closer, I breathed a sigh of relief when I heard voices inside.

I entered, the warmth from the space heater a welcome reprieve from the bitter cold of early January, and found Kat standing in the middle of the room. She held her hands in the air with a large sphere of water floating over her head. Sweat beaded on her forehead, and her arms trembled. Coleman and Jason stood off to the side, watching.

"Hey," I said, dropping my backpack by the door.

"Sup," Coleman replied, glancing my way. Kat grunted a greeting, and Jason crossed the room to me.

"While she does that," Jason said, "let's get you started."

"What *is* she doing?" I asked, letting him lead me out of the warm barn.

"Coleman claims it will help with magical strength and dexterity," he answered. "I don't know if that's true, but I don't envy her. And I fear that Coleman might make me try that as soon as this rune is off my neck."

"Speaking of, what are you planning for me? You can't summon swords or heal us if we get hurt."

"I'll watch while you run drills." He let out an irritated huff. "I hated Morgan before, but now, I have to *manually* put toothpaste on my toothbrush!"

"Oh, poor baby. I can't imagine what it must be like to not be able to use magic for every simple task throughout the day!" I said.

Jason turned toward me with a sorrowful gaze and put a consoling hand on my shoulder. "It is indeed a difficult burden — one I would wish on no one in a thousand years. And yet . . . it is my burden to bear."

"Oh, shut up." I rolled my eyes but retrieved a sword from the rack in the old wooden shed by the barn.

I fell into the drill's familiar rhythm until Coleman approached, and I stopped to wipe my brow, my sweat still beading despite the cold air.

"Do you have a moment?" he asked. "Kat wanted to work on planning our next move."

Jason and I followed him back inside the barn where she was setting up maps of the coliseum and the council chambers.

"Time to talk," she said. "We need a plan, and we need allies. Are we building an army or not? When can the UK dragons join?"

Coleman shrugged. "Tythan said it could be a bit."

"Can we get anyone else?"

"Not yet," he answered.

"That's fine. A small group is all I need," Kat said, pointing at a map of the council chamber. I recognized most of the lines we had drawn across it, but she had added a few more. "Coleman, do you know how often he meets with his Court?"

"Every other week or so. In the evenings."

"Good. How many people attend?"

"A dozen, give or take."

She frowned. "Is he ever in there alone?"

"No."

She pondered the map before tracing a circle around the chamber. "I'll need you guys to get the attendants out of the way and give me enough time to fight him alone. Can you do that?"

I sat back against the wall and frowned. It wasn't the real plan, but I still didn't like it.

"Kat, you're not *ready*," Coleman said. "Not by yourself. *I* can't even face him alone."

Her eyes burned with determination. "Trust me. Give me time alone with him and an army outside the door to keep others out, and I'll finish this."

"But..."

"Do you have any other ideas?" Kat asked. "These attacks on us aren't going to stop unless we do something."

Coleman, Jason, and I shared a look full of trepidation and anxiety. After some hesitation, Coleman and Jason nodded.

This deception felt like a curse. One I hoped we wouldn't see the effects of before the end of this. I'd joined this fight to try to keep Kat safe and stayed to save the rest, but now, I wasn't sure I *could* help with either.

Grand Prize

Kat

The attack on New Year's a month ago haunted my every waking moment, and even my non-Dream Realms dreams weren't safe. Jason's scars, Morgan's face, and her parting words threatening Aaron and promising another fight played on repeat until finally Jason called me to the Dream Realms.

Jason's mouth opened in surprise as he looked me over. My body still trembled from the nightmares, and as much as I tried to hide it, I was certain I didn't look great.

"What's wrong? What happened?" Coleman asked.

My hands curled into fists at my side, trying to hide the shaking. "Have you heard from Tythan yet? It's been weeks since we agreed to act, and we haven't *done* anything! We have to move *now*. No more waiting. No more training." My voice was harder than I meant it to be. I didn't intend to face Aurakbahor alone like I'd suggested before, but we needed to do *something*. We weren't safe anywhere; we couldn't trust anyone, and it was only a matter of time before one of us died.

And that? That scared me more than any egotistical king.

"Still no word from Tythan," Jason said. "But Kat, even *with* Tythan, we're not ready."

"That's not good enough!" I shouted, surprised at the anxiety and fear behind my words.

Coleman paced behind Jason, looking concerned.

"I've spent months training," I yelled. "I've been in more life-and-death situations than I can count. I've fought other dragons, and I walk away every time. The four of us make a great team. We can take on at least one of them!" I was *sick* of waiting around, and training and training and training and *still* being attacked. And now, knowing that the kings could listen in on their dragons — on Coleman and Jason — the stronger I got, the stronger *Aurakbahor* would know I'm getting. And the more reckless he'll get. The New Year's Eve celebration proved that.

Coleman frowned. "Aurakbahor and Balaskad are stronger than anything you've faced."

I crossed my arms with a huff. "I combine two clan lines! *Two*! If it's their lineage that makes them strong, then I should be stronger than at least one of them alone."

"They're never truly alone though," Jason insisted. "They command *armies with their minds!*"

"Then we'll bring an army ourselves!"

He sighed. "If you're so inclined to go to war, you better go train with Coleman. We can talk battle plans tomorrow after I've had time to think."

The student body buzzed with a strange energy the next

morning. For a moment, I thought it was my own anxiety for the war, but then I remembered the raffle assembly was today.

The school had confirmed on Monday that the grand prize was indeed a new car, and the smaller prizes ranged from ten dollar gift cards to thousand-dollar scholarships. We skipped first period and headed straight to the auditorium. Jason, Coleman, Aaron, and I filed in behind swarms of other students. Lily noticed us and waved us over to stand in line next to her.

Pushing our way through the crowd, I grabbed Aaron's hand to make sure we didn't get lost in the large auditorium that also doubled as our town's community theater stage. We found seats but got separated from the others. Jason and Coleman sat with Lily and Miranda a few rows behind us. They smiled and waved.

The first half of the assembly crept by as the student officers and cheerleaders tried to entertain the restless audience. Their part ended, and the dozens of school sponsors walked onto the stage one at a time.

One by one, the gift cards, scholarships, and small electronics were raffled away to various gleeful students. With each gift, the tension swelled.

The final sponsor stepped up, and my stomach twisted in inexplicable knots. The odds were against me, and I didn't even *want* a new car, but a stubborn bubble of hope formed anyway.

"You students," the spokeswoman said, smiling, "are inspirational! You've raised *eight thousand* dollars for our partner charities!" She paused for a polite smattering of applause. "You've also raised your grades and attendance! Your generosity, determination, and unification are overwhelming! And I am" — her voice cracked, and she wiped at her eyes — *"overwhelmed* to be here with you. I am so excited to award this car to one very special, inspirational, dedicated, and generous student today. But now, I'm standing here in front of you, seeing your faces, and I know that each and every one of you deserves this prize!" She actually broke into tears this time. "I wish we could give a car to all of you inspirational students today!"

"If she says *inspirational* one more time . . ." Aaron whispered.

I elbowed him and rolled my eyes at her dramatics, but my butterflies got more agitated.

She finished telling us about all the charities the donations would go to, and she walked over to a comedically massive upside-down top hat. Her microphone picked up the sound of ruffling paper in the otherwise silent auditorium.

"And the winner is . . ." She opened the folded piece of paper. "Aaron Johnson."

Aaron jumped out of his chair and shouted for joy. Most of the audience joined in, but a loud few expressed their disappointment.

"Congrats!" I said, grinning.

He smiled at me before making his way to the stage, a spotlight following him down the aisle.

The woman pulled a small box out of her pocket, lifted off the top, and let the bottom fall theatrically to the floor. She held onto the keychain for all to see, smiling.

The spotlight glinted off the bronze keychain, and a shiver ran down my spine. It reminded me of something; I couldn't remember what or why, but it caused my adrenaline to spike.

She stepped forward to hand the key to him. My heart pounded in my ears, drowning out the world except for the *click-click* of her heels on the stage.

He reached for the key.

My racing heart stopped as realization dawned. The bronze

reminded me of the dragon that Morgan rode. It matched his scales. Her parting words echoed in my ears, highlighting the threat I hadn't expected.

I wonder what would have happened if that was your boyfriend.

The grand prize was a trap.

"Aaron! No!"

Puppet

Aaron

Kat's scream echoed around the auditorium. I snatched the key fob from the sponsor, the bronze keychain slapping against the back of my hand, and pressed the silver button on the top, causing the metal key inside to shoot out. I held the key between my fingers like a push dagger and pitifully braced for an attack. My body *burned* with adrenaline, and my eyes watered as I tried to scan the audience for the unknown threat, but the stage lights made it impossible to see.

Light refracted around the room. Even with the bright lights, Kat's dragon form was unmistakable. People screamed, but the noise dulled in comparison to an overpowering itch across my body. My eyes suddenly recovered from the lights, and I saw clearly again. Clearer than ever before. A buzz filled my bones, sending chills up and down my spine. Energy — raw, unfiltered *power* — burned in my blood.

I got bigger. Or everyone else shrank. The sponsor ran screaming.

Kat landed on the stage as a dragon in front of the entire student body. A tiny part of me hoped Jason or Coleman were able to put up a shield in time.

Kat's reflective eyes filled with sorrow as she approached me, but my eyes were drawn to the reflection in her mirrored scales.

Where I had stood moments before — where I was sure I still stood — was a vibrant green dragon. My own black talons bit into the floor. My powerful wings lifted.

The keychain must have been a token.

Oh, *no*.

"*Oh*, yes." A mocking voice boomed in my head. "*Welcome to the family Aaron Johnson. Now go kill your girlfriend.*"

The words grated my mind and lurched in my stomach. My whole body moved against my will toward Kat. I tried to fight it, but it was like trying to redirect a runaway bus with my hands — impossible, overpowering, and *painful*.

Beyond the first voice, at least a dozen other voices roared to stop fighting and get it over with. Hundreds laughed at my struggle. Some seemed sympathetic. None were helpful.

I always thought Kat was ginormous as a dragon; she was at least seven feet at the shoulder. Her body length alone was closer to eight with her tail and neck adding another ten more feet — but I was bigger and clumsier by far.

My body dove at her, and I could only watch in helpless horror, my own body a prison. My massive jaws snapped around empty space as she darted away, and I could only feel relief that she was faster than I was.

Somehow, she made herself heard above the others. "*Aaron, change back!*"

I tried. Holy *crap*, I tried. "*I can't!*" I shouted. I don't know if she heard me.

"*I'm so sorry, Aaron.*"

"*Me too.*"

My massive wings lifted me off the stage, scraping against the backstage wall and reaching across the audience. My talons spread, aiming for her throat, but she reared back, took to the air, and tried to force me into the catwalk.

Against my will, I pursued her above the stage, knocking down lights, breaking boards, and ripping ropes out of the ceiling. Her mirrored scales reflected my terrifying face.

"*Stop fighting us, boy! Use your fire!*" the voices in my head demanded.

Something convulsed within my gut, forcing fire from my mouth. Kat's scales had the disorienting effect of appearing to send the fire back at me as my flames raced after her. She dodged, flying higher.

The auditorium had emptied, and the fire alarm blared, echoing around us. We wove through the catwalk, my wings tangling in the ropes. She tilted her head up and breathed fire against the ceiling. Without hesitation, she slammed against the burning layers of wood and drywall and crashed through to the roof.

"*Leave her alone!*" I screamed. "*You already have me. Stop!*" But no one listened, and my body was forced to follow her through the burning wreckage. I burst into the open air and glanced around, trying to find her. But the sky was devoid of her silver wings.

As I turned, a streak of blue and gray barreled straight into me with the force of a semi-truck.

I fell, shrinking.

"*I am so, so sorry.*" Kat's voice was finally the only one I heard.

ASHLEY N.Y. SHEESLEY

Local High School Evacuated After Explosion

The most recent explosion in a stream of serial outbreaks happened yesterday at a local high school during a scholarship assembly. It seems to have been triggered by a thrilling light display to celebrate the occasion. Authorities still will not confirm if they believe the recent explosions across the country are connected.

Two students were initially reported missing after the explosion; one was the grand prize recipient who was on stage where the explosion is said to have started. They were later found outside the auditorium. One student was taken to the hospital with possible head injuries, though is now in stable condition.

The sponsors and stage crew have been taken in for questioning. Mr. John Mordious, the high school principal, assured us that increased security measures will be taken, and the school will reopen at the end of next week. Students are encouraged to speak with one of the school counselors if—

THE ARTICLE WENT ON, but my hands shook. I dropped the newspaper onto the ground and tried to make them stop. I slid my hands down my face, trying to get my vision to return to normal. Failing that, I clasped them together and leaned against the porch railing, exhaling slowly.

The others had suspected the explosions around the country were related to the war.

I guess I was living proof they were right.

Someone stepped up behind me and stood there. I

remained silent. I didn't want anyone near me. I didn't want to hurt them.

Kat sighed and sat next to me. The screen door closed moments later. "I know you could hear me. We have the same super hearing now."

"Don't remind me," I said, trying to scoot away.

"Aaron..."

"Kat, please."

"No. I know what you're going through." She placed a hand on my shoulder. For the first time in months, we were the same temperature.

I almost laughed. "You know what I'm going through, Kat? You're a beautiful creature — a beautiful person. But me? I'm a monster. Yes, you have emotional changes, but at least you are free to do whatever you want when you do change. I went on a rampage against my will!"

"Aaron..." she said repeated, blinking away tears.

My vision sharpened. I shook my head, terrified I might change. "I can't hurt you again."

She took my face in her hands and stared into my dragon eyes. "I am *not* afraid of you. You didn't hurt me. If you want to keep me safe, keep training with us. Learn to control your emotions and how to use magic. Keep being my rider and go with me into battle when the time comes."

"It doesn't matter if I hurt you this time or not. I don't think you understand. I. Was. Trying. To. *Kill*. You."

The corner of her mouth curled into a half-smile. "Good thing I'm fast then."

"Don't. Please. Just... just don't."

Her gorgeous, silver-flecked eyes searched my face like she was reading something there. "Stay with me, Aaron. I love you."

My hands clenched to control the emotions roaring inside

me. "That's the exact reason I have to get away from you! Don't you see that? I have to stay away because I love you. Okay? I love you! I care about you. I'll fight for you. I will *die* for you if I have to. But I will *not* fight you. And right now, I'd just put the resistance in danger. Maybe someday . . . someday, I can join you again, but for now . . . go. Just go." I took a deep breath. The words burned in my throat and tasted bitter. "I don't want you here."

Her eyes swam with tears, and she shook her head. "You don't mean that."

My stomach clenched, and my mouth went dry. "Get out."

She grabbed her locket like she does when she's distressed but stood. "I love you. Don't forget that."

She ran down the stairs and around to the back gate, her movements precise and controlled. Her hands stayed clenched by her sides as she worked her way through the icy snow.

"I love you too," I whispered once I saw her car pull away. For the millionth time in a few hours, I found myself blinking back tears and counting my breaths to get my eyesight back to normal.

The screen door opened and closed again, and my mom sat next to me. Prince followed close behind, wagging his tail as I greeted him.

"How are you doing?" she asked, brushing my hair off my forehead. "The bruise seems to be gone, but you're burning up." She pursed her lips as I pulled away. "Oh, hon . . ."

"How much did Kat tell you?" I asked, staring at the newspaper on the step below me.

"What do you mean? She asked if she could see you. Where is she?"

"She left. I told her to go."

"What? But why?"

I pressed the heels of my hands against my eyes, trying to

make everything go away. Everything from the too-loud noises and too-sharp smells to everything that had happened in the last twenty-four hours. Something scratched my face, and I realized I was still wearing the ridiculous bracelet the hospital made me wear. I tore it off, the plastic cutting into my wrist.

"Aaron?"

"Mom, I need to tell you something. I haven't been completely honest with you for the last few months..." *But it isn't my secret to share.*

"What are you talking about?"

I buried my face in my hands and shook my head. *Maybe it's still not my secret.*

"Aaron, honey, you can tell me anything."

I nodded, still refusing to look at her. "I know."

She put her hand on my back. "What's up?"

"I . . . Kat and I broke up." I don't know what made me chicken out, but I figured the words "Mom, I'm a dragon" shouldn't leave my mouth anytime soon. Besides, it wasn't a lie. My stomach twisted, and my hands trembled.

Mom met my eyes that I prayed were still human. She seemed to see through my veiled truths, but her face softened with pity. "What happened?"

"A lot of things. We've both kind of . . . changed a lot recently. Hopefully, we can be friends again. It's my fault. I should have noticed . . . She tried to . . . she tried to tell me." I buried my head in my arms folded across my knees. "I ruined everything."

"Oh, baby, no," Mom said, pulling me into her arms. "I'm so sorry."

I didn't return the hug, but I didn't fight against it either. "Me too..."

She pulled away and searched my face. "Is there anything I can do? Do you want anything?"

My humanity? My freedom? Kat. "No. I just need to be alone right now."

She seemed to see something in my face because she pursed her lips but patted my back and stood. "Okay. But come inside. It's freezing, and you have a fever."

"I'll come in later. The cold helps me clear my head." In truth, I hadn't even noticed the cold.

She frowned but went back inside. Prince nudged me with his head but followed her.

I closed my eyes and propped my head against the railing.

My phone buzzed. I tried to ignore it, but it buzzed two more times, so I checked it out of sheer annoyance. Jason and Coleman wanted to talk. I would rather listen to them than Kat, but I didn't answer.

I was frustrated and hurt and furious and a million other emotions I couldn't figure out, but I was also painfully aware of the consequences of responding to those emotions beyond recognizing their existence. I couldn't let them control me. It was too dangerous for everyone.

I was too dangerous for everyone.

BLOOD IN THE SNOW

KAT

I made it a block from Aaron's and had to pull over on a forested section of road.

My whole body shook, and my vision blurred with tears.

This was all my fault.

I sat in the car for a moment, running my tether over my lips, before throwing the door open. It slammed behind me, and I stalked off.

I might have changed and flown until my body cried for mercy, but guilt weighed heavy in my chest. Aaron was right. I didn't know what it was like for him. He *couldn't* change, no matter where he was.

I changed all the time. Because I could. Because it was *fun*. Because it was an *escape*. The only thing stopping me from changing all the time was the number of witnesses. He *couldn't*.

I shouldn't change just because it was easy.

I *wouldn't*. Not until he was free.

With a cry of frustration, I expelled the building power into a snowdrift, melting it away.

"Mmm . . . temper, temper, Kitty Kat," a voice hummed behind me.

My hot blood turned to ice. "I will kill you, Morgan," I promised through clenched teeth.

"Murder, Katherine? What would your mother say?"

"She'd do it herself if she knew."

"Oh, so she doesn't know. So, if she found your dead body in the—"

I spun around, fire encasing my fists like gloves. "*Shut up!*"

Two tall, menacing figures in black cloaks and bird-like masks stood next to Morgan. Despite the extra threat, I stalked up to her, shoved her against a lamp post and lifted her off the ground with a burning hand clenched around her throat. My voice came out cold. "Do not push me right now."

Her face reddened as she tried to pull away. My fire licked up the sides of her face, but my anger strengthened me, fueling the burning in my shoulder and forearm. The other two charged at me, but I stomped the ground, sending a shockwave of earth and snow to throw them off their feet and used the motion to build a wall around Morgan and me.

Morgan choked out indecipherable words, and I was slammed against my own wall, shattering it. She still leaned against the lamp post, coughing and rubbing her throat, while I stood. The two assassins rushed at me.

I searched for something I could use as a weapon. Finding nothing, in desperation I combined the words I knew for *sharp* with the phrase for *practice swords*, hoping against hope it'd work. "*Ma adamas chalybs haerent.*"

A rough, painful energy rushed through me with a chill, but a solid, sharp *metal* sword materialized in my hands. I slammed the butt of my hilt into the first assassin's mask. The mask shattered, his nose crunched, and he crumpled to the ground.

I thrust my blade forward, meeting the second assassin's sword. "*Ally eathia*," I yelled, and my sword burst into flame, slicing through his.

He tried to kick at me, but I jumped out of the way and spun, slashing my sword through the air. Fire arced off my blade, racing toward him.

He stumbled backward, his hood falling back as he erected his own shield to take the brunt of the attack, but the force still sent him sprawling backward against a tree. He slumped, unconscious.

The first assassin climbed to his feet and helped Morgan to hers. She reached her hands out to me, chanting.

I lifted my hand in response, preparing my own counter, but the man charged. His sword flashed in the air, and I caught his blade against mine and sent a curse after Morgan.

I lunged. He parried and sent out a ball of red energy from his free hand. I dodged the spell and blocked his riposte. I turned and sent my foot into his stomach, throwing him into the path of Morgan's latest curse. He screamed and arched his back before collapsing to the ground, quivering and unconscious.

I dropped my sword, letting it disappear into thin air. "*Ally aira!*" I commanded, and the wind screamed around us.

Morgan withstood the blast with obvious effort. Her lips moved, but the wind ripped her words away. She reached out her hand, and a thick stream of blue streaked toward me. I jumped and rolled to get closer to her.

"*Eathia cor.*" My curse hit true, though my hands were getting cold. She clutched at her chest, gasping for air. Her skin turned red as her body tried to put out the literal fire burning in her heart.

She gasped out what must have been a counter curse. Moments later, she straightened, her breaths coming out in hitches.

I didn't have time to block before a bolt of lightning struck my left shoulder.

Electricity coursed through my body, causing my muscles to seize. I fell to the ground, unable to force my body to obey. More spells slammed into me, and smoke spiraled off my shirt. My skin steamed against the snow. My stomach ached like I'd been hit with a battering ram.

I tried to sit up, but Morgan kicked my arms out from under me. She turned me over and sat on my stomach, igniting the pain her spells had sparked. I tried to throw her off, but she slammed my head into the dirt, and my vision blurred.

I threw my right arm up, fist clenched for a wild strike. But she drew a knife faster than I could blink and slashed it across the inside of my elbow. My punch made contact, yet it made no difference.

She let out an inhuman snarl and pressed her fingers against my neck, sending hot pain coursing through my veins. I tried to recoil, but my muscles froze and fell limp, refusing my demands to move.

She took my bare arm and dragged her knife like a paintbrush along my upper arm, using my body as her bloody canvas. Pain like fire engulfed my arm. I tried to move. I tried to scream. But my body lay still and mutinous against my will.

"You know," she said as my blood dripped down my arm, "Jason screamed a lot more."

Anger coursed through my body, drowning out the pain and returning my draconic vision. I managed to make a toe twitch.

She noticed my eyes. "Ah. That's usually the reaction I hope for, but it won't do at all for you. But for Aaron . . . That's his name, right? That's exactly what I'd want now. Sadly, we have other plans for him."

The thought of her even touching Aaron broke her spell.

I jerked my hips up. Her knife slid up my arm as she fell forward. My eyes filled with reflex tears as I shoved Morgan off of me. Her spell dulled the full extent of the pain in my arm, but once it broke, the pain flooded in full force.

I fought back a wave of nausea, blinking away the dark fog in my vision. I dragged myself to my feet. Morgan stumbled away, seeming stunned that I could move. I stalked toward her, blood dripping down my arms and into the snow. She tried to scramble to her feet, but I kicked them out from under her.

She collapsed against a tree and threw up a force field. But I kept coming, my palm filling with power. I pressed it against the field and broke through as though it never existed. Her eyes widened, and I fell on her with the full force of my rage.

"Why" — I kicked her in the ribs hard enough to hear them crack — "won't you" — I slammed my bloodied fist into her chin — "leave us" — I shattered her nose — "*alone?*" Something inside me snapped, and with each hit, I wanted to hit her again, only harder.

I kept attacking, even after she slumped against the ground, and her eyes rolled back. My knees pinned her shoulders down, holding her in place, as I continued my attack. Blood dripped from her nose and smeared across her face. How much was her blood and how much was mine, I couldn't tell, but I *wanted* to keep going.

You're going to kill her, the little voice in my head said. *Stop it!*

I pulled up short and stared down at my horrendous handiwork. My hands trembled, and my body ached. My arm was a steady stream of blood. Bile rose in my throat. I had almost killed her! Maybe she deserved it, but I kept fighting after it was no longer a fair fight.

Would that be so bad though? another voice whispered in the back of my mind.

I stumbled backward, staring at my blood-covered arms and quivered. I reached for my phone in the dirt, streaking blood across the screen, and called Jason.

"Help me."

It was all I could get out before I began to cry. I crawled behind a tree, hiding from Morgan's half-dead form, and sobbed gross, heavy sobs, barely clinging to consciousness, until Jason and Coleman arrived.

Coleman immediately went to work on cleanup, dragging the two masked, unconscious attackers deeper into the woods. Whether he was hiding them or finishing the job, I didn't dare ask.

Jason ran to me, steering clear of Morgan's limp form. His eyes dropped to my blood-soaked arms. Recognition darkened his face. He pulled off his jacket, tearing several strips before using them to apply pressure to the deeper wounds and tying a tourniquet on both arms.

"Kat . . ." He had the air of someone about to give very bad news. "What she did . . . I can't fix it. I don't know what kind of magic she uses on her knives, but it resists magical healing."

I stared at my arm, feeling like I was seeing it in a dream. The carving was too thickly coated in congealing blood to make out what Morgan had done. "Can't you at least try?"

"The only thing I can do is make sure you don't bleed out. But then we can only clean it up, the same way humans take care of injuries," he answered, using a water bottle to drench a clean strip of fabric. "It will hurt."

He wiped away the blood on my arm, pulling at the tender skin. It stung, and I flinched. I tried to stop myself from crying out, but tensing made my arm throb and tingle from the tourniquet. I shifted my head to avoid watching, only to catch Morgan's swollen eyes flicker open.

I jerked, trying to warn Jason. But before I could get out a single word, Morgan vanished, just as she had when I'd fought her before. An almost inhuman sob escaped my throat as I watched her flee *again*. Dark spots danced in my vision.

"You have to relax," Jason said, barely glancing at the now empty-bloody patch of snow. "Stay with me, Kat. Breathe."

Coleman reappeared and put a soothing hand on my right arm, above Morgan's first cut. He held me down, speaking words of comfort laced with magic. My breathing slowed, and my eyelids drooped. I slumped forward, and he pulled me toward him.

My arms throbbed. I groaned and opened my eyes.

Groggily, I sat up, realizing I was in my bed. Bandages wrapped up my left arm from my mid-forearm to my shoulder and across my chest. My right arm was wrapped at the elbow. Both sets of bandages were already red. My ruined shirt had been removed, leaving me in my blood-stained sports bra.

The door opened, and my dad walked in. He hesitated when he saw me and held up a first aid kit. "I'm going to change the wrappings. Jason and Coleman are headed over to help with the pain. How are you feeling?"

"Like I got hit by a truck," I answered. "Why am I home? Won't Mom see?"

"I asked my sister to call her and ask for help with her baby. She won't be home for another few days," he said.

"How long have I been out?"

"Only a few hours, but we already have to change the bandages again." His sympathetic face turned dark and angry. "If I ever get my hands on whoever did this, they will pay."

I sniffed, leaning further into my pillows. "Trust me. You should see the other guy."

Dad didn't laugh. "I'd ask you to tell me what happened, but I imagine your friends are curious to know, too. Want me to call Aaron—"

"No!" My eyes flashed mirror. Dad seemed taken aback, and I realized how sharply I had spoken. "We . . . we got into a fight after what happened. He's really upset at me. I don't blame him. It was my fault. Completely my fault. But . . . I think he broke up with me. It wouldn't be a good idea to let him know about this. I was leaving his house when it happened. Knowing him, he'll blame himself and he'll probably get worked up and change and make everything worse." Thinking about him made tears spring to my eyes. I blinked them away.

Jason and Coleman knocked and opened the door in one movement.

Jason smiled. "Hey! You're up!"

"Barely," I said.

"What happened?" Coleman asked.

"Um . . . Aaron dumped me. Morgan jumped me."

Jason put his hands up. "Wait. Aaron *dumped* you? That was not a part of the story I expected . . ."

Coleman scowled at him. "What he *means* to say is he's very sorry, and are you okay?"

"Okay?" I asked. "Not even sort of. Surviving? Sure. But I guess you want to know more about Morgan?"

"Tell us first, then we can clean up Morgan's grotesque approximation of body art," Coleman answered.

Jason's eyebrows furrowed, and he rubbed the shoulder with the dragon's head scar. He glanced at me apologetically.

Coleman looked between us and blushed. "Sorry. That . . . wasn't the most tactful bedside manner. What *happened?*"

I started my story but only got as far as summoning a sword when Coleman interrupted.

"Wait. You summoned a *sword?* Like, a legit I'm-going-to-cut-your-head-off sword?"

"Well, yeah."

"But . . . how?" He seemed at a loss for words. "You can't make something from nothing! You can create illusions and summon elements but a *whole entire sword?* Magicians stronger than me have *died* attempting that stuff. It can't be done!"

"It wasn't even that hard. I asked for a sharp practice sword. It just . . . happened. I didn't know it wasn't possible."

Jason frowned. "Even with the materials, it takes hours for skilled mage-smiths to make swords."

"I can do it again! Here. *Ma adamas chalybs haerent.*" That rough energy from before tugged at my gut as magic ran through my body. My head spun, but the sword materialized in my hands, heavy, solid, and sharp, just as before.

Jason stretched his hand forward and tested the edge of the blade on the side of his thumb. He jerked his hand back, blood welling up.

Coleman's jaw dropped. I passed him the sword, and he whistled. "How in *Tasalgré?*"

"I don't know!" I said. "Until two seconds ago, I didn't know this wasn't supposed to happen. Can I continue my story, please?"

He passed me the sword without a word. I dropped it off the bed and let it disappear before resuming.

I managed to finish this time without interruption, though it was not without obvious restraint from the others. "Okay. That's it. Questions, comments . . . death threats?"

Coleman raised his hand. "Question."

"Comment," Jason said.

Dad listed off streams of death threats under his breath. "Coleman?"

"You set her heart on fire?" he said, flashing a small smile.

A thousand atrocious puns about warming up her icy heart jumped to mind, but I pushed them back. "It was all I could think of." I shrugged then winced in pain. "Jason?"

"She used the paralyzing spell on me, too. I couldn't break it, no matter how much she pushed me. Remind me to never get you mad. You're terrifying."

Unsure how to respond, I shrugged again, though my cheeks burned. "I'm sorry, Jason."

"It's in the past. Just a bunch of scars now. I'm sorry, though. The next few weeks are going to *suck*. Coleman is able to dull the pain at least."

"I also have some ideas to try to work *around* whatever it is that blocks magic that might help speed up healing," Coleman added. "But I can't promise anything."

Dad picked up his first aid kit. "Coleman, work your magic. Then we'll set to work on cleaning it up again."

Coleman leaned forward. "Can I touch you?"

I nodded but still flinched as he pressed his fingers against my throat. His eyes flashed red, and he muttered a couple words. My vision flashed at the touch, much like Morgan's earlier, but instead of burning fire came cooling water, relieving more pain than I realized I had. "Whoa."

He nodded, his eyes sad. "Ready to see the damage or would you rather look away?" he asked, lifting the end of the wrap on my right elbow.

"I need to see it," I answered, determined to get it over with sooner than later.

He unwrapped the dressing. It wasn't too bad. Just swollen

and red around a thick gash. Someone had placed a butterfly bandage over the cut. I took a deep breath.

Dad put a towel under my arm and cleaned off the blood. After, he applied a topical antiseptic and a new bandage over it. He wound fresh wrappings around it, hiding the laceration from view once again.

The big one on my left arm took longer to unwrap. The bandages pulled in the places that had begun to scab over, causing me to hiss and blink back tears. I turned away, not wanting to see until they finished.

Jason whistled once they cleared the bandages. "She hit you with that lightning hard. You have a . . . What's it called when lightning leaves lightning-shaped welts?"

"Lichtenberg figure," Coleman answered quietly.

"Yes, that. You have a Lickin-thingy mark down your arm and across your chest. Those don't stay around for long, and we should be able to heal some of it, but she traced the larger branches with her knife."

I took a deep breath and looked down at my arm. It was bad, and I couldn't make sense of the twisting wounds. Frustrated and panicked, I stumbled out of bed to reach the mirror on my door and twisted to see it better.

Jason's dragon breathed the scars of real fire.

Mine spewed actual lightning.

The mark from the lightning strike left a terrible, branching tree fragmenting across my arm and torso. The ridges on my arm started just below my armpit and down to my elbow. The dark, lightning-shaped bruises then reached across my chest and down my back, disappearing beneath my sports bra, but reappeared across my stomach, running through my dragon and compass tattoo. The more lightning-esque branches on my arm had been cut open, and a dragon curled up my arm from a few inches below my elbow, snaking around the different lightning sections and up to my shoulder where its head curved. Its mouth opened around the base of the figure. The top half of the dragon had scales, spirals, and tiny designs, but from my elbow down, it was blank. A long, jagged line raced from just above my elbow to my deltoid, where her knife had dragged when I threw her off me.

It would have been beautiful if it hadn't been so graphic.

Someone had placed a few uneven stitches across some of the bigger gashes, blood trickled through a couple deeper regions that hadn't begun to scab yet, and my whole arm felt swollen. Staring at it though, I realized with horror that Morgan hadn't just been an artist.

She'd been a surgeon.

Every knife stroke had been made with precision. The more I looked, the more I realized Morgan had no intention of letting me die.

Not from this anyway.

My back itched, and my vision blurred. I tried to look at something else. Anything that wasn't a bleeding dragon on my arm, but that was all I saw. My breath came out in short gasps as my stomach churned.

"How do you do this, Jason?" I asked, trying to keep my voice even as tears streaked down my face. I lifted my less-damaged hand to my mouth, trying to muffle my hitching gasps of air.

"Do what? Cope?" he asked. "I don't. I shower in the dark to avoid seeing mine. I am a dragon with the body temperature of fire, and I wear long sleeves in one-hundred-degree weather because I am horrified. I've lived with mine for well over a decade, and I haven't figured it out yet. I'm not ashamed of the scars, but I'm afraid of the memories."

My dad tried to pull me into a hug while avoiding my arms. I lifted them up and wrapped them around his neck, letting his familiar, comforting scent fill me as I sobbed into his shoulder. "Dad, what am I going to do?"

"Right now," he answered, "we're going to clean it up. When it heals, you can decide if you'll let it show or if you're going to hide it. But we'll move past this. And if you get another chance to destroy this horrible woman, do it. But don't let revenge — or rage — consume you."

Promises to Keep

Coleman

Kat's front door closed behind us, and I pulled Jason along the side of the house and hid behind a pine tree.

He rubbed at the scars hidden under his sleeve. His face was a sickly gray, and his eyes were black. His breath came out in short gasps, and I worried he might collapse.

"Can I touch you?" I asked, reaching out.

He grasped my hands like a lifeline and nodded, his eyes far away.

I drew him closer, grabbed his shoulders, and looked up into his face. "Hey, hey, breathe," I said as calmly as possible. "You're not there anymore. You're here. With me."

He nodded, swallowing hard and blinking back tears. "I know, I know," he said. "I . . ."

I pulled him into a hug. His body was tense and burned with the fever of dragon fire, but I trusted his ability to stay human through this. He'd made it through Morgan's torture without changing; he could do it again now, no matter how real it felt.

I knew the memories that haunted him. They weren't the same ones that haunted me, but they were close enough. We'd both been in cells carved from stone. We'd both screamed until we couldn't anymore. We'd both clung to our humanity like it was the only thing that mattered.

"Can you still hear me?" I asked, my voice hoarse.

He nodded but didn't speak.

"Right now, I can feel the snow crunching under our feet, and the pine needles poking my back." His body released some of the tension as I spoke, so I kept rambling. "I can smell the tree too. The wind is gentle and cold. But *I'm* not cold. You're warm."

He broke down, crying into my shoulder. I held him as tight as I could, wishing I could ward off the waking nightmares. I rubbed circles into his back, slow and firm, trying to pull him back to me.

I wanted to assure him he was safe now, but Kat's still-bleeding wounds were proof that we *weren't*.

I let him cry and collect himself for as long as he needed. But my stomach twisted with anger and fear. Kat would be down for the count for who knows how long while the cuts healed. Aaron would need help, assuming he ever *talked* to us again, but he couldn't fight either.

We couldn't go after the kings yet, no matter how much Kat wanted to, but I had no doubt this wouldn't be their last attack.

And my watch sat heavy on my wrist, reminding me that a time *would* come when I'd be defenseless for sixty seconds — and that might as well be an eternity if it happened during a fight. I needed a way to protect the people I cared about, even if I didn't have magic.

Jason's tears stopped, but he still held me tight, letting his breathing settle.

"I have to tell you something," I whispered once his body temperature came down a little more. "Promise not to hate me?"

He pulled away and gave me a hard look. "You blew up a geyser to try to kill us, and I still couldn't hate you."

I flushed. "I told you about meeting Kroll and how they weren't very helpful, but they told me where to find Tythan and Hope," I said.

"I remember," he said.

"I didn't tell you . . . about the bet I lost."

His face softened. "Cole . . ."

"It didn't seem like a big deal at the time." It had seemed like my only choice at the time, but even then, it didn't seem *this* dire. Hindsight was cruel that way. "I told them they could have sixty seconds of my power at any time and without warning, so long as it reverted back to me exactly as it was." I'd not spoken the terms out loud since the casino. I cringed at my bad decisions. "I thought they'd use it in the next day or two or something, but it's been months, and they haven't used it yet. But the attacks keep getting worse, and I'm *terrified* it will happen during a fight. I'm scared I won't be able to protect you . . ." I swallowed down my guilt like a pill. I'd figure it out. *We'd* figure it out.

He looked up at the sky, lips pursed. "That . . . was not the smartest thing you've ever done."

"Well . . . rude," I muttered.

He laughed — oh *Tasalgre* he *laughed*. It was a dark laugh, but he somehow mustered the courage to laugh in the face of *everything*. "What are you going to do now?"

I thought for a minute. "Until Aaron and Kat are ready to

fight again, I think you and I need to keep a guard over them—"

"Oh, Kat will *hate* that."

"That's why we're not going to *tell* her," I said. "But because I don't know when I won't have my magic, I think I need to call Tythan and try to move up their timeline. Maybe if they can join our guard duty, I won't feel so helpless all the time."

He wiped his eyes and squinted at me. "I remember what happened last time I left Tythan alone with you."

I held up my hands, fending off the accusations. "Whoa. It was fine. We didn't get caught!"

"You burned down a building!"

"It was scheduled to be demolished *anyway*."

He let out the most long-suffering sigh I had ever heard. "Promise me no arson this time."

I huffed. "I won't make a promise I can't keep."

He smiled and started back to the car. "I guess that's the best I can ask."

I caught his hand. "I am going to find a way to keep us safe," I said. "I am going to find a way to keep *you* safe."

He opened his mouth.

I met his tear-stained gaze and raised my chin. "I promise."

SPICED CITRUS AND DRIED BLOOD

AARON

Breathe. Calm down. It's just calculus. Just an easy, little derivative. Don't change. Relax. The itching stopped, and when I opened my eyes, the world was back to my fuzzy, human vision.

I tried to return to my homework, but my pencil disintegrated into ash when I placed it on the paper. The paper itself had burn marks from my fingers.

I sighed and surveyed my room, taking in all the damage from my most recent power leak and trying to ignore the older damage. My lamp had fallen over, an old picture frame of my family had shattered, one of my light bulbs had exploded, and a poster on my wall had fallen off. The bottom half was burned and curled around itself.

"That was signed . . ." I complained, picking up the poster. I threw it in the trash with my other destroyed things before I slumped to the floor to lie on my stomach.

You could always call Jason and Coleman. Or Kat, an annoying voice said inside my head.

"Shut up and let me sulk and destroy stuff," I grumbled, the words muffled by the carpet pressed against my face.

Great. Now I'm talking to myself. Or maybe not. I didn't have my mind to myself as a dragon. If Kat was right, Aurakbahor could listen in at any time. *"Aurakbahor, if you're listening, at least pull your weight and help with my calculus."*

But even in jest, the thought that he was listening sent shivers down my spine. Ice squeaked around me, and I pulled my face out of the carpet. My room had turned into an ice rink.

Perfect. Exactly what I needed.

I heaved another sigh, and the ice evaporated. *Maybe I should call someone.*

My fingers pulled up Kat's contact. I froze, hovering over the call button.

Not Kat, I thought. *Anyone but Kat.* I couldn't face her yet.

I swallowed my pride and found Jason's number. Just before I hit call, my phone rang.

Jason.

I'm not saying it's some weird dragon mind connection thing, but it's definitely some weird dragon mind connection thing.

Or the fact that he'd called four times in the past two hours.

"Hey," I said.

"You answered!" he exclaimed.

"I need help. I basically only have an ugly Christmas sweater left undestroyed."

"Coleman and I will be over in a minute."

He left Kat out. Was it clear I didn't want her here? Or did *she* not want to be here?

A second light bulb exploded, plunging me into darkness. I groaned and buried my face in the carpet again.

My door opened a little later, and the light switch clicked twice. Coleman hissed something, and the room filled with light. I glanced up to find a glowing orb around my light fixture.

"Holy Tasalgré, Aaron," he said, taking in the damage.

"If you have any ideas on how to rein it in, that would be great. Also, tips on how to keep from changing every time I'm asked to use the chain rule in calculus would be nice."

Jason walked over and held out a hand to help me up. "It takes practice, but I'm impressed you haven't changed! It's been four days. I'm pretty sure I hadn't even figured out how to change *back* yet."

"I've never met anyone who has had this much control at first," Coleman added.

"This is great, guys," I said bitterly. "It's really beneficial and helping my feelings of being completely helpless and out of control a lot." The mirror on my closet door cracked.

"Whoa."

"Yeah. I may not have *changed*, but I have no control over anything."

"We get it. Trust me. I know how hard this is," Jason said. "But we can't undo it. So, are you going to keep exploding things in your room, or are you going to learn how to control it and come back to help us?"

"I'll get control, but I'm not coming back. I can't hurt you guys. I don't want Kat to get hurt."

"Too late—" Coleman started, but Jason jabbed him in the ribs.

"What is that supposed to mean?" I asked.

"Nothing. Coleman thinks it's super uncool that you won't come back. But it's up to you."

I glared. "Are you going to help or just pitch your cause?" I had no idea why I had become so rude since Friday, but I was bitter and tired, and restraining my tongue took too much effort.

"We'll help," Coleman replied.

"Let's get you a tether and then go outside to practice. We'll start with some nondestructive magic to expel instead of changing," Jason said.

"Just teach me something," I begged and accepted a hand up. I looked around my room, hoping to find something small and unbroken I could use as a tether, and my eyes landed on a small gray rock on the ground beside my desk.

I picked it up, feeling a twinge of guilt. Kat had given it to me all those months ago before I knew any of this. Maybe it was disrespectful to have it as my tether, but it posed as a reminder of what — *who* — I was fighting for.

I pocketed the rock without a word and led the others outside.

Once in my backyard, Coleman turned to me. "Yeah. Forget this nondestructive stuff." He put his hand out to stop Jason's protests. "Fire is easiest anyway. Let's blow stuff up."

I almost smiled. "Did you not see my room? I've been blowing stuff up for almost a week."

"Let's *intentionally* blow stuff up. The word for fire is *eathia*. Extinguish it with *gasić*. Go."

I did as he said, and flame danced across my fingers for a few seconds before disappearing.

"Great! Now . . ." He whispered something, and most of the snow in the yard piled itself into a decent-sized mound. "Blow it up."

I smiled and held my hand out. "*Eathia.*"

Fire and ice are a beautifully destructive duo. The fire melted the snow, and the water made the fire sizzle. But the fire raged stronger as the pile grew smaller. Soon, the pile melted completely.

"*Gasić*," I muttered, worried I'd set the yard ablaze. The fire obeyed my command. My head spun, but a weird, giddy thrill filled my veins. Things weren't ideal, but I *did* that.

"Why'd you have him take away winter?" Jason complained. "Winter isn't hot. Let's please teach something nondestructive."

"What do you have in mind?" Coleman asked.

"I don't know! Water or something."

"Oh, well then, by all means, teach him." He leaned toward me and mumbled, "You can still break stuff with enough water. Don't worry. It will be okay."

Jason looked at the sky for a moment. "Are you ready?"

I nodded, and Coleman backed away.

"Okay. Water is tricky, so you need to be more specific when you command it. It also takes more energy than fire, so using water to subvert the impulse to change will be stronger. We'll start with lifting water and redirecting it elsewhere, so you won't have to hold it for long. *Lefterni mizu* will lift that puddle you've just made and then you can use it to spray Coleman in the face."

"Wait!" Coleman's head snapped toward us. "No!"

I grinned. "*Lefterni mizu!*" The water lifted off the ground, snaked around my arm, and jumped off my fingers toward Coleman.

"*Ally key!*" Coleman shouted, crossing his arms in front of his face to create a shield of ice.

My knees shook, and I sank to the ground, exhausted and freezing.

His shield shattered against the ground as he raced to me. "This is why I started with fire!"

"Well . . ." Jason said, "on the bright side . . . he won't change for a couple hours!"

I used Jason's arm to pull myself to my feet. "Painful bright side," I complained.

"You'll get stronger," Coleman said. "I promise. But start with smaller bodies of water. Try keeping two bottles with you — one with water in it and one without. If you're close to changing, just redirect the water into the other bottle. It'll work the same, but you won't be so tired after."

"Thanks," I muttered and started back to the house.

"Get some food and water. Then take a nap!" Coleman called after me as I stumbled up the back steps to my house.

I waved over my shoulder, not bothering to say anything in reply.

My enhanced ears picked up Jason's voice as they left through the back gate. "Why didn't we teach Kat that trick?"

"You're the one who trained her," Coleman replied.

I closed the door, shutting out the rest of their conversation.

THE SCHOOL REOPENED TOO SOON. The hole in the ceiling was repaired, but everyone was subdued. Many students didn't come back at all. Despite the solemnity, Kat and I found ourselves minor celebrities. Word had spread that we were the missing students, but no one said anything about dragons.

The bell rang for classes to start, and I trudged down the hall, regretting that Jason, Coleman, Kat, and I coordinated our class schedule. Even worse, we sat next to each other.

Kat sat on my right in calculus. She pretended I didn't exist while I tried to ignore the bloody bandage poking out the bottom of her sleeves. I tried not to notice how she smelled like cinnamon and citrus and dried blood.

I played with my rock and water bottles as subtly as possible.

Putting Out Fires

Coleman

I sat in the branches of a tree at the edge of Kat's front yard. Dark clouds rolled overhead, threatening rain — maybe snow — but for now, it was dry. I had her grandma's book propped open in a forked branch just ahead of me, and I carefully braided stamped strips of leather together while I attempted to decipher the ever-shifting text. I thought I'd caught something earlier in the book about some Council or other, and I still hadn't forgotten Aurakbahor's avoidance of the term after I'd met Kroll. I'd been able to find mentions of other magics and was hoping I could find out more, but the book was like trying to catch a butterfly — the more I chased it, the harder it became to catch.

But when I held still, sometimes I could catch another word or two. *Curse. King. Pact. Ancients. Mages.* None of the words I caught meant anything to me in isolation, so I worked on the bracelets while I waited for the book to trust me with more.

If I'd done the enchantments on the bracelets correctly,

they *should* be able to block a sneak attack, giving us more of a chance against the kings. Maybe if we'd had these already, Jason wouldn't have been hit with that curse at New Years. Maybe Kat wouldn't have been tortured by Morgan in the woods.

Maybe now I could keep my promise to protect my friends.

I'd been trying to add a way to enchant longer-lasting armor into them. I hadn't had much luck yet, but I wasn't going to stop just because it was hard.

Maybe we wouldn't have to be so scared while we took turns guarding Kat and Aaron.

It'd only been a couple weeks since the assembly, but so far, Jason and I had managed to fend off over a dozen minor attacks as Aurakbahor sent his followers to test our defenses.

So far, those defenses were just Jason, me, and some magic walls up around both neighborhoods that warned us of magic users entering the area. Tythan had only confirmed that they were coming, but they hadn't shown up yet.

I muttered frustrated incantations under my breath, weaving silvery-blue threads of Tasalgré in with the leather plait.

Something tugged at my magic — the warning sign that someone had crossed my wall. I sighed, setting aside the leather strips and drawing my sword.

I dropped from the tree, hissing out another ward to shield the potential fight from sight and to protect the rest of the neighborhood from any stray curses. I stalked off in the direction of the warning.

But another tug came from behind me.

And another to my left.

My heart quickened. This was more coordinated than usual.

My racing heart skid to an abrupt halt when a figure in a black cloak and a beaked mask stepped onto the street.

I reached for my phone, hoping to signal a quick SOS to Jason, but my pocket was empty.

Maybe it's for the best that he doesn't come...

"Any chance you're here to surrender?" I asked the Knight as she approached.

I only managed to narrowly dodge the cracking orange spear hurdled at me in reply.

"Well, I gave you a chance..." I muttered. My chest burned with the icy fire of Dragonstongue as I called on my magic, wrapping the threads around my chest, my arms, and my legs. I hadn't yet figured out how to enchant the leather with this armor, but I'd gotten pretty good at summoning it on my own.

Too bad one day I might not have the magic to call for it.

I pushed the magic down my arm and out through my sword and charged forward. Lightning flashed from the blade, but the first Knight rolled underneath it and jumped to her feet. Her blade met mine hard enough to rattle my teeth.

The others would be close behind, but for now, it was one-on-one.

And that was all I needed.

Our clashing blades echoed through the empty street. The masks were supposed to help guard against projecting their next moves, but I'd trained with the Knights since I was big enough to hold a knife. I knew what to expect.

She swung her blade with a flourish, and I ducked under the hex I knew would come next and met it with my own. She caught my spell with her cloak, not missing a beat.

"Think we could speed this up before your buddies get here?" I asked.

She snarled. I caught a blow against my armor and decided to fight dirty.

I summoned the winds, letting them howl around us, then directed them to pull the assassin into the sky. She screamed, flailing upward. A roaring gust of wind pushed her into the distance.

She'd be fine. But she was no longer my problem.

The other Knights had arrived.

Two-on-one wasn't my worst odds.

The taller one on the right set the street on fire.

I let the flames dance around me, pulling them toward me, twisting them around my body, and coaxing the flames to obey *me*.

"Aww, all this for me?" I asked, putting a hand to my chest as the fire draped itself off my shoulders. I smiled as it harmlessly licked at my armor before I threw it back at the Knight.

His cloak caught fire, and he screamed, spinning and trying to put out the flames encircling him.

"Sorry!" I yelled. "It wasn't my size! It looks good on you though!"

The other Knight put out the fire with a hissed command, drew a bow, and shot an arrow in my direction.

I threw up a shield. The arrow shattered against it. The slightly crispy Knight charged forward. Green, ropey magic curled around his arms and extended out his hands, forming thick vines with massive, lethal-looking thorns.

He whipped it against my shield, and it curled around the magic barrier. I jumped back, but a vine cut across my cheek, narrowly missing my eye. I hissed and dropped the shield and my sword but grabbed hold of the vines and pulled the Knight into my welcoming knee.

He gasped and buckled over involuntarily, so I drove my knee into his face for good measure. His buddy lifted their bow again. I grabbed the vine-Knight by the shoulders and shoved him in the path of the arrow.

He screamed and dropped to the ground, back arching around the arrow.

My ward around the neighborhood sent two more tugs. "Papa Aurak really sent five of you after me? I'm flattered!"

"What?" the archer asked.

It was always great to get them to crack in combat, but I wasn't expecting confusion. "*Oh*," I said. "So, he sent backup because he didn't *trust* you. Neat."

I kicked my sword back to my hand with a flick of my foot and leaped over the fallen Knight.

The archer dropped his bow and fumbled for the knives at his side as he spat out a spell.

I skidded to a stop to avoid the sudden wall of thick smoke between us. My stomach churned in fear for just a moment thinking it might be a death wall, but the smoke moved and rippled and the dark mists of a death wall wouldn't.

I made a mental note to teach Kat and Aaron about that particular piece of cruelty and slashed my sword through the smoke, stirring the air enough to break up the thick plume. It dispersed but the assassin was gone.

The ashen remains of a set of transport beads dispersed on the wind.

Cowards. All of them.

My armor shattered, pain exploded at my side, and the tip of a blade emerged from the front of my stomach, just above my hip.

I screamed and summoned a shockwave to push my attacker away.

The skewered and roasted assassin rolled as my wave knocked him back.

With trembling fingers, I pulled the dagger out of my back and advanced on the assassin. Each step sent a wave of agony ripping up my side, and the blood poured hot and thick from the wound, even as I pushed a healing spell into it. My Dragonstongue began to slip as I put all my focus on reaching the assassin, and my vision turned blue.

The Knight scrambled to get away from me. His mouth twisted in fear beneath the mask as I approached.

I'm sure I looked like quite the nightmare.

Good.

I caught a fistful of his cloak and pulled him toward me.

He screamed as I pushed his own dagger into his stomach. I brought my bloodstained and Dragonstongue-streaked face close to his, driving the dagger deeper. "Tell my father I send my regards."

He fumbled for his own set of transport beads and disappeared.

I stood, panting through the pain shooting through my body with every heartbeat and blinking back the blackness that consumed my vision.

Through my graying vision, a tall figure with long, dark hair approached, and for just a moment, I thought it was Jason.

But I managed to fight back the wave of dizziness, and my vision cleared.

"You look disappointed to see me," Tythan said, taking in my bloodied form.

"You could really work on your timing," I said, but another wave of dizziness rocked me to my core. "Now, if you'll excuse me . . . I think I'm gonna . . ." My eyes rolled back, and Tythan caught me, grumbling about having to save my sorry butt while they set to healing me.

"You're . . . late," I slurred as they finished healing my stomach. My head immediately began to clear as the bleeding stopped.

They healed my cheek and helped me to my feet.

"I felt two people cross my wall," I said, leaning on them

for support. The wounds were healed, but there was only so much that could be done for a Dragonstongue flare-up like this. "Any chance Hope's with you and not another assassin."

They nodded. "Yeah. Hope's here." They gestured back toward the tree I'd been working in where Hope waved from up in the branches. "I don't want her fighting, Coleman."

"I know," I said. "I don't want her involved either."

"Good. So long as we're on the same page, I'm here to help. She's just here to learn."

Hope swung out of the tree and approached us. "No," she said, crossing her arms. "Tythan doesn't even *want* to be here. *I'm* here to help."

Tythan and Hope

Kat

Jason wasn't at practice.

I checked my phone to verify I was supposed to meet him at the rec center today. I had healed enough over the last month or so that I could start training again, but considering Aaron wanted nothing to do with me, we had to trade who trained where and with whom. According to my calendar, Jason was supposed to be here.

I traced my locket against my lips, trying to remain calm, and I called him.

Voicemail.

I paced, reassuring myself that Jason was fine. My scars still throbbed even though weeks had passed — a sore reminder of the danger we still faced.

As my heart pounded against my rib cage, I snatched my bag off the floor and stalked out to the car. *If he just overslept, I'm going to murder him for the heart attack he's giving me.*

I drove to my grandma's old house and threw the door

open without knocking. I called out for him, my voice echoing around the house.

A little girl with curly black hair and dark brown skin poked her head over the banister and darted away.

Coleman and Jason both walked down the stairs a moment later and froze, looking surprised to see me.

"Oh! Kat!" Jason said. "We were just getting ready to leave."

A tall, thin person with red-tipped black hair, a black leather jacket, and fingerless gloves trailed behind them. The little girl followed, clinging to the new person's pant leg. Their gloved hand rested protectively on her shoulder.

"Who are they?" I asked, gesturing at the newcomers.

"Tythan and Hope!" Coleman said as he walked past me and headed toward the kitchen.

My stomach sank. "In light of recent events, I didn't think we'd, you know, muster the troops."

We hadn't planned our attack or talked about gathering the resistance in weeks. I hadn't planned anything either since Aurakbahor would know my old plans through Aaron by now. We trained, but we were just going through the motions. We'd lost. I was trying to prolong the finale.

"They actually got here a while ago," Jason answered, rubbing the back of his neck like he was embarrassed.

"Why didn't you say something?" I asked, hurt.

"Because, like you said, in light of recent events..."

"Right..."

"Anyway. Meet Tythan. They're the best pyrokinetic we have."

"You say that?" I scoffed. "After meeting me? Rude." Rude but also intriguing. I wondered how good they actually were. And if they'd give us an edge against the kings.

"I wouldn't say it if I didn't think it was true," Jason said, a warning in his voice. "I wouldn't challenge them."

I laughed as an idea struck me. "Too late. Tythan, you and I are going to have a fire fight."

"Deal," Tythan said, fire dancing across their fingertips.

Jason jumped between us. "Whoa! Whoa! Let's finish introductions first, and you can try to deep fry each other later — *preferably outside*. Tythan, meet Kat."

Tythan inclined their head with a small smirk. "Pleasure."

"You too," I replied. I knelt to be on the same level as the little girl who couldn't be older than five or six. "Hey."

She peered out from behind Tythan's leg.

"Are you Hope?" I asked.

She nodded.

"Good to meet you, Hope."

Her dark eyes avoided mine. I stood to talk to Jason, but she pulled on my sleeve and motioned for me to come closer, so I bent next to her again.

She put her lips against my ear. "I can't fly."

Stunned, I asked, "Why not?"

"Balaskad took my wing. But I'm *really* good at magic." She rushed through the last bit like she had to prove she was still useful. Her eyes searched my face, begging me to accept her anyway.

My throat went dry, but my will to fight came back. This wasn't over yet. "We're going to stop her. I promise."

She grinned. "Tythan says the same thing."

I stood. "All right, Tythan. Jason says you're good with fire. Let's see how true that is." *And maybe conjure up some hope for the resistance.*

They started toward the yard. Jason pressed his hand against his face in disappointment as I followed.

I stopped in the middle of the backyard, feet shoulder

width apart. *"Ally eathia!"* A semicircle of fire ten feet tall roared around me. A cloak of flame trailed off my shoulders, and fire encased my hands.

I smiled smugly. "Your move."

A massive explosion behind Tythan formed into giant wings of flame coming out of their back that stretched out across the yard and up toward the sky.

"Holy..."

They pressed their wings forward, lifting their whole body off the ground. The hot blast of wind extinguished the flames around me.

"You win!" I squeaked.

Their wings folded in and disappeared. They dropped the last few feet to the ground, landed in a crouch, and straightened up, unsmiling. "Nice cape."

"N-nice wings," I stammered.

Jason jumped over the porch railing and walked toward us, shrugging. "I told you, Kat."

I stuck my tongue out at him.

Hope ran over to Tythan, grinning. "Your wings are really pretty!"

Their face paled, and they turned on their heel, stalking back to the house without a word.

"What—" I started to ask, but Hope's face fell, and tears welled up in her eyes.

Jason rushed forward and pulled her into his arms as her lip quivered.

I stalked after Tythan, ignoring Jason telling me to wait. I slid through the back door just before it closed and grabbed Tythan's hand. "What was that?" I asked, my voice low.

They looked shocked that I would confront them, but their face hardened defensively, and they jerked their hand away from me. "Why would you care?"

"Because you just blew off a kid when she tried to compliment you, and now she is *crying*."

"She is *my* little kid," they said. "You don't know anything about either of us, so I don't know why you think you have any right to question me, but since you *have*, I'm trying to make sure I don't do more harm than I already did."

My face twisted in confused disgust. "You hadn't *done* any harm."

They crossed their arms across their chest. Their eyes flashed to their dragon eyes — one black and one blood red. "I didn't?" they asked, arching an eyebrow. "Because you know us *so* well, and you know what does and doesn't cause harm? Tell me, *Kat*. What did Hope tell you *just* before we went outside?"

"What do—"

"She told you Balaskad took one of her wings, and then — in the heat of the moment," — they paused, their hands curling into claws — "I summoned *the very thing that was stolen from her*. You've never heard her cry out in her sleep. Never seen her tears as she relives one of the most traumatic things a dragon can endure."

I took a step back, and my stomach sank. "Oh, Tasalgré..."

They raised an eyebrow. "You see?"

I tossed my hands up, exasperated. "You still let your emotions control you. You could have apologized, but instead, you hurt the person you cared about even more."

Jason poked his head in, carrying a sleeping Hope against his chest. "Um, I don't mean to interrupt... whatever this is."

"It's fine," Tythan said and stomped up the stairs.

Jason eyed me like *I* was the one at fault, but he just carried Hope to the old guest room that used to be my room when I'd stay over as a kid. He reemerged a little later and gestured for me to lead the way to my car.

"Tythan would jump in front of a bullet for her, you know," he said softly as we started to drive to the rec center. "But . . . they're not quick to forgive *themself* if they hurt her."

"But they assumed they hurt her, then hurt her *worse*."

"Tythan has their own things too. The rule of the kings has not been pleasant to many, as you know. *You* know how hard it is to control your emotions as a Rhaegynne. It's even harder when you're trying to resist the mind control. Now imagine you're on your own *and* you're responsible for keeping a child alive who's been through so much, and well . . . it's hard to be the person you used to be. They shouldn't have been so harsh, but don't take this out on Tythan. We need them."

"Hope too?" I asked. "She's a kid."

"So are you," Jason said.

"I'll be an adult this summer," I said. "And it's *different*."

He nodded. "It is. And don't worry. We won't let her anywhere near any fighting. She's here to learn."

I sighed. "I'm not ready for the fighting to start again. I want this over as soon as possible, but I . . . I'm not ready. Those two can stay, but let's . . . let's wait before we try to find others. How many are we anyway?"

"Umm . . . we have . . . a decent amount," he replied, turning to look out the window.

"Which is how many?" I pressed.

"Including Coleman, Tythan, Hope, Aaron, you, and me?"

"Sure."

"Well . . . that's about it."

"*What?*"

"We were bigger a few years ago! But people got captured or killed, and Jamie got sick, and a lot of people got scared, and . . . it was only Coleman and me stubborn enough to stay. That's why it's taken so long to contact everyone. They're all afraid and hiding or dead. Everyone *wants* us to win. There are only a few of us willing to die to make it happen."

My blood ran cold. We were dead before we even started. What was even the point of Coleman trying to find others if this was all that was left in the first place? "How common are Rhaegynne?"

"One in a million."

"So, worldwide, there's eight *thousand* Rhaegynne. And all but *six* want to kill us?"

"Well," Jason said, his voice still light like he didn't understand how upsetting these statistics were, "considering we're resisting, I'd say we're trying to kill us too—"

"*Jason!*"

"Sorry! No, most are just trying to live their own lives. And we have twenty to thirty members possibly still alive in prisons on either side. The rest are distracted with trying to kill each other under their king's commands, so they're not *all* out to kill us *specifically*."

"How comforting."

"But hey! You combine two royal clan lines, so that's got to count for something!"

We're so screwed.

The Floor is Lava and the Walls are Alive

Aaron

I leaned against the hood of my new silver sedan — at least that part wasn't a trick — in the driveway of our practice field. Coleman usually got there before me, but I was alone.

Ten minutes passed. I checked my phone. No missed calls. Was training canceled? Did something happen? My insides twisted. Was I at the wrong place? Did I do something to make the others leave me?

I checked down the road and saw nothing. I stood and opened the door, ready to leave. Before I could even climb in, another car sounded about a block away. *Curse these dragon ears! And eyes and nose and body while we're on the subject.*

I closed the door as Coleman's car appeared around the bend and pulled up next to me. He parked, and three doors opened. My heart stopped in fear — hope — that it would be Kat and Jason. Instead, someone with red and black hair climbed out of the front passenger seat, and a little girl with dark, curly hair slid yawning out the back.

"Who's this, Coleman?" I asked.

"This is Tythan. They're going to help add some . . . *fire power* to our side. And this is Hope. She's probably going to save us all to be honest. Kat wanted to train with them, but she and Jason left without them, so here we are."

"Why'd they leave them?"

Tythan raised their leather-clad hand. "She and I had a bit of a fight."

My hands itched, my vision sharpened, and I reached for the rock in my pocket, automatically siding with Kat.

They took a startled step back. Fire caught in their palms.

"Is she okay?" My voice came out in a choked snarl.

Their eyes widened. "She's fine. We had a bit of a show-off competition, then some other stuff happened, but she's unharmed."

My body relaxed, but my draconic eyes remained. "Show-off competition?"

"She didn't believe Jason when he said I'm the best pyro this side of the war," they said proudly.

"It's a claim I don't believe either," Coleman added. "I'm better than Kat. Just because you beat her doesn't mean you're the best."

They gave a sly, crooked smile. "I'm game for another round. Let's go."

"Bring it."

"Take it over there," I said, shoving them away from my new car.

Coleman laughed and led the way to the field. They set up several dozen yards apart.

"What are the rules?" Coleman called.

"Anything goes as long as it's fire. No maiming, I guess," Tythan said, sounding bored.

"But maiming is fun!"

"Whenever you're ready."

Coleman shot three large balls of fire into the air and juggled them.

"Starting out easy?" they called.

"Do you have something better?" he asked, throwing a fourth fireball into the air.

Tythan inhaled deeply before spewing a thick tongue of white-hot fire into the sky.

"We are *dragons,* and you decide to breathe *fire?*"

I turned away from them, rolling my eyes.

The girl gave me a strange look. "Why do you care so much about Kat? Do you have a crush on her?"

I flushed, and she giggled.

"You *do* have a crush on her!" she cheered. "Why aren't you with her then if you like her so much?"

"She's . . . mad at me," I confessed.

"She's mad at Tythan, too!" she said gleefully. "What did you do? Why not apologize?"

I blinked. "Uh, after I got changed, I told her to stay away from me, so I didn't hurt her."

"Tythan's always trying to protect me. But they forget I can breathe fire!" She let out a massive breath of fire just to prove her point.

I shifted uncomfortably. Kat could breathe fire, too. Maybe she didn't need as much protecting as I thought she did either.

"Do you want help learning to control it?" Hope asked, watching me with suddenly somber eyes. "I've had a lot of practice, I could help."

I raised my eyebrow. "How old are you?"

"Six. But I'm *almost* seven!"

"How *long* have you been Rhaegynne?"

"A couple years."

My stomach sank. "How?"

"It was an accident. But I've gotten really good at not changing. It hurts me differently."

"What do you mean?"

"I don't have a lot of practice as a dragon, but I do with magic. Wanna see?" She turned, figuratively and literally avoiding my question, and ran toward the barn.

I trotted after her but got distracted by the battle raging in the field. Both magicians hovered in the air, supported by jets of fire shooting out of their hands and feet like rockets. Coleman wore a flaming crown, and Tythan wore a cloak of fire billowing out behind them.

I wandered over to the barn, mesmerized by the skill each Rhaegynne utilized. Once in the doorway, I froze, mouth falling open.

In the barn, Hope climbed on a playset made of vines. Each one writhed, springing from the wood paneling on the floors and walls. A wet, earthy scent filled the room.

"Where did this come from?" I gasped.

"I made it," she said, leaping from a vine near the ceiling. Vines shot out of the walls and caught her halfway down.

"How long did it take you?"

Her vines turned into a ladder, then turned sideways into a set of monkey bars. "Um . . . Not very long."

"When did you start?"

"When you didn't follow me."

I looked around again, taking in the magnitude and complexity of her playground. Each vine came to life as she approached it, seeming to bend and shape to her will. I glanced back at the fiery silhouettes outside. I had been amazed by their skill earlier, but Hope's legitimate child's play made their magic competition seem childish. "Nice job," I managed.

"It wasn't hard. Do you want to hear a joke?"

"Sure," I said, taking a step over the threshold.

She screamed, and I jumped back, calling fire to my fingertips as I spun around to face whatever threat she saw. But nothing was there.

My flames died, and I turned back to her. "What's wrong?"

"The floor is lava! You almost died."

"Oh, um . . ." I searched the room to find something to jump on, but everything was just out of reach. *Was this the joke or . . .*

She laughed. "Use magic, silly!"

"I don't—"

She clapped her hands, and the floorboards came alive with vines shooting out and grasping for each other. Branches and leaves grew out of the ceiling and walls. When the floor stopped moving, small platforms, ropes, and ladders provided pathways throughout the room.

"I'll only help you this once!" she warned.

"Where were you when I used to play this game as a kid?" I muttered, shocked.

"Not born yet. Come and get me!" She squealed and jumped onto a ledge. Her monkey bars dissolved and reformed into a series of hanging rings behind her.

I reached for a hanging vine. It felt *alive*. I expected something fabricated like the practice swords, but these were very real. I tested its strength and swung to the closest platform. Hope reached for a vine and swung across the hanging rings.

I jumped and swung over to her as fast as I could. I made it to a point where I could grab her feet, but she turned upside down and pulled herself on top of the bars of the playground. The ring closest to me disappeared as I reached for it.

"That's cheating!"

"We didn't make any rules!" She giggled, scampering across the bars. She disappeared into the leaves.

I stood on my isolated branch podium, defeated. "What is this supposed to teach?" I asked.

Her head popped out of the branches above me. "To have fun!" she declared and disappeared again.

The leaves around the room rustled, making it impossible to track her movements. I sighed and leaped for the remaining ring to reach the other side of the room, but my hand slipped on the last bar. My feet hit the ground with a thud.

The vines around the room recoiled from my feet, retracting back into the walls. Hope landed next to me, laughing.

"You lose!" Hope said. "Good game, though!"

"Well, what if I had on lava-proof shoes?"

She squinted up at me, then down at my shoes. "You don't."

"Oh. Okay. Will you teach me magic or how not to change please?"

Her face fell. "I guess so." She grabbed my hand and pulled me back outside. "Let's play with ice," she suggested.

"Uh, sure."

She spoke a million miles an hour on how to summon and shape ice in an intricate explanation that didn't quite match her age. I caught maybe four words. She stopped talking and smiled at me like it was the easiest thing in the world. "You try!"

I sat and used a couple of the words I thought she had said. I'd gotten pretty good with water and fire, but new stuff still intimidated me. So, when I summoned a small disc of ice on the first try, I proudly turned to show her, but she was busy running in a giant circle, throwing ice at random.

Light danced off the small disc. I frowned and decided to not be shown up yet again by a six-year-old, no matter how skilled she might be.

Desperate for inspiration, I looked to the field for Coleman, but their battle still raged. Tythan had encased themself in a four-story-tall dragon avatar. They laid siege to Coleman's massive palace of fire. Six-foot tall knights in flaming armor broke off from the fortress and threw javelins at the dragon. Ballistae shot massive fireballs, and little archers from the highest turret loosed arrows and set fire to the ground around the dragon.

I sighed in resignation, tapped my pathetic disc against my thigh and made two more. I put them together and laughed. "Look, Hope! It's a snowman — Holy Tasalgré."

Hope was perched in the frozen crow's nest of a full-scale pirate ship. She watched me through a telescope of ice. "Good job!" she shouted down and gave me a thumbs-up.

"How on earth . . ." I shook my head and let my ice shatter against the ground.

An explosion, a roar of pain, and a blast of heat split the air. I spun to find Tythan's dragon lying on the ground while Coleman's minions kicked the beast repeatedly.

"Hope, I'm going to go . . . help," I called up to her.

She nodded and pulled herself out of the crow's nest.

"Enough!" I shouted, running to them.

The fires extinguished themselves, and both Rhaegynne slumped to the ground.

"I think I'll have to call Coleman the winner on this one, Tythan. Sorry."

Coleman's hand pumped the air weakly from the ground. "Champion!"

Tythan only let out a halfhearted moan.

"Let's not do this anymore, please?" I begged.

Coleman smiled, a strange glint in his eyes. "I will promise to refrain from challenging other skilled magicians to petty competitions if you promise to come back to training with Kat."

Hope snuck her cold hand into my own. She wiggled her eyebrows knowingly when I looked down at her. Glancing at the scorched field and the small heap of exhausted pyromaniacs, I swallowed my aching pride. It would've been better to have Kat and Jason here to prevent this.

I took a breath, my eyes changing and my heart racing at the prospect of even *talking* with Kat again. "I'll come back," I said. "But I want one of those dragon and compass tattoos."

I'd joined the resistance to help Kat.

But it was personal now.

And I was ready to make Aurakbahor pay for what he'd done to me.

Scars and Death

Kat

"No! Absolutely not!" I protested while we left the rec center. Jason still had his phone with the message from Coleman displayed on his screen.

"I thought you'd be excited for Aaron to come back!"

"It's been two *months*, Jason! He hasn't even talked to me outside of classes. I'm past sad. I'm past hurt. I am *furious*. Why now of all times?"

"We need the whole team together. Besides, you're nowhere near as focused since he left."

"Are you *suggesting* I need a *man* to make me *better*?" My left shoulder itched, and my vision shifted. Magic lifted my hair off my back. I glanced down at my hands, half-surprised to find my entire body glowing with energy.

Jason stumbled backward. "N-no! Not at all! You've been distracted and depressed. It has nothing to do with him being your *boy*friend but because he was your *friend*."

"Key word there: *was*."

He put his hands up. "I get it! Trust me, I do! But we need everyone together again."

"*Fine.*"

Jason's eyes scanned my face, trying to find some answer I didn't have. "One practice, okay? You can leave if it gets bad."

Pulling a jacket over my tank top, I ran out the door, carrying my shoes with me. My heart pounded thinking of all the different ways Jason could and would kill me for being so late to practice. It was the first day of spring break, and he'd wanted to start early. *I* had wanted to sleep in.

But . . . maybe not as much as I had.

I sped most of the way there and screeched to a stop in the driveway. Shoes half on, I jumped out of the car and ran. Jason, Tythan, and Aaron were running fencing drills while Coleman and Hope sat quietly in a circle of blue light.

I finished tying my shoes, summoned my sword, and jumped into the drills.

"Nice of you to join us, Kat," Jason chided.

"I overslept! I'm sorry!" I replied, still panting from my run.

The corner of his lip twitched before he pressed them together. "Well then. That will be three laps around the entire property."

I dropped my sword but jogged over to the fence.

"Hey, Kat?" Jason called.

I flinched and turned. "Yes?"

"Run."

I ran hard around the property without verbal complaint, but I contemplated several death threats as I completed each lap.

They finished drills and switched groups before I finished. Hope practiced martial arts with Jason while Coleman and Tythan helped Aaron with magic. I returned to Jason's station.

He hardly looked up from correcting Hope's form when I walked over. "Practice with Tythan. Good luck."

Tythan glanced up in surprise as I approached.

"Hey, fight me," I said. My sword materialized by my side, solid and heavy.

"All right." They picked up a nearby sword and led me away from the rest of the group.

"Do we want magic and punching this round or just swords?" I asked.

"No magic, though I'm game for it turning into a fistfight."

"Deal." I lifted my sword moments before they did.

They danced to their right, trying to reach for my less dominant side, but I skipped out of range, then ducked and moved closer. Tythan stepped back gracefully. I feigned forward, but they barely reacted. Both of us stood poised with our swords pointed at the other's throat. I tried to read their body to predict where they would go, but every muscle was relaxed and revealed nothing. Even stalking each other, not a single twitch revealed their intentions. But their face betrayed a faint irritation that I hoped meant they couldn't get a read on me either.

Bored of our study, I lunged forward, plunging my sword straight in. Faster than lightning, their blade met mine with a metallic clang, and we fell into our deadly dance.

It was good to fight someone new. I had become accustomed to Jason's and Coleman's personal flares. They were elegant, but their tiny flourishes made it easy to catch them off guard. Tythan was all attack and power. They were graceful, but it wasn't beautiful. They fought with the speed and agility of a knife fighter and the brute strength of an ax wielder.

I found myself out of breath much earlier than I ever would with Jason. Luckily, Tythan was panting too. I caught their blade in my cross guard, and they stepped in, locking our hilts together.

Their foot swung behind them before planting into the ground and jerking our swords downward. I sucked in a breath of fear as their blade dropped only a few inches from my face.

I yanked my sword up and out, freeing my blade and regaining control in time to parry. I turned with the momentum, spinning to try to land the elbow of my sword arm into their chest. They dodged but walked straight into my chambered free arm.

Somewhere in the fight, we both lost our swords, and our match devolved into a fistfight. I managed to wrap a foot around Tythan's leg and pull it out from under them. They fell but caught hold of me and pulled me down too. They wrapped their arms around my neck in a chokehold I couldn't break. I struggled and thrashed but had to tap out when spots danced in my eyes. They let go, and I rolled off them, massaging my throat.

"Where did you learn to fight like that?" I asked after catching my breath.

They shrugged. "I've been around."

"Around *where?*"

They laughed darkly. "Well, that's a story for another time."

I changed the subject. "What's your dragon name?"

They seemed irritated by my questions. "Why? Aren't you supposed to free us before you'd ever have a chance to meet that version of me?"

"Jason made it sound important that I know his dragon name is Aerolan, and Coleman is Sa'hranet," I said with a shrug.

They clenched their jaw but answered anyway. "Rorivan. What about yours?"

"I never picked one."

"A dragon named Kat? Do you have whiskers, too?"

I rolled my eyes. "Very funny."

A branch snapped behind me, and we both turned. The others had finished their drills and were headed toward us.

"Nice fight," Jason said.

"Thanks," I answered. Tythan grunted.

Coleman pursed his lips. "Kat, you should have a dragon name."

"Why? I'm still me."

"We don't know what will happen if you take a throne before the curse breaks."

"Let's say I figure out the curse first, or we worry about that when it happens," I suggested, uncomfortable about the idea.

Jason broke in. "It's good to have something picked out now, just so you can get used to it. Aaron, you should pick a name too."

"I've kind of already thought of one," he admitted. "Something like Aryxon or something. I dunno. I like it. It's close enough to Aaron to not be hard to get used to, but strange enough to not be linked to me."

"That works! Kat?" Coleman said.

"Can I still wait on this?" I asked.

"Of course."

"Thanks," I said, weirdly embarrassed. "Do you have a dragon name, Hope?"

"Maxyre."

"That's beautiful," I said.

"Thank you," she whispered, staring at the ground.

Tythan glared at Jason. "Is there a reason you all came over, or were dragon names this important?"

"Nah. I have a magic lesson for today. I wanted to share with everyone," Coleman replied.

"Well, by all means," Tythan answered, motioning with a gloved hand for them to take a seat.

Coleman's eyes darted to Hope. "Hey, Jason? Take Hope away," he said softly and passed him something I couldn't make out.

"Hope!" Jason beamed, pocketing the item. "Let's go play with knives, okay?"

Her face broke into a grin before she bolted to the target and knife set by the barn.

"Why'd you send her away?" Aaron asked.

"I'm going to teach you about death curses. It's not age appropriate."

"How do you expect us to practice this?" I asked.

"I guess I'm not so much going to teach you *how* to kill. More like teach you how to *avoid* being killed by one."

"That's helpful," Tythan commented dryly.

Coleman shot them a glare. "Anyway, there are plenty of spells that *can* kill. Kat's already found out about turning blood to fire and how dangerous that can be, and we know things like the Assassin's Leech can siphon off life until nothing's left. But only a few spells can *guarantee* death — can *demand* death. The Tasalgric command for death is *dumort*. All the killing spells I know use some variation of that word. Common ways are *dumort mizu* and *dumort aira*. It's easy to poison most basic elements. You can poison the ground, but due to its density, it's more difficult to curse a large area. You can also just touch someone and speak the command for death, but that requires convincing the living thing to die, which is much harder than convincing the elements to kill for you." He shrugged. "Nature is neutral about death and can be easily convinced. Living things don't like to die.

"If encountering this sort of curse, the most effective way to counter it — though it can only be countered in the first few moments — is with the word for life: *vito*. It's not going to bring back the dead, but it can stop death before it arrives."

I raised my hand. "Can you use *ally* at the end to make a wall of death? Or at the beginning to kill several things at once?"

Tythan's mouth curled in disgust like they couldn't believe I'd think of something so macabre.

Coleman frowned. "Killing everything in an area is theoretically possible, but the spell would likely fail to discriminate between the target and the caster. And there's a chance it wouldn't be strong enough to do more than knock a bunch of people unconscious for a few minutes. As for the death wall ... It's a thing. It's what I wanted to talk to you about it."

"What?" I asked.

"Yeah. Aurakbahor likes it. It creates a dome-shaped shield over the caster that's got this ... misty, glowing darkness to it."

His description stirred at a memory I couldn't place, almost like a strange sense of déjà vu.

"It does have limitations," Coleman continued. "It can't be broken unless a living creature passes through it or the caster drops it. It only has one 'hit,' so using it as a shield in the middle of a big battle wouldn't be very effective. It can, however, block spells while letting the caster's spells go out. So, if you're cornered, it's not the worst tactical move you could make, but I still wouldn't recommend it. You can't hold the wall forever, and if you fall from exhaustion, it goes with you."

"Could you use *vito ally* and just plow through it?" Aaron asked.

He shook his head. "No one's survived trying. Your best bet is to hide until they drop the wall. I mean, maybe against someone like Aurakbahor, you'd have a bigger problem, but hopefully we can take him out first."

A cheer came from across the field. Hope danced around, a knife in each hand. Jason kept a clear distance from her flailing arms.

He noticed us and smiled. "Bull's-eye!"

Everyone but Tythan cheered. I glared at them, and they clapped their hands twice.

"Any other questions about death commands?" Coleman asked, returning to the lecture.

No one answered. Coleman reached for his bag and pulled out several braided strips of leather. "I've been working on a project. They can't protect us from death commands, but they can protect us from other attacks." He gave one strip to each of us, and I could finally tell that they were bracelets. "They'll automatically activate to block a sneak attack, but—" He finished putting one on his own wrist, then tapped his wrists together in an *X*. Silver-blue translucent armor sprang to life around him.

Aaron's mouth dropped open in awe, and he tapped his own wrists together, the armor forming around him, too. "These are *sweet!*" he said.

"It will only last a few minutes at a time," Coleman said. "But the enchantment should last for a while and won't draw on your own magic."

"Aww, how sweet," Tythan said dryly. "You made us friendship bracelets."

Coleman crossed his arms. "Bold of you to assume I'm friends with any of you."

"Aww," I said, mimicking Tythan's dry tone. "You made us nemesis bracelets."

Tythan almost smiled at that. I counted it as a win.

Jason and Hope trotted back over to us. "Just about

finished, Cole?"

Coleman stood and brushed the dirt off his pants. "Yeah, I think we can call it for the day."

I climbed to my feet and started toward my car.

Aaron fell into step next to me. "Hey."

"Hi." I walked faster.

"Can we talk?"

"No."

"I wanted to make sure I could control my emotions," he said anyway, "but I realized you can protect yourself, and I'm sorry . . . I thought I was making the right decision. I didn't want you getting hurt."

I spun around to face him. "Your absence did *nothing* to prevent me from getting hurt, Aaron." I didn't know what made me do it, but I yanked my jacket off, revealing my bare arms. My dragon was still red and raised. The yellowing lightning bruises arched across my chest and shoulder blades. The Lichtenberg ridges hadn't faded at all. The inside of my right elbow had a large, red rope-like scar across it. "Don't you *dare* claim you did it to protect me because it changed *nothing*!"

His light green eyes turned emerald and slitted. He pulled a small gray stone out of his pocket, but it slipped from his trembling fingers. "Who . . . Kat, I-I didn't know. I'm sorry." Flames sparked on his fingertips but extinguished almost immediately. The air around him warped.

"Aaron?" My stomach sank as my anger dispersed. "Wait! No! Control it! I'm sorry too." I threw my arms around him, desperate to restrain the dragon within. "Stop it!"

Someone grabbed my shoulder and pulled me away from him. "Kat, get back!"

I fought against at least two sets of arms as Aaron stumbled away from me, his face pale and his dragon eyes wide.

"*No!*"

He looked at me with fearful, apologetic eyes and shuddered. Aryxon's emerald form stood in his place.

"Aaron!" I sobbed.

He made a weird choking noise and took off into the air. Jason and Coleman still gripped my arms, trying to keep me away. The fire inside me died, and I slumped into them. I shut my eyes and tried to sink all the way to the ground.

The two Rhaegynne on either side of me kept me somewhat upright.

"Kat . . ." Jason spoke cautiously.

"I know," I muttered. "It's my fault. I'm so sorry."

"No, Kat . . . L-look," Coleman's voice shook.

I opened my eyes and turned toward the sky. Aaron's tiny speck flew in the distance, but two other dragons were closing in.

I'm Not Yours

Aaron

Oh, Kat. What have I done?

The image of her scars was seared in my mind. Not even the hundreds of voices could cover it. I pressed my wings hard, surprised by the ease with which I could run away from her before someone could stop me.

I searched for some place to change back. To the south, I spotted a cluster of trees, but before I fully decided to turn toward it, someone else forced me that way.

My heart pounded, and I screamed out in protest. I severely underestimated the danger of leaving if my puppet strings dragged me where I wanted to go. I tried to force myself to the ground, but I only rose higher.

Two dragons, one gold and one ruby, darted out of the cloud cover miles away from the field. They circled me, shepherding me onward. I struggled against the bonds that moved my wings, but I just kept flying, sandwiched between two large, angry dragons.

"*Coliseum.*" The word echoed in my head repeated by

dozens and spoken louder and louder until the chant was taken up by every voice in my head, blinding me with the mental volume.

"*Coliseum.*"

Kat and I had planned to attack at the coliseum. Of course, that would be where I'd end up.

I felt broken and shattered. The battle was already lost. Aurakbahor knew everything, he had me, and he'd found Kat. I wanted to stop fighting and give up.

But I couldn't.

I needed to change back, but I would fall to my death if I did.

Somewhere in my head was a link to Aurakbahor. I just had to find and destroy it.

Steeling myself against what I needed to do and using the jagged shards of my soul as a weapon, I closed my eyes, trusting that I'd go where I was commanded anyway.

I pushed into my own mind and shifted through the voices screaming in my head, touching each and moving on. They faded as I found the one I sought. His energy was like a black hole — at the center of everything, holding it together, and promising destruction if one got too close.

In the chaos, I pinpointed Aurakbahor. My puppeteer.

"*I am not yours,*" I growled as I met him in my head.

"*But you are,*" he answered. Amusement dripped from his voice and rang in my head. "*You are* mine."

I focused on him. "My name is Aaron Levi Johnson. I am not Aryxon. I am not a puppet. And. I. Am. Not. Yours." Some confusion stirred around me, but I pushed those voices aside, focusing on Aurakbahor's energy. "*My name is Aaron Levi Johnson. I demand my freedom!*"

I reached out with my mind and yanked the connection between us.

Nothing happened.

Fear filled my stomach as Aurakbahor's laughter filled my head. "*Fool,*" he whispered. "*You are not the first to try. You are not the first to fail.*"

"*No!*" I screamed. "*I belong to me!*"

"*Not yet.*"

A tail whipped across my face, and lights danced behind my eyelids. My wings fell limp, and the voices went quiet.

A Dragon Named Kat

Kat

I helplessly watched Aaron fall.

"Aaron..." I croaked, intimately aware this was my fault.

Jason pulled me back to my feet. "Come on, Kat. We have to go."

"Where are they taking him?" Rage came so easy these days. It had become a weapon, a well of strength to draw upon for the battle ahead.

But I'd used it to hurt the people I cared about most.

And I couldn't find it now.

I wanted to throw up.

Coleman and Jason glanced at each other.

"*Where are they taking him?*" I asked.

"Kat..." Jason said.

My arms throbbed. "I don't want him anywhere *near* Morgan's knife!" I tried to control the panic burning inside me. I tried not to lash out at Coleman and Jason.

I clutched at my tether. I didn't care to stay human, but I

needed to remember who the real enemy was. And it wasn't my friends.

Jason avoided eye contact. "Aurakbahor's coliseum. That's what he's been doing with traitors. They'll make him be a gladiator."

My stomach sank. "The coliseum," I whispered, horror causing my voice to catch.

Coleman nodded. "He might survive the first few fights if he's human, but the second he changes into a dragon, he's at the mercy of Aurakbahor. And trust me when I say this: Aurakbahor has no mercy."

My stomach sank. "I'm going after him."

He grabbed my arm before I could step away. "You can't take on both those dragons alone!"

"Then come with me!" I snarled.

"I'm coming too!" Hope shouted.

"What? No! It's too dangerous!" I said. "My dad can watch her."

Tythan stepped in, putting a protective hand on her shoulder. "We don't have much time, and whoever watches her will be in danger. I can't risk that."

I shot a glare at Jason. "You said she wouldn't be near any fighting! She's *six!*"

"It's her birthday today . . . She's seven," Tythan said as though that changed anything.

I forced a smile at the young child. She didn't deserve to be in the middle of this. "Happy birthday, Hope." I turned back to Tythan. "She can't come. Besides, I can't carry all of you!"

"I have transport beads at home," Coleman said. "We just need to make it there and—"

My vision slipped to my mirrored irises, my panic making it hard to stay human. "Coleman, I will *destroy* the car. I'm going after Aaron with or without you."

Coleman took a step back, hands up in surrender.

I took a deep breath, and for the first time in weeks, I became a dragon.

Hope let out a small *wow* before I took to the skies.

I pushed myself faster than I had ever flown before. Guilt gnawed inside me, but I didn't have time for that. Aaron was already out of sight.

The clouds embraced me, and for a moment, I allowed myself to revel in the strength of my dragon form. I hadn't been allowed to shift for the first few weeks after Morgan attacked. But even after that, I hadn't *let* myself shift. None of my friends could change whenever they wanted, so why should I change at every whim? Aaron said I didn't understand, so I tried to prove to myself that I could.

I went nine weeks without . . . *this*. It was beautiful to fly. To feel the raw power coursing through my veins. To have the muscles through my chest and back strain against gravity to keep me airborne.

To be truly me.

It dawned on me then that flying through the sky fast enough to pass passenger airplanes, that I *wasn't* human. I never had been. My blood had always been Rhaegynne, back to the first of us. Back to Rhaegynne herself.

The others might feel better as dragons, but they were all humans masquerading as dragons. They were all someone else: Jason was Aerolan, Coleman was Sa'hranet, Hope was Maxyre, Tythan was Rorivan, and Aaron was Aryxon.

But I was Katherine Victoria Lance. A dragon named Kat. I was meant to be a dragon.

I was meant to take two of the four clan thrones. I was meant to be king.

The kings had taken this feeling from the rest of the Rhaegynne. And Aurakbahor had taken Grandma from me. And now, he wanted Aaron.

I finally found the anger I'd lost in my panic.

Fury built up inside — lethal but focused this time — and erupted out of me in a white-hot flame. I barreled through the fire and burst through the clouds. The two dragons spun around in surprise, still some distance off, but I'd closed the gap. As they turned to flee, I let out another breath of flame and scorched the gold dragon's tail. He twisted around, spewing fire before he cleared his companion, searing the ruby dragon's side.

They both faced me, teeth bared and eyes glazed. Aaron's human body flopped in the red dragon's talons.

The red dragon held him out like a rag doll.

"*Surrender, or he dies,*" Aurakbahor's voice said in my head.

I lunged toward him, darting between the dragons.

The gold dragon attacked, slicing his talons across my side. Screaming, I lashed out as hot blood dripped across my body.

I spun in the air, whipping out with my tail. It hit his face with a satisfying crack.

Teeth sank into the back of my neck, piercing my throat. The gold dragon watched as I struggled. His claws reached out and encircled my throat from the front as blood ran hot down my chest.

"*Oh,* Kitty," Aurakbahor said. "*What will you do this time?*"

I squirmed and thrashed, but I couldn't escape. My wings were pressed against my back by the ruby dragon's body. I couldn't change or I would lose my head.

Aaron . . .

Spots danced in my vision. I couldn't breathe.

Aaron dangled beneath me.

"*Surrender, Kitten* . . ."

I gasped for air and succumbed to the darkness.

I didn't expect to wake up.

I lay against a red stone wall. Thick, cold metal manacles cut into my wrists and clung to my neck. The wounds from the fight were gone, but my tank top was still damp with my own blood. Some of the still-healing scars on my arm had reopened and beaded with blood. There was a cold ache in my chest.

The fire of my magic was gone.

A blue light flashed on the manacles, drawing my attention. Carved and painted into the metal was the same anti-magic rune I had seen on Jason's neck and the old broken pendant from Grandma.

I closed my eyes and sighed. "Of course . . ." I groaned, pushing myself upright. The chains clanked as they dragged across the ground.

The cold, damp cell smelled of mildew and iron, leaving a harsh metallic taste in the back of my mouth. Water dripped from a small stalactite above me and fell into a thin stream snaking its way along the dungeon's wall.

Shuddering, I pulled my knees into my chest, fighting back the tight grasp of fear.

Coleman once warned me that if they ever captured me, Aurakbahor could curse me the way they cursed him . . .

Would I even know if they'd already done it?

I shook off the thought and glanced around, taking in my surroundings. The cell was more like a cave; it extended out on either side of me, stretching into the darkness. Empty sets of manacles like mine dangled from the wall every few feet.

I tried to stand, but the chains were too short and bolted in too low. I couldn't even straighten my knees. Gasping, I fell back to the ground.

"Careful," a quiet voice rasped from the shadows.

I jumped, biting back a scream. A form hunched against the far wall. Covered in orange dust and grime, they were camouflaged almost perfectly with the wall at first glance. Squinting, I could make out a scraggly beard, a bare, emaciated chest, and hundreds of scars — new and old — across his body.

"Who are you?" I asked.

"Henry," he answered.

"How long have you been here?"

He glanced back at the wall behind him which had hundreds of tiny scratch marks carved into the stone. "I lost track."

"You're Rhaegynne?" I asked, noticing his manacles didn't glow.

He shook his head. "No, but my son is. Or was. I assume he's dead by now."

"You're human? How are you still alive?"

His chains rattled as he shrugged. "I didn't feel like dying."

"Do they torture you?"

He studied his cracked knuckles. "They use me to train their assassins and throw me in the coliseum when they feel I need to remember my place."

I clenched my fists. "I'm going to get you out of here."

He grunted. "How are you going to do that?"

The cold pit inside throbbed at the reminder of how powerless I was. "My friends are coming."

"They're fools if they do."

I let out a humorless laugh. "We kind of make it our job to be fools, I guess. Fools stand up when the odds are against them. Making things happen through stubborn persistence and hope alone."

"I must be a fool to still be alive then," he muttered.

"What are you fighting for, Henry?"

He stayed quiet for a long moment. "It's *foolish* to voice these things aloud when there are ears trying to learn what it will take to break us."

I slumped against the wall, the chains dragging in the dust. "They'll come, Henry. They'll get us out of here, and I'll save us all."

THE KING EATS CHARCUTERIE

AARON

My head throbbed when I woke up on a red dirt floor in a cramped stone cell. *Will I ever get the chance to turn back without being knocked unconscious first?*

Chills ran down my spine at the hopelessness of it all. I didn't want to die here.

I took a deep calming breath, refusing to give them the satisfaction of knowing I was terrified.

I stood, my body announcing new pains. I tried the bars on my cell. They didn't even rattle.

Footsteps echoed down the hall. A tall man in armor with a long black coat dropped a tray with a roll and a brown banana on the floor and kicked it through a small slot under my cell door. He didn't even look at me before continuing down the hall.

My stomach growled as I kicked the food back out of the cell. *I'm not about to eat food from someone who wants me dead.*

I leaned back against the wall and closed my eyes, waiting for my doom.

I'd dozed off at some point, but the door slammed open with a grating clang, and I jerked awake, frustrated I'd let down my guard in a place like this. Armored men in cloaks stood in the doorframe.

"Get up," the one in the front demanded, kicking me when I failed to comply fast enough.

I fell, and he yanked me to my feet. "I said get *up*." He jerked my arms behind my back and dragged me into the hall.

Cuffs tightened around my wrists. I tried not to wince as they pinched my skin. Someone shoved me forward.

I walked forward, trying to orient myself within the cell block. This whole place was a labyrinth, but Kat and I had spent weeks memorizing the maps. We passed a distinctive intersection of five tunnels. I knew where I was.

But the arena was the other way.

I ran through the map in my head, trying to figure out what horrors lay ahead. My stomach sank as I mentally traced this tunnel to the end of the map.

Which is worse: the torture chambers or Aurakbahor's private study?

My palms began to sweat, but I curled my fingers into fists and lifted my chin. *Isn't this what the resistance is all about? Being trapped, cornered, and controlled but facing it head-on anyway? Aurakbahor may have my body, but he cannot control my mind, and I will resist and revolt with every thought I have left. If all I can do is annoy him, then I've won.*

I could feel my new dragon and compass tattoo warm on my right shoulder blade at the thought.

I clenched my jaw as the guards directed me down the fork toward massive metal doors large enough for a dragon to pass through. More guards stood at attention outside the entrance. They parted without a word and swung the door open.

Rough hands pushed me forward, and the chains around me rattled. Two guards escorted me into the large cavern.

The cave's rocky red floor had been covered with marble tile. Intricate mosaics of mythical creatures adorned the walls and ceiling. Silver and gold gilded every piece of furniture in the room.

At the center of the room, Aurakbahor lounged upon his throne. A scarred woman stood by his side, holding a plate of food.

His cold brown eyes cast a disinterested glance in my direction as he reached for a grape from the plate. "Unbind our guest and leave us," he commanded, inspecting the red grape between his fingers.

Blood flooded back into my fingers as the guards removed the cuffs. I rubbed my wrists while they left the room. The heavy doors closed with a note of finality.

My heart remained surprisingly calm as I stared down the man who had ruined my life. I longed to attack him, but even though my hands were free, my every move was known. I would be dead before I could take my foot off the floor. So, I stood where I was, seething.

He popped the grape into his mouth. "So," Aurakbahor said around the fruit and paused to chew. He swallowed and turned back to his plate. His ringed fingers glittered under the lights as he selected another grape. "What do you think?"

I blinked, unsure how to respond.

He put the grape in his mouth and chewed. "Oh. How rude of me. Did you want some?"

I glared.

He placed a slice of cheese on a cracker. "Listen, Aryxon."

I flinched at the use of my dragon name.

"The way I see it, this is going to end in one of two ways." He took a bite out of the cracker, crumbs falling into his beard.

"I could use you and your friends to help me take down Balaskad."

He finished the cracker and leaned toward me. "I know you act under some false confidence that because Katherine is free that she's the chosen one or whatever you want to call it, but she's not. Her grandmother was assumed dead when the curse fell, so she was missed. It has nothing to do with this daughter of Rhaegynne, child of the dragon nonsense she's used to inspire hope in her followers. Coincidence and *luck*." He spat the word like a curse.

I made a face, and he paused to put on a sympathetic façade.

"Jamie was no hero, Aryxon. She was a liar at best and a murderer at worst. And your friend Katherine is on a dangerous path to being just like her.

"Aryxon, I need you to help her see the truth. Rhaegynne's *firstborn* was supposed to lead the rest of her descendants. But there was a schism, even back then, between her four children and their descendants. They split apart, claiming their own families as clans and nations. But none of the others had any right to rule. It was *my* great ancestor who was supposed to be their king, and it was only by his grace that he allowed the others sovereignty."

Aurakbahor picked a strawberry off the plate and put everything but the stem into his mouth.

"Splitting the Rhaegynne was one of the worst decisions they could have made. Ours is not the first war between us, but through my efforts, it will be the last." Strawberry juice dribbled into his beard. He flicked aside the top. "The prophecy your friends cling to? Freeing the dragons calls for the reinstatement of the rightful heir. Aryxon, don't you see? *I* am the rightful heir — the *chosen one* if you prefer. I'm the only one with a right to rule, the only one with the training to lead, and the only one who can free the dragons.

"I cannot do that until Balaskad is dead. And with Katherine leading the resistance, I'm losing brave warriors who can help me stop the real threat. I'm not the bad guy, Aryxon. I've been backed into a corner, and I've been forced to be harsher than I have ever wanted to be. But a king must act in the best interest of the kingdom, no matter how hard it is to sleep at night."

He paused to study his newest piece of fruit.

"Join me, Aryxon. Let us put an end to Balaskad's reign of terror, and, together we can free the dragons."

"I'm not Aryxon," I hissed.

"Aaron then," he said with a dismissive wave. "I don't care which version of you I get on my side."

"Over your dead body," I growled.

Aurakbahor set his berry back onto the plate and sighed. "Aaron..." He pushed himself to his feet.

My feet stumbled backward as he approached.

"Aaron . . . the other option is I put you in the arena. I cannot tolerate treason."

He put a fatherly hand on my shoulder, and I spat in his face.

Aurakbahor reached up and wiped the spit from his cheek. His expression didn't change, but his eyes shifted to black. "I like you, Aryxon. So, here's what I'm going to do." He waved his hand, and a suit of black armor hanging on a wall flew forward. "I'm going to protect you. I'll give you an edge. I'll make sure you win your first fight."

The large chunk of armor slammed into my back, forcing me to my knees. I gasped. The piece wrapped around my torso as other pieces latched onto my arms and legs. I cried out, and the helmet closed around my face.

Knights of the Raven's Vigil

Coleman

We watched in horrified silence as the dragons disappeared with Kat and Aaron.

"We have to go," Jason said, tugging my arm and dragging me to the car.

We sped to the house, my heart pounding, head spinning. I barreled through the front door and raced into my room, tearing through it like a hurricane to find the last transport beads.

Note to self: Always keep at least one set of transport beads with me.

I sprinted outside to where the others waited anxiously.

"Did you find them?" Jason asked.

I held up the beads, breathing too hard to respond and dizzy from the exertion.

"Where do we go?" Tythan asked. "Straight to the coliseum?"

I shook my head, gulping down air until I could speak

again. "No. We can't transport directly in. There are only a few places inside where Aurakbahor allows transport beads. I'll have the beads take us to a more remote area of the park. There should be an opening to the tunnels there. Best I can tell, Aurakbahor doesn't know the entrance exists."

I tossed out the beads, aware we didn't have a second set for the return trip. I watched them glow with my magic and prayed there *would* be a return trip.

I really hope I don't have to destroy another *National Park...* I thought, stepping through the beads to Zion National Park. I led the way, barely checking my watch before staring down the trails I'd all but memorized as a kid. The path narrowed as we descended the canyon — rock wall on one side, sheer drop on the other. I felt exposed, but there was nowhere to hide, and we didn't have time for stealth. So, we ran...

We rounded a corner and came face-to-face with several masked figures hooded under black robes in a wider portion of trail. One held up a glowing force field between us while the others prepared curses and weapons. I jumped back, pushing my friends behind me. Red dust showered down on us as the arrows and spells hit stone instead.

More Knights came from behind, and I set a shield around our small group.

"What do we do?" Jason asked while spells pounded against my wards. They somehow sounded like rain on a tent rather than the bombs they were.

"It's twelve of them against four of us. How hard can it be?" Tythan asked.

I swallowed my fear and checked my watch. "Those are Knights of the Raven's Vigil — Aurakbahor's personal team of assassins. I don't like our odds."

A blast threatened to shatter my shield, but Jason summoned one of his own to support mine. "Those losers have *names?"* Jason asked. "We've faced them before, Cole. Why do you look so scared?"

Now is not the time! I looked away. "Because . . . I used to be one. They scare me."

"Then they scare me too, but we have friends down there being tortured or already dead. So, what are we going to do?"

I studied the forms converging on either side of us through our shields' warped blue glass. "Tythan and Hope, you take point. Jason and I will take the ones behind us. Once you get through, run. You'll want to get to the base of this cliff. There's a cave entrance hidden under overlapping boulders. Go that way, then follow the tunnel to the arena."

Jason and I made eye contact. I nodded and tapped my wrists together to activate the Tasalgric armor. After others did the same, Jason and I dispelled our shields and came up shooting. I threw fireballs and lightning while Jason deflected. Behind us, Tythan and Hope encased the assassins in fire and ice. They broke free at the same time I felled the last assassin on my side.

That felt too easy . . .

Ten more assassins swarmed the trail, and a large bronze dragon rose up from beneath the rocky cliff.

Ah, there it is.

Morgan laughed from the dragon's back, and the Knights of the Raven's Vigil attacked.

We met the onslaught with our own, but one of them grappled Jason from behind and pressed a black rag over his mouth until he fell limp. I screamed and tried to summon a bolt of energy.

Magic rose inside me and coursed through my arm. Dragonstongue squeezed at my chest and arm, but the spell sputtered out with blue-tinged sparks at my fingers.

My chest was cold but not from Dragonstongue.

I tried to summon my magic again to stop another Knight who'd grabbed Tythan with a black rag pressed to their mouth.

Nothing happened.

I swore and checked my watch. *Sixty seconds. You can hold out for sixty seconds.*

Anger smothered my fear. *I will kill Kroll when I get out of this.* I drew my sword and rushed forward, but an icy burning in my chest made me stumble.

I wasn't using magic; why was it—

Because, I realized with a sinking dread, there was no longer any magic to keep the toxins in check...

Jason was right. This was certainly not my smartest decision.

I clenched my teeth against the pain and swung my sword, killing one while the burning toxin crawled up my neck.

Morgan slid off her dragon's back, and Hope rushed forward, glowing with a blinding, golden light that lifted her off the ground. Hope screamed and threw daggers of light at Morgan. She blocked most but one pierced her stomach.

Morgan dropped to a knee, clutching at her side, but I forced my attention to the closest Knights. Only two remained. The others were dead or were fleeing with my unconscious friends.

I took deep breaths, trying to keep my eyes open as the poison turned my vision blue. I tried to swing my blade, but pain flared through my body, and my legs gave out.

Somewhere behind me, Hope screamed.

Rough hands seized me, sending stabbing agony through my paralyzed body. They dragged me backward down the trail so I could see Hope face Morgan alone before my vision was engulfed in burning, icy blue.

Reunion

Kat

The sound of a struggle outside broke the dungeon's eerie silence. I looked to Henry, hoping he could explain what was happening, but he shrugged.

"Probably got someone new," he said. "Most people stop fighting eventually."

But the shouting got closer. The door flew open, and hooded guards entered, dragging a squirming Jason, a glaring Tythan, and a screaming Hope with them.

Before I could even react, three sets of manacles sprang to life on the walls, reaching out with hungry, grasping tendrils to restrain my friends. They struggled, but one by one, the blue lights turned on and pulled them to the floor.

The door slammed shut.

"Are these your friends?" Henry asked over Hope's impressive display of swear words.

Dejected, I slumped against the wall. "Most of them . . . Henry, this is Hope next to me, Tythan in the middle, and Jason across from you."

"Jason?" Henry said.

Jason leaned toward the man, eyes squinted to see through the dim. His eyes widened, and he lifted his hand as far as his manacles would let him. "Dad?" he choked.

"*Dad?*" I repeated. Hope's cursing died off as we all turned to watch.

Henry strained against his chains, stretching toward his son. The tips of their fingers barely touched. "You've grown so much," he whispered.

"What have they done to you?" Jason asked, his voice cracking. Tears glistened on his cheeks, reflecting the rune's light.

The chains creaked as they reached toward each other. Tears left clean tracks through the grime on Henry's face. "*Jason,*" he sobbed. "How many years has it been? You're so much younger than I thought you would be."

"Thir-thirteen years. My birthday was a couple weeks ago. I'd be twenty-three now if not for my Rhaegynne blood," Jason answered.

"They told me you were dead..." Henry whispered.

"I thought *you* were dead! I searched for you!" Jason cried. "I should have looked here."

"No, then they would have captured you again," he answered.

"I'll get you out."

He glanced at me. "Your friend keeps promising the same thing."

Jason smiled weakly. "We're an ambitious lot." He frowned. "Where is Aaron?"

I stared at my hands so I wouldn't have to look at anyone else. "I don't know."

"We'll find him, Kat," Tythan insisted.

I smiled half-heartedly. But my stomach sank again. "Where is Coleman?"

They shook their head. "We were ambushed when we arrived."

Jason sat back, resting against the wall but not taking his eyes off his dad. "We fought back, but they picked us off. They got me first, but *Morgan* was there. And a bunch of assassins that Coleman called the Knights of the Raven's Vigil."

I groaned. "Aaron's missing. Coleman's probably dead. We're all prisoners without magic. And Aurakbahor knew we were coming. He knows everything."

"When did you become the pessimist?" Tythan asked.

"What do you mean he knows everything?" Jason asked, staring me down.

"Aurakbahor can still hear your thoughts even when you're human," I said, too defeated to care to keep it a secret anymore. He would have found out I knew the second Aaron became Rhaegynne.

Jason paled, the blue light of his runes casting a sickly shadow across his face. "What do we do now?"

I rubbed my eyes. "I don't know."

"Hope?" Tythan said.

She sniffed, wiping the tears off her face. "What?"

"Do you think you could pass the clip in your hair to me?"

Her chains rattled as she strained to get the glittering hair clip to Tythan. Dark curls fell into her face, and she pushed them back.

Tythan pulled the clip apart and set to work trying to open the cuffs. "I got her a hair clip with a lock pick set hidden inside but haven't had the chance to teach her yet," they said while twisting their hands around the cuffs. "It was intended for this kind of situation. And would work, except these manacles are sealed with magic and don't have a keyhole." They slumped and put the clip back together. "I'll keep trying. I bet if I find a sharp enough rock, I could scratch out the runes and then work from there."

"Will we have to fight each other?" Hope asked, her voice trembling.

I clenched my hands into fists, the metal biting into my flexed wrists. "I'll do anything in my power to make sure that doesn't happen."

"Coleman's alive," Jason whispered, his voice carrying in the cave. "He has to be. He'll figure something out."

"We'll have to figure something out in the meantime," Tythan said.

The door opened again, and two guards entered. Hope shrank against the light in their hands, and Tythan moved to try to protect her, but the chains caused them to pull up short.

The guards cast uncaring eyes across our defeated and pathetic group before settling on me. I tried not to flinch as the front guard motioned toward me.

The second guard crouched down and grabbed my hair, yanking my head up to see him. "This is what Aurak's so obsessed with?" he hissed then spat on my face.

"Quit wasting time," the first guard said.

The guard in front of me smiled cruelly, breathing putrid air into my face. He lifted another set of chains from his side. He clamped them to my ankles and attached them to the chain between my hands before undoing the connection to the wall.

He jerked me to my feet. I staggered under the weight of the shackles around my wrists, neck, and legs, but he pushed me forward.

"Kat!" Hope cried, but Tythan hushed her.

"I'll be okay," I lied as they dragged me into the hall.

Four other guards waited outside the dungeon and fell into place around me. The second guard dragged me along like a disobedient dog. Someone kicked me from behind, but I held my head as high as the metal around my neck allowed.

They led me through a series of tunnels and cells. I caught glimpses of emaciated big cats, rabid wolves, and tormented Rhaegynne behind the bars. I shuddered to think of fighting any of them.

A large metal door came into view ahead, and my heart pounded in anticipation for the fight on the other side. What was I even supposed to fight out there? A human like Jason's dad? One of the diseased cheetahs? Maybe there were other prisoners who weren't on the verge of death. Maybe there would be volunteers from the audience. Is there even an audience?

I didn't come to kill any prisoner, and I'd rather not kill a volunteer. In fact, I didn't want to kill anyone, but what if I didn't have a choice? This was a fight to the death, and I wanted to die even less than I wanted to kill.

Bile rose in my throat at the thought.

The massive metal door loomed at the end of the hall, and my heart skipped a beat as it lifted off the ground and rolled up against the ceiling. I was met by blinding light and deafening applause.

I stepped out into the round amphitheater, blinking in the light. I scanned the rocky arena, my heart sinking as I realized the several hundred spectators all supported Aurakbahor's rule.

Stadium seating surrounded the arena. The ceiling reached higher than I could see. A judge's box sat in the middle of the seating in front of me.

I scanned the box, and my throat went dry. I didn't care about what waited for me behind the other door anymore.

I knew who I could fight.

The guards pushed me to the middle of the amphitheater

and shoved me to my knees. I lifted my head up to the box, locking eyes with the dark-haired man sitting on the throne.

I knew who I could kill.

Aurakbahor stood and smiled. "Kitty!"

"I challenge you, Aurakbahor!" I shouted.

He laughed. "I am an old man! But I did select a prized champion to stand in my place just in case!" He waved his hand, and the door on the opposite side of the coliseum opened.

Three guards dragged a struggling figure incased in black armor. They brought the shackled knight forward and stopped a few feet away. A guard reached up and ripped the helmet off.

Aaron gasped around a dirty rag shoved into his mouth.

"*No!*"

"I accept your challenge, Kitten," Aurakbahor said, his low voice somehow carrying across the arena. "Defeat my champion, and the throne is yours."

One of Aaron's guards pulled out a rod crackling with electricity and slammed it into Aaron's side. I screamed as his knees buckled. His eyes rolled back and turned emerald. Ice crackled out around him, but his eyes turned human again as he gasped for air on the ground.

"Aaron!" I struggled against my guard's restraint, but the rune leached even my draconic strength.

The guard lifted the rod again, but Aurakbahor put up his hand. "Enough," he said. He lifted a vial of sludgy liquid, and another one of Aaron's guards pulled out a matching vial. "This vial contains clay from the geyser my *son* destroyed." He glanced over his shoulder.

A figure in the shadows behind Aurakbahor stepped forward. Morgan's face twisted with a sadistic glee as she dragged a bloodied and half-conscious Coleman into the light with her. Blue veins covered his face, and my stomach flipped — *Dragonstongue*.

Aurakbahor sneered, watching the potion move sluggishly in the vial for a moment. "Yes, this would help access the link between myself and my dragons, but it can do so much more." He pulled the cork out with his teeth and downed the vial's contents.

The guard beside Aaron ripped out the gag and tilted Aaron's head back. Another guard poured the vial down Aaron's throat while he sputtered. His eyes slitted again, and a vein in his temple bulged.

I lunged forward, but they jerked the chain around my neck, yanking me backward. I fell hard against the stone but scrambled to my knees, reaching out as far as my chains would allow.

Aaron's body quivered as a guard covered his mouth and nose, forcing him to swallow.

"Yes, this does so much more than help me focus. Because when another drinks from the same batch, it gives me just—" Aurakbahor stopped and sounded like he struggled for breath, but I couldn't keep my eyes off Aaron.

"I'm so sorry, Aaron," I said. "I'll make this right."

Aaron looked at me with wide, fearful dragon eyes. "I—" He groaned and bucked forward.

"It gives me just enough power to force a change," Aurakbahor finished.

Aaron screamed, and his armor exploded, expanded, and rearranged around his massive dragon form.

Aryxon stood panting in front of me, mouth frothing with the potion's remnants and his head down and forearms spread wide. The armor gave his face a fierce appearance, but his eyes darted around the room in fear before freezing on me. He breathed out small puffs of steam.

My manacles fell off, and magic surged through my body like a dam breaking. I was relieved to find the leather bracelet pinned beneath the cuffs.

"I'm cheering for you, Kitty," Aurakbahor purred before sitting back onto his throne and kicking his feet up.

Aryxon lunged, letting out a feral snarl. I rolled forward, ducking under his stomach and tapping my wrists together to summon the armor. I wasn't willing to hurt him, but I couldn't let him hurt me either. His jaws let out a pop like a gunshot as they snapped around empty space. I sprinted away as he whipped around.

Fire burned at my heels. I threw up a shield, letting the fire part around me. He pounced, and I dodged, narrowly avoiding his talons. The audience booed as I ran.

"I gave your powers back! *Use them!*" Aurakbahor screamed as more fire poured from Aryxon's mouth.

I ran toward Aryxon and slid between his legs again, forcing him to turn around.

"What do you *want*?" I screamed at the box.

"I wanted you!" Aurakbahor shouted back.

I stomped the ground, sending a thick wall of rock up between Aryxon and me. "Then *take me*!" I screamed. "Let my friends go!"

Aryxon froze, and Aurakbahor leaned forward. "Kitten, I don't think it works that way anymore."

I stared at the dragon in front of me, hoping to see anything of Aaron left in this form.

Disgust curled in my chest. That potion gave Aurakbahor too much control. I eyed the remnants on Aryxon with distaste and suspicion, but I wondered, too, if Dragonstongue wasn't the only poison Aurakbahor had given Coleman before . . .

"What else does that clay do, Aurak?" I asked, confident I already knew the answer. I let the armor disperse around me.

He glanced at the potion in his hand, and his eyes widened in realization, confirming my suspicion. "Oh. *Oh.*" He gestured toward one of the servants behind him, and she ran off. "I offered you my throne if you'd just kill my champion. But instead, you offer me..."

"Freedom for freedom," I said, sounding a lot calmer than I felt. "Your potion can do that, right?"

"You'd offer yourself as my servant in Aaron's place?"

"Kat, no!" Coleman shouted. Morgan slapped him, and he fell out of sight.

"Release my friends. All of them. Lift their curse, leave them alone, and do them no further harm. But keep me."

The woman entered the arena carrying another vial of potion. I reached out with shaking fingers.

Aurakbahor leaned against the railing of the judge's box, a hungry look in his eye. "I agree to the terms."

I pulled out the cork and shot back the chalky liquid, trying not to taste it. My head buzzed as I swallowed, and I felt Aurakbahor probe inside.

"*Where are your weaknesses, Katherine?*" he asked, shoving his way through my brain. My shoulder itched, and my vision slipped as he sifted through my thoughts like a magazine. He pulled on the memory after the assembly on Aaron's porch. "*Aaron?*" he scoffed. "*How... uninspiring.*"

He grabbed the memory and yanked, pushing me over the edge. I gasped and shifted. I struggled to change back, but Aurakbahor just laughed inside my head and kept a firm grip on the memory. "*Not yet.*" He stretched the memory, twisting and pulling. "*This is mine now. This is me.*"

"*Free Aaron first,*" I managed to beg through the pain.

Aryxon whimpered beside me, and I reached out with my mind to find Aaron cowering inside.

"*What are you doing?*" Aaron asked.

I glanced at Aryxon — at *Aaron* — and longed to do more. "*Saying goodbye,*" I answered.

Aurakbahor yanked on my memory, and he lifted my wings. But I could still feel Aaron, and even as his connection to me strengthened, I could tell it lessened for Aaron. His taut muscles relaxed, and his snarl faded, but my muscles tightened, and my lip twitched.

"*Aaron,*" I groaned, trying not to cry.

Aurakbahor pulled harder, and I let out a scream. "*You. Are. Mine!*" he shouted as my connection to Aaron weakened.

"*You can't have her!*" Aaron snarled.

I grunted as Aaron pulled back on his connection, dragging Aurakbahor away from me.

"*What are you doing?*" I hissed.

"*I'm not about to let you do this,*" he said, tugging on the connection between our minds.

I pulled back. Aurakbahor joined me, and I stopped. Aaron yanked again, but I found the strength to shake my head.

"*Together,*" I said.

Aaron turned to me with those wide, fearful eyes, but they narrowed, and we both pulled.

"*No,*" Aurakbahor said, his tone frantic.

Aaron and I heaved on the connection at the same time. Aurakbahor pulled back, fighting against us with a desperation that made me confident we were close to winning.

We struggled, locked in a mental battle, pulling against each other, neither side willing to surrender.

But the link, being stretched and twisted, pulled in two different directions, couldn't hold.

The threads binding Aaron and I to Aurakbahor snapped, abruptly cutting off his mental screams. The three of us recoiled, free from the telepathic tug-of-war.

And, more importantly, free from Aurakbahor.

Wait — To the Death?

Aaron

Aurakbahor screamed as his puppet strings snapped. He climbed atop the railing and *jumped*. His black coat billowed out behind him in the few moments before he shifted. He caught his fall on massive smoky gray wings and landed in front of me, making the ground shudder under his weight.

He put his head close to mine and curled his lip, revealing large white fangs. He turned his massive head toward Kat, but she stood firm, her chin held high and her wings raised in defiance.

"So, you accept my challenge?" she asked.

"To the death?" he asked.

"To the death."

A woman in the judge's box stood. She glanced nervously at the silent audience. "Begin."

Aurakbahor sprang toward me like a bullet, and the crowd roared with excitement.

I barely had time to react but managed to roll out of the way. I pushed myself off the ground and circled his head, spitting fire at him. He growled and met me in the air. I flew under him, pulled myself close, and slammed my head into his chest. He thrashed his tail across my back.

Kat circled above him and dove at his head. He twisted onto his back and caught her in his talons. She growled and lunged at his neck, but he caught her wing in his jaws. She screamed as he bit into the joint. Bones snapped. He threw her off him, letting her spiral to the ground, blood falling behind her. She hit the dirt in her human form with a heavy thud. The king turned to me while the crowd went wild.

I dodged a torrent of flames and attacked. He tried to slip away, but I caught his tail in my mouth and sank my teeth into it. He roared in anger, and I shook my head, throwing him off-balance. I flung him to the ground where he landed with a crash.

I landed on top of him, somehow pinning the much larger dragon to the dirt. Kat sat up and stared in shock.

"*Are you going to help or just watch?*" I asked as the king struggled beneath me.

"*I don't know how to heal my wings! I don't have magic as a dragon, and I don't have wings as a human!*" Her mental voice was tight with panic. "*I can't fly.*"

"*I can!*"

She smiled and tapped her wrists together. A sword formed in her hand as the armor materialized, and she charged forward, summoning lightning as she ran.

Aurakbahor dodged the bolt, but Kat scrambled up my forearm, using the armor to pull herself higher and onto my back.

I launched us into the air. Kat let out a small squeak as her arms wrapped around my neck. *"How do you stay on and fight at the same time?"*

"Remember the bull? Remember the saddle?"

Aurakbahor took off again, a dangerous glint in his eyes. He opened his mouth, and his maw glowed white.

"*Bol protect!*" Kat cried, and the fire arced around us. She grunted and set the fire raging back at the king.

I maneuvered around the dragon, letting Kat throw out spells and block attacks. Rocks fell from the ceiling and rained down on Aurakbahor's head, but still he raged on, blood dripping from his face. Beneath us, the audience screamed and ducked for cover.

I couldn't say I particularly cared.

I dodged another breath attack, but Aurakbahor bit into my leg and clawed my side. His teeth ripped through my leg as I pulled away, but Kat quickly healed the wounds.

Despite Kat's healing, my wings grew heavy, and I struggled to breathe. I had watched Kat train, and I had fought as a puppet, but I had never been in a real fight before. Let alone a fight in heavy armor. Aurakbahor, however, was a dragon familiar with the fight. He was ruthless, every inch a weapon.

My stamina failed, and I struggled to maintain altitude.

"*We have to get him on the ground somehow!*" Kat said, stabbing her sword into Aurakbahor's side.

"How?"

"*Attack his wings,*" she said, throwing her sword like a knife. It flew end over end toward Aurakbahor, but he tucked his wings in and dove. Her sword blinked out of existence as it fell.

Aurakbahor stretched out his wings, catching his fall, but as he rose, I dove, reaching out with my talons. They caught the thin membrane between the wing bones and ripped through.

He let out a pained screech and fell, his tail a terrifying

mace as he spiraled to the ground. I followed, spitting fire at the falling king and causing smoke to curl off his injured wings.

He landed, changed back, stumbled forward, and drew his sword.

As soon as Kat's feet hit the ground, I dropped my dragon form. The black armor collapsed around me, still dragon-sized. I extracted myself from the heavy plate and leaned against a tall rock for a moment, trying to catch my breath.

Kat charged forward, a sword materializing in her hands. Aurakbahor rolled out of the way and shot a red bolt of magic. I sighed in relief as Kat dodged it, but the bolt ricocheted and hit me in the gut before I could summon Coleman's armor.

I screamed and collapsed. Pain made my vision turn white and red around the edges. It deafened my ears to the cheering crowd and magnified my racing heart. Every inch of me burned as my body seemed stuck between trying to change into a dragon and trying to remain human. I tried to let the change happen, but the pain burned deeper. Aurakbahor's curse slid through my body, clinging to my magic.

I tried not to throw up.

Kat turned to me, then back to Aurakbahor. She was so close. She stomped her foot, and a shockwave made the earth shake. The ground between the two Rhaegynne erupted with jagged rocks reaching at least ten feet tall. Instead of using them to attack, she ran to me and lifted my head off the ground.

"What are you doing?" I gasped.

I couldn't hear her voice, but I could read her lips. "Saving you."

She pressed her fingers against my temple, and her eyes turned mirror. Cooling magic ran through my veins. For just a second, her eyes flashed green, and she was in my mind, easing my body's tension. She gasped and drew back like she had been burned, and the pain returned.

She took a deep breath before pressing her hand against my sternum.

Her mouth moved, but I couldn't hear. The pain faded, but Kat's back arched, and she threw her head back. My hearing returned, but Kat didn't scream. She gasped like the pain took her breath away. Her face twisted in a grimace, and I pulled away from her in horror.

Her fingers trailed smoky black and green magic as she clawed at her throat, her eyes rolling backward. She screamed and sent fire toward the ceiling, scorching the stalactites high above us.

I scrambled to my feet and reached my hand out to help her, but she jerked away.

"*Don't touch me*," she spoke aloud and in my head. Her eyes opened. They weren't mirrored, and they weren't brown.

They were emerald and black.

I stumbled backward. She stood, glowing with strange green-black energy. She turned, and her barrier collapsed, the curse flying back toward Aurakbahor. The ground rumbled as he fell to his knees, clutching his head. Blood dripped from his nose. The audience's jeers turned into screams.

I stepped forward, but my legs nearly buckled like all my energy had been drained. Like I had used magic instead of Kat. My ears rang as I staggered to her. "What did you just *do*?"

"Coleman made lifting curses look so easy!" she huffed, breathing hard. Her eyes were mirrors again. "The curse was binding to your magic. I had to release some of yours to get his out." She passed me a sword and charged at Aurakbahor.

The king's sword flashed up, the familiar clang of metal on metal joined the crowd's uproar.

I found the strength in my legs, summoned my armor, and charged to join Kat's fight.

We fought side by side, just as we had practiced countless times before. We fell into a rhythm as though no time had passed since we had last been together. But even with us working in harmony, Aurakbahor still pressed forward, backing us up against one of the rock formations.

I set my blade on fire and redoubled my attack. Kat rose to match my efforts, her sword sparking with lightning.

We pushed back against the king. He yielded ground, only to replace it with shimmering barriers or ripping open chasms between us. Kat's focus switched from offense to building bridges and breaking down walls. As we backed him against a wall, someone handed him a second sword.

We split up and circled him, forcing him to spin and keep his attention split between his front and flank. But he still blocked both of us as though he could see us even when he faced away.

He lunged toward me, stepping on one of Kat's bridges. The bridge crumbled with a flash of light, and he fell forward, his arms and swords flailing as he tried to catch himself. I dodged backward, but his sword slashed through my pants, biting deep into my shin at the base of my knee and sliding to my ankle. I bit my tongue, trying not to cry out as I fell.

Aurakbahor swore as his knee slammed into a rock's edge before falling onto his face. Kat leaped across the chasm, her sword glinting off the light. She landed next to him and lifted her sword over her head.

He turned and spat out a curse, sending her flying backward. I scrambled to find my sword, stood, and closed the last few feet between Aurakbahor and myself.

He glanced at me, and his magic sent me flying.

I slammed against a boulder and slid to the ground. My

armor disappeared, but I struggled to my feet and looked for Kat.

She was an unmoving heap a hundred feet away.

Aurakbahor struggled to get back up. His knee was swollen and bloody. Blood smeared across his mouth and nose. His eyes burned with fury, and a vein pulsed on the side of his ruddy face. I pulled myself to my feet and limped toward him, using my sword like a cane. The crowd seemed to hold its breath.

Something like fear crossed Aurakbahor's face. He dropped his swords and lifted his hands up in front of his face

His lip twitched into a half-smile. "*Dumort ally!*"

The crowd gasped as a ring of black mist shot out around him like a shockwave, stretching out ten feet in all directions. My heart stopped for a moment, watching his wall of death spiral toward me. I sighed in relief when it stopped inches away and expanded into a dome, meeting high above Aurakbahor's head. Through the mist, I saw him sit on the ground and inspect his knee.

Kat shakily climbed to her feet. Her armor was gone, but bright white light spiraled off her hand, and she charged forward.

"*Kat! Stop!*" I shouted with both my voice and my mind. She slid to a stop, too close to the wall for comfort. I limped as fast as I could toward her and pulled her into me. A sob escaped me.

"What's wrong?" she asked, pulling away to look at my face.

"Remember the death spells Coleman taught us?"

"Yeah?"

I pointed at the wall a few feet away.

Her eyes widened as her face paled. She pulled me away from the wall, pressed her hand against her mouth, and let out a shaky breath. "I've seen that wall before. Aurakbahor used it at the—" Her voice caught. "I think this is what killed my grandma."

My own hands shook, but I pulled her cold body toward me.

"I'm sorry for everything," she whispered against my chest. "I miss you."

"Me too." She pulled away and met my eyes. "What are we going to do?"

"Wait it out until he gets tired?"

She shook her head. "He can hold this for — Look out!"

She pushed me to the ground and landed on top of me. A ball of red light soared overhead and crashed into the floor behind us, leaving a deep, smoking crater behind. The crowd cheered.

Kat dove into the crater. I followed her, ducking as Aurakbahor sent more hexes through his wall.

Muttering a couple words, Kat stood and mimed pulling a bow back to full draw. A smoky arrow materialized between her hands before she released. The arrow shattered against the wall. She gasped and dropped down. I tore my attention away from the smoking wall and fixed my eyes on a flash of green coming straight at my face.

Kat pulled me down as the curse sailed overhead. "Holy Tasalgré..." she whispered. She was panting, and she ran her locket along her purple-ish lips. A strange look fell across her face.

"You have a plan?" I asked. I hadn't realized how cold I was until Kat shivered.

She chewed on her lip for a second. "Part of one."

"What are you thinking?" I brushed a piece of hair out of her face, and she smiled sadly.

"An awful thought. Can you still fight?"

"I'm getting tired. Cold. But I think so. What's your plan?"

She didn't answer. She noticed my legs and grimaced at the blood on my shin. She reached out, but instead of healing my leg, she grabbed my feet and pressed her hands against my shoes.

"What are you doing?" I asked, pulling a foot away from her.

"*Turēsies ne se miči*. I'm so sorry."

The muscles in my feet and ankles tightened, and my legs felt like lead. I gasped and fell to my knees. "What—" I tried to move forward, but my legs wouldn't listen.

"Finish this for me."

My blood turned to ice. "Kat, don't do this."

She pulled herself over the ledge. "You're free now. The prophecy can be about you. I have to clear the way or we'll both die. I love you."

"Wait — Stop!" She kept walking toward the death wall. She didn't look back.

"This isn't the only way!" I shouted.

"*Can you think of another?*" she whispered in my mind.

Her mind brushed against mine, and I sobbed at her stubborn resolve. Her whole soul believed this was her only choice.

I screamed and shouted and tried to break free from her spell, but I couldn't move. "Katherine! This doesn't help!" I screamed. "Stop!"

I threw a spell out toward her. Aurakbahor laughed behind his shield, dispersing it before I could stop her.

I sent up a prayer to anyone who would listen, praying that something — *anything* — could stop her. I thrashed against her magic, but her bindings didn't break, and she was too close now.

She reached out a hand toward the wall, and Aurakbahor threw back his head with cruel laughter.

Movement flickered out of the corner of my eye. One of the double doors flew open, and Tythan bolted through, sprinting as fast as they could. They somehow half changed, unfurling only their black wings with a crest of red running down their back and through their tail. It propelled their human body forward, arms reaching out to Kat and coming to answer my prayer.

Dumort Ally

Kat

Strong, scaled arms slammed into me, pushing me to the side. We fell mere inches from the wall. Tythan — half human, half dragon — glared at me.

"Get off me!" I cried. The inches between me and the wall felt like a chasm now that I'd been distracted from my goal.

But someone had to pull it down for the war to end.

"I'm not about to let Hope lose her future because you *killed yourself!*" They snarled, still holding me down with their body positioned at an angle to keep me from reaching the wall. Their half-transformation gave their face a terrifying edge.

I opened my mouth to reply, but movement behind Tythan made my stomach drop with dread.

"Watch out!" I cried, trying to pull Tythan away.

But Aurakbahor pushed the wall toward us too fast.

The wall of black mist dissolved, and Tythan collapsed on me.

And suddenly, it was like I was holding Grandma's body

again in the hospital after she'd passed through this same wall trying to save me all those months ago.

Tythan's tail and wings disappeared, and I clutched their fully human body to my chest.

"No. No, Tythan! Stay with me! Stay for Hope!" I swore and turned their face toward me. Somewhere, I could hear laughter, but I could only focus on Tythan. "*Vito!*"

Their eyelids fluttered, trying to focus on me. They smirked. "You're welcome."

"Tythan!" I sobbed.

They shook their head weakly and spoke. "Tell Hope . . . happy birthday for me. Save them . . ." Their eyes rolled back, and they let out a soft sigh.

"No!"

Their lifeless body offered no response, but Grandma's words echoed through my head.

Save them.

I finally looked up.

Aurakbahor chuckled with a smug, gleeful face. "Bravo, Kitty. Using your friend as a shield for your doomed cause."

Meticulously, I slid Tythan's eyelids closed, set their body on the ground, and stood, summoning the last bit of my strength while the audience jeered. I let my hold on Aaron's feet slip and heard him jump out of the crater, but I didn't look back.

I tapped my wrists together, hoping to call the armor one last time, but warmth surrounded me. Instead of the silvery-blue armor from before, armor made of crackling flame encased my body. Strength flooded into me, and I smiled sadly. *Thanks, Tythan.*

I charged forward, my hand tightened into a fist. A sword of fire erupted from my clenched hand.

Aurakbahor's eyes widened. He took several steps backward, reaching for his swords. I flicked my wrist, pushing the swords away from him.

He lifted his hands defensively and backed away. I stormed forward to close the distance. Movement from the doorway revealed Jason and Hope trying to edge into the arena.

"No!" I shouted, slashing my hand through the air. A bright blue screen appeared across the doorway's threshold. "No one else comes in!" I glared at Aaron, and he hesitated before backing into the crater again.

Trying to take advantage of my distraction, Aurakbahor shot electricity at me, but I felt it coming. Something snapped in me when Tythan fell. I felt them next to me, fueling my fire even if I couldn't see them.

I blocked the curse and sent it back. It struck Aurakbahor's chest and knocked him to his knees. I marched up to him and kicked him to the ground. I pressed my fiery sword against his breastbone. "It's over, Aurakbahor."

I thrust my blade through his chest.

He gasped, but his face softened, and he smiled. Blood spilled out as his lips parted. "Enjoy my curse." His eyes glazed over, and he fell limp.

The fire encasing my body died, and I felt very, very cold. I stared at his body in the arena's stunned silence. I stepped away but froze as I noticed movement from Aurakbahor's corpse.

Black mist rose from him and materialized as a dragon. I stumbled backward as the head turned to face me.

I ran, but the mist dragon darted forward and enveloped me. I fell to my knees and tried to scream, but I was consumed by the mist. My brain burned with a fiery inferno raging inside, splitting and growing all at once.

A thousand voices pressed themselves into my skull. Thousands of awarenesses. All begging for my attention. I tried to press my hands against my head to keep the pain at bay, but my arms were too weak.

I fell to the ground as strength left my legs and the voices overpowered my mind.

Peaches

Aaron

The audience screamed as black mist exploded from Kat's and the king's fallen bodies and shot around the room. People ran, climbing over seats and each other to escape.

"*Kat!*" I leaped out of the crater and limped toward her. A bolt of mist rushed toward me, and I rolled under it. When I stood again, the mist around the room was gone, though most of the crowd were still scrambling toward the exits.

I fell to my knees beside Kat, barely feeling the pain in my shin, and lifted her head into my lap. I brushed her hair off her bloody forehead and felt for a pulse. Her heart pounded beneath my fingers, and I sighed in relief.

She muttered something.

I leaned closer. "What?"

She mumbled again, but it was just as unintelligible as before. Her eyes shifted beneath her closed eyelids. Her face twisted in pain.

I didn't have much magic left, but I cast small spells to try to wake her as I ran my fingers through her hair. The bloody bump on the side of her head healed, but her eyes stayed shut, her lips whispering words I couldn't hear.

Jason, Hope, and an older man ran over to us in the now deserted coliseum.

"Is Kat okay?" Jason asked, helping support the older man. But his eyes were on Tythan a few feet away.

"I'm not sure," I answered, finally managing to look at Tythan's body too.

They were so young without their usual scowl.

Jason held onto the man as a tear rolled down his cheek. He turned to shield Hope from the view — too late.

She pushed past him and ran toward Tythan. She shook their shoulder. "We won, Tythan! Wake up!" She shook them again. "Come on. Wake up!"

The old man tried to gently pull her away, but she clung to their arm and refused to leave.

"Why won't they wake up?"

Jason knelt in front of her, moving her to look at him. "Hope... listen. Tythan did a very brave thing. They're a hero." Tears welled in his eyes, and his voice cracked. "But they're not going to wake up."

Her brow furrowed. "Why?"

He chewed on his lip for a moment. "Tythan is dead."

She pressed her hand against their cheek. "No." Her lip quivered, and the temperature dropped. Her warm brown eyes changed to green and gold. Her breath hitched, and she screamed their name, her cries wrought with magic as she tried to shake Tythan's body.

A thick sheet of ice spread out from beneath her, coating the ground and up the walls.

Her outburst ended as quickly as it came, and she fell back to the ground, collapsing into a weeping heap on Tythan's body. The ice immediately around us melted, but squeaking ice still cracked around the coliseum.

Kat shot up. "Make it stop!" she screamed.

"Kat!" I cried in relief and fear.

She turned, her eyes wide and searching for something.

Seeing her eyes slitted and draconic was expected, but these weren't her normal dragon eyes. Instead, a thick black ring at the edge of her irises surrounded the normal silver.

I touched her shoulder. "Kat?"

She gripped my hand and held it close. Her eyes focused on me, and she reached her hand out toward my face. "Aaron?" Her hands flew back to her head and clutched her face. She let out a groan. "Make it stop..."

"Make what stop?" I asked, trying in vain to calm her.

"The voices! All the voices..."

"Voices? There are no voices." But my stomach twisted into knots of anxiety. *What happened to her?*

She held her ears and covered her face, curling in on herself.

Jason looked around, a growing panic rising on his face. "Where is—"

"Coleman?" she finished then pointed without looking up. "He's up there."

"How do you—"

"I can feel him. Go."

He seemed stunned but ran the best he could across Hope's ice rink and climbed up the empty seats to the judge's box.

I turned to Kat and frowned. "What's—"

"I don't know. Yes, I do. No, I don't. What's happening?" She groaned and put her hands over her ears again. "You're all so *loud!*"

"No one is—"

"I know. I know no one's *talking.*"

Before I could say anything, Jason emerged from the judge's box with Coleman's limp body in his arms and slid down the stadium ramp. He climbed over the barrier and laid Coleman on the ground beside us before dropping to his knees next to him.

Ignoring us, Jason poured healing spells into Coleman until the Dragonstongue markings faded, and Coleman's eyes opened.

Jason let out a teary laugh. "Don't *scare* me like that!"

Coleman sat up and wiped a tear off Jason's cheek before leaning in and kissing his forehead. "It's just a little Dragonstongue." But his whole face had turned pink.

Jason seemed taken aback.

Coleman's eyes widened. "I-I'm sorry. I'm just glad to—"

Jason cupped Coleman's face in his hands. "Coward. Kiss my mouth next time." This time, Jason leaned in and pressed his lips against Coleman's.

A crack of an explosion overhead caused me to jump, and Coleman and Jason broke apart. I scrambled to my aching feet as a large boulder broke free from the ceiling.

But Kat jumped into action, chanting incantations like Tasalgré was a first language. She held her arms up and out, and a beam of light shot from her hands and flew up to the ceiling. She swept her arms open, and the light spread across the entire room like a net and caught the falling boulder. The webbing slid out the door, running along the ceiling and lighting the tunnel.

Jason helped Coleman to his feet, and they both looked as panicked as I felt.

Coleman leaned heavily on Jason. "What's happ—"

"Hope's ice is getting into the cracks and collapsing the cave." Kat sounded almost calm.

"Can you stop it?" I asked.

She shook her head, then frowned. "Where is Morgan? I saw her up there. But I can't hear her. Is she dead?"

"Wait. What do you mean—"

"I don't know." Another boulder cracked and shattered against the shield. She jumped. "Now is not the time!" She grabbed my hand and pulled with more force than I expected. She broke into a run, the ice melting in front of her. "It won't hold forever. We have to save the prisoners!"

"Kat!" Jason called after us.

She slid to a stop, her face falling.

"Tythan . . ." She pressed her hand over her mouth. "Oh, Tythan . . ."

Tears streamed down Hope's face. "We can't leave them here."

Kat moved with inhuman speed to stand in front of Hope. She wiped tears off Hope's cheeks and blinked some of her own away. "You're right, Hope. Where should we take them?"

"Some place pretty. Some place with fire, so they never have to be alone."

She swallowed. "That's a good idea. We'll find a place." She bent down, pulled Tythan into her arms and effortlessly lifted them up.

"What about—" Coleman started.

"Aurakbahor can rot for all I care." Her face turned dark. She swept out of the room, leaving us to follow her.

I limped behind Jason, the old man, and Hope but turned to make sure Coleman was coming. Coleman stood over Aurakbahor's body with an odd expression. He reached down, grabbed one of his discarded swords, pulled the scabbard from Aurakbahor's side, and sheathed it. He slammed the tip into the ground, where it transformed into a dark wooden cane. He leaned on it and hurried to catch up.

Once in the dimly lit tunnels, I noticed the light in the

tunnel seemed to bend and wrap around Kat, dusting her shoulders with a shawl of light and circling her head in the crown of a queen — king? The cell doors opened as she passed. People stumbled out of their prisons in astonishment and followed us through the hall. Even the animals we freed followed docilely.

Several tunnels converged, and four more freed prisoners joined us. She stopped.

"*Aurakbahor is dead.*" Her words echoed in my head, and I assumed she was projecting her declaration to Aurakbahor's dragons. "*As descendant of the first Rhaegynne, a child of the dragon, and granddaughter to two fallen kings, I, Katherine Victoria Lance, claim my birthright to the thrones of the unruled clans. As far as I am concerned, you are free. Though if you'll stand by me, I will gladly have your aid to fight Balaskad and break our curse.*"

A cheer rose from our small gathering. Kat stepped out of the way, leaned against a wall, and smiled. "Go on then. Be free." Once they were gone, her smile fell, and her glow flickered. "We should go. We should really go." Her eerie eyes swept around the tunnel before she closed them and shook her head like she was trying to clear her thoughts. Abruptly, she started walking out of the cave again.

"What happened to you?" I asked.

She shook her head. "I don't know."

I touched her shoulder and nearly burned my fingers against her skin. "You're glowing and reading minds, and—"

"What do you mean glowing?" She stared at me as if trying to read something on my face. "Oh. I see. I don't know. I just... I feel... *stronger.*"

"Are you *okay?*"

"I just killed a man," she whispered. "I am carrying my friend's corpse. And I have the world's worst headache."

"What's wrong with your head?"

She pressed her lips together but didn't respond for some time. "The better question is: Which of us is the prophecy about? You broke the chains more than I did."

"Do you know the exact wording of the prophecy?" Coleman asked.

"The Council to keep the peace / Will force the war of kings / With one left and all to remain, / All agency shall cease / Until salvation soars on willing wings. / A free dragon, one to break the chains, / Will release them from the snare / And take their place as rightful heir," she recited. She looked just as startled as I felt that she could do that.

"Well, if you think about it," Coleman said, "the line 'a free dragon, one to break the chains,' doesn't necessarily imply they're one and the same." He turned to me. "Kat could be the free dragon, and you're the one to break the chains. You're both essential to the prophecy. Besides, Jamie always said it was more important to be willing to be chosen than being the exact fit for the prophecy."

Jason chuckled darkly. "So, the chosen one *was* the friends we made along the way..."

We reached the cave's opening. Jason climbed through first, and Kat passed Tythan's body through the thin crevasse.

Our group crawled out of the cave and into the light of a fading sunset. The soft pink light made Zion's red rocks glow above, but the western side cast a long shadow through the canyon to where we stood.

Several prisoners stood outside the cave, seemingly waiting for us.

A woman with long, tangled hair stepped forward. She appeared old, but under the layers of dirt, she could have been much younger. "Did you mean what you said?"

"Yes," Kat said.

"Can we be dragons? Or did you just mean to set us free from those cells?"

"Go ahead and change. I'm not going to stop you."

The woman's eyes glistened, but she limped off to join the others. The freed Rhaegynne basked in their physical and mental freedom, turning into dragons of every shape and color. They spread their colorful wings and took flight.

Kat let out the tiniest whimper as they left.

"What's wrong?" I asked.

"It's nothing. Just my head." She handed Tythan over to me and rubbed her temples. "I can fly us home. My wing healed itself."

"Actually, Kat . . ." Jason said. "I'd like to change if I can."

A muscle in her temple jumped. "Of course."

He grinned. "Watch this, Dad!"

The older man watched with pride as the air shimmered around Jason, and he changed into his dragon form. His black scales had an iridescent sheen the Dream Realms never showed. He opened his wings but froze and looked down at Kat. Her face twisted in pain.

He shrank back down to human.

"What the *crap*, Katherine?"

"You have your freedom. I swear it. Just . . . not your privacy."

"What do you mean?" Coleman asked.

She sat on the ground, pulled her knees in close, and kneaded her knuckles against her forehead. "Change, Coleman."

He hesitantly handed his cane to Jason. Coleman took a couple steps away and changed. Confusion flashed across the dragon's face. He shifted back. "I don't understand."

"Don't understand what?" I pressed.

Kat stared at the ground between her knees. "Until we

break the curse . . . I took Aurakbahor's throne . . . and power. I can control his dragons. But I won't! I can grant you your freedom, but I can't stay out of your heads, and I can't keep the others out either."

"So . . . you can read minds now? Even when we're not dragons?" Coleman asked, taking back his cane.

"If the mind is one of Aurakbahor's — one of *my* — dragons, yes. I can't hear Hope."

"What am I thinking right now?" he asked smugly.

"Peaches."

"Dang it."

"Change if you want," she said, pushing herself back to her feet. She reached out and grabbed my hand. "Let's go home."

Embers and Ash

Kat

My best friends stood before me, majestic and grand in their dragon forms. No longer Aerolan, Sa'hranet, and Aryxon, but Jason, Coleman, and Aaron.

My head throbbed, trying to rob me of our victory. I tried to shield my pain from them; they didn't need to know how much it hurt to hear them. At least my connection to Aaron was muffled.

But Aaron, of course, noticed. He noticed everything.

He dropped his dragon form and rushed over to me. "What's wrong?"

Aaron's concern drew the others' attention. Jason and Coleman shifted back.

"It's nothing," I said, waving off their pity.

Jason's face softened with sympathy. "It's worse when we're dragons, isn't it?"

I carefully schooled my face, lifting my chin in defiance. "If this is the price for your freedom, I will gladly pay it."

"If you need us to—" Coleman started.

"No." I cut him off before he could suggest they just stay human.

We fell silent for a moment. I didn't know how to reassure them I was fine — I wasn't, and they knew it.

"Legally, what are we supposed to do with Tythan?" Coleman asked, watching the freed prisoners fly away. He stared numbly at Tythan's body.

I looked away, fighting back the crushing wave of emotion from the others. I felt it all. Every thought, every emotion. From *everyone*. I tried to hide my own tears and guilt from them. I closed my eyes, trying to think.

One of the voices in my head belonged to a doctor. She soared through the air over a beach, celebrating her new freedom. I reached out to her. *"Hey, don't panic,"* I said. She jumped but didn't seem surprised. *"I lost a friend today. They don't have a home or family. What are we supposed to do?"*

"Magic-related deaths have the worst paperwork. I'll take care of it. You take care of the body. I'll sort it out for you. Thank you for my freedom."

"We just need to find a place for them," I said, interrupting my friends' conversation. "I've got the rest covered."

The others looked concerned but didn't ask questions.

"How are we supposed to get home?" Jason asked. "We don't have transport beads."

"We'll—" I spoke for Coleman but then clamped my mouth shut. "I'm sorry."

He frowned but left it alone. "We'll have to fly the rest of the way."

I bit my tongue to stop myself from speaking for Aaron.

In their dragon forms, the connection between us showed me how I could control every aspect of the Rhaegynne under me. The connection still existed in their human forms — I felt the synapses in their brains before they even finished firing, and I knew their every thought and move — but instead of me knowing how to control them, it felt more like they controlled me.

"We could always take turns riding dragonback and sleeping that way," Aaron said.

My body buzzed with energy that didn't belong to me, but the others ached with exhaustion. The pain from Coleman's Dragonstongue flare shook him to his core — and to mine by extension. None of them would make the flight home on their own.

But I could.

"I'll carry everyone. Jason, could you stay awake for a bit to keep a ward up around us. I don't trust my ring that much."

He nodded, looking relieved, but he rubbed at his scar. The words formed in his head, and I hummed a nursery rhyme to keep myself from speaking for him. "I'm worried we'll fall if we sleep."

I messaged my temple. The leather bracelet brushed against my face and sparked an idea. "Hold on," I said, excitement and magic mixing in my veins.

"What?" Coleman asked.

"Hush. Thinking." I stepped away from them and reached for my fire to shift.

My left shoulder itched, but nothing seemed to change. Confused, I hesitated, but I was already a dragon. My eyesight didn't change, but my ability to tune out all the different minds in my head expanded, and the pressure dispersed slightly.

"*Were my eyes mirrored the entire time?*" I asked Aaron.

He sent me an image of me carrying Tythan as I walked through the cavern. My eyes reflected the dark red rock around the pupil, but the outsides were smoky black. "I wouldn't call it mirrored. And I don't think you can call yourself mirror anymore either."

I saw myself through Aaron's eyes. I was at least a foot taller, and my coloring was all wrong. I still reflected everything like a mirror, but the mirror was tarnished. Hundreds of my scales were now dark gray. Others had black smudges and flecks across them. I looked like an antique mirror.

"What happened to me?" I gasped.

"I don't know," he answered. *"But she looks beautiful,"* he thought.

"Shut up . . ."

He blushed. "You weren't supposed to hear that part . . ."

I turned my head to my forearm and scraped at the small scales below my wrist, ignoring the pain as I pulled a couple off.

"What are you doing?" Aaron sounded horrified.

I changed back into a human and picked the scales off the ground, wiping away the pinpricks of blood on my arm.

I explained how the scales could be manipulated with magic to fuse with the bracelets and form a sort of connection to me to keep anyone from falling off. I was met with blank stares.

Poking into Aaron's mind, I backtracked to see what I had done wrong. Watching through his eyes, I realized I spoke too fast for them to understand. I don't know where that came from. Maybe some side effect of sharing my mind with three thousand four hundred and seventy-two minds, but I could think faster, move faster, and — apparently — talk faster.

"What's happening to me?" The words tumbled out of my mouth. They were my own, but they all thought it too.

Coleman shook his head. "I don't know. Some . . . consequence of taking the throne?"

I pressed my hand against my eyes, trying to work out the pressure in my head. "I hate this."

Aaron walked over, put his arm around my shoulder, and pulled me close. "I know. We'll get through it. But for now, tell us your idea again."

I held out the scales. "I can enchant the scales, so you won't fall off."

He grinned. "Brilliant!"

I frowned and chewed my lip. We'd eventually have to take turns on the way home if I needed to sleep. "I think I'll need scales from everyone but Hope."

Jason nodded and immediately changed to collect a couple scales. Coleman and Aaron followed suit, and soon, I held a small collection of dragon scales in my hands.

"Could I borrow everyone's leather bracelets?" I asked. "I can link the scales to those. Henry, we'll just have to keep yours loose for now, sorry."

They all passed me their bracelets. I cupped the scales and leather in my hands and started an incantation. The words came naturally, though I had never learned them before. *"Tarisnae morgathala sorka ma silane corsna roka."* Light shot out from between my fingers, and my hands burned from the magic. The others shielded their eyes, but I watched for the light to go out.

I held out the bracelets, each now with four softly glowing dragon scales embedded in the plait. The last set of scales had a small hole through them for a chain, and I passed them to Henry before returning the bracelets to the others. I should have felt drained from the amount of magic I used, but, if anything, I felt rejuvenated.

"As long as you and the dragon you're riding have this, you can't fall off." I put my own bracelet on, then changed into a dragon. My head hurt less to be a dragon. Like everything *fit* better.

Coleman clasped his bracelet and turned to Jason to help him with his.

Jason blushed and gave him a little smile. "I'm glad you're alive."

He reached for Jason and wrapped him in his arms. "I thought I'd never see you again," he whispered, but I heard it in his thoughts more than I heard it with my ears. I turned away to grant them as much privacy as I could.

I worried the five of them would push my strength, but with the extra energy coursing through my body, I barely felt them on my back. I spread my wings and lifted into the sky.

I wandered the scenic route on the way home, to try to clear my crowded head as my friends slowly drifted off to sleep.

I flew over the mountains, aimlessly following along a mountain road leaving the park. My dragon eyes were able to make out the path despite the darkness of the night. The paths led me to a road that circled a lake below that glittered with starlight. The trees were beginning to blossom, but stubborn piles of snow still lingered around tree trunks and along the side of the road. Ancient lava rock and the burnt trees from an old forest fire somehow made the landscape even more beautiful. The air hummed with magic.

It was pretty and had the memory of fire. Just like Hope wanted for Tythan.

"*We're going to stop here,*" I said, gently waking the others. "*I know where we can bury Tythan.*"

I landed in a clearing near the lake and let the others slide off my back before changing. "Help me find the right place for them," I said.

Henry looked ill and lacked our night vision, so I told him to stay with Tythan while the rest of us split up to look.

Jason, Coleman, and Hope found a small clump of evergreen trees in the middle of a lava rock field.

"Here," Hope said, her eyes draconic and rimmed with tears.

Coleman's irises were red and matched the rim of his eyes as he blinked back tears. "We should cremate them. I think they'd prefer that."

I nodded and gestured for Aaron to follow me. We returned sometime later with bundles of broken branches and kindling. Hope clenched her jaw but helped us arrange the pyre.

We laid Tythan on top, arranging their already stiffening limbs. They could have been sleeping if not for the stillness of their chest.

I stepped back, reciting the first magic spell I had learned. *"Contra mortabalis ally."* Ghostly blue flames spread around us, encircling our private funeral grounds.

The six of us just stared at the unlit pyre in silence, tears running down our cheeks. I reached for a branch. *"Eathia,"* I whispered, alighting the end. I raised it like a torch. "Tythan was a hero. They're the reason Aurakbahor's Rhaegynne are free. At the end of the day, they were selfless, strong, and constantly watched out for Hope. I held them as they died. I heard their last words. They spoke only of Hope. They loved you."

Her little hand wiped tears off her face.

"We'll miss them, and I will forever be in their debt." My stomach clenched as I turned to ignite the pyre.

"Wait!" Hope called. She reached out and took a branch of her own to light. "Not yet."

Henry knelt, grabbed a branch, and lit it from Hope's torch.

"I didn't know Tythan for long. But I can see how much Jason respected them. I know they will be missed."

Jason knelt and grabbed two branches before passing one to Coleman and igniting both with a word. Jason spoke of Tythan's strength and courage, and Coleman thanked Tythan for saving him more than once and praised their pyrotechnics.

Aaron lit his own torch. "I will forever be in their debt." His voice shook. *This would be Kat if not for them,* he thought. I suspected I wasn't supposed to hear it.

Hope stepped forward. "They saved me." Her voice cracked, but she pushed on. "So many times." She reached out a hand to touch Tythan's. She opened her mouth to say more, but nothing came out. She just stared at them and cried, her arm shaking as she held her torch aloft. Coleman placed a hand on her back. Her lip trembled. "I love you."

She dropped her torch on the pyre.

"*Ally eathia,*" I whispered, adding my torch to the pyre and convincing the fire to burn hot enough.

The others dropped their own torches, each adding their own magic to the fire, then stepped back to watch it burn. The fire illuminated the night, and the sparks danced toward the stars.

Too soon, the fire consumed the pyre, leaving behind nothing but embers and ash.

Coleman wrapped his arms around Hope and pulled her into a hug.

She let out a quiet sob. "I don't want to go."

"We don't have to yet," he said, watching the last of the fire flicker and die.

I picked up a small stone by my foot and spoke an incantation to carve it into a box. I carefully collected a handful of ashes. I knelt and offered the box to Hope. "We'll find something better to hold their ashes later, but for now..."

She accepted the box but then turned, handed it to Coleman, and walked up to the field of lava rock. She selected one, returned, set it on the ash, then went back for another.

I climbed to my feet to help her. The others joined, bringing more rocks and stacking them high. When we finished, the shrine reached my waist.

We stepped back to judge our work. It was beautiful. But something was missing.

It was like Hope could read *my* thoughts. She stepped forward and pressed her hand against the base of the pile. A tongue of fire ignited at the bottom and climbed to the top of the headstone, snaking through the lava rocks.

I swallowed a lump in my throat and held out my hand. "*Permanere.*" The flames flashed blue for a moment, then back to orange. "It will burn forever but never destroy."

Hope stood and took my hand. We could have stayed there, gathered around Tythan's eternal fire until the flames died out. Minutes passed in silence. Then an hour came and went, and the sun began to rise, but none of us moved.

"What are you doing here?" an angry voice said from behind us.

We spun around. I took a step backward as a sword tip pressed itself against my throat.

For Better or For Worse

Coleman

A young woman stood in front of us. She wore black leather riding pants, boots, a brown leather corset over a white, long sleeve shirt, and a cloak with the hood drawn up, covering her vibrant purple hair. A brown quiver strap ran across her chest, and green fletched arrows peaked over her shoulder. Her dark brown eyes squinted into a glare as she held the sword to Kat's throat.

I stepped in front of Hope, shielding her with my body.

Kat lifted her hands to her head. *"No one attack,"* she told us telepathically. "Who are you?"

"I asked you first." The woman's lip curled into a sneer.

"I'm Kat. This is Hope, Jason, Coleman, Aaron, and Henry. We just . . . had a funeral."

"I saw you use magic. Who are you with?" she asked.

"What? We're—"

She pushed the tip of her sword against Kat's throat, drawing a drop of blood. I flinched, but Kat held still and shot me a warning look.

The newcomer sneered. "You reek of Council magic."

My stomach dropped. *Council?*

"I—" Kat started.

"You're one of *them!*" She swung her sword, and Kat darted back.

"What are you *talking* about?" Kat yelped, ducking under another blade swipe. I drew my sword, but Kat flashed me another look. *"Not yet."*

I clenched my jaw but nodded, reaching out to stop Aaron from lunging forward anyway.

The woman looked murderous and attacked again. "I've only ever met one woman on the Council, but she had the same aura and" — she fluttered her free hand around her head — *"mind thing* you do, *Kat."*

Kat took another step away. "Calm down! My, uh, mind thing is new. Like last night new. I killed a dragon king named Aurakbahor. He was evil and—"

She froze, and her sword drooped to the ground mid-strike. "You . . . *killed* . . . Aurakbahor? He's . . . dead?" She looked to the rest of us for confirmation.

I nodded, and she scanned my face, the buddings of a long-lost hope beginning to form on her face.

"He's dead." She covered her mouth and *laughed.* "Aurakbahor is dead!" She reached out and shook my hand. "It is an *honor* to meet you. Call me Zed."

"What sort of name is that?" Kat asked.

"Like the letter," Z said.

"Well, call me K," Kat scoffed.

"Look. It's the name I told you to call me. On more important matters . . ." She gestured her sword at us. "What *are* you?"

Kat furrowed her brow. "Rhaegynne. Aren't you?"

"What's that?"

"Huh?" Kat asked.

My heart was racing. I knew about Kroll. I'd seen mentions of other magical creatures in Jamie's book. But Aurakbahor seemed terrified about this Council, and as much as I hated him, his fear made me nervous.

"I've not heard of Rhaegynne magic before. I'm a dragon rider, a psychic, and a magician."

I *could* smell the smoky sweet cinnamon and pine scent of another dragon nearby, but when I scanned the area around us, I couldn't see them.

"Where's your friend?" Kat asked. Whether she picked up on the scent by herself or if she noticed from me, I couldn't say. "He's not one of Aurakbahor's. Is he Balaskad's?"

I flinched at the fact she even knew the difference now.

"What? He's *mine*. We're against the entire Council of Mages. You know, big guys who control every magical creature that's ever existed?"

My head was spinning. Aurakbahor wouldn't tell me anything more about the Council, but I did know what a mage was. Or at least . . . I knew some of the definitions of the word. Aurakbahor had taught me a very *specific* definition of the word when I was a kid.

But if Z was using the term the way I thought she was in relation to the Council . . . why would Aurakbahor be so afraid of it?

Was he only afraid of *me* finding out about it?

"Kat . . ." I said cautiously. "I think . . . we've been lied to."

"What? By whom?"

I hesitated, and Jason took my hand in his. "I met a couple imp things a few months back. I asked Aurakbahor about it, but he got scared and tried to wipe my memory. I don't know why, but he didn't want me knowing." I shuddered.

"Do you *want* to know?" Jason asked.

"I . . . don't know," I confessed. "I feel like we're missing something. Something important."

A massive peridot green dragon dropped from the sky, and Kat stumbled backward.

"It's okay," Z said after looking her way. "He's a friend if you're a friend."

"Is your friend going to shift and introduce himself?" Kat asked.

"He can't."

"He's stuck?" Kat asked.

Z frowned. "Are you all shifters?"

I nodded.

A deep rumbling voice filled my head. "*Hello. Unfortunately, this is my only form.*"

"It takes a while to get used to learning there are different magics out there," Z said. "It took me years to just accept it. So, you're all Rhaegynne?"

Everyone nodded except Henry.

"Are you here to sign up for the rebellion?"

"Rebellion?" Aaron asked.

"Against the Council of Mages. You said you killed Aurakbahor to free the Rhaegynne, but what about the rest of us?"

"Z," I said cautiously, as if approaching a feral cat. "Could you . . . define the word mage real quick?"

She furrowed her brow. "An exceptionally powerful magician. Why?"

I nodded. Maybe that's all it was this time. But then . . . why does she know who Aurakbahor is? "Who's on the Council? Do you know?"

"Aurakbahor was one. There's a woman called Balaskad, and—"

"*Tasalgré*," I swore under my breath. Jason squeezed my hand, but I couldn't look at him. I looked up to the sky. "In some mythologies, a true mage was a wizard who could transform into a dragon — or perhaps a dragon who could transform into a wizard." I squeezed my eyes closed so I wouldn't have to look at my friends. "A mage is a Rhaegynne."

"What are you saying?" Kat asked.

"I'm saying that I think Aurakbahor and Balaskad kept the rest of the magical world a secret from the Rhaegynne but have likely been just as cruel to them as they were to us."

"*The Council to keep the peace / Will force the war of kings,*" Kat repeated.

I turned the words around in my head, wondering how I never considered what the Council to keep the peace might have meant. But somehow the magical world was bigger and more connected than any of us had ever imagined.

I gulped and looked at Z, feeling a strange mix of apprehension and hope. "If I'm right . . ." I said, eyeing Z and Kat. "I think we might make extremely powerful allies. And if I'm wrong . . . well . . . Aurakbahor didn't want us knowing about each other for a reason. For better or for worse, I *personally* want to know what that reason was."

Kat stepped forward and offered a hand to Z. "What do you say?" she asked. "Save the dragons, save the world?"

They clasped forearms, and, for better or for worse, something told me there was no going back.

Acknowledgments

It's been said millions of times in millions of acknowledgment sections that it takes a village to make a book happen, but I will reiterate that sentiment: It truly does take a village to make a book happen. The thing about writing the very first versions of this book in high school almost fifteen years ago is that there has been a massive village of some of the greatest people along the way who have helped shape this book. The terrifying thing is that means I will absolutely miss people (or not be able to fit everyone in, as these acknowledgment sections are supposed to be kept brief) who made a huge difference to this story and to me personally.

But I do want to take a moment to thank my village. If you were someone along the way who supported my writing in any way, please know I love and appreciate you more than words can tell. And if you were one of the people who read the earliest drafts . . . I am very, very sorry, and I hope you are proud of how far this has come since then. (Janessa, your disco dragon comment has haunted me for over a decade. I hope I addressed that better this time.)

But there are people I can thank specifically, and I would like to highlight them for all their help and support over the years.

I want to thank my family first. Mom and Dad, thank you, for always just accepting my strange fantasies. Sorry, I will likely never write a full out spy thriller. Dad, hopefully Coleman's espionage is close enough. Natalie and Emily, I know you're not readers but thank you for cheering for me along the way. J, thanks for reading almost every draft. Katie, James, Maddie, and Jacob, this story wouldn't exist without our old adventures. And Evie, thank you for reading my books, liking my posts, and helping me figure out what high schoolers still like these days.

For my husband Drew, sorry for all the late nights and endless obsessions. Thank you for joining this ride with me.

To my various writing groups — The Ace Writer's Discord, The Disabled Author's Circle, and the 2026 Debut Author's Group (May the goose be with us!) — I wish you all lived closer because I owe you cookies or something.

To Conner, Harper, and Janessa, thank you for panic reading my edits behind me and helping me through all my breakdowns. Thank you Robin for getting this book into shape enough for it to be ready for querying and always being around for grammar questions. (Commas are not meant to be understood by mere mortals like myself. You are a wizard.)

Austin, thank you for giving me the name Rhaegynne. I think you gave me some of the other dragon names too, but it's been so long now that I can't remember which. Danielle, thank you for your care editing an early version of this story. Coleman's POV wouldn't exist without you and that would have been a tragedy.

Thank you to every coworker I have ever had who put up with my constant ramblings about this book, and a special thanks to Beck and Sydney for reading it and going on the querying roller coaster with me.

Michaella, thank you for being one of my longest supporters. Rachel, that sleepover all those years ago created the very premise for the conflict here. Thanks for staying up too late talking about dragons with me. Sam, thanks for wandering around with me, talking about stories and keeping me entertained. Jess and Danielle, your support means so much to me.

To everyone who's ever looked over a query letter or gave me a positivity pass, I wouldn't have made it without you. Thank you Mercedes for being my first mentor as I took the plunge into pursuing publication.

And to everyone at Inked: Thank you, Lauren, for taking a chance on me. Kota, thanks for always being willing to let me bug you about book stuff. And thank you Vanessa for the copy edits, understanding exactly what I meant, and sending me cat photos along the way.

Also, a formal apology to the National Park Service: Sorry my dragons caused significant damage to two fictionalized versions of your parks. And also, a formal thank you to all of Montana for letting me dump an entire fictional town in the middle of your mountains.

Ashley N. Y. Sheesley is a disabled author, scientist, animal lover, and a big fan of all things fantasy. In fact, she is only a scientist because she can't figure out how to be a wizard in real life. When she's not studying diseases or writing about dragons or werewolves, she loves to draw, paint, crochet, knit, spin wool, or venture out in the dead of night to Dark Sky zones and take photos of the stars.

She lives with her husband and her small army of animals — a bearded dragon, two rabbits, and three cats. Her writing has been featured in Knee Brace Press Magazine and in *Artifice & Access*.

She can be found on Instagram and Bluesky @ashintheashes and Tumblr @chronicallydragons

If You Enjoyed Child of the Dragon . . .

If you enjoyed *Child of the Dragon*, please consider also reading **Artifice & Access: A Disability in Fantasy Anthology** featuring a story by Ashley N.Y. Sheesley or any of the other Inked in Gray novels and anthologies. Support our small business by buying direct at InkedinGray.com

We also appreciate any and all reviews! You may leave a review on Goodreads, Amazon, IndieStoryGeek, or on our site at Inkedingray.com